Praise for *The Pacifist*

"Written by a Pulitzer-Prize-winning journalist, this fast-paced crime novel is set in the era of hippie communes, draft dodgers, and protests against the Vietnam War...it seems inevitable that this book will soon become a popular television series."

–Jerry Griswold, author of *Feeling Like a Kid*

"Lyn Bixby manages to accomplish something that is enormously difficult to pull off: to write a novel whose narrative thrust drives multiple storylines forward like a detective crime thriller. The dilemmas the novel's characters face moved me because the moral choices that drive the novel's actions and story lines are very real to me."

–Basil T. Paquet, poet, Vietnam War veteran, cofounder of First Casualty Press, publisher of and contributor to *Winning Hearts and Minds: War Poems by Vietnam Veterans* and *Free Fire Zone: Short Stories by Vietnam Veterans*

"Lyn Bixby has penned a rocking tale of the tumultuous 1960s, wrapped in a mystery that will keep you guessing until the very end. His compelling characters hold plenty of lessons for our own time as they try to resist the forces of war and repression without losing their way."

–Lawrence Roberts, author of *Mayday 1971*

"A novel about the death of a pacifist at an Army base in 1968, it fueled a rebellion in New England against the Vietnam War that would spread swiftly and lead to shocking mysteries and secrets and deaths. This anti-war thriller, with fictional characters resisting the war surrounded by a factual background, will keep you reading through the night. Bixby's skills as an investigative reporter are on display throughout the action. A very impressive first novel. Here's hoping another one is on the way!"

–Mike Waller, Pulitzer Prize winning former senior editor at *The Courier-Journal*, former editor of the *Louisville Times* and other newspapers, and former publisher and CEO of *The Sun of Baltimore*

THE PACIFIST

Lyn Bixby

Rootstock Publishing

Montpelier, VT

For the young American draftees and soldiers
who had the courage to defy their government
to end an immoral war in Vietnam.

Author's Note

This is a work of fiction. The storylines and characters are products of my imagination. With that said, real historical events, people, and places form the backdrop.

The 1960s was an extraordinary decade in America, fractured by the Vietnam War, political assassinations, brutal police beatings of nonviolent civil rights demonstrators, and fierce racial protests in cities set on fire across the country. At the same time, the 1960s ignited an environmental awakening and historic advances in civil and voting rights, in social and health care programs, and in the arts, highlighted by the explosion of rock and roll.

In the 1950s the United States assumed control of the Vietnam War from France on the premise that if communism wasn't stopped on the other side of the world, it could spread everywhere. Many Americans didn't realize the US had soldiers in Vietnam until 1965 when a relatively dormant military draft was reactivated. The government, lacking enough volunteers to fight, conscripted men from age eighteen to twenty-six for two-year Army commitments.

The reimposition of a draft sparked an anti-war movement that coalesced with the civil rights movement, and the government became obsessed with trying to crush all dissent as the power of public protest became evident. Early anti-war demonstrations took place on college campuses, where students burned their draft cards. Then students banded together into regional and national groups. In 1968 large off-campus protests extended across the country and grew more confrontational. Resistance to the war also began to take hold within the military.

1

Sunday, September 29, 1968
Thompson Farm, Vermont

She didn't see the stranger until he was a few feet away. She first spotted his shadow. It was dark and dangerously close in the afternoon sun. She finished her cut and looked up. He was smiling and waving a hand to get her attention. She shut off her chain saw and set it in the dirt by the pile of logs she was cutting for firewood. She checked him out while taking off her gloves and earmuffs. She guessed he was in his midthirties, possibly a lost hiker, judging by his knapsack. The Appalachian Trail wasn't far away and through-hikers who started last spring in Georgia should be entering the most grueling part of the trail by now, the stretch run through New Hampshire and Maine, pushing to reach the finish line at Mount Katahdin before it was encased in ice and snow. Most men who were through-hiking would have full beards by the time they made it to Vermont. He was clean-shaven, his knapsack didn't seem to have much in it, and he didn't have a hiking pole. He was wearing a flat cap, the kind you'd expect to see in Scotland or Ireland, a flannel shirt, shorts, and boots. His body was stocky. His legs looked strong.

"Hi," she said.

"Hi. Sorry to interrupt. Looks like you're getting ready for winter."

"It's that time of year. How can I help you?"

"I came here to talk to Lisa Thompson."

"That's me."

"One of your friends at the farmhouse said I'd find you down here by the barn. My name's Johnny Dollar."

"Really," she said. "With a name like that I'm hoping you're here because

I won some kind of contest. But your outfit says otherwise."

"I'm a friend of your brother Chris."

"That's better than winning a contest. Nice to meet you."

"Likewise. From what Chris told me, I figured you might be working, even on a weekend. Where'd you learn to run the saw?"

"My grandparents. Chris must have told you this was their dairy farm. They always told us Vermonters have to be good with tools and able to improvise when something goes wrong because, you know, help isn't just around the corner."

"That's for sure. The farm is just as Chris described it, isolated and peaceful. This is my first trip to Vermont. What a beautiful state, the topography, the mountains, the streams, the fall colors."

"We like it," she said. She reached for a thermos by the chain saw and took a sip of tea. "Did you come up from Boston?"

"Yes, yesterday."

"You're dressed like a hiker, but you don't look like you hiked very far. Did you hitchhike?"

"Good one." He grinned. "No. I drove most of the way. I camped last night at Quechee Gorge, which was simply gorgeous." His voice had the slightest hint of an accent, probably Spanish.

She returned his grin. "Nice."

"Thanks. Boston is where Chris and I got to know each other and where we do some work together."

"Anti-war work?"

"Yes."

"I don't think Chris has ever mentioned you. I'd remember a name like Johnny Dollar."

"I try to keep a low profile. I've asked him not to talk to other people about me."

"Is it your real name?"

"It's more like a persona."

Lisa took another drink of tea. Her hair, the color of a wheat field, was pulled back in a ponytail, and her blue T-shirt was sweat stained under ragged brown bib overalls. She grabbed a long-sleeved shirt off the woodpile and put it on.

Johnny looked around the barnyard and spotted a man barely visible behind a dusty barn window. He was watching them. Lisa saw them eye each other. Johnny seemed to be on alert, taking stock of his surroundings. She wondered if he could be a fugitive. Too old to be a draft dodger. His movements were athletic, controlled, not nervous. The way he introduced himself was respectful. His eyes were penetrating. He could probably handle whatever life threw at him without freaking out. His face suggested he'd already taken quite a few of life's punches.

"Tell me about your relationship with my brother."

"Oh, it's very professional. I mean it's not a business relationship, like where money changes hands. He does the kind of work I respect, and I try to help him with that. We rarely see each other, but we've become friends. I kind of operate in the background. In newspaper lingo, I'd be a confidential source."

"Sounds mysterious. Does it involve breaking any laws?"

"That's the kind of question I'd rather not answer for a variety of reasons. Most important is I don't want to get you or your brother in trouble. If anyone ever wants information from you about me you won't have anything to hide because you don't know anything. You can be truthful, with one exception, my phone number. I'd like you to have it if you agree not to share it."

"Why would I want it?"

Johnny glanced toward the barn. The man was no longer there.

"If we go for a walk would your friends get alarmed?"

"Did you see one of them watching us?"

"Yes, but not any longer."

"Did you tell them you're a friend of Chris?"

"Yes."

"I don't think they'd mind."

"Then I have a request. Would you take me to Turtle Rock?"

"Why?"

"From the way Chris described it, I'd love to experience it. I'd also like to talk to you without an audience."

"OK. It's a good place to talk. I'll tell my boyfriend where we're going and we can hike up there. Do you want something to drink?"

"I'm good. I've got water."

She said she'd be back in a few minutes.

When she returned, they set out from the woodpile and skirted a massive garden that had recently been harvested. It was easily more than half the size of a football field, bordered by young fruit trees and bushes. Johnny asked about it, and she told him it provided most of the vegetables she and her friends would need through the winter. They crossed a pasture and headed into the woods on a rugged old logging road that narrowed to a path and climbed through cedars and white pines and maples to the peak of a high ridge. Lisa set a quick pace. The trail was steep in spots, but Johnny had no problem keeping up. The trail flattened as it turned to follow the height of the ridge. Soon Johnny saw what appeared to be a clearing through the trees and asked about it. "That's our destination, Turtle Rock, our special place." When they reached the clearing, Johnny was stunned by the dramatic view of the surrounding western mountains and the size of the domed boulder in the center of the clearing. "Spectacular," he said as he circled Turtle Rock. He reached out to run his hand along the smooth surface. "Do you think it would mind if we climbed up on top and sat down?"

"It's never complained before," said Lisa. The rock was more than twenty feet across and nearly ten feet high. "It's a nice place to meditate if you can stand sitting on stone." She showed Johnny a convenient foothold and climbed onto the rock. He took off his pack and followed. They sat in the center, facing the western view in silence for quite a while. Johnny was the first to speak. "I'd love it if Chris was here," he said, "but I thought it would be best if I came alone. He doesn't know I'm here. I'll leave it up to you to tell him. As you know, he plans to defy the draft. Has he mentioned Lincoln Freeman to you?"

"I've heard the name," she said. "A young civil rights lawyer I think sometimes works with Boston Draft Resistance."

"That's him. He's going to represent Chris to challenge the constitutionality of the draft. I think he's a good choice, but their odds of winning are ridiculously low."

"That's never stopped Chris before. It's comforting he has a good lawyer. What I'm worried about is what'll happen when he goes to that Army base and refuses to be inducted. What are they going to do to him?"

"He should be fine. If they try to arrest him or take him into custody, Mr. Freeman will be able to handle it. Chris calls him Link. I haven't met him, but I've provided information and documents through Chris for him to use for various purposes. What worries me more than the Army is the FBI. That's why I came up here."

"What does the FBI have to do with anything?"

"I don't want to alarm you, but J. Edgar Hoover, the head of the FBI for what seems like forever, as you probably know, is very powerful. He's also ruthless and is out to destroy the anti-war movement. He calls anti-war leaders public enemy number one, just ahead of civil rights leaders. Never mind organized crime. That doesn't seem to be on his hit list. Under cover of law enforcement, Hoover is turning America into a combat zone going after anti-war protesters, who aren't out to hurt anybody."

"Is he after Chris?"

Johnny said Hoover's agents were gathering as much information as they could on anti-war and civil rights activists in cities all over the country. "Chris has a pretty high profile in Boston. A few months ago, as you probably know, Benjamin Spock, the pediatrician, was convicted of promoting draft resistance in Boston. Think about it. The government is trying to put America's leading authority on raising children in prison because the doctor wants to save lives. Spock and Chris know each other." Johnny said that Hoover had ordered his agents to recruit informers, meaning mostly criminals, to act as spies and infiltrate the anti-war movement. "He wants to know what anti-war leaders are planning so agents can stop them or harass them or manipulate them or, like Spock, prosecute them, whatever it takes to shut them down. I know that's happening right now in Boston."

"How do you know that?"

"That's another one of those questions I'd rather not answer, to protect Chris and you as well as myself."

"What would they want with me?"

"With Hoover anything's possible. With other activists, he wants to know everything about them and their families, from traffic tickets to criminal records to drug use to romantic affairs, pretty much anything that could be compromising and used against them."

"I don't have anything to hide."

"I'm not saying you do. But if strangers like me come around here asking questions, I'd like you to let me know because it could mean trouble for Chris or others. That's why I'd like you to have my phone number."

"You don't work for the CIA or something like that do you?"

"No, no, no. I don't work for any government agency. I work for myself, for what I believe in, which is that the draft is incredibly unjust and the war is totally immoral. The war is killing and maiming our children and corrupting our country and our government, and I'm doing whatever I can to prevent it from ruining what most of us value. For me, it's personal, not business."

"How do you support yourself?"

"That's another one of those questions I'd rather not get into."

They stretched their legs and shifted positions and returned to silence. This time it was Lisa who spoke first. "I'd like your phone number," she said. "I won't share it. I'm out here in the mountains in the middle of nowhere doing a back-to-the-land thing, as I expect Chris has told you. I won't be part of an economy that's exploiting and polluting and eventually probably destroying the planet. All for greed and power. I want to show that we don't have to live like that, that it's possible for us to save ourselves from ourselves, to live responsibly and find ways other than wars to settle our differences. I'm sure it sounds naïve and stupid when I say it like that. But I like it here. I support Chris and the anti-war movement from afar."

"You two are kindred spirits."

"We do share some genes," she said. "If you give me your phone number, are you going to ask me to keep it secret and not say anything about you to other people?"

"Yes."

She cocked her head and looked up above the trees. "Listen," she told him. He looked around and was about to say he didn't hear anything when he detected wingbeats and then squawks and then watched two big black birds soar above Turtle Rock, one after the other. They squawked again as they passed overhead and flew out of sight down the valley.

"That does it," said Lisa. "They also think I should have your phone number."

"Were those crows?"

"No. Ravens. They've been here ever since I can remember, which is almost twenty-five years. They like it here. I think they like our family."

"I can understand why." Johnny reached into his shirt pocket, pulled out a card and handed it to her. "Here's how to reach me. It would be best for both of us if nobody sees this and you only call from a pay phone."

* * * *

Shortly before midnight, the tidal air at the South Boston Army Base was heavy with fog and the stench of dead fish and diesel oil. Three figures dashed across a stretch of blacktop to the backside of a hulking, six-story building. They were college graduate students, but they were outfitted for something else. Two wanted to make headlines. They wore black ski masks and backpacks and carried crowbars. The third lagged a few paces behind. He preferred to avoid publicity. He was tall and slim with long black hair tucked inside a dark, hooded sweatshirt.

A military police cruiser had just circled the building and drove on. It looked like one of the routine patrols they saw while planning their raid. If so, the patrol was not expected to return for close to an hour.

On a Sunday night, thousands of Boston-area college students were studying or working on assignments or catching some sleep ahead of morning classes. But the guys sneaking through the Army base only studied or went to classes when they had to, when they needed a grade to retain their student deferments that shielded them from the draft.

The office building they were about to attack appeared identical to other nearby buildings. It was the place where draftees and recruits were ordered to show up for physicals and testing and were then sworn in to the Army to be turned into soldiers, most likely bound for Vietnam. In military lingo it was called AFEES, a regional Armed Forces Examining and Entrance Station. Among the young, it was known by other names, frequently accompanied by obscenities.

Few lights were visible inside the building. The raiders moved quickly along the outside wall from one first-floor window to the next, switching flashlights on and off to check what they could see inside. They tried opening each window, but none budged. They reached the corner of the building and conferred. Each corner had a spotlight illuminating the outside area from above, except for their corner where the spotlight was dark. They turned back and stopped in front of the second window. One of them tried to pry it open with his crowbar and backed off frustrated.

The other masked man said "fuck it" and grabbed his crowbar with both hands. Holding it like a baseball bat, he swung. The window exploded, shattering the stillness of the night. It sounded like a car crash.

The thin man cringed and looked around nervously. The other two used their bars to clear the debris and climbed through the opening into a room with a desk and a couple of chairs. They stood still inside, trying to quiet their breathing while listening for alarms or guards. Based on their surveillance, they didn't expect guards, but they weren't sure about alarms. They didn't hear anything.

One of the masked men told the thin man outside, "Stay where you are while we're inside. If you have to use the whistle, blow it as long and loud as you can. One whistle means time's up and we come back here. Two means something's wrong and we get the hell out any way we can and meet back at the apartment."

"Ten four," said the thin man, fingering the whistle in his pants pocket.

The masked man turned to his partner in the room, raised his arm in a signal of solidarity, and declared, "I'm ready. How about you?"

"Let's do it."

They bumped fists, switched on their flashlights, and moved to the office door. One lifted his crowbar and told his partner to stand back. "No. Wait," said the other one. He reached out and opened the door. His partner smashed it anyway and they disappeared down a hall, breaking doors and windows as they went.

Outside, the thin man shook his head. His name was Ian MacPherson and he felt sorry for the other two. He was good at calculating odds, and he would never bet on those two accomplishing anything other than self-destruction. He checked his wristwatch. They had set an inside time limit of thirty minutes to do whatever they were going to do. He didn't know or care, as long as they didn't kill anybody and he didn't get arrested. It sounded like the others were above him now, on the second or third floor. They had a rough idea of the inside layout from students who'd been there for draft physicals.

MacPherson rechecked his watch. He tried to count the minutes and guess how much time was passing. He was surprised how quickly he counted and how slowly time moved. He didn't sign up for this. He'd been drafted by the guys who were inside. He smirked at his own joke.

The other two imagined themselves as radicals, reckless and eager to change the world. A couple of hours ago MacPherson was playing cards and drinking beers at their apartment when they asked him to be their lookout. He said it depended on what they were going to do. They told him they wanted to spray paint anti-war slogans at the Army base. He'd reluctantly agreed, only because someone else had ordered him to cozy up to them.

Now, standing alone outside the building, listening to the demolition, MacPherson felt like he'd been sucker punched. He should have seen it coming. He knew all about deception. This raid could become a complicating factor in his life. But he'd figure something out. He usually did.

Inside the building the others reached the offices where draftees were tested and given physicals. They smashed everything in sight. They knocked over file cabinets and pried the locks open and tossed draftee medical records across the floors and spray-painted anti-war slogans everywhere—floors, walls, and ceilings. In a bathroom they used Army paperwork to clog sinks and toilets and left the water running. One of them checked his watch and told the other they'd better leave soon. He said he wanted to wreck one more office that looked like it belonged to whoever was in charge. They broke through the door where a nameplate identified the officer by name, Lt. William Sanders. They smashed his desk and phone and pictures on the walls, including a large framed image of the president. They toppled file cabinets and pried them open and scattered the contents. "Hey man," one shouted as his partner was spray-painting "SDS" on the president's face behind the desk. "Check this out." He held up what looked like an ammunition vest. "They're running drugs out of here. It's packed with bags of powder and thousands of dollars." His partner told him to bring it. "Time to go." They hustled toward the stairs. The floor was covered with running water cascading down the steps. They slowed to a walk, but the one with the vest slipped turning the corner, fell sideways, and reached for the railing. He missed and slid, bouncing down the stairs on his butt.

Outside, MacPherson checked his watch again. Not much time left. A siren sounded in the distance. It grew louder, coming in his direction. He wouldn't have time to run. He couldn't lay on the ground because it was covered with broken glass. He flattened himself against the side of the building, his arms outstretched, glass crunching under his shoes. He looked like a scarecrow. A Boston police cruiser raced by on the other side of the building. MacPherson's heart pounded as the siren receded.

He checked his watch. A phone rang. It was inside the office behind him and it kept ringing. The others burst back into the room and switched off their flashlights. One of them picked up the phone and shouted into it, "SDS. We're busy. Leave a message." Then he smashed the phone with his crowbar and shouted for MacPherson to get away from the window. They threw their backpacks through the opening, as well as a third bundle, and scrambled out. They were breathing hard. They pulled off their ski masks, grabbed their backpacks, and passed the bundle to the thin man. It was olive drab. He asked what it was.

"A bonus. Something we found. A vest. It got wet, but don't let anything fall out of the pockets. It could be worth a lot of money. You need to hide it in a safe place, like a storage locker. With a key. We gotta get out of here."

They'd agreed to split up and take different routes back to the apartment. They took off, slowing down only to look over their shoulders.

2

Friday, October 4, 1968
Cape Cod, Massachusetts

The jobsite on a sandy hummock was speckled with wind-torn pitch pine and scrub oak. It overlooked the coastline and Nantucket Sound south of Boston. The view could be enchanting or threatening or something entirely unforeseen, depending upon the New England weather and the mood of whoever was doing the looking. On this sunny fall afternoon, a framing crew of five carpenters, their hammers hanging from their belt hooks, gathered around a table saw on the first floor of the house they were building. It would become an elegant weekend getaway for a wealthy family, the kind of place nobody on the crew could ever afford. They hoisted beers to toast one of the carpenters on his last day of work, Jud Stillman, who'd been drafted and was supposed to report for induction into the Army in a few days. They also passed around a bottle of whiskey, which intensified the mood.

Two of the carpenters were military veterans, recently back from Vietnam, discharged from the Marines. They delighted in telling war stories during breaks. To listen to them, Vietnam was the highlight of their lives and always would be. They bragged about the harsh conditions they endured and the dangers, the land mines, booby traps, and ambushes that killed and maimed their buddies. Those lucky enough to survive bonded in a brotherhood of war, tense with fear and crazy for revenge.

On the afternoon of Stillman's going-away party, one of the marines recalled how his unit routinely killed Vietnamese civilians because nobody could tell the good guys from the bad guys. He warned Stillman to be on guard because women and children or grandmothers and grandfathers could be carrying grenades or planting mines. The other marine recalled the time he killed a Vietnamese farmer's water buffalo for sport, shooting it from a helicopter while the farmer was working his field. "Target practice," he said with a grin. The marines laughed together as they hoisted their beers to Stillman and encouraged him to "make sure you kill some gooks for us."

He didn't return the toast. "I'm not gonna go to Vietnam," he said. "I'm not gonna kill anybody. At least not over there."

"When you're drafted, that's where you're going."

"No. That's where I won't go."

"So you're a draft dodger."

"No."

"Then he's one of them conscientious objectors."

"A fucking coward."

"I knew it. The college boy is a commie coward."

"He thinks he's better than us."

"That's why he hangs out with that other longhair."

They closed in, like a snarling pack of animals.

The foreman, a master carpenter, worked his way around the table saw and got in Stillman's face.

"Are you a draft dodger?"

"No."

"Then you're going to Nam."

"I'll go into the Army, but I won't go to Nam."

"'Cause you're scared?"

"Because I won't be part of an immoral, fucked-up war."

"That's bullshit."

"The Vietnamese haven't done anything to us."

"Bullshit. They're the fucking enemy, fucking communists taking over the fucking world."

"We're the invaders. We're taking over their country."

"Fuck you."

"The British tried to do the same thing to us about two hundred years ago. You remember what we did to them?"

"So you're not going to defend your country?"

"Our country isn't under attack."

"I say it is. I say real Americans are under attack by hippie fucking commie fags."

"Like me?"

"If that's what you are. 'Cause I'm not sure I know you anymore." He put his beer on the table saw and pulled his blue knit cap down across his dark eyebrows. "Looks like somebody needs to teach you a lesson. Remind you who you are. You're a fucking American."

Stillman didn't move. They glared, eyeball to eyeball. They had been working together for almost a year. They trusted each other. When the crew was split between two jobs, the foreman would stay at one site and put Stillman in charge at the other. The marines resented that the college kid could tell them what to do. The foreman was Irish, short and stocky. No doubt he could handle himself in a fight. Stillman was at least twenty years younger and slightly taller with an athletic build. He had a mustache and his long brown hair curled around his neck at his shoulders. He didn't have much experience fighting. Keeping his eyes on the foreman, he cautiously put his beer on the table saw and said, "I guess you gotta do what you gotta do."

One of the marines edged behind Stillman and grabbed his arms. Stillman reacted instantly, elbowing the marine hard in his side, then spinning and hitting him with two quick punches to the face. The marine stumbled backward and the foreman stepped in between them. Stillman had been around a few street and bar fights. He'd seen that anyone who hesitated lost.

The foreman raised his arms with open hands like a referee, directing the fighters to move away from each other, indicating the confrontation was over.

"This didn't turn out like I wanted," he said. "It was supposed to be a send-off." He told the marine to stand down. He shifted his cap and relaxed his shoulders, then his expression. He grabbed the whiskey bottle off the table saw, took a swig, and said, "Here," holding it out to Stillman.

"Thanks." Stillman took a drink and handed it back.

"You were dependable," the foreman said.

"We built some good houses together," said Stillman. "You taught me a lot."

The foreman nodded and turned away. The others followed his lead.

They picked up their tools in silence and headed for their trucks. They drove off, one after another. The last to leave, the marine who grabbed Stillman from behind, rolled down his window and shouted, "America. Love it or leave it you fucking asshole commie motherfucker."

Stillman thought about blowing him a kiss, but didn't. He just wanted them gone. He'd avoided talking politics with the crew. It would only create tension. No minds would be changed. He was sure he'd never see any of them again. He picked up their empty bottles and put them in a trash box.

The ocean sparkled in the afternoon sun. He loved the view. He loved the work. It was physical, stimulating, satisfying. At the end of each day he could see and touch and smell what he built and be proud. This would probably be the last house he'd ever build. He hadn't set out to be a carpenter. He wanted to be a writer. He figured the best way to do that was work for a newspaper. He had talked with a few editors, but they wouldn't hire him because he had passed his draft physical and would soon be in the Army. He found work as a construction laborer and after a few weeks was promoted to carpenter to work with the foreman to start a new framing crew. He hated the draft, but he had the draft to thank for the chance to learn how to build houses.

Stillman finished his beer and opened another that had been left on the table saw. He hoisted himself onto a sawhorse and took a swig. The fucking draft. It had ruled his life since his student deferment ended at graduation. Friends had extended their deferments by going to graduate school, whether they wanted to or not. They had the money. Stillman didn't. Plus, he didn't want to be in school anymore. He wanted to get on with his life. He considered the draft unconstitutional, but knew courts had ruled otherwise.

He'd been ordered to report for his Army physical less than two weeks after graduation. The government didn't waste time. At his physical an Army medic told him he should have been exempted from military service for head and face injuries suffered in a car accident. But the Army had cut back on medical deferments because the war was raging. Now he only had two more days of freedom before he was supposed to report for induction at the South Boston Army Base.

It was decision time. He figured he had three choices—go into the

Army, go to prison, or go to Canada. He didn't want prison. He'd told friends he'd move to Canada, but that was back when the decision was hypothetical. He liked Canada. He'd lived in Montreal with his family when he was a kid. Now, looking out over the ocean with the sun sinking and shadows lengthening, he decided to delay the Canada decision. He'd go into the Army. He'd only go to Canada if he was ordered to Vietnam. He figured it wouldn't make much difference if he went to Canada as a deserter or a draft dodger.

He finished his beer and walked around the inside of the house, imagining how it would look when it was finished. He reached out and grabbed a stud on an interior wall. The foreman had asked him to rebuild that wall because the marines had messed up the framing. The foreman was a perfectionist. Stillman didn't like having to fix other people's screwups. He thought those marines might not be so careless if they had to fix their own mistakes. But he knew that wasn't true. Those marines didn't care about the quality of their work. They never would.

He scanned Nantucket Sound for what might be the last time. He grabbed his tools, made his way down a plank to the ground, and headed for his car, a faded blue Volkswagen Beetle. He put his tools inside, where he had removed the passenger seat to make room for them. He looked back at the jobsite. He was going to miss building houses. It was a relief he didn't have to fight the foreman. But he was determined to fight the Army. He would create as much trouble as he could without putting himself behind bars. He'd been a passive anti-war protester, going to marches and demonstrations. Now his opposition to the war would be personal.

His grandfather had been in the cavalry on horseback on the Mexican border before World War I, the war that was supposed to end all wars. His father was in the Army Air Corps in World War II. He was born a child of war, one of millions of baby boomers fathered by soldiers returning from the second world war. Then came the Korean War. Then the Vietnam War. And spanning the Korean and Vietnam Wars, there was the Cold War, when the prospect of nuclear annihilation became frighteningly real. That was four wars and counting in just twenty-one years since he was born. And that didn't count the dozens of smaller wars being fought around the rest of the world.

War, he figured, must be an essential building block of the human genetic makeup. Look at kids. They instinctively played war games. Then in schools they were forced to memorize the names and dates of generals and battles and wars. That's how adults told time. Counting the days between wars. We're prisoners of war. We always will be. Until we destroy ourselves. Look at religions. They had savaged each other for thousands of years to rule the world. Religion was a license to kill dressed in fancy clothes. As it was in the beginning, it is now and ever shall be. Wars without end. Amen.

"A-fucking-men."

He shouted it out loud. To nobody.

He thought about the teenagers drafted to fight in Vietnam. They couldn't drink or even vote against the politicians who were sending them to kill and be killed. They had no voice. How unfair was that?

He opened the driver's door and dropped heavily into his seat, ready to put the key in the ignition. He would miss his car. He was giving it to a friend until he got back. He had distanced himself from a girl he really liked. He planned to look her up when he returned from wherever he was going. If he returned.

He started the bug and put it in first gear. The radio was on and the Beatles new hit song "Hey Jude" was playing.

He had a flash of anxiety about his decision to report. He didn't know anything about the military, other than listening to those two marines. He learned more about war from them than he ever did from his father or grandfather. He had figured he could never do the horrifying things those marines bragged about. Now he wasn't so sure. He might be capable of anything if it could end the war. He had heard reports about American soldiers killing their own officers in Vietnam with grenades. They called it fragging. He imagined he should have felt a chill at that thought. But he didn't. He stepped on the gas.

3

Saturday, October 5, 1968
Downtown Boston

Saturday night foot traffic was picking up, and Johnny Dollar was on the prowl, looking for a particular pair of shoes to come his way. He was on the sidewalk with one foot propped on top of a stained wooden box, a rag draped over his shoulder, checking out shoes as people passed by, trying to make eye contact. "I can do something about those scuffs," he'd say. "I'll clean 'em up in no time." Sometimes several people would turn toward him all at once and look down at their shoes. "Who wants to go first?" he'd say.

He liked that some people still cared about the appearance of their shoes and were even willing to pay for a shine. Rock and roll music and hippies were changing the world, rebelling against the middle-class make-believe Disney lifestyle of their parents. They grew long hair and beards. They wore tattered Salvation Army hand-me-downs, the counterculture uniform of the time, anything to piss off anyone who thought they knew everything about everyone else based on how they looked. Johnny knew all about people making assumptions. He'd learned how to use it to his advantage. He'd also learned that he really could judge some people based on their shoes.

"Good evening, Johnny," said a man in a suit wearing a fedora. "How's it going?"

"So far, so good. How 'bout you?"

"Weekend work."

"That's too bad. But your offices are sparkling. We cleaned 'em this morning. Thanks for getting me on the crew."

"I hear you fit right in."

"Yeah and the money really helps. Why don't you step over here and let me take care of those shoes. If you take a bullet tonight, you're gonna want 'em to shine when they wheel you into the ER with your toes pointed toward the heavens."

"I can always count on you to cheer me up."

"It's part of the service."

Johnny pointed to his box. The man's shoes were already nicely polished, but he put his left foot on the stand and Johnny went to work.

"So what's the FBI got going tonight?"

"You know I can't talk about cases."

"Unless it'll get you something. With you guys, it's always get. Never any give."

Johnny put the finishing touches on the left shoe and signaled him to switch feet.

"What are you seeing these days?" the agent asked.

"Lots of shoes. Big shoes. Little shoes. Brown shoes. Black shoes. Some of the ladies like colored shoes. Red seems to be catching on. Just like those magic ruby slippers in *The Wizard of Oz*."

"Suppose you had a pair of magic slippers. What would you do?"

"I don't know. I don't have time to dream. It doesn't pay."

The agent reached into his pocket and pulled out a one-dollar bill, then another. He handed both to Johnny, stepped back, and looked at his shoes. "Nice job," he said. Johnny thanked him for the tip.

The agent turned to leave, then stopped. "One more thing," he said. "As we've talked about before, there's a lot of anti-government shit going on. Student radicals, like those SDS assholes, they're doing stupid, dangerous things. You know what happened with those Democrats in Chicago this summer. Lots of people were hurt. It didn't look good. You know what I mean. It's those anti-war agitators. The director wants to shut 'em down before they do any more damage. It's a high priority. If you hear or see anything, you can tell me. Just between us."

"With you guys, it's never just between us."

"We protect our informants."

"What makes you think I know anything about that kind of stuff? When's the last time you saw one of those SDS guys get a shine?"

"We both know there's more to you than a shine, Johnny. You're a smart guy. We're on the same side. You know where to find me. Hell, now you probably even know where my desk is. I'll see you later."

He stepped into the flow of foot traffic.

"Later," said Johnny. He took off his gray tweed newsboy-style flat cap and put it in his box. He waited until the agent was almost out of sight and headed off after him at a safe distance. He was easy to follow in his trademark fedora.

4

Wednesday, October 9, 1968
South Boston Army Base

"Stillman. Judson Stillman."

The command echoed off the walls and hung unanswered in the gleaming barren room. The lieutenant scanned the young faces in front of him. His fingers gripped a podium displaying a gold United States Department of the Army insignia. The podium was flanked by flags, the room's only decorations other than a picture of the president on the wall. Two soldiers were positioned rigidly to either side of the podium.

"Judson Stillman," the lieutenant repeated. "Step forward. Now."

Nobody moved.

The lieutenant paced to the center of the line of draftees and recruits, his heels cracking on the polished floor. He turned sharply and stopped, looking sternly up and down the line. Almost all had already taken a step forward, as ordered, after their names were called. Seven were left behind.

The officer scanned the back row, pausing to look at each one.

"Which one of you is Stillman?"

Nobody answered.

"OK. Listen up. Here's what we're going to do. You men in the back who haven't had your names called, you're going to sound off with your full name, last name first, first name, middle name last, and step forward. From right to left. Sound off now."

Two young men at opposite ends of the row—they looked more like boys—started to speak at the same time and stopped. They glanced nervously at each other, and then at the officer.

"Starting on my right," the lieutenant barked. His arm shot out to his right. "Sound off. Now."

Three called out their names in order and stepped forward.

The next one said nothing. He had the look of a resister. His clothes were scruffy, his hair was long, and he had a drooping mustache.

"You're next," the lieutenant said, looking him up and down. "What's your name?"

Still nothing.

The lieutenant moved in front of him, leaving just inches between them. He imagined this renegade's head and face being shaved. It would take seconds. That task would be performed at his next stop.

He leaned closer and rose up to whisper into the renegade's ear, "Keep this up and you will suffer. The Army will break you."

No reaction.

The lieutenant's mission was to induct this latest batch of conscripts and send them on their way to training and then the war. This renegade was an irritation. The lieutenant reminded himself to maintain his composure. His uniform was pressed perfectly, his shirt decorated with medals and ribbons. His black shoes sparkled under the fluorescent lights. He was short, made all the more apparent as he pressed close to the ragged recruit. The recruit smelled of marijuana. The lieutenant smelled of cigarettes, coffee, and perfume.

He took one sharp step back and said, "It's obvious you have a problem, son. But it's not a hearing problem or you wouldn't be here. What's your name?"

Still nothing.

Stillman wasn't sure how he wanted to handle his introduction to the Army, other than by challenging authority. His indecision had something to do with the joint he smoked before he was dropped off an hour earlier by a friend outside the decaying South Boston Army Base, a waterfront relic of World War II.

He expected the other draftees would be college graduates like him. But most looked like they were still in high school, and a lot of them were Black. He hadn't known any Black kids in high school and had only passing contact with a couple of Black students at college.

He thought about Muhammad Ali, the brash young boxer who refused induction. Ali said the US government was his enemy, not the Viet Cong. He was willing to go to prison. He said his people had been in jail for hundreds of years and could handle a few more. But most people didn't have Ali's courage, or his prestige, or his money. If everyone who was against the war refused induction, there wouldn't be a war.

"I'm going to give you one more chance," the lieutenant said. "What's your name?"

"What do you think of the draft?" Stillman asked.

"I'm the one asking the questions."

"I think it's a reasonable question since you're sending all these kids off to die. What are they going to be fighting for?"

"For our country."

"That wouldn't be the same country that's stealing our freedom would it?"

The lieutenant's expression tightened. "Son," he said, "you're delaying this induction. If you don't answer, I'll have you escorted to a place where we'll find out your name one way or another. Now, are you going to tell me who you are, or do you want to do it the hard way?"

"Jud Stillman."

"Outstanding, Stillman," said the lieutenant, moving another step back. "Now take one step forward."

"Wait," shouted one of the other draftees. "Don't do it." He was a white guy, about the same age as Stillman, wearing glasses, a crumpled tweed sport coat, and faded blue jeans. Another troublemaker, thought the lieutenant.

"Who are you?" the lieutenant demanded.

Rather than answer, the draftee ignored the question and sat down on the floor. He took off his glasses and cleaned them with a red bandanna. He then looked at Stillman and said, "You should think carefully about that step before you take it."

"Why is that?" Stillman asked.

"Hold it," said the lieutenant. "I'm in charge here."

The man on the floor dismissed him with a wave of his hand and continued talking to Stillman. "Because it's a really big step. What this Army guy doesn't want you to know is what that step means."

"Stop talking," demanded the lieutenant.

"That step means you're volunteering to be in the Army and you're inducted and you don't even know it and you don't have any constitutional rights anymore."

"That's enough," said the lieutenant.

"That's how the politicians and the Army see it. That's how they get around the Thirteenth Amendment that ended slavery. The theory is you can't be forced into bondage if you volunteer, even if you don't know you're volunteering."

"Sergeant," barked the lieutenant. One of the soldiers by the podium marched forward and snapped to attention next to the lieutenant.

"That sure sounds like slavery," said Stillman. "I didn't volunteer for anything."

"Are you two together?" demanded the lieutenant.

"Never seen him before," Stillman said. "But he seems to know what he's talking about. Is he right?"

"Join me," said the man on the floor. "Sit down and join me. If everyone sits down, we can end the war."

Stillman shifted his feet, and his shoes squeaked on the floor as he looked around the room.

"Stillman," the lieutenant thundered. "Get this straight. You either signed an enlistment contract or you were drafted and you passed your physical. It doesn't matter. Either way, you're gonna be in the Army or you're gonna go to prison. It's your choice. If you want to talk about it, step aside, and you'll be taken to another room."

Stillman stood his ground in silence.

The officer moved toward the man on the floor.

"What's your name?"

"Thompson."

"First name?"

"You can call me Chris. What's your name?"

"It's on my uniform."

"I can't read it from here."

"Sanders."

"First name?"

"It's lieutenant to you. Are you going to stand up and step forward or are we going to do this the hard way?"

Thompson put his glasses back on. "Why do you think I'm sitting here on this floor? I'm not going to be part of your duplicitous little ceremony and your imperialist war. I'm going to fight you and your draft with whatever it takes."

"Then we need to send you to another room." The lieutenant nodded over his shoulder. "Sergeant."

Thompson kept talking. "You're inducting kids who should never be in the Army and you're doing it illegally because you have ridiculous quotas to fill because nobody supports this war."

"Take him away."

"And you're pissed off because the SDS trashed your little induction station."

The lieutenant raised his hand to stop the sergeant. "What did you say?"

"You heard me."

"Where did you hear that?" he demanded.

"I work with Boston Draft Resistance. We hear a lot."

"Sergeant." The lieutenant motioned with his arm. "Get him out of here and get as much information as you can."

"Yes sir." The sergeant stepped forward and motioned to the other soldier by the podium for help. Together they reached under Thompson's arms, hoisted him to his feet, and spun him toward the back wall. "This way," ordered the sergeant, pushing him toward a door marked "Authorized Personnel Only."

As he was led away, Thompson twisted and shouted back to the others. "Resist. Call Boston Draft Resistance. Tell them Chris sent you. You can stop the war." Then to his escorts, he said, "Hey guys, take it easy. This is America, you know."

The door thumped shut behind him and the room was silent.

Stillman looked down the row of draftees. They were so young. They appeared dazed and afraid. Nearly all were watching him to see what would happen next. He was thinking about the step he had been ordered to take and about the guy who had just been hauled off and how he had to be careful.

The lieutenant continued with the induction. He called the names of the last two recruits. Both cooperated and took the step. Stillman took the step with them. All the inductees were ordered as a group to repeat an oath of allegiance to the United States, to defend the Constitution and obey orders. Stillman didn't say anything. It was a meaningless gesture. He knew it didn't matter. He was now in the Army, beyond the reach of the Constitution. He took grim satisfaction that he didn't obey the Army's first order, the oath, even if nobody knew or cared.

The lieutenant told the new soldiers the Army would turn them into men. He warned them that the penalty for disobeying orders or causing trouble was a court martial under the Uniform Code of Military Justice and a dishonorable discharge. Their lives would be ruined. Now that they were in the Army, he said, it wouldn't do them any good to whine to their parents or write to their congressmen. Nobody could bail them out. In the Army, they would be part of a disciplined team, and the men on the team would depend on each other for their lives, and if one of them stepped out of line, the team would make sure he wouldn't do it again or the entire team would suffer.

A door opened behind them, and they heard a commotion.

Everybody turned around to see what was going on. The sergeant who had taken Thompson away was walking sideways toward them through the door, telling someone they couldn't see to keep applying pressure. He told the lieutenant, "Sir, we had to call for medical assistance. The draftee fell."

*   *   *   *

The newly minted soldiers were herded to a loading dock and told to wait for a bus that would take them to eight weeks of basic training at Fort Dix, New Jersey. At one end of the dock was a pay phone mounted on a wall. Stillman got in line to use it. An old man in a rumpled uniform circulated through the crowd, passing out packages. He offered one to Stillman.

"What's this?"

"These are a few things to help you on your way, toothpaste, toothbrush, soap, shaving supplies, that kind of thing. It's a comfort kit."

"I'm not interested."

"It also has a Bible."

"A fucking Bible?" Stillman said, loud enough for all to hear. "Look around. What do you see? They're kids. You're sending these kids to the other side of the world to kill and be killed so some filthy rich capitalists and politicians back here can make more weapons and stuff tons of money in their pockets to buy more yachts and mansions. And you're justifying it with a Bible?"

"Some people find it comforting," said the old man.

"You can't be serious?"

"You don't have to read it."

"That's a bonus." Stillman grabbed the package from the old man's hand and hurled it off the loading dock. It slapped the oil-stained pavement below and slid to a stop. "That's where your comfort kit and your Bible belong."

"I didn't mean to upset you," said the old man, backing away. "We're just trying to help."

"Then stop the war."

"I wish I could."

"Bullshit. You need the war. You need misery. Without war and misery, you and your religion wouldn't have anybody to save. You're part of the fucking war machine."

"I'm not in the Army."

"You're supporting it. Go find somebody else to save."

The other draftees were frozen in place, watching the drama. One of them in the phone line ahead of Stillman, a big, young Black man jumped down off the loading dock. He picked up the comfort kit, brushed it off, and returned it to the old man. Then he said to Stillman, "Hey man, take it easy on the old guy. He doesn't mean you no harm. We're all part of the war machine now."

Stillman took a deep breath. The kid had a strong voice, broad shoulders and stood out in the crowd. His face was youthful, tender, but his look was tough. He had a black leather jacket and a black beret, like the Black Panthers, and he had big bushy hair. "You're right," Stillman said. "I got carried away, but this isn't the place to peddle religion."

"Nobody wants to be here."

"I get it," Stillman said. "Thanks."

"It's cool. But if you keep pissing everybody off, ain't nobody gonna wanna be around you."

"I'm not gonna roll over and do whatever the Army wants."

"I'm not saying you should, but you gotta be smart. Otherwise, the Army's gonna squash you like a bug."

"How do you know so much?"

"I know what it's like."

"Are you from around here?"

"Roxbury."

"I've heard of it. Is that the combat zone?"

The kid laughed so hard he shook. "That is funny," he said. "Roxbury, the combat zone. You must not be from Boston."

"Not from the city. No."

"The combat zone is where sailors and soldiers get laid and beat up and robbed. Roxbury's different. It's where Black folks live."

"That's where you grew up?"

"Yeah. Where're you from?"

"Lots of places, mostly the suburbs. My parents moved a lot. I feel like a visitor on this planet."

"Hell of a time to stop by."

"Yeah, just in time for the draft. Were you drafted?"

"No. A judge gave me a choice. Army or prison."

"What'd you do?"

"Are you fucking with me?"

"No man."

"It's obvious what I did. I'm here ain't I."

"No, I mean how can a judge do that?"

"I was born Black."

"Yeah. I'm learning that can be tough."

"You don't know."

"You must've been arrested."

"That's why you go to prison."

"What'd you get arrested for?"

"Rioting."

"Here in Boston?"

"That's right. Roxbury. Twice." He took a deep breath. "The first time I was with my mother."

"Holy shit."

"She was at a sit-in protesting welfare rules, and the cops got carried away. The second time was after Dr. King got shot."

"Were you rioting?"

"I was trying to protect my mother. The cops were beating on people. The second time there was no riot. I was just out on the street, like a lot of people, sad, pissed off they killed our leader because they were scared of him."

"Yeah. It's a dangerous time to be a leader. King. The Kennedys. You think things might get better and they don't. I feel guilty for saying it, but I was in Florida on vacation when Martin Luther King was shot. It was like the whole country was ready to explode."

"It did."

"I know. I saw it. All the cities along the coast were on fire the night we drove back to school. I was there for spring break."

"So you were partying in Florida when he was murdered."

"Yeah."

"How many people at that beach party looked like me?"

The question left Stillman stunned. He raised his eyebrows, took a deep breath and exhaled through his mouth. "I can't believe I didn't even think about it," he said. He ran his fingers through his hair while looking around at the others fearfully awaiting their next orders on the loading dock.

Turning back to the Black kid, he said, regretfully, as if confessing a sin, "Nobody partying down in Florida looked anything like you and these others about to be sent off to war."

"And what does that say?" He prodded.

"Wow. It's just wrong, man."

"It says people like me don't get invited to your beach parties or your houses or your schools or your jobs unless we play basketball or football or fight your wars."

"Yeah. You're right."

"The only invitations we get are for your jail parties and your war parties."

"Yeah. I'm beginning to see that."

"How many guys do you know who went to Nam?"

"One."

"I know six, and I'm only nineteen years old. How many do you know who didn't come back?"

"One."

"I got three, including my brother. And there's two others who came back with body parts missing. What's that tell you?"

"Oh man. That sucks," Stillman said. "I'm really sorry to hear that. I can't even imagine how that feels." He reached out. They exchanged a fist bump.

"My name's Jud. Good to meet you."

"Same here. I'm Clarence. Some call me Bear."

The other draftees had resumed talking among themselves. Bear told Stillman his big brother was drafted into the infantry and got killed in Vietnam during the Tet Offensive weeks before Martin Luther King was killed. Bear got a letter from his brother a few days after his mother was notified he was dead. A letter from the grave. His brother told him the war was lost and nobody wanted the Americans there and all the soldiers had turned against the war. He said he was going to join the Vietnam Veterans Against the War when he got back to the states.

"So you're against the war."

"You got it."

"Same here," Stillman said. "Look at us. We grew up in totally different worlds, but we're here together. We're even thinking the same."

"Don't get carried away," said Bear.

"We could build on that."

"We can try, my man."

Bear said his brother hadn't paid any attention to the war until he dropped out of high school and was drafted. After he was in the Army, he told Bear to get serious about school so he wouldn't get drafted. He said racism was a lot worse in the Army than in Boston. While his brother was in Vietnam, their father, an auto mechanic and a heavy smoker, died of a heart attack. Their mother worked two jobs to keep the family together. Bear had a younger brother and an older sister who were deeply affected by the deaths of their father and brother. Bear followed his older brother's advice and got serious about school. He said he was accepted at a community college, but the judge wouldn't let him go. He said he had to go into the Army first. Bear did well in school, but his real passion was music. He taught himself to play the guitar, piano, and saxophone. He played in a school band, but mostly he loved the blues. He'd jam with friends and had played in some clubs around town. He talked about the power of music. He brought up James Brown, who had a Boston concert scheduled the night after Martin Luther King was assassinated and saved the city from burning. Boston officials had wanted to cancel the concert, but Brown insisted he had to play to keep the peace. It worked. The concert was broadcast live on television, but Bear didn't see it because he was in a jail cell.

"That was a turning point," said Stillman.

"The TV broadcast?"

"No, I mean King's assassination. It energized the anti-war movement. Maybe it'll bring Black and white people together. It could change everything."

"What you been smoking?" Bear laughed.

"It was different from the Kennedys. They were the government."

"And white."

"King was a nonviolent preacher who wasn't threatening to hurt anybody."

"Except the whites down south by letting Black folks vote."

"You got me."

"Amen."

The line for the phone moved slowly. Stillman and Bear, carried away with their own thoughts, looked around the loading dock. It was crowded with clusters of recruits separated by color and language, whites with whites, Blacks with Blacks, Spanish-speaking with Spanish-speaking, some sitting on benches, some standing, shifting from one foot to the other, looking lost, waiting for the bus, waiting to be told what to do next. A siren shrieked, and an ambulance drove by, its emergency lights flashing.

"What's up with the beret and the jacket?" asked Stillman. "Are you a Black Panther?"

"Not really. I like the look, what it says."

"Like Black pride, identity, power?"

"Something like that. It tells the Army don't fuck with me and my people."

"That'll only last until they take our clothes and cut our hair."

"I'll still be Black and my eyes will still say don't fuck with us."

"I don't know too many Black people."

"No shit."

The line for the phone shifted forward. It was Bear's turn. He told Stillman to go ahead of him.

"Thanks. Don't you want to make a call?"

"Not really."

Stillman said he wanted to call the newspaper to tell them about the guy who was supposed to have fallen. He flipped through a directory hanging next to the phone.

"He sure pissed 'em off," said Bear. "Must've been that thing about SDS. I don't know much about that."

"Students for a Democratic Society," said Stillman. "They organize demonstrations, sit-ins, strikes at colleges. They do some crazy stuff. They're pretty combative."

"You think that guy was SDS?"

"I don't know."

"You think he was pushed?"

"Maybe."

"You think he was in the ambulance?"

"Probably."

Stillman dropped a dime in the slot and dialed the number for one of Boston's newspapers, the *Boston World*. He asked to talk to a reporter and was put through to an editor in the newsroom.

"Roger McAlister."

"Hi, Mr. McAlister. I'm told you're an editor?"

"Yes. How can I help you?"

"I'm calling to let you know a draftee was injured, maybe seriously, at the Boston Army Base today when he refused to be inducted."

"How do you know that?"

"I was there when it happened."

"What's your name?"

"Jud Stillman."

"Are you in the Army?"

"I'm a draftee. I was just inducted, so yeah, I'm in the Army and I'm about to be sent to basic training at Fort Dix, New Jersey. Oh shit. It's here. The bus is pulling in now."

"How did the draftee get injured?"

"He fell or he was pushed down some stairs after he sat on the floor and refused to be inducted. We think he might have been pushed."

"Who is *we*?"

"Me and another guy."

"Did you see him pushed?"

"No. They took him through a door in the back of the room, where the stairs were."

"Do you know how badly he was hurt?"

"No, but it sounded bad. They called for medical help. An ambulance just came by with a siren and flashing lights. Look, I'm being ordered to get off the phone and get on the bus. I'd like to know what you find out."

"You can call back when you get a chance. What was the name of the draftee who was hurt?"

"It was Chris somebody. They know him at Boston Draft Resistance. He mentioned something about the SDS. I've got to go. What's your name again?"

"McAlister. Roger McAlister."

"Thanks, Mr. McAlister. Gotta go."

5

Thursday, October 10, 1968
Thompson Farm, Vermont

The screen door on the old Vermont farmhouse slapped shut behind Theo, a long-haired bearded man in jeans wearing a Henley sweatshirt hanging open at the neck. He went to the edge of the porch holding a spatula and called out toward the nearby barn.

"Lisa," he shouted. "You've got a phone call."

She leaned around a corner of the barn and said she'd only be a few more minutes. "Who is it?"

"It's your mom. I think you should take it now. She sounds like it's important."

"OK. I'll be right up."

Lisa ducked back behind the barn and came out through its massive sliding doors, heading for the house. She slipped out of her boots on the porch and swept back her hair as the screen door closed behind her. The phone was on a table next to the couch. Theo, standing by the couch, looked grim. He handed her the receiver without saying a word. She lifted the cord over a lamp on the table, moved a guitar off an armchair and eased into it.

"Mom?"

"Honey. I'm sorry to call so early."

"It's not a problem. I was in the barn."

"I've got dreadful news."

"Oh no." Lisa sat up and shifted forward in her chair.

"There's no easy way to say this. Your brother is in the hospital. He's in a coma."

"What?" She stood up and stared at the phone. "No. That can't be. No."

"I know. We don't want to believe it either, but I'm at the hospital right now with your father. We're at Mass General. We've been here all night and we're praying."

"What happened?"

"Chris went to the Boston Army Base yesterday, you know, because he was drafted. They said he fell down some stairs. We didn't find out until last night."

"He was going to refuse to be inducted."

"That's what we thought."

"Did it happen after he refused?"

"We don't know."

"I didn't want him to go."

"I know."

"I called him last night. Now I know why he didn't answer. Those bastards. The Army did this."

"The Army said it was an accident."

"That's a lie. The Army did this. Chris doesn't just fall down stairs. The Army must have known he was with Draft Resistance. And those bastards probably knew he ignored his first induction notice. They were trying to kill him."

Lisa realized she was on her feet. Her body was quivering and she was looking wildly around the living room and saw Theo and two friends watching her with alarm. She dropped back into the chair to try to stop shaking. Her mother assured her she and her father were both as upset as she was and didn't believe the Army's explanation. They had been unable to talk to Chris because he'd been unconscious since he got to the hospital. Her mother said his face was cut and terribly bruised and swollen and there was no way to know how long the coma would last. The doctors said they might have to operate to relieve swelling in his brain.

"Goddamn." Lisa was on her feet again, walking around with the phone cord in her hand. "The fucking Army. We need to talk to Chris. What are the chances he'll recover?"

"We don't know. One doctor said he could have brain damage, even if they operate. We couldn't ask for a better hospital, but we have to pray for a miracle."

"We have to find out what really happened."

"We will honey. We will."

"I'll try to get there as soon as I can. I've got truck trouble."

"Your father can come up to get you."

"No. You should both stay there. I'll find a way."

"Don't hitchhike."

"I won't. I'll fix the truck or find a ride."

"If you can't find a ride, don't hitchhike. Call us."

"I will. When did you find out about Chris?"

"Yesterday." Her mother was crying. "We decided to wait until we knew more about his condition before calling you. We hoped we'd know more by now."

"Who told you?"

"Somebody from the hospital called. And then somebody from the Army. A captain or lieutenant, I think. We've got his name written down at home with a phone number."

"Have you talked to the police?"

"No."

"You should. We need to get a lawyer."

"We will. But first we need to do everything we can to help Chris."

"Yes. Is there anything I can do?"

"I'm sure Chris would like you here, to be here when he wakes up. But before he wakes up we need to show him how much we care, how much we love him, and just hope he can hear us and know that we're with him."

"Of course. We do love him. And I love you. At least you and I love him. And I'll be there as soon as I can."

"You know your father loves him, too, even if they don't agree about some things."

"I hope so. I can't believe this happened. I didn't even consider the Army would do something like this. For opposing the fucking war."

"I know. But right now, we've got to think of Chris and do what we can to help him get better. We'll let you know if anything changes down here."

"OK. And I'll let you know when I can get there. Right now, I've got to get out of the house. It's dark in here. I need some air. I need to go for a walk."

"That's a good idea honey."

"Bye mom. I love you."

"We love you too. Bye sweetheart."

Lisa put the phone back on the table and looked out through the screen door.

"That sounded bad," said Theo.

Lisa didn't look at him. "It's bad. Real bad. Chris is in a coma. It's the Army. It's the government. It's the politicians. It's the fucking war. I've got to go for a walk. And then I've got to get to Boston."

"Want me to walk with you?" Theo asked.

"No. No thanks. I need to be alone."

"Remember, we're all here to help with whatever you need."

"Thanks." She left the house.

She walked in a daze past the barn and the garden, through pasture to the woods and the path to Turtle Rock. She climbed aboard the boulder and sat with her arms wrapped around her knees. Pockets of mist hung over the valley's still-green fields and pastures bordered by autumn's scarlet, orange, and gold forest colors. She closed her eyes and thought about her brother and how the two of them had camped overnight at Turtle Rock at least once every year, sometimes with family and sometimes just the two of them when they were older. Their grandparents' farm had been their favorite escape from the suburbs growing up. They had collected eggs and fed chickens and pigs and helped with the cows and the crops when they weren't playing in the barn and the woods and pastures. She remembered the aroma of fresh-cut hay bales in the loft as they stacked them in the crisscross pattern they had been taught to keep them from tumbling down. They helped cut, split, and stack firewood for winter heat. They tapped maple trees and collected the sap and boiled it into syrup. Lisa loved to watch the steam clouds billowing from the sugar house roof, signaling the start of spring. She and her brother bonded through their visits and learned from their grandparents about how farmers had to provide for their own needs because most of them didn't make enough money to pay somebody to help. Self-sufficiency was a matter of pride in these mountains. Probably in all mountains.

She heard wingbeats and lay back on Turtle Rock and looked at the sky. The ravens squawked as they flew over the clearing. She waved and called to them, "I wish Chris could be here. I wish we could fly with you." They squawked and flew on. Each spring their babies were so loud calling for food that it was easy to spot their big nests high in the pines.

The farm had been in the Thompson family for generations. Their grandparents had operated it, always as a dairy farm, until they retired to Florida while Lisa and Chris were in college. Their mother and father bought the farm as a second home to keep it in the family. They hired nearby farmers to hay the fields and brush cut the pastures to keep the forest from closing in. Chris had graduated from college in May with a degree in government. He planned to go to law school after taking a year off to work with Boston Draft Resistance, counseling young people unsure about their rights and options. He was sure he would probably be drafted, even though he had already been accepted at law school. Lisa, two years older, hadn't seen Chris in months. He favored city life, where he wanted to try to make a difference.

She stood up and declared out loud, "You did make a difference." Then she realized she had just talked about Chris in the past tense and corrected herself. "You are still making a difference," she shouted. She remembered the last time she was on Turtle Rock she was with Johnny Dollar and he gave her his phone number, swearing her to secrecy. Johnny knew Chris was going to refuse induction and would be represented by the lawyer he and Chris knew. So either the lawyer or Johnny or both of them would know something went terribly wrong at the Army base. She was confident they would find out what happened. She'd wait to talk to the lawyer until after she got to Boston. His name was easy to remember. Lincoln Freeman.

She jumped down to the grass and twisted her ankle when she landed. It stung. She lay on the grass for a few minutes, testing how far she could bend and turn it. It was a struggle to get back on her feet. She circled Turtle Rock slowly, using the boulder for support while limping to keep her throbbing ankle moving. She picked up a broken branch to use for a cane. That helped. She remembered that Chris broke his ankle one summer jumping off a hay wagon. Both of them had been hurt at the farm, but never seriously. Now Chris was unconscious, fighting for his life. She imagined him in a hospital bed hooked up to machines with tubes running in and out of him. She thought about an awful morning at the henhouse when she and Chris were ten. They had gone to collect eggs and walked into a massacre. Half of their grandparents' chickens were dead. The others were barely alive, their bodies ripped open, their insides hanging out in the blood-splattered dirt. She didn't know about weasels before that. They can squeeze through the smallest openings, and they seem to kill and mutilate for no reason. She and Chris raced back to the house that morning, screaming through tears. Looking back, she mostly remembered how she admired the courage of those mangled chickens. They struggled to stay upright as long as they could and shivered silently as they dropped and died. Recalling that image, she wondered whether any animals other than weasels killed when they weren't hungry, and why they did it. The similarities between the henhouse massacre and the nightly television news photographs from Vietnam were chilling.

Lisa stopped hobbling, leaned back against the rock, and looked out at the view across the valley. In the distance the top of a far ridgeline was highlighted in the morning sun. She loved this farm. It was so peaceful that it didn't seem real. She knew it couldn't last. Nothing does. She had to get to Boston. She could feel the tension in her face and realized her teeth were clenched. She didn't know what she was going to do, but she couldn't do nothing. She wished Chris had continued to ignore his induction notices. He could have come to the farm. But she knew how passionate he was about openly opposing the war and the draft. She told him she would have joined him in refusing induction if they drafted girls. He predicted that would probably happen someday. He told her he wasn't afraid to go to court, or to prison.

She'd had her sanctuary in the mountains. At least until now. In college she started out majoring in biology and was inspired by Rachel Carson's book *Silent Spring*. After that, she was drawn to environmental studies and the movement it was spawning to clean up and preserve the earth and its creatures.

She and Chris saw themselves inheriting a world driven by power and greed, destined to destroy everything they valued. Chris was determined to confront destiny and change it, while she had withdrawn to their special place to set an example to save the planet. But even at the farm she couldn't escape the consequences of war. Their father was an executive at a weapons company that profited off the war. His salary was paying the farm's mortgage. She was haunted by that and couldn't stop feeling guilty about it. Chris and their father rarely saw each other or spoke anymore.

"Fuck that fucking war," she shouted from the clearing at Turtle Rock. "Fuck the Army."

With her brother in a coma, she knew what she had to do. She would leave the farm to help him and to find out what had happened and do something about it. She felt rage building again through her body. Before this morning, the rational part of her personality would have rejected anger and revenge as a waste of time that clouded good judgement. She was surprised she was already thinking about how to get even. The flower child takes on the Army. The Army wouldn't see her coming.

6

Friday, October 11, 1968
Boston

In a stale third-floor apartment in the Brighton section of Boston, Roy Hodges lit a cigarette and put the Rolling Stones' *Beggars Banquet* on the turntable. He flopped into a shabby chair with a newspaper in his hand. The windows were open to air the place out. It was Friday and the afternoon light was fading.

Conga drums pulsed from two large speakers as the Stones' bad boy singer Mick Jagger picked up the beat on "Sympathy for the Devil."

Hodges was a grad student who shared the apartment with another grad student, Bruce Franklin. They dressed and acted like students, but considered themselves vigilantes. They had joined the local SDS chapter, but grew frustrated that anti-war protests weren't producing results and broke away to operate on their own, convinced a cultural revolution wasn't going to change America.

They didn't go to Chicago in August to protest at the Democratic National Convention. They were sure it didn't matter which political party won the presidential election. The military-industrial complex was going to be the only winner, and the war would go on. After seeing national TV coverage of the convention, where protesters were saturated with tear gas and dragged away bloody from having their heads bashed in by police goon squads, Hodges and Franklin decided to strike back on their own terms in Boston.

While the Stones played in the background, Hodges scanned the pages of his newspaper. Franklin was on the couch, rolling a joint. Behind him was a wall poster of Che Guevara, the Marxist revolutionary who had been captured and executed a year earlier in Bolivia. Hodges threw down his newspaper in disgust on a pile of other papers and magazines on the coffee table between them. "I can't find anything about Chris," he said. "It's like he doesn't exist. We wouldn't even know what happened if his sister hadn't called Draft Resistance. What's happened to the news?"

Franklin lit the joint, took a deep hit, and passed it to Hodges. "It's like when we trashed the Army base," he said. "How can that not be news? We tip off the newspaper and they ignore it."

"It's the establishment man."

"We need to ramp it up. I've talked to a couple of people about explosives."

"No man. Cool it. We've got to lay low for a while. We're in enough trouble already."

Hodges got up and went to the only window in the room. There was nothing to see except the side of the next building, which was so close he could almost touch it. The paint was peeling, the alley below was splattered with trash, and the Stones were singing their song. He blew a stream of smoke through the window and passed the joint back to Franklin. "You know they're coming for us."

"Yeah. It's that fucking vest. We should have left it there. Ian should be here soon. Then we'll find out what we're dealing with."

Only two other people knew they had raided the Army base. One was MacPherson, who was staying with them while his apartment was being fixed up after a fire. They met him through anti-war demonstrations and convinced him to be their lookout. They tried to solicit help from another guy they met at a coffeehouse who was against the war and seemed to have some kind of connection to the Army Base. He introduced himself as Johnny Dollar, but they were sure that wasn't his real name, which is why they thought he might be the kind of guy who would help them. They told him they wanted to break into the induction center, but they didn't tell him what they wanted to do. He said he didn't want any part of their plan.

After the raid, they wanted to boast about what they had done. But they didn't because they couldn't trust anyone. They congratulated themselves for jamming the gears of the Army's war machine and managing to do it without getting caught, but their only reward was forced isolation. They were sure they stopped the Army from drafting anyone for at least a few days. And their calling card placed the blame right where they wanted it, on the Boston SDS chapter. But their pride turned to disillusionment when they didn't see any newspaper headlines. Confined to their apartment, thinking about what to do with the vest, their decision to steal it started looking like a death sentence.

They remembered the name on the office door where the vest was found, Lt. William Sanders. They were sure he'd be coming for them. They had checked out his picture before they smashed it. In the photograph, he was in uniform, adorned with a chest full of combat medals. He looked tough, ready to kill anyone who got in his way without any second thoughts.

After the raid, MacPherson stashed the stolen vest in a locker at South Station, a transportation hub near the Army base. They left it there untouched. One of them stopped by every couple of days to try to see if the locker was being watched. It had been two weeks without any indication of trouble. They asked MacPherson to get a sample of the powder so they could try it and know what they were dealing with.

"I wish we'd never found that fucking vest," Hodges said.

"Where we fucked up was stealing it," said Franklin. He took a final drag on the roach and dropped it into an overflowing ash tray. "How much do you think it's worth?"

"Who knows?" said Hodges. "Thousands, tens of thousands, could be a hundred thousand or more. Enough money to kill for. That's for sure."

"Those Army pigs don't know who we are yet," Franklin said. "If they did, we'd already be dead."

"They'll find us," said Hodges. "We blew it. We shouldn't have claimed we were SDS. That's how they're gonna find us."

"We could call that lieutenant and tell him where the vest is. Or we could go underground."

Hodges didn't respond. They'd had similar conversations over the past two weeks. They always ended with the soldiers finding them and killing them no matter what they did. They sank into their seats in stoned silence.

A knock on the door and a key turning in the lock was followed by MacPherson announcing his arrival and telling them he had a drug sample for them. Hodges asked him if he could have been followed.

"I made sure I wasn't. I zigzagged my way here and ducked in alleys to look back and check." He pulled a small plastic bag from a pocket inside his sport coat and gave it to Hodges.

"I'm done with this revolution stuff," MacPherson said. "My apartment is fixed and I'm moving back in. I need to put some distance between us." He reached into his jeans. "Here's the locker key. This stuff is too dangerous."

Franklin took the key into the kitchen and put it in the refrigerator freezer.

Hodges opened the bag of powder and raised it to his nose. "Doesn't have a smell," he said. "What do you think, Bruce?"

Franklin took a whiff, shrugged his shoulders, and looked at MacPherson. "How about you?" he asked.

"Probably cocaine."

"There's one way to find out," Hodges said. "I'm thinking we snort it. Are you with me Bruce?"

"I'll try it."

"What about you, Ian?"

"No. Like I said, I'm done. I'm going out tonight, but I'll hang around a few minutes to make sure you guys don't die from whatever's in that bag."

Hodges rummaged through the newspapers on the table. "Can't find the mirror," he murmured. He went into the kitchen and came back with a plate and razor blade. He sprinkled the powder on the plate, chopped it, and separated it into four long lines. He rolled up a dollar bill and inhaled two lines. He passed the plate and the bill to Hodges, who snorted the other two.

They eased back into their seats and looked at each other in questioning silence while MacPherson flipped through the newspaper. After a while, Franklin asked Hodges how he felt.

"I don't know. I think I'm feeling something. Not sure what."

"Me too."

"The music's great. Sounds like we got new speakers."

"Dig it."

The Stones were on their last song, and soon there was nothing but street sounds.

"More music," Hodges said slowly, as if coming out of a dream. "More music." He started to get up, but dropped back into his chair. "Ian, can you do it?"

"Any requests?"

"The Doors."

MacPherson sifted through a stack of records and put one on the turntable. The music started. An organ set the melody as drums picked up the beat in a prelude to a primal scream.

Franklin and Hodges closed their eyes. They looked so content that MacPherson wondered whether he should try some.

After a while, Franklin shifted on the couch and stretched out on his side. He started to say something and gave up. He shifted again and rolled off the couch onto the floor. He crawled across the floor on his hands and knees. MacPherson asked if he felt OK. Franklin convulsed, crawled a bit farther, and threw up on the floor.

The Doors played on.

Hodges struggled to get out of his chair, stood, unsteadily holding onto the back of the couch, and stared blankly around the room. He worked his way toward the bathroom. He didn't make it. He bent over and vomited next to Franklin, who was still on his hands and knees, staring at the foul puddle on the floor.

MacPherson said he was going to call an ambulance.

"No," Franklin protested. "No. No, it's cool. I think. I'm good."

MacPherson asked Hodges how he felt.

"The Doors man," he said.

MacPherson went to the kitchen to get a towel to clean up the puke.

Franklin crawled back to the couch. He wiped his face with his arm and turned toward Hodges, who had made it back into his chair. A conspiratorial grin crept across Franklin's face. "Guess what man," he said. "This ain't cocaine."

They melted into the cushions, closed their eyes, and soaked in the music.

7

Sunday, October 20, 1968
Fort Dix, New Jersey

Bear and Stillman weren't church-goers, but they made sure they were on time for Sunday morning chapel at Fort Dix. They were wearing green fatigue uniforms and combat boots, and their heads were covered with stubble. The church service was voluntary. They didn't pay attention to what was said. They just wanted an hour or so of peace, their only chance for relief from two weeks of relentless harassment and abuse by drill sergeants.

After the service, they waited while the chapel emptied out because Stillman had requested a meeting with the chaplain. It would be his second. He had asked the chaplain the previous week to help him get out of the Army because he opposed the war and would never be turned into a soldier and was afraid of what he might do if he didn't get a discharge. He called it a potentially explosive situation. The chaplain reacted with indifference and told Stillman he had to give the Army a chance to prove itself worthy of his respect.

Bear was joining Stillman for his second meeting to report an extreme case of brutality in their unit. They were escorted to the chaplain's office and directed to sit in chairs in front of his desk, where he was shuffling paperwork. Overweight and balding, with a pale complexion that didn't go well with his formal Army uniform, he was as uninspiring in his office as he was from the pulpit. Stillman thought he looked like a figure in a wax museum. Bear looked across the desk and saw a corpse ready for burial.

"Trainees," the chaplain said, looking up, "what can I do for you this morning?"

Bear did most of the talking because the chaplain had been so unsympathetic to Stillman the week before. Bear told him that three trainees in their unit had gone AWOL Saturday night and were found by New York police in a city park, blotto after shooting up heroin. Shortly after midnight, the trainees were returned to the base, where drill sergeants put them through punishing physical workouts and beat them before locking them in a room on the third floor of their barracks, where they were chained to a metal bed frame. Bear said he heard they needed medical attention, as well as food and water, but nobody was sure because the drill sergeants who had the key were nowhere to be found.

The chaplain, who had impatiently drummed his fingers on his desktop while Bear was talking, asked why Bear and Stillman came to him.

"If you can't figure that out," Bear said, "you don't deserve to be a chaplain. You need to do something else, like find a new job that doesn't require compassion or sympathy." He stood up, turned his back, and moved toward the door.

"Wait," demanded the chaplain.

Bear turned back toward the chaplain. "Why?"

"That's not the way you leave a meeting with an officer."

"If you're looking for a salute, you don't deserve one," said Bear. "But I'm feeling generous this morning, so here you go."

He snapped off a salute and left, leaving the door open behind him.

The chaplain rose, trembling, from his chair, reached for his desk to steady himself, and followed Bear down the hall. "Wait," he demanded. "Stop."

Left alone, Stillman took the opportunity to check out the paperwork on the chaplain's desk. He saw his name on one document, a report written by the chaplain to Stillman's company commander about his attempt to get a discharge. He folded it and stuck it inside his shirt. Then he saw a memo titled "Coffeehouse Bombing." Bear had talked about a coffeehouse. He folded that memo and put it inside his shirt. He heard the crack of footsteps in the hallway and sat back down.

The chaplain appeared at the doorway. "This meeting is over," he said. "If you have any more problems with anything from now on, you will follow the chain of command." He stepped aside so Stillman could leave. Stillman stood and asked to use the bathroom. The chaplain reached into his desk and held out a set of keys. "It's the red key," he said. "The toilet's around the corner, the second door on the right."

Stillman took the keys and moved down the hall without saluting or closing the door. The chaplain slammed it shut behind him. Stillman turned around and stood quietly outside the door. He heard the chaplain dial his phone and tell someone, "They just left. They wanted to talk about the AWOLs. I'll get the equipment, but they've made me late."

Stillman headed for the bathroom, opened the door, looked around, and closed the door without going in. Then he left the building.

Bear was waiting outside. With nobody else in sight, he fired up a joint and handed it to Stillman as they walked. Stillman took a hit and said, "I'm such an idiot. I thought he'd have some compassion for those guys locked in the barracks."

"He might if those guys weren't Black," said Bear. "You know they're brothers, right?"

"Yeah, but nobody deserves to be treated like that."

"We've been treated like that for hundreds of years."

"But that's changing."

"That's what some people want you to believe."

"You make me feel so stupid."

"Just letting you know how it is on my side of town."

"Thanks. I'm learning more from you than I did in four years of college. You know, you'd hope a chaplain might be different."

"Some probably are. When I walked out of that motherfucker's office, all I could think about was my father."

"Wasn't your father a mechanic?"

"That's what he did for work. But he did a lot for kids in the neighborhood. If they got into trouble or their parents were fighting or something was wrong, they could always come to our house. They'd get fed and find a bed if they needed one. Both my parents loved kids. My dad was a good man. Compared to that chaplain, he was a saint."

"Why would anyone even want to be a chaplain in the Army?"

Bear took a deep drag on the joint—"To stay off the battlefield"—and passed it back.

"Just like the draft," said Stillman. "There's lots of college guys going to divinity school just to keep their student deferments and stay out of the draft."

"Praise the lord."

"Can you give me an amen?"

"How about a fucking A."

"Hey, at least we didn't come away empty handed," said Stillman. He dug into his pocket and pulled out a key ring. "He gave me these when I asked to go to the bathroom. I forgot to give them back. Maybe one will open his office so I can use the phone next Sunday and find out what happened to that guy in Boston."

He passed the joint to Bear, unbuttoned his shirt, and pulled out the memos. "I got these off his desk while he was chasing you."

"What a loser," said Bear.

"There's no shortage of those in the Army," said Stillman.

"I don't have a problem with that so long as they're not in charge of anything."

Bear passed the joint and a hot ash fell onto the memos Stillman was holding. He tried to shake the ash off, but it burned a hole through both memos before it dropped to the ground.

"Hot stuff," said Stillman. "One's about me and the other's about a coffeehouse. I think it's the one you told me about."

"The one that got bombed?"

"Yeah."

Bear reached for the coffeehouse memo and read it. "That's it, the anti-war coffeehouse," he said. "It closed 'cause of the damage. The Army'll do anything to stop another coffeehouse from opening. It's all here in this memo. Can't let soldiers talk and think for themselves."

He passed the memo back to Stillman.

"How'd you know about the bomb?"

"Brothers talk. Folks hung out there to get off the base and listen to music and talk, you know, about racism and the war and the Army."

Stillman tucked the memos back inside his shirt. "What about those AWOL guys?" he asked. "What's gonna happen to them?"

"The stockade."

"Why'd they go to New York?"

"To get drugs. That's where they're from."

"Guess what," Stillman said, holding up the roach before taking a last drag and ditching it. "You can get drugs right here."

They started walking back to the barracks. Stillman asked Bear what he knew about the stockade.

"It's hell in there."

"It's probably hell in any Army stockade."

"It's worse here. A lot of brothers are jammed in that stockade. People at that coffeehouse were trying to help 'em with protests and stuff. You talk anti-war. That stockade has a lot of guys who refused to fight, refused to go to Nam or went AWOL. It's a shithole. They rioted over the brutality."

A basic training platoon, led by a drill sergeant, marched past them on the street, chanting.

> *Mama Mama can't you see*
> *what the Army's done to me.*
> *Put me in a barber's chair*
> *And spun me around.*
> *Now I have no hair.*
> *Mama Mama can't you see*
> *what the Army's done to me.*
> *I used to date a beauty queen.*
> *Now I love my M16.*

Stillman asked why so many Black soldiers were in the stockade.

"We're standing up for ourselves," said Bear. "We're tired of fighting the rich white man's war."

"That takes guts."

"We're fighting for justice."

"What's justice look like for those guys locked up in the barracks?"

"They're fucked."

"What can be done?"

"Nothing. They fucked themselves."

"Who's gonna stand up for them?"

"Nobody."

"We could report it."

"We just did."

"That fucking chaplain. What if there's a fire or something while they're locked and chained?"

"They're fucked."

"What about a fire alarm?"

"What about it?"

"We could set one off, like a high school prank. It would be juvenile, but at least we'd be doing something and we could tell whoever shows up that they're locked and chained."

"Who would care?"

"The firefighters. They'd have to break down the door."

"Nobody would care. They'd keep it quiet. Just like that chaplain."

"We could do more than pull an alarm. We could set a fire and yell smoke and somebody else would pull the alarm. They can't ignore a fire."

Bear held up his hand and stopped walking. He looked at Stillman. "Where you gonna set a fire?"

"How about the bathroom, in a trash can?"

"Make some smoke."

"What if someone puts it out and doesn't pull the alarm?"

"We don't give them the chance."

"We smell smoke and yell and pull the alarm if no one else does, all at the same time."

"The barracks gets evacuated."

"Where's the fire alarm?"

"At the end of each hall."

"Who tells the firemen about the brothers chained in that room?"

"I don't know. Somebody."

"We could tell them."

"We're going to get questioned."

"All we know is we smelled smoke."

"One of us has to be the lookout while the other lights something and drops it in the trash can."

They neared their barracks, where some trainees were hanging out around the door, smoking cigarettes. Stillman bummed a cigarette from one of them.

Bear said he'd be the lookout. They climbed the stairs to the second floor where they shared a private room, a privilege they had earned by scoring well on the Army's tests.

"If we get caught, we're gonna lose our room," Stillman said.

"We'll lose more than that."

"Are we gonna do this?"

"It's risky."

"Ready?"

"No time like now."

Bear sauntered down the hall and into the bathroom. Stillman felt his pants pocket for his lighter.

Bear returned with a grin. "We got trash and nobody's in there."

Stillman headed for the bathroom. He lit the cigarette, opened the trash can, balled up some trash, lit it, and dropped the smoldering mass, along with the cigarette, into the can just before he heard Bear in the hallway ask another trainee what time it was and whether he had any cigarettes. Stillman dropped his pants and sat on one of the toilets. Smoke began seeping out of the trash can. He could hear Bear still talking. The smoke thickened. A wind gust through the bathroom window swept the smoke toward the hallway. Stillman jumped up, half pulled up his pants with one hand, and stumbled into the hall.

He looked toward Bear and the other trainee. "Where's the fire alarm?" he shouted. "We got smoke in here."

Bear sprinted down the hall and set off the alarm. Other members of their unit scrambled out of the dorm and started filing down the stairs to the outside door. A few of them checked the bathroom, where Stillman was at a sink running water on his hands. He told them, "The fire's in the trash can. It's hot. We need a bucket."

Somebody found a mop bucket. The smoke smelled awful. Sirens sounded in the distance. Stillman started a shower to fill the bucket. Bear kicked the trash can to tip it over. The lid came off and charred debris scattered across the floor. Somebody poured water on it from the mop bucket. By the time firefighters hustled up the stairs and reached the bathroom, the fire was out, but lingering smoke made it difficult to breathe.

They directed everyone to leave the barracks and gather outside. Bear told them some trainees might be trapped upstairs, locked in a room.

"Which room?"

"I don't know, it's just what we heard."

"We'll check. Who put this fire out?"

"We did," said Bear.

"Who found it?"

"We did. We smelled smoke."

"OK, good work. We'll take it from here. You have to leave."

Bear and Stillman worked their way downstairs around other firefighters and out into the bright sun. They exchanged triumphant glances.

While they were waiting to march to lunch, an ambulance pulled up along with MPs in their cruisers. Medics went inside with a stretcher. One of the three trainees who'd been chained was helped from the building by MPs who took him to a waiting van. He was in civilian clothes, grimy and torn. He wasn't handcuffed, but he was limping and had a bloody gauze bandage wrapped around his head.

"He looks like he's coming from a war," Stillman said.

"And going straight to the stockade," said Bear.

"Somebody should take him to the hospital."

"Yeah, right. We didn't do him any favors."

"At least we did something. Seeing him makes you wonder which is worse, here or the stockade."

"Not even close."

Medics came out of the barracks with the second of the New York trainees on a stretcher. He looked unconscious. They put him in the ambulance, which sped away with its siren blaring and lights flashing.

"At least one of them is headed to the hospital," Stillman said.

"What's sad is the Army could be good for those guys if we weren't fighting the stupidest fucking war ever. People been knocking 'em down so long they don't know which way is up. They got no hope."

Stillman reminded Bear about a Black trainee who passed out in a bathroom stall in another barracks a few days earlier with a bag wrapped around his head. He had been trying to get high on shoe polish fumes. "It's like he didn't care if he died," Stillman said.

"That's no hope. But some of us got to keep trying."

"Fuck the Army," said Stillman.

"Fuck 'em all."

Later, after lunch, they were told the third trainee who ran off to New York had been carried out of the barracks in a body bag.

8

Monday, October 21, 1968
Cambridge, Massachusetts

Climbing the stairs out of an MBTA subway tunnel at Harvard Square, Lisa heard the street traffic before she could see the sky. She had traded her farm overalls for a more formal look, a short skirt and blouse under her beat-up brown leather jacket. A colorful Native American parfleche bag hung from her shoulder. She sidestepped hustling students to get her bearings. She thought about what it would be like to return to campus life. But only for a moment. Mostly, the city, the crowds, and the traffic made her wish she was back in Vermont. A chilly fall wind swept the streets. She imagined the farmhouse, the warmth of the woodstove, the smell of fresh-baked bread, Theo playing a folk song on his guitar, and their friends gathered around. It had been two weeks since she left Vermont to be with Chris and her parents.

She had just spent a frustrating hour sitting by her brother's bedside with her mother. They tried to carry on a cheerful conversation when they were with him and cried together after they left his room. It was getting more difficult every day to put on a happy face. She had tried reading stories to him from the newspaper, but gave up, unable to find upbeat news. Mostly when Lisa talked to Chris she tried to remind him of pleasant memories from the good times they shared growing up. She hoped he would squeeze her hand or blink or twitch or do anything to indicate he could hear her. He didn't. Lisa wanted to tell her brother she would not rest until she found out what happened at the Army base and she would dedicate her life to making sure that whoever hurt him would never do it to anyone else ever again. But she didn't. She didn't want him to relive the pain and suffering of that day.

Now, after crossing the Charles River on the subway from Mass General to Cambridge, she was on a mission, looking for the law office of Lincoln Freeman, who had been recommended by Boston Draft Resistance and had worked with her brother and probably knew something about Johnny. She hoped he would represent Chris. She wanted to sue the Army.

She found the street where Freeman's office was supposed to be after a long walk from Harvard Square. Many of the neighborhood's buildings needed paint and repairs. They looked like cheap student housing, not suitable for an attorney. She checked the notepaper where she had written the address and approached the door. There was a number on it, but no sign for Freeman's office. A Black man wearing a leather jacket and carrying a brown paper bag edged up beside her. "Can I help you?" he asked. His voice was pleasant, but she was startled.

"Ahhh, no, I don't think so," she said, backing away. "I must have the wrong address."

"Who're you trying to find?"

"It's a law office. I must be on the wrong street."

"You wouldn't be looking for Lincoln Freeman would you?"

"Well, actually, yes, I am."

"Then you found me," he said, opening the door. "You must be Lisa Thompson. I've got an extra coffee here if you'd like one."

She thanked him for the offer, but declined, saying she'd just had some tea.

He apologized for the lack of a sign on the street. He said his landlord had promised to put one up listing all the offices in the building, but that was almost a year ago. Freeman's office was up one flight of stairs on the second floor. His nameplate was on the door, which opened to a waiting room with a couch, a couple of chairs, and a desk, where his assistant, as he called her, was on the phone. He waved to her, put a coffee on her desk, and led Lisa to his inner office, which had a window overlooking the street. Two walls were lined with file cabinets and bookcases. His desk was a jumble of file folders and paperwork.

He hung their leather jackets on hooks on the back of his office door and invited her to sit in a chair facing his desk. She put her bag in her lap and pulled out a notebook and a pen. He was wearing a red tie with a paisley pattern and a pressed blue shirt. He had sympathetic eyes, a trimmed mustache and goatee, and big hair in the Afro style. He opened his coffee, sat down, cleared a space on his desktop for a pen and legal pad, and smiled at Lisa.

"From what you said outside, this is not what you expected."

"I didn't know what to expect," she said. "I got your name from Boston Draft Resistance and Chris mentioned you. I didn't know you were Black. You're the first Black lawyer I've ever met. There can't be too many of you."

"More than you might imagine, but not enough. We're making headway."

"What I'm hoping to find is a lawyer who isn't afraid to go up against the government."

"Then you're in the right place. I'm a sole practitioner. I don't have the resources of a big firm, but what I do have is independence. That's really important to me, not entirely by choice. Many firms don't hire lawyers who look like me." He grinned. "It could be my hair."

"I like your hair," said Lisa. "I apologize for the way I acted when you came up to me on the street. I didn't see a lawyer carrying coffee."

"We all make assumptions," Freeman said.

"Then let me ask you about your name. I don't want to make any more assumptions. Does it refer to the civil war and the president?"

"Yes. I'm descended from slaves and one of my ancestors changed his last name to Freeman to celebrate emancipation. My parents came up with Lincoln. I was Link when I was growing up."

"I'll go with Mr. Freeman."

"I'm good with that. Chris told me you live in Vermont on a family farm that's sort of a commune."

"Some people think of it that way, but not really. It's just a few friends who come and go, and some help out and stay for a while."

"I've never been to Vermont, but I hear it's beautiful."

"And peaceful, usually, until now, for me, until this happened."

"So let's talk about Chris and why you're here. I know Chris because I represent some people with draft issues he sent my way. I like your brother a lot, and I want to help if I can. How's he doing?"

"Actually, not well. He's still in a coma. The doctors are worried about brain damage. I was with him this morning and I'm going back after we're done. I'll tell him you were asking about him."

"I tried to visit, but was told only family was allowed. Please give him my wishes for a full recovery."

"I will. As you know, I don't believe the Army's story about him falling down stairs. I think they went after Chris because he's an activist and a resister. I want to sue them and I want to stop them from hurting anybody else who's against that insane war."

"A lawsuit's one possibility," Freeman said. "I haven't researched the issue yet, but my basic understanding is that since Chris was not a member of the military, a lawsuit is possible. If he had been inducted before he was hurt, it would be a lot more difficult to hold the Army accountable."

Lisa opened her notebook and jotted a few words. She had been thinking about Johnny Dollar on and off throughout the morning. To honor his request for anonymity, she decided she would not mention him or their Vermont conversation. But she did want to know how her prospective lawyer felt about the FBI. She asked him if she should call the FBI to request an investigation about what happened to Chris.

Freeman reached for his coffee and slowly took a drink. He said the FBI would probably have to take a back seat to the Army's Criminal Investigative Division, known as the CID. "The Army doesn't want an investigation," he said. "It wants what happened to Chris to go away. The FBI is another story. It's supposed to be impartial, but it's not. And it's not our friend. The FBI considers the anti-war movement public enemy number one."

"I've heard that before. Wow. You—I mean we—we'd be going up against some big guns."

"The biggest," said Freeman.

Lisa leaned back in her chair. "So, is this something you might want to do, represent me and Chris?"

"Absolutely."

He asked if the family had received any written reports from the Army about what happened to Chris.

"Not yet. The only thing my parents were told is that he fell down stairs. They asked for a report, but they haven't received anything."

"Do you know who told them he fell?"

"It was a phone call from a Lt. Sanders."

"Has anyone tried to reach him?"

"I have. He's never available. So I went to the Army base, but that didn't go well." She told him she wanted to see Sanders face-to-face to size him up and get him to show her where Chris was hurt. But the soldiers told her Sanders was busy and they didn't know where the accident happened. "That's what they called it, an accident, not even an incident." She said she tried to keep her composure, but was frustrated. "I might have been a little confrontational."

"Did anyone threaten you?"

"No. They just kept telling me I had to leave because I wasn't supposed to be there. Actually you might say I threatened them. I told them I was going to sue and get our congressmen to help me find the truth they were trying to cover up. That didn't seem to worry them."

Freeman asked if she took notes about what happened. She didn't. He asked her to put it all in writing as soon as possible, including any phone calls to or from the Army.

"It's important for you to write about any contacts you have with anyone if we're going to build a case or accuse them of a coverup. Get names and ranks and phone numbers and dates and times. That way we can develop a chronology."

Lisa promised to write everything down that evening. She told him she'd like to hire him. They settled on a modest retainer. Freeman asked her to insist that the Army give her a copy of its full written report and any supporting documents. He also told her that he and Chris had been working together on a special case to accuse the Army of wrongdoing, specifically recruiting fraud. Lisa hadn't been aware of that.

"We have some documents confirming abuses in the Boston area," he said. "Some of them may have grown out of a government program called Project 100,000, created to get more bodies for the war by inducting men who would otherwise fail enlistment standards. A lot of the violations are down south, but it's happening here too. About half are Black. We're talking about kids with criminal records or low IQs or very little education. Some can barely read or write, if at all. Others hardly know any English. The government says it's helping those boys by giving them jobs and lifting them out of poverty and advancing civil rights. We say that's bullshit."

"That's unbelievable," said Lisa. "That sounds like murder."

"That's how we see it. That's one hundred thousand unqualified recruits every year. We suspect most are shipped to Vietnam. We think the Army took Project 100,000 as a license to do whatever they want, including going after a disproportionate number of Black folks."

"Does the Army know what you have? Could that be why Chris was hurt?"

"As far as I know, the Army doesn't know about this case. We've got more work to do before we'll be ready to go to court. But you and I have the same question about what happened to Chris."

He reached for his coffee. "There's another thing that happened," he said. "Are you aware the Army induction station got trashed by the SDS a few weeks ago?"

"No."

"The Army got so pissed off about it that they cut way back on medical deferments, practically eliminating them. Since then they won't let anybody out of the draft, Black or white, unless it's a really extreme case."

"How do you know that?"

"Because of Chris. He met somebody who knows a lot about the Boston Army Base and tells him what's going on there. The guy calls himself Johnny Dollar, if you can believe that. We think he might have a connection with Army medics because he's familiar with medical records and reports. He might even be a medic."

Lisa stayed silent.

Freeman said he suspected Johnny Dollar was the source of a lot of the internal Army documents that Chris gave him for their special lawsuit. He said some documents were from the Pentagon ordering medics at the South Boston Army Base to lower their "flunk rates."

"What are those?"

"That means Washington wants the medics in Boston to cut back on the number of people they let out of the draft. If you flunk your physical, you're free. You get a deferment from the draft, usually a medical deferment, like flat feet or bone spurs or high blood pressure, that can make people ineligible for military service."

"So lowering flunk rates," said Lisa, "would mean more soldiers for the war."

"That's right. Being a medic is a very powerful position at processing stations, like here in Boston. Medics determine who does and doesn't go into the Army. It can be a life or death decision."

"Wow."

"Officers at Army headquarters in Washington keep tabs on deferment statistics from around the country. Washington is saying Boston is letting too many people out of the draft. The pressure falls on medics to put more people in the Army because the government needs bodies for the war. It's like a butcher demanding fresh meat."

"That's vivid," said Lisa. "It sounds like the butcher doesn't trust the medics."

"That's right. Chris told me Johnny Dollar told him a lot of medics are draftees who are against the war, which makes sense. So they sympathize with other draftees who want to stay out of the Army and out of Vietnam."

"Chris knows his stuff," said Lisa. "So, it seems, does Johnny Dollar. Cheers for the medics. They're the ones who deserve medals. And as long as we're handing out medals, one should go to Chris."

9

Tuesday, October 22, 1968
Boston

In the Tuesday issue of the *Boston World*, a brief item was buried deep inside the metro section of the newspaper:

Heroin Overdose
Death Toll Rises

The bodies of two college students were found in a Brighton apartment over the weekend after the city received a complaint about odor.

Police said the students are believed to be the most recent victims of a deadly batch of heroin that claimed at least a dozen lives in September.

The men were identified as twenty-two-year-old Roy Hodges and twenty-three-year-old Bruce Franklin, graduate students at Boston University. Police said they appeared to have been dead for some time before the complaint was received.

Syringes and other drug paraphernalia were found in the apartment, according to police, who said the heroin is believed to have come from Southeast Asia. It is known on the streets as "Mekong gong." Police said most of the overdose deaths were in Roxbury.

10

Sunday, October 27, 1968
Fort Dix

Through closed doors at the Fort Dix trainee chapel, Stillman heard the start of the Sunday service and slipped down the corridor to the chaplain's office. He hoped the locks hadn't been changed since the chaplain misplaced his keys. One of the keys worked. He unlocked the door and stepped inside, closing the door behind him. He picked up the phone and dialed the number for the *Boston World*, hoping Roger McAlister would be working on a Sunday morning. A woman who answered said McAlister was not in the office, but put him through to an editor.

"News desk." It was another woman.

Stillman explained who and where he was. He said McAlister told him to call about a draftee who got hurt at the South Boston Army Base.

The woman said she didn't know anything about it. "If you can hold on for a few minutes," she said, "I'll try to reach Roger."

"OK," said Stillman. "I'm kind of rushed, but I'll hold as long as I can."

He looked around the chaplain's office. He didn't see any changes from the previous week. The office was compact with a desk, a bookcase, file cabinets, and a Xerox copy machine. Several photos of Asian children were on the walls. One showed youngsters gathered around the chaplain in front of a low-slung building. The chaplain had told Stillman on his first visit the building was an orphanage in Vietnam he helped build and was still supporting with military money. In front of the desk were a couple of cushioned chairs for visitors, the chairs he and Bear had used. He tucked the phone between his shoulder and ear and looked through the paperwork on the desk. He felt his gut tighten when he saw his and Bear's names on a memo with a subject line that said "Insubordination."

It was from the chaplain to their company commander and other high-ranking officers, reporting how Bear walked out of the chaplain's office a week ago after claiming the AWOL trainees were brutalized. Stillman wasn't surprised the chaplain would run it up the chain of command.

He stepped to the Xerox machine to make a copy of the memo. When he opened it he saw that someone had forgotten to remove the last sheet of paper that had been copied. It was actually four sheets. He turned them over and was stunned. The phone slid off his shoulder and hit the floor. He was holding two photos of naked Asian children in sexually suggestive poses and two contact sheets of negatives of adults and children in various stages of undress, engaged in suggestive poses and sex acts. "Holy shit," he whispered. He scanned the contact sheets quickly, but didn't see the chaplain in any of the pictures.

He pulled the phone off the floor by its cord and made copies of the memo and the photos. As he was putting the pictures back in the machine, the editor at the *Boston World* got back on the phone.

"Mr. Stillman," she said. "Sorry it took so long. I talked to Roger. He said he assigned a reporter to contact the Army base and the Boston police and they said nothing happened."

"So the Army claimed nobody got hurt that day."

"That's right," she said.

"They're lying. Do you know if the reporter called Boston Draft Resistance?"

"No, I don't. But Roger said you could give him a call if you want. I've got his home phone."

Stillman wrote down the number, using a pen and paper from the chaplain's desk. "I'm kind of limited in how much time I can spend on the phone," he said. "Could you look up the Boston Draft Resistance phone number for me?"

"Sure." It took another minute. She gave him the number and wished him luck.

Stillman checked his watch. He had been in the chaplain's office for more than fifteen minutes. He figured he had another ten to fifteen minutes before the service would end. He dialed the number.

"Boston Draft Resistance," said a woman who picked up.

"I'm so glad you're answering the phone on a Sunday," he said.

"We try to have someone here seven days a week," she said. "What can I do for you?"

He explained he was calling from Fort Dix about what happened at the Boston Army base to a guy named Chris.

"Were you there?" she asked.

"Yes," he said. "Do you know him?"

"Very well," she said. "His name is Chris Thompson. He's one of our best people. He's been in a coma at Mass General for weeks. I'm sure his sister, his family, would want to talk to you as soon as possible. Did you see what happened?"

"I didn't. That's why I'm calling you."

"The Army told his family it was an accident, that he fell down stairs."

"So the question is whether he fell or was pushed," Stillman said, checking his watch, then looking nervously at the door. "Nothing adds up. On the day it happened, I called the *World* to tell an editor that a draftee got hurt bad enough for an ambulance to be called. He asked a reporter to find out what happened, and the Army told him nothing happened and nobody was hurt."

"Why don't you give me your phone number and I'll have his sister give you a call. Her name is Lisa."

"I don't have a number. We aren't allowed to use phones here, and I won't have a number even when we can use them. Can you give me Lisa's phone?"

"How are you calling me today?"

"I'm on a phone I'm not supposed to be on, and I've got to leave here very soon."

She told him Lisa lived in Vermont, but was staying at her parents' house in Lexington for a while. She gave him both phone numbers. He thanked her and hung up. He looked around the room to be sure he hadn't moved anything or left anything. He tucked the copies he'd made inside his shirt, straightened the desk, and stepped to the door. He opened it just a crack to listen and then looked to see if anyone was in sight. He made sure to lock the door as he closed it and hustled down the corridor. He paused at the corner. He knew the chaplain's phone bill would show the calls. He hoped the chaplain made lots of out-of-state calls and that the Boston calls would blend in with the others and that he and Bear would be long gone and forgotten before questions were raised. But what really concerned him was the photos and how he and Bear could protect the children, wherever they were now.

When the chapel doors opened, Stillman stepped around the corner and eased into the line of trainees filing out. He saw Bear and gave him a conspiratorial nod.

11

Wednesday, November 6, 1968
Lexington, Massachusetts

The upscale suburb where Chris and Lisa Thompson's parents lived was about ten miles from Boston's Roxbury neighborhood, where Bear grew up. But the two communities were separated by far more than miles. Roxbury was a ghetto, predominantly poor and Black, struggling to build a middle-class, with dilapidated housing, little access to health care, and elevated rates of disease, crime, and unemployment, reflecting neglect by the city's leaders and institutions. Lexington was a tidy town, white and wealthy with a nationally recognized school system. Most of its young people went to college, more than a dozen each year to Harvard, and relatively few were drafted, although their lives were enriched through parents whose paychecks came from Boston-area defense companies that profited from the war.

It had been more than three hundred years since Massachusetts was colonized, largely by Puritan families from eastern England during what was known as the great migration. A much larger migration took place after World War I, as more than five million Black people left rural southern states to move to northern cities, fleeing racial injustice and seeking job opportunities.

It was back at Fort Dix where Stillman had learned that from Bear. Black migration was not the kind of history routinely taught in white suburban schools. Black history was passed down through families, by word of mouth, from generation to generation. While many moved north and found work, they couldn't escape the discrimination ingrained at all levels of American culture and business and government. The jobs were largely low-wage, and Black workers had limited options where they could live. Roxbury was one of the Boston neighborhoods where Black folks found housing.

The Thompsons' house was a short walk from the route of the Patriots' Day parade, which commemorated the battles of Lexington and Concord, and the Lexington Green, where the first shots of the revolution were fired. The house had a colonial look with modern conveniences, a two-car garage, and a large yard.

On this night, the Thompsons' house was dark except for a single outside light illuminating a porch between the house and the garage. Inside the house, a phone rang—once, twice, three times, four. Someone answered. A woman screamed. The lights came on.

The call was from Massachusetts General Hospital. Chris was dead. He had never regained consciousness. He was alone when he died. His body shut down during the night. The machines had alerted the nurses. The nurses had notified the doctors, and one of them called the Thompsons shortly before sunrise.

Chris's mother, Mary Lou, had visited her son every day during the weeks since he was admitted to the hospital. His father, Art, joined her at the hospital when he could after work and on weekends. Lisa had also spent many hours sitting with Chris, who never showed any signs of consciousness. The call from the hospital left them all numb.

They cried and hugged and dressed and drove to the hospital in silence. They were allowed to spend time in Chris's room before his body was moved. Lisa wanted an autopsy, which might provide a clue to what had happened at the Army base. Mary Lou and Art went along with her request. The doctors knew Lisa did not believe the Army's accident story.

Lisa and her mother left the hospital and returned to the Lexington house to notify friends and relatives. The first phone call Lisa made was to the Army to once again demand the report on Chris. The call lasted only a couple of minutes. She slammed down the phone, turned to her mother, who was crying, and declared, "They're lying. They're covering up. Now it's the chain of command. They won't give us the report until it goes through the whole fucking chain of command. I'm ready to sue them now."

Mary Lou, a petite woman with short dark hair, was sitting in a chair leaning over the dining room table, holding her head in her hands. She had been listening to Lisa's end of the conversation and her body was heaving with sobs. "I'm sorry," Mary Lou moaned. "I'm so sorry. I just wish we could go back to the way it was before that damn war. Maybe we could have done something different. I can't believe I'll never talk to my son again."

"Mom, I'm sorry I yelled. I'm just so mad." She grabbed a box of tissues in the kitchen and put it on the table next to Mary Lou.

"I know honey. I understand. We're all hurting."

"I'm going to tell our lawyer to go ahead and sue to force them to give us that report. Our lawyer and Chris knew each other. I think you'll like him."

Mary Lou straightened up in her chair and looked at Lisa. "You should do whatever you think is right. Your father and I will support you. I can't help thinking if only Chris had let your father help him."

"There's no way Chris was going to use dad's connections to dodge the draft. He wanted to fight the government. That fight's not over. We're going to finish it. The Army killed him, and the Army's gonna suffer."

Lisa's father worked as a lawyer for a defense company that made military equipment and weapons. He was responsible for managing the company's political relationships and its government contracts. Some of its products were being used in Vietnam.

Art was a World War II veteran who had supported America's involvement in Vietnam without thinking much about it. In his mind, it was a legitimate extension of the Cold War rivalry with Russia to contain communism and promote democracy while fueling the US economy. But over the past year, in response to Chris's anti-war activism, Art had begun to doubt the claims made by the president and the Washington politicians and the generals that America was winning the war. He had also begun to feel uneasy about his own role in the defense industry, which he knew engaged in unethical and possibly illegal tactics concealed behind claims of patriotic dedication.

Earlier in the year America's most trusted television newsman, Walter Cronkite, widely known as Uncle Walter, went to Vietnam. The Viet Cong had launched their Tet Offensive, a massive series of coordinated attacks on cities and American military bases across South Vietnam. When Cronkite returned, he declared in a sobering broadcast that the war was a stalemate and the only way out was to negotiate. Mary Lou and Art had watched Cronkite's broadcast and it altered their outlook.

A few months later, Mary Lou grew distressed about the government's federal prosecution in Boston of Dr. Benjamin Spock, the renowned pediatrician and author of a bestselling book. She felt indebted to him for his child-rearing advice. Spock was convicted by an all-male jury of encouraging draft resistance. Mary Lou was stunned that a jury would not have any women after they became eligible to serve in 1957.

At home the evening after Chris died, Mary Lou and Art retreated to their bedroom and closed the door. They collapsed on their bed and shared treasured memories of their children. They talked about how proud they were of Chris and Lisa and how they worried about Lisa's determination to extract revenge from the Army. They didn't want Chris's death to consume her. They vowed to each other to honor Chris by devoting what was left of their lives to protesting the draft and the war. They were willing to be arrested and even prepared to go to jail. Their first demonstration would be just over a week away, a rally at Boston Common organized by the SDS. The anti-war movement was becoming a force in Boston, gathering strength from the abundance of college students.

Mary Lou and Art had never before protested about anything. They were surprised when they thought about it and ashamed that it took the death of their son to shake them out of their apathy about the war. They got excited at the chance to make up for lost time.

Art got off the bed and shuffled toward an easy chair by a window. He stood silently looking into the darkness outside. His body was showing his age. He was balding and his midsection had ballooned and he was frequently short of breath. He blamed his wheeziness on seasonal allergies. He eased slowly into the chair and looked back at Mary Lou, who was adjusting a pillow under her head. "It's time for me to do what we've been talking about," he said. "I'm going to hand in my resignation letter next week and cut my ties to the goddamned military-industrial complex for good."

"Thank you," said Mary Lou. She pulled her pillow under her chin and turned so she could look Art in the eye. "You know I love you and I always will. It's the right thing to do. Chris would be thrilled. And Lisa as well. We'll have to cut our expenses, but I'm ready to make the change. We'll be fine. We'll live on love and work for peace."

Art smiled. "And live on wild hickory nuts," he said. He started to laugh, but it turned into a hacking series of coughs. "Look at us," he said when he caught his breath. "We're going to turn into a couple of aging hippies."

He'd already been making copies of company and government documents as evidence to support his suspicion that payoffs were made to win military contracts. He'd never discussed military-industrial corruption with Chris. He regretted that, but he'd make up for it. Quitting his defense job would give him time to volunteer to help Lincoln Freeman and Boston Draft Resistance with legal issues if they wanted him.

Art was proud of Chris, although he couldn't remember telling him that before he lay comatose at Mass General. Art would carry that guilt for the rest of his life.

12

Friday, November 8, 1968
Boston

Ian MacPherson scanned the crowded platform before he stepped into the subway car. He found an open spot on a bench seat. The train lurched to a start and swayed as it picked up speed. He scanned the other passengers and did not see any uniforms or military haircuts. He figured they wouldn't be wearing uniforms while trying to find him. He didn't know their faces, so he looked for any kind of warning sign. His only salvation was that, as far as he knew, they didn't know what he looked like either. He took off his backpack and set it in his lap, allowing him to lean back and try to relax for a few minutes. He was living out of his backpack, sleeping only when he couldn't stay awake. His eyes were hollow and radiated desperation.

He'd grown a shabby beard and cut off contact with friends and relatives. He didn't want to put their lives in danger. He'd stopped seeing anyone associated with the anti-war movement. He'd parked his car in a rented garage so the Army guys couldn't find him through his license plate. He'd been walking or using public transportation to move around the city. He was running low on money. He was running low on hope. But he still had one card. He was the only one who knew where the heroin was. He just wasn't sure how to play it or when. He was tempted to take some of the cash, but he hadn't yet.

He hoisted the backpack onto his shoulder before the subway slowed for the Harvard Square stop. He had heard about Lincoln Freeman through Boston Draft Resistance. He wasn't sure how much to tell the lawyer. It would depend on how they got along, except for one obligation he couldn't talk about, no matter what.

He found Freeman's building and looked up and down the street before he went in. He climbed the stairs and saw the nameplate on the office door. Below it was a handwritten note saying Freeman was at court but would return soon.

MacPherson took off his backpack, sat on the floor, and looked around. Not much to see or hear. The building was old and dark. The floors and the stairs creaked, which was good. He would know if anyone was coming. He figured there must be a back door or a side door, but from what he could see, the only way out was the way he came in. He couldn't believe he was thinking about escape routes. He thought about his parents and what they would say if they could see him now. Bearded, scruffy, sitting on the floor outside a lawyer's office. They would be devastated. They had paid for him to go to college and then grad school. They'd invested in him, financially and emotionally. Now his life was probably over. Death or prison. Those were his options.

He'd made his share of mistakes. He wished he had never got mixed up with Hodges and Franklin. Now they are dead. He could be next. The guys who killed them would have killed anyone else who was there that night. The only good decision he'd made was to leave the apartment when he did.

A door opened and closed and the stairs creaked. MacPherson tensed as a head appeared through the railing, an Afro. Their eyes met. "Hey," said Lincoln Freeman with a friendly smile. "You must be Ian. I'm Lincoln. Sorry I'm late. There was a backlog in court."

"Hi," MacPherson said, pushing himself up from the floor. "No problem."

"Normally the office is open, but my assistant had a sick child this morning. I told her to take the day off. I hope you haven't been waiting too long."

"Not at all. My schedule is pretty open these days."

Freeman unlocked the door and led the way to his inner office. He motioned toward a chair and told MacPherson to make himself comfortable while he took off his coat and settled in behind his desk. He grabbed a pen and a legal pad from a stack of paperwork and asked, "What's up?"

MacPherson felt ashamed. He looked like a bum. In recent days, he'd seen his reflection in subway windows and the cracked mirrors of filthy public bathrooms.

"For starters," he said, "I'd like to apologize for my appearance. I've had a rough few weeks. I'm sure you're wondering how I could possibly afford you."

"That's not at all what I'm thinking. Forget about money for now. Tell me what happened to bring you here on a Friday afternoon."

"As you probably know, I heard about you through Draft Resistance. They said you're a good lawyer, a good person. I've been involved in the anti-war effort. First I should tell you I'm a grad student, I was a grad student. Something happened a few weeks ago that changed that. I got caught up in something that I shouldn't have, and now I think I've got people trying to find me and kill me and I don't know what to do."

"Have you reported that to the police?"

"No."

"Why?"

"Because they'd arrest me."

"What for?"

"A raid at the Boston Army Base."

"By the SDS?"

"Yes. You know about that?"

"I heard something about it. Were you involved?"

"Sort of. I was asked to be a lookout."

"Did you go inside?"

"No. I was outside. I was supposed to alert the guys who were inside if anyone showed up."

"Did anyone show up?"

"No."

"Do you know what happened inside?"

"Just from what they said."

"What did they say?"

"That they trashed the place, smashed everything in sight with crowbars, spread medical records on the floors, and clogged sinks and left water running. They hoped to shut it down."

"What happened when they came out?"

"We took off."

"Did anyone see you or try to stop you?"

"Not that I know of."

"Who was with you?"

"Two guys."

"Where are they?"

MacPherson shifted uncomfortably in his chair. "They're dead."

"Dead?"

"Dead."

"What happened?"

"They died from overdoses."

"Where?"

"In their apartment. It's in Brighton."

"Were they addicts?"

"No. They were killed."

"How do you know that?"

"I was there."

"You saw them get killed?"

"No. I was with them before they got killed and then I left for a while and when I got back, I think, they were dead."

"You aren't sure."

"I didn't see them. I saw and heard other guys in the apartment through an alley window."

"What did they say?"

"I only heard a few words from one guy who sounded like he was in charge. He told someone else something like we're not going to get any more out of these guys."

"Then what?"

"I was scared shitless. I got out of there. I was at the back of the alley because when I was walking down the block I saw someone hanging out by the front door, like a lookout. He looked just like me that night at the Army base, you know, kind of nervous, not sure how to act to seem like he belonged there. I didn't want him to see me. So I went around back to find out what was going on. But when I heard that guy through the window I took off."

"Who do you think they were?"

"I think it was Army soldiers."

"Why do you think that?"

"Because of what we did."

"At the induction center?"

"Yeah. The Army base."

"They wanted to kill those two because they trashed the place?"

"That might have been part of it."

"What would be the rest of it?"

"We had something they wanted."

"What was that?"

"Drugs and cash."

Freeman dropped his pen on the legal pad, got up from his desk chair, and gave MacPherson an angry look before turning away toward the window. He wanted to say something, but let silence speak for itself. He didn't like surprises, though lawyers get them all the time. He didn't want any from clients. Or in court. Especially in court. He prided himself on anticipating surprises and preparing for them. He wasn't sure how he felt about MacPherson. Obviously, he was nervous and was holding something back, maybe many things. Experience had cautioned Freeman to trust few people. Trust had to be earned. A line of cars moved slowly on the street below. It was getting dark. The streetlights were on. He heard MacPherson shift in his chair behind him.

He turned back toward MacPherson. "If you got any more bombshells," he said, "lay 'em on me now."

Macpherson shook his head. He said he was just trying to tell what happened.

The lawyer turned back toward the window and launched a series of rapid-fire questions without looking at MacPherson.

"Where did the drugs come from?"

"The Army base."

"The induction center?"

"Yes."

"Your friends took them?"

"They weren't my friends. But yeah, they took the drugs."

"During the raid?"

"Yes."

"Where were the drugs?"

"In an ammo vest in the back of a filing cabinet, along with some cash."

"How do you know that?"

"That's what they told me."

"Have you seen the drugs?"

"Yes."

"Do you know what kind of drugs they are?"

"It's powder. I think it might be heroin."

"Why heroin?"

"Because of what happened to the other guys."

"Do you know how much cash there was?"

"They said over six thousand dollars."

"Do you know where the drugs are now?"

"In a locker."

"How do you know that?"

"Because they asked me to put them there. I put the vest in a locker with the cash and the drugs. They're in pouches in the vest."

"Is the locker locked?"

"Yes."

"How do you know?"

"Because I have the key."

Freeman returned to his desk chair, facing MacPherson. He massaged his forehead with his fingertips.

"How can you be sure those guys were killed?"

"Because I was with them when they tried a sample of the powder. They snorted it. They got sick real fast. They threw up. I didn't take any. I thought it might be cocaine, but it wasn't. They seemed to be OK after they threw up. When I say OK, I mean they were alive. They didn't want to move. They couldn't really do much except listen to music. That's all they wanted. To listen to music. So I felt like it was OK to leave. When I got back, those other guys were there."

"How long were you gone?"

"A few hours."

"And you didn't see any bodies when you got back?"

"No. I didn't go back in. The police found their bodies. There was an item in the newspaper. It identified them and said they overdosed on heroin. It said the cops found needles and other drug stuff. It said the heroin was the same stuff from Southeast Asia that had killed a bunch of people in Roxbury. I never saw any needles in the apartment. I didn't go back after that night because I figured the Army guys would be watching, looking for me to come back so they could grab me."

"Where did the police find the bodies?"

"Inside the apartment."

"How do you know those two guys weren't addicts?"

"I lived with them for a few weeks. I needed a place to stay after my apartment building got damaged by a fire. They only smoked pot. They were just a couple of guys who wanted to start a revolution and end the war. They were frustrated. They wanted to do something dramatic. They wanted news coverage."

Freeman spun his chair toward the street and looked out the window again. MacPherson wondered what Freeman was thinking. He hadn't told the lawyer everything, but it was more than he'd planned to say.

"What do you think I could do to help you?" asked Freeman, still looking out the window.

"I don't know, maybe tell me how much trouble I'm in and what I can do about it."

Freeman was silent as he considered the situation. He'd agreed to see MacPherson primarily because he was referred by Draft Resistance and MacPherson had mentioned Chris's name when he called for an appointment. Freeman hoped MacPherson might be able to help him find out what had happened to Chris. But after talking with MacPherson he didn't think he could trust him. Freeman was reminded of his past conversations with prisoners accused of crimes. It was always a challenge to sort fact from fiction.

He turned back toward MacPherson, looked directly into his eyes, and asked "Have you ever been in jail or accused of a crime?"

MacPherson was stunned by the question, hesitated, and asked, "Why?"

"So the answer is yes," said Freeman. "Tell me about it."

MacPherson shifted in his chair. "It was a few years ago. I got set up for a pot bust for a few joints I gave to some friends."

"What happened?"

"It went away. It was settled as a breach of peace with a small fine."

"Who represented you?"

"A lawyer hired by my parents."

"Name?"

"I don't remember."

"So you've dealt with the police and the courts before."

"Yes."

"Well, this time obviously it's a much bigger deal. You're implicated in a bunch of crimes and you're a witness to murder if those guys were killed."

"Implicated in what kind of crimes?"

"A combination of state and federal crimes. Conspiracy, breaking and entering, vandalism, causing significant property damage, possibly sabotage, theft, possession of illegal drugs, for starters." Freeman was silent for a moment. "But if you're right and Army soldiers killed those other guys and they want to kill you to get their drugs back, that's obviously your biggest problem."

They eyed each other in silence. MacPherson stood up and paced slowly around the office. He stopped behind his chair and grabbed the back of it with his hands to keep them from shaking. "I'm fucked, aren't I?"

"That depends on you. Why don't you sit back down."

MacPherson sat.

Freeman asked whether he would recognize the soldiers he saw at the apartment.

"I only saw one, the lookout on the street, and he was too far away to see what he looked like."

"Do they know who you are or that you were involved in the raid?"

"Probably. They could have followed me to the apartment when I got the drug sample for those other guys. But I was careful and I checked and didn't see anybody following me. They could have found the apartment by getting the names of SDS students. I wasn't big in SDS, but they could have got my name that way."

"If soldiers killed those guys, they must have tried to get them to say where the drugs were."

"Yeah. And whether anyone else, like me, knows where the drugs are. I'm sure they suffered. If I hadn't left, I would have been killed too. I gave them the key just before they took the heroin."

"The locker key? I thought you said you had the key."

"I do. What happened was I thought I gave them the key, but it turned out I gave them the wrong key. It was the key to my apartment. I didn't realize it until I tried to get back into my apartment."

"What do you think happened after you left their apartment?"

"Those guys were so wiped out they couldn't put up a fight. They must have told the soldiers everything before they were killed. The key, the locker, me. So now they must be looking for me and they know the drugs are in a locker. I haven't moved them. The locker is—"

Freeman held up his hand to cut him off. "I don't want to know where the drugs are. Not now."

"The soldiers have to know where the locker is and they'll be watching it. I don't think they know the locker number because I'm the only one who went into it."

Freeman swung his chair back toward the window. Lights flashed faintly outside as cars passed by. "Where are you staying now?" he asked.

"Any place where people don't know me. I'm on the run. I slept a few hours last night in a cemetery. I don't want to put anyone else in danger."

"Does anyone know you're here?"

"No. I heard about you before those guys were killed. It might have been from Chris Thompson or other people at Draft Resistance."

"Did you know Chris?"

"Not really. I was introduced to him once at the Draft Resistance office and I knew he was well-respected."

"Was Chris aware of the raid?"

"No, not that I know of."

Freeman stood up, stretched his arms, and said, "Give me a minute."

He walked to his outer office with his legal pad and a pen. He wanted time alone to think. He sat in his assistant's chair and doodled at her desk. MacPherson was running scared. He looked like a fugitive. He needed a lawyer and a safe place. It wasn't the type of case Freeman anticipated when he concentrated on civil rights law, but he'd already decided to represent MacPherson, mostly because the Army base was involved. He didn't trust MacPherson, but he believed his story about the raid and the ruthless soldiers chasing him down. The issue now was how to keep him alive while developing a strategy for his case. Freeman picked up his assistant's phone and called his cleaning service. He cancelled its regular weekend cleaning and rejoined MacPherson in his inner office.

He opened a drawer on his desk and took out a ring with three keys. "I'm going to do something I've never done before," he said. "I'm going to let you stay here for the weekend unless you have other plans."

MacPherson's eyes brightened. "Wow man. Thanks. I'm blown away. I mean I don't know what to say. Thank you."

Freeman handed him the key ring, saying he could sleep on the couch in the outer office. "The keys open the street door, the office door, and the bathroom in the hall. I have a separate key for my personal office here, which I won't give you for obvious reasons. Nobody should bother you until Monday morning. I just cancelled the usual Saturday cleaning."

He told MacPherson not to answer any phone calls or knocks on the door.

"I need some time to think about your situation," he said. "I'll tell my assistant you're here, and she'll be the only one who knows. She may get here before me on Monday. We can continue this discussion when I return."

"Thank you, Mr. Freeman. Thank you so much. I'll be able to pay you for this when I get back in touch with my family."

Freeman put on his coat, grabbed his briefcase, and guided MacPherson to the outer office. He closed and locked the door to his inner office and checked the file cabinets in the reception area to make sure they were all locked. He pointed to a closet and told MacPherson that sheets, a blanket, and a pillow were in it. "You can use the lights. I've spent a few nights here myself, so people shouldn't be surprised to see lights on."

"Thanks. I have a sleeping bag in my pack that I can use."

"That's fine. Get some sleep. You look like you need it."

"Thanks again, man. Do you think there's a way out of this for me?"

"We'll talk on Monday."

13

Saturday, November 9, 1968
Wrightstown, New Jersey

Bear and Stillman stepped off an Army shuttle bus and walked uneasily toward the Fort Dix gate. After being confined for a month of basic training, they didn't trust anything about the Army, including whether their day passes would get them past the gate. The guards checked their passes and waved them through. They lightened up. The passes were their tickets to spend a few precious hours in the civilian world, to breathe and talk freely, maybe even see some women. It was noon on a Saturday, the first time they were allowed to leave the base.

"Welcome to Wrightstown," said a sign just outside the gate, leading to a street lined with cheap commercial buildings containing the kinds of businesses that come and go like mushrooms around the edges of military bases—bars, pawn shops, sex shops.

"So this is what we've been missing," said Stillman.

"Which way is the museum?" asked Bear.

They wore jeans and their Army field jackets to shield them from the chill November wind. They were halfway down the block, less than two hundred yards past the gate, making their way along a sidewalk when Bear bolted across the street. Stillman swiveled to see where he was going. Someone in an Army field jacket, likely a trainee, was curled up on the sidewalk at the entrance to an alley trying to protect himself. He was white and he had three Black men standing over him. "Hey," Bear yelled as he sprinted toward them. Two of them took off down the alley and the third, a tall skinny guy dressed in a tight-fitting purple sharkskin suit, eyed Bear. He kicked the victim on the sidewalk and then casually followed the others. Before he reached the end of the alley, he looked back and flashed a long knife in his left hand, daring Bear to come after him. But Bear was tending to the victim.

Stillman crossed the street and helped Bear lift him to his feet. His face was bloody and he was so woozy that they each took an arm to support him. He said he was in basic training and it was his first time off the base. He said he was walking down the street when his attackers asked him if he wanted to buy drugs. He said no, and the punches came out of nowhere, one to his gut, another to his face. They threw him face down on the pavement, kicked him, and took his wallet.

"Can you walk?" asked Bear.

The GI nodded.

"What's your name?"

"Bailey. Walter Bailey."

"Let's get you cleaned up, Walter," said Bear, keeping a hand on his arm as they walked. Stillman followed behind, watching for the attackers.

Bear led Walter into a bar a few doors down the sidewalk. He asked the bartender for a towel and helped Walter to the bathroom. Stillman asked about contacting the police. The bartender offered to make a call from his office. The barroom was long, narrow, and dark, with stools along the bar and a dozen tables with chairs. At the back, two overhead lights illuminated a pool table. A customer was stalking the table. Balls clicked quietly as he lined up shot after shot until only the cue ball was left. He grabbed his beer off the side rail with one hand and plucked a jacket off a chair with the other and walked slowly toward Stillman. It looked to Stillman like a scene out of a western movie—the rugged loner hired to defend a town terrorized by a brutal criminal gang. The pool player was wearing cowboy boots, jeans, and a T-shirt barely able to contain his bulging upper body and arms. He was good-looking, clean-shaven with short dark hair, a no-nonsense square jaw, and eyes that didn't know fear.

"How's it going?" he asked.

"Not so good," said Stillman, "for the guy we just brought in here."

"What happened?"

"He got beat up. They stole his wallet."

"It's a tough town."

"Looks that way."

"You guys in basic?" the pool player asked.

"How could you tell?" Stillman grinned, running his hand over the carpet of stubby hair covering his head. "You in the Army?"

"Yeah, short time. Back from Nam."

"How was it?"

The pool player was the same height as Stillman and appeared to be about the same age. He took a long drink from his beer and stared at the bottle while considering the question.

"Fucked up, man. Really fucked up." He took another drink. "It fucks with everybody. Doesn't matter who you are. You know what I mean? It just fucks you up."

"The war or the Army?"

"All of it."

"I got drafted," Stillman said.

"That sucks."

"I'm gonna make 'em sorry."

"Right on."

"They're forcing kids to fight a war nobody wants except for the fat cats making money on it." Stillman glanced toward the door.

"You worried those guys are gonna come after you?" the pool player asked.

"Just staying alert."

"You're safe here. But when you're new to the Army on the street in this town, it's smart to be with a buddy."

"You're alone."

"Yeah. But I can take care of myself. I'm a bad dude. I didn't used to be. The Army did that to me."

"You sound like you're against the war."

"Right on."

"Are a lot of soldiers against the war?"

"Just about everyone who's been there."

"If so many of them are against the war, how can it keep going?"

"I don't know man. Ask the lying dudes in Washington. The guys in Nam are just trying to stay alive, you know, keeping their heads down so they can get back to the world and get on with their lives. Trouble is so many of them are so fucked up that when they get home, they don't know who they are anymore."

"Too bad they don't all get together and say fuck off, we're not gonna fight anymore. This war is over."

"Some do that. Or they go AWOL. Either way, it's a one-way ticket to the stockade. Or they frag the motherfucking officers who keep sending them out to get butchered. I've known about patrols that refuse to go into certain areas and get away with it. But to get a whole Army to walk away, that'd take a union. There's talk about unionizing, but it'll never happen."

"Yeah, but what an image. Soldiers striking, passing out flowers, singing protest songs, ending a war. Something to shoot for."

"Right."

"I must sound pretty naïve."

"Yeah, but that's OK. You'll learn."

"Hey, it's great to meet you. My name's Jud Stillman."

"Good to meet you Jud. I'm Peter Ransom."

Stillman told him he and Bear came into town to look for an anti-war coffeehouse they heard was bombed. Ransom said he knew the place. He started to describe it, but the bartender interrupted to say the police were sending an officer over.

Bear came out of the bathroom with Walter, who was holding a bloody towel. Bear asked the bartender for a clean towel and ice for Walter's face. Stillman introduced Bear to Ransom, who offered to show them the coffeehouse.

A uniformed police officer showed up. He asked them about the attack, took a few notes, and said he had a good idea of who did it. "Fucking n—s," he snorted, staring at Bear. Bear didn't respond.

The cop suggested Walter go to the hospital for a checkup, but he declined. The officer asked if he wanted to prosecute. Walter said all he wanted was his wallet back. The officer said it might be somewhere down the alley, empty. He and Walter left.

"The cops don't like the coffeehouse," Ransom said.

"Or Black folks," said Bear.

"All these businesses, they make their money off the war," said Ransom. "They don't want anybody fucking with that. War brings a shitload of money to Wrightstown."

Bear asked who blew up the coffeehouse.

"It was like a homemade bomb. Nobody's been arrested. And nobody will be."

"Why is that?"

"This town doesn't want anything anti-war."

"Was anybody inside when it happened?"

"I was there. In the back, right place, wrong time. Or something like that. A couple of people out front were hurt, nothing serious. One of them was a disabled vet in a wheelchair. The owners say they'll repair the damage, but they won't let the coffeehouse reopen. They got the message."

"Somebody could have been killed," said Stillman.

"Yeah. I suppose. The war fucks with everything."

Bear said he'd talked to Black soldiers who went to the coffeehouse because it was about the only place where they could be themselves. Ransom said it was run by a committee, but mostly by a young Black woman, an anti-war activist studying to be a lawyer. He said he keeps in touch with her and she might be around when they get there. He said the coffeehouse was popular, even though everybody knew the Army planted spies there. The local cops would also be nearby to harass anyone who went in.

Ransom said appointments could be arranged at the coffeehouse for counseling, and there was a mimeograph machine for printing underground GI newspapers with stories about anti-war resistance and the Army's rampant racism. He said underground papers were banned on military bases and were part of an anti-war GI movement that was just getting started. Only one GI newspaper, called *About Face*, had been printed so far at the coffeehouse. It was just a couple of pages, and it had only lasted one issue.

Ransom said the soldier who put out *About Face* was set up for a drug bust. The Army claimed marijuana was found during a search of his locker. Ransom said the newspaper really pissed off the Army brass.

"So much for the free press," said Stillman. "What blows my mind is how the Army can take away all your rights. I mean what happened to the fucking Constitution?"

"Brothers ain't never had constitutional rights," snorted Bear. "You can't take away what you never had."

"Right on," said Ransom, plunking his empty beer bottle on the bar.

"Let's go to the coffeehouse."

* * * *

On the way, Stillman stopped at a bookstore that had a rack of used books out front on the sidewalk next to a phone booth. He bought a secondhand copy of *Catch-22*.

"Great book," said Ransom.

"Yeah," Stillman said. "It's my second copy. The fucking drill sergeants took my first one when we got to Dix. They made a big deal about it. They held it up so all the trainees could see it before they threw it in the trash. They said the book showed I thought I was better than everyone else. They promised they'd cut me down to size."

"Welcome to the Army," said Ransom.

"Fuck the Army," said Bear.

"Right on."

Stillman said he wanted to call Chris Thompson's parents to find out if he'd come out of the coma. He stepped into the phone booth, put a coin in the slot, and dialed. Lisa answered. Stillman explained who he was.

"I've been hoping you'd call," she said. "Thank you so much. Draft Resistance said they gave you our number. There's no easy way of telling you this, so I'll just say it. Chris is dead."

"Holy shit."

"Yeah."

"Holy fucking shit."

"Yeah."

"Sorry for the language."

"It's OK."

"Did he ever wake up?"

"No. You were one of the last people to see him alive. I mean really alive."

"Oh man. I don't know what to say. I just wish I could have had a chance to get to know him. I only saw and talked to him for a few minutes, but I felt like we could be friends. I really admired how he handled himself that day. He was so brave."

Lisa asked him to describe what happened. He told her about the encounter with the lieutenant and how angry he got when Chris brought up the SDS raid. She asked for the lieutenant's name. He said he only knew his last name, Sanders. He was about to tell her the lieutenant refused to give his first name, but was interrupted by the voice of an operator telling him he had to pay more money to continue the call. Lisa said she'd pay and reversed the charges.

Stillman told her he had called the *Boston World* about Chris getting hurt and the Army had told the newspaper that nothing had happened and nobody had been hurt.

"Those fucking liars," Lisa said. "The Army told us it was an accident. I was sure it wasn't an accident and now after what I'm hearing from you, I'm even more sure. We asked for the accident report and we still don't have anything. They killed my brother. I'm going to find out who did it."

Lisa told him she hired a lawyer who knew Chris, but the lawyer didn't want to make a move until the Army produced a written report. Stillman offered to have the newspaper follow up, but she asked him to hold off until they got something in writing from the Army. She said the family was also waiting for autopsy results. Stillman asked about a memorial service, saying he and Bear wanted to go if the Army would give them a pass. She said she'd let him know and then took down his address. She said she was looking forward to meeting him and talking more.

After hanging up, Stillman and Bear filled Ransom in on the details. He had heard Stillman's end of the call and was standing close enough that he could also hear some of what Lisa said. He thought of his own sister and how she would react. He was sure she would be just as skeptical as Lisa and just as determined to uncover the truth. They'd both be out for revenge.

Ransom told Stillman and Bear he was due to be discharged in less than two weeks and didn't have any plans. He said he'd be willing to help them and Lisa if she was still being stonewalled. He grew up in West Virginia and said he wanted to see other parts of the country. He'd never been to Boston. He warned them Army reports couldn't be trusted because officers routinely lied and faked paperwork to cover their asses.

They said they were beginning to understand that and resumed their walk to the coffeehouse. On the way they probed Ransom about the Army and Vietnam.

"The first thing you need to understand," he said, "is the reason why we'll never win the fucking war. The Vietnamese are so determined to defend their country they'll never give up. They've been doing it for decades, for a long time against the French and now us. They're farmers by day and Viet Cong by night. They're masters of guerrilla warfare. Just look at what they're doing. They're standing up to the strongest fucking military power in the world and they're holding their own. They whittle us down a few soldiers at a time with their mines and their booby traps and ambushes. They're in no hurry. For Americans, it's terrifying. Every step you take could be your last. It messes with your mind. It fucks you up."

He brought up the Ho Chi Minh Trail, the military resupply route built to get soldiers, weapons, and equipment from North Vietnam as far as the Mekong Delta near the southern end of South Vietnam, a journey of almost a thousand miles. He described the trail as an engineering marvel—a network of roads, rugged paths, and tunnels that weaved through mountains and jungle. It was regularly bombed and defoliated by Americans and immediately got rebuilt by the Viet Cong. The trail had its own fuel lines and barracks and hospitals.

"A VC we captured said he walked over two hundred miles completely underground while coming to Saigon," Ransom said. "You have to admire people who would dig hundreds of miles of tunnels."

"That resonates with me," said Bear. "My people have been oppressed for hundreds of years, but we aren't giving up. A lot of brothers identify with the Viet Cong. It's not just Ali."

Stillman asked Ransom why he became a soldier.

He had been drafted after dropping out of college, having decided it was a waste of time and money. What he really wanted was to take a break from school to clear his head and have some fun. He knew that was unlikely because of the draft. He didn't know much about the war before the Army put him in the infantry. In Vietnam he had endured more than his share of combat, had been wounded several times, and had seen fellow soldiers die agonizing deaths, their bodies ripped apart by mines and shrapnel. The hardest part, he said, was trying to curb the craving for revenge.

"That's where I might be able to help Lisa," he said. "With her brother dead, she's so hurt and angry I get the sense she might do anything to get even, maybe even put herself in danger. Revenge can make you so crazy it's hard to think."

He brought up a vengeful lieutenant who ordered him to shoot a suspected Viet Cong prisoner, captured in a sweep of a village where two members of his squad were killed. Ransom said he refused to do it. The lieutenant threatened him with a court martial if he didn't shoot the prisoner. He refused again. Then the lieutenant threatened to shoot Ransom if he didn't obey the order. Ransom called his bluff. It was a standoff, and the lieutenant backed down.

"Wow, man," said Stillman. "That took balls."

"Yeah, but you don't think about it that way," Ransom said. "There's no time to think. You react. You operate on instinct. It's hard to explain. It's not real, man. But it doesn't get more real. You know what I mean? It's like one of those zombie movies, only it's in technicolor, a battlefield of tortured souls, condemned to linger between life and death, following orders or dealing with conflicting orders or ignoring orders from officers who pretend to know what they're doing but don't. Those kids get splattered with blood and guts and they can't control whether they live or die and some of them are so lost they don't care. It's hard to come back from that. Some never do."

Ransom stopped walking and looked around, like he needed to get his bearings. "Man," he said, "how did we get onto this? Let's change the subject. Do you get high?"

"When we can. You bet."

Ransom reached into his jacket and pulled out a joint. "Then let's take a detour and fire this up."

"Dig it."

They turned onto a side street and smoked, passing the joint as they walked. "Potent shit," Bear said after his second toke. "Distinctive taste. What is it?"

"Thai stick," said Ransom. "The best dope in the world, courtesy of the US Army. I brought some back with me."

"Might make me change my mind about going to Vietnam," said Stillman.

"Think about it," said Ransom. "The military has all these planes and ships and trucks all over the world. It's the biggest drug network anywhere, with access to the best shit everywhere. In the Army just about everybody's high on something all the time. It could be booze or weed or acid or smack, all day, every day. That's what the Army does to you. Guys get so deep into smack that they OD and die, and they know that's what's gonna happen to them but they don't care because they're trapped in the Army and the war is gonna kill 'em anyway. They probably aren't even in the list of American casualties, but they are. They're casualties of war. They sure are. Like I said, it's not real, man, but it is."

They walked on, each in his own world, passing the joint until it was almost gone. Ransom detached an alligator clip from a belt loop on his pants and used it to continue passing the roach until it was ash.

He led them to an intersection where he stopped. "The man is waiting for us," he said, pointing ahead. "That's where the coffeehouse used to be, and that's the cop from the bar."

The officer was leaning against his cruiser, parked in front of an ugly light-green wood-frame building. The windows were covered by plywood, spray-painted with dueling graffiti:

> STOP the war, FEED the poor
> COMMIES Go Home
> Make LOVE, Not War
> MY COUNTRY, Love It or Leave It.
> Hell NO, WE WON'T GO

"Good afternoon soldiers," the officer said as they approached. "I heard you might be coming this way. This building is off limits. It's private property and a crime scene."

"We'll stay on the sidewalk," Ransom said.

"I wouldn't stay too long," said the officer. "That would be loitering."

"What happened here?" asked Stillman.

"I expect you already know," the officer said. "The building was damaged and had to be shut down."

"Is it going to reopen?"

"You'll have to find that out from somebody else. My job is to make sure the property stays secure."

"Looks like somebody with paint got past you."

A faded multicolored VW bus pulled up and parked behind the

cruiser. A Black woman with an Afro got out from behind the wheel and approached the officer. She was slender, wearing tight jeans and a stylish jacket. She introduced herself and asked the officer if he was there to open the building for her. He demanded identification and escorted her to the door, which was padlocked. He opened it. She pulled a large flashlight from her handbag and disappeared inside. The officer followed her in and left the door open.

"Who would she be?" Bear asked.

"Angela Williams," Ransom said. "She's the law student who helped start the coffeehouse and managed it."

"Nice looking," said Bear.

"Smart too," said Ransom. "She's at Columbia."

"What's that?" Bear asked.

"A law school in New York, one of the best."

"She must be tough. Can't be too many Black women going up against rich white guys."

"Right on."

She made several trips from the coffeehouse to her van carrying cardboard boxes. She asked Ransom for help with some heavier items. Bear volunteered. The officer said only one of them could go inside with her. Bear helped her carry out a couple of chairs, a small cabinet, a record player, and a mimeograph machine and put them in the van. "What about the piano?" he asked.

Angela laughed. "We'll need a bigger van for that. We'll move it to the new place when we find one."

They went back in for another load. Angela came out alone with two more boxes and took them to the van. The officer followed her. Then, from inside the bombed out coffeehouse, a single piano cord sounded. It was followed by another. Then another and it became a melody. Then Bear started singing.

"Oooo, yeah," sang Angela. "Sing it, Bear. What a voice. Respect. What a song. I love Aretha and the late great Otis Redding."

The cop marched toward the door. "Get the hell out of there," he shouted to Bear. But Bear played on, even more forcefully.

The officer stomped inside the building, his hand on his sidearm. "Stop. Now," he demanded. "Get your n— ass outside or you're going to jail."

The piano went silent, its last chord reverberating in the air as Bear came out. Stillman, Ransom, and Angela started clapping. Bear was imposing in front of the shorter officer. He acknowledged the applause with a bow, a grin, and a wave of his hand as the officer padlocked the door behind him.

"I knew you played music," said Stillman, "but not like that. Man, you got talent."

Bear said music took him to a special place where nothing else mattered. Then he corrected himself. "Almost nothing," he said, glancing at the cop.

The officer approached Angela and declared, "You're never going back in that building if I have anything to say about it."

"Is that because Bear played the piano and sang a beautiful song?" she asked. "You must be jealous. You have to admit, he's very good."

The officer ignored her, returned to his cruiser, picked up the microphone, and started talking into it.

Angela asked Bear about his musical tastes and favorite instruments. He said he liked different kinds of music and was partial to jazz and blues, which his dad really liked. He usually played the piano, the saxophone, or the guitar and would love to play professionally, but didn't think he was good enough yet.

"You've got three fans here," she said. "That's a start."

The police officer swung his cruiser across the street like he was making a U-turn, but stopped and raised a camera in their direction. "Smile guys," Angela said, "you're on *Candid Camera*." They waved and made funny faces.

The officer pulled up beside the van with his window rolled down. "You need to leave now," he said. "All of you."

"Would you please send me copies?" Angela asked. "I'd love them for my scrapbook."

He drove off.

Angela told the others she'd offer them a ride but didn't have room in the van. She suggested Bear and Stillman walk down the street with her for a few minutes so they could talk. Ransom could follow in the van.

Stillman asked about the connection between the coffeehouse and the underground GI press.

She told them the coffeehouse was opened by civilian activists to build anti-war support inside the military. It was going to be one of the first of many at bases all over the country. She considered Dix an obvious location because so many Black soldiers were crammed into the stockade. "You've got blatant racism and a senseless war," she said. "We expected harassment, but we didn't expect a bomb. I guess you know about that."

"Peter told us," said Bear. "A couple of weeks ago me and Jud found an Army memo about the coffeehouse and ways the Army could shut it down."

"Really," said Angela. "I'd like to see that."

Bear offered to get her a copy.

Stillman said the memo might make a good article for the next GI newspaper. He asked what happened to *About Face*. She said fewer than a hundred copies were passed around the base, but it got soldiers talking about the war and what happened to the soldier who started it. He was shipped to the West Coast for an Army trial on the bogus drug bust. "They isolate anyone who challenges them," she said, "and then they move you all over the country. You might have an hour to pack up your stuff and you're gone and nobody knows where you went."

Stillman wondered what would happen to the *About Face* guy. Angela said the drug charges would probably be dropped and he'd be discharged. Stillman said that sounded like a good way to get out of the Army. He couldn't imagine how a few dozen copies of mimeographed GI newspapers passed around military bases could stop the war.

"We do what we can," she said. "A little here and a little there adds up. We'd like to see it grow into a movement that shakes the Army to its core and demolishes morale. That's the way to win a war. It's about truth and lies. The politicians and the Army lie about everything, from body counts to casualties to who's winning and losing. It's the GIs on the ground who know the truth, that the war is already lost. Their lives are being sacrificed for a lie. If they have a way to tell what they know, the truth spreads. Guys who didn't realize other guys were refusing to go to Nam or refusing to fight, they see the truth and they join the resistance. It turns the Army against itself. Eventually the politicians and the generals will have to end the war because if they don't, the war will destroy their Army. That's the theory. I think it's a good one."

"Right on," said Bear.

"I'm in," said Stillman. "I'll start a newspaper if I'm in the Army long enough, but I'll need some help."

"I'm with you," said Bear.

"Maybe we can do it before you get shipped out of Dix," said Angela. "I've got some material for another issue, including letters from GIs who saw the first issue and wrote to offer support and say what they knew. We could run them as letters to the editor. How much longer before you finish basic?"

"Four weeks," said Bear.

"I think that gives us enough time," she said. "I've got to get going. Don't forget about that coffeehouse memo." She stopped walking and signaled to Ransom to come up with the van.

She pulled a notebook and pen out of her handbag, wrote her name and phone number on a page, tore it off, and handed it to Bear. "The best time to reach me is the evening," she said.

"We don't know when they'll let us use a phone."

"If I'm not there, leave a message with a time when you can call back and I'll try to be around."

Bear handed the paper back and asked her to add her mailing address. He said he'd find a way to make a copy of the coffeehouse memo and send it to her.

Angela said she'd be driving back and forth between New York and Wrightstown to find a site for the next coffeehouse. "We're not feeling the love here," she said, "but we're not going away."

She climbed into the driver's seat and rolled down the window. "It's been great to meet you guys," she said. "Write a story about that memo and anything else you can think of, and I'll write a story about what happened to the coffeehouse. See you soon."

Stillman and Bear wished they had more time to talk to her about how to write a story and also about the pedophile chaplain. A law student might have good advice on what to do about him.

Overall they were upbeat after their first afternoon off base. They learned more from Ransom about Vietnam and the Army than they ever would from drill sergeants. They got to see the coffeehouse and talk to Angela about underground GI papers. Bear played the piano and sang and pissed off a cop. It was such a thrill to see and talk to a woman after four weeks confined with teenage boys and nasty drill sergeants. It was obvious Bear wanted to get to know Angela better. Quite a day.

On the walk back to the Fort Dix gate, they told Ransom about the chaplain. They wanted to do something to protect the kids. If they reported him to the Army, they doubted anything would be done. Nobody would believe them and he'd just be moved to another base, where he'd keep on doing what he did.

Stillman asked Ransom for advice.

"First I need to know who you guys are. You're in the Army for a month and somebody from your induction is dead and now you're going to expose a pedophile chaplain. What the fuck is going on?"

"It's the Army, man," said Stillman. "From what we've seen, it's like the place where psychos, racists, and perverts run wild. We're new to the Army, but we're learning."

"There's more," said Bear. "Our drill sergeants beat up three brothers who went AWOL, locked them in a room, and chained them to a bed. One of 'em died and another one's in the hospital. Add that to the list."

"Fucking A. You guys know I'm short. Less than two weeks to go. I'm not gonna mess that up."

"Right on."

"Which doesn't mean I won't help. I mean I have time and you don't. I could just drink beers and shoot pool and count the days, but that's a drag. I could try to keep an eye on that chaplain, see where he goes, where he lives, what he does."

"Far out."

"We plan to hit him tomorrow with what we know," said Bear. "Flush him out."

"After you do that, I could follow him. I've got a bike."

"The Harley near the bar?"

"That's me."

14

Sunday, November 10, 1968
Fort Dix

The next morning, Stillman and Bear went to the chapel to confront the chaplain after the service. They agreed Stillman would do most of the talking.

When the service was over, they stayed in their seats, waiting for the chaplain to reappear. They were the only trainees left except for the chaplain's assistant who was doing something at the altar. Stillman was thinking about what he would say to get things started. He and Bear figured exposing the chaplain might even be their ticket out of the Army. The tricky part would be staying out of the stockade if the Army tried to go after them instead of the chaplain.

They were uneasy when the chaplain's assistant turned away from the altar and walked up the aisle toward them. He asked why they hadn't returned to their unit. Stillman told him they needed to talk to the chaplain. The assistant said the chaplain was busy and couldn't be disturbed. He said his job was to deal with most trainee issues without burdening the chaplain. Stillman insisted they needed to meet with the chaplain privately. The assistant said that was not possible. He had sergeant stripes on his sleeve and his name tag said *Youngblood*.

"Sergeant Youngblood," said Stillman. "We don't mean to be rude. We understand we don't have many rights here in this here Army, but I expect we have a right to meet with the chaplain."

"You certainly do," he said. "Just not today."

"Then we'd like to make an appointment."

Youngblood scanned the chapel. He sat down in the pew in front of them and rested his arm on the back so he could face them. At first he looked sympathetic, then his expression turned hard. "I've got to be honest with you," he said. "I think I know why you're here. It's about the orphanage and the kids isn't it?"

Stillman and Bear looked at each other in disbelief. "That's, that's part of it," Stillman stammered.

"And it's not to compliment the chaplain on his commitment to the orphans of Vietnam is it?" Youngblood asked.

"No."

"I know you've been here before," Youngblood said. "And I know you've been in his office before when he wasn't there. You took his key and used it. You used the phone."

Stillman didn't respond.

"That's breaking and entering," Youngblood said. "That's a court martial offense. That's stockade time."

"That's nothing compared to what that chaplain's doing to innocent kids," countered Stillman.

"Outstanding," said Youngblood. "Now we're getting somewhere. I can't tell you who I work for, but we're investigating the chaplain and I'm undercover as his assistant and I will continue to be until we wrap this thing up. I compliment both of you for your tenacity and your desire to do the right thing. But you are jeopardizing our investigation, which goes well beyond what you think you know. That's why I can't let you meet with him. Do you understand?"

"This is," Stillman struggled for the right word, "unexpected."

"Nothing will happen to either of you if you go back to your unit and keep quiet," Youngblood said. "If you create any problems for this investigation, you will be brought up on charges. Do you understand?"

"Yes," said Stillman.

Youngblood looked at Bear. He nodded grudgingly.

"Say it," said Youngblood.

"I understand," said Bear.

"Now it's time for you to get back to your unit. You will forget this conversation ever took place. Good day, trainees. If we ever have to meet again, it will not go well for you."

Stillman and Bear left quietly.

* * * *

Ransom was waiting for them down the street. They told him what happened. His first question was whether they believed Youngblood.

They didn't know what to believe. Stillman said it was like they'd tumbled into a whirlpool sucking them into a sewer of shit and there was no way out. "Fucking Army," he said.

"We've got to do something," Bear said. "We can't do nothing." He wished kids weren't being hurt. Otherwise, he might walk away. He asked Ransom if there was any way to check Youngblood's story.

If Youngblood was telling the truth, Ransom said he was probably with the CID, the Army's Criminal Investigative Division. But regardless of whether he was being truthful, Ransom pointed out Youngblood admitted that something bad was going on and it involved children. He said he could check out Youngblood through a friend at a West Coast Army base who had access to all sorts of records. Ransom said his friend might be able to get Youngblood's personnel file to find out more. But that would require his full name and date of birth and Social Security number.

Stillman offered to go back to the chapel to see if Youngblood's full name was posted there. "Bear's right," he said. "We can't just do nothing."

"We got to remember why we're here," said Bear. "We're here to fight the fucking Army and cause as much trouble as we can and end a war. It's time to get started."

"Right on," said Stillman.

Ransom asked what they wanted to do.

Bear and Stillman looked at each other with uncertainty.

"Wait," said Ransom. "Here we go. Two uniforms just came out of the chapel."

"That's them," said Bear. "The chaplain's the older one."

"I'll take it from here," Ransom said. "You guys get back to your unit. I'll be in touch to let you know what I find."

15

Monday, November 11, 1968
Cambridge

Lincoln Freeman didn't sleep well over the weekend. He couldn't get Ian MacPherson out of his mind. He called a few lawyer friends for advice. Then, Lisa called to tell him Chris had died. That meant three young men were dead after going to the Boston Army Base in the past month, and MacPherson was scared he could be number four.

Freeman had planned to meet friends at a Celtics game Saturday night and go out with them afterward. He went to the game, but wasn't into it. All he could think about was the unfolding murder mystery. With the Celts well ahead, he apologized and said he had to leave because of work. He returned to his apartment in Boston's Dorchester neighborhood and opened a beer.

MacPherson wasn't blameless, but he didn't seem like a bad guy. He was intelligent and had done something stupid that made him an accessory to a bunch of bad shit. But he could also be seen as a victim, caught between two dead would-be revolutionaries and a gang of drug-running battle-hardened soldiers. If you believed his story, you had to think that MacPherson was lucky to be alive. Then there was the heroin. He said he had it. That could be his ticket out of the mess if he was willing to work with the cops. Then there was Chris, who, according to Lisa, mentioned the SDS raid while refusing induction. She got that from the draftees at Fort Dix. Freeman couldn't imagine Chris had anything to do with dealing drugs. So why was he killed? This was not the kind of law Freeman had planned to practice.

On Monday morning he left early for his office to get there before his assistant. On his way, he picked up an extra coffee for MacPherson, who was waiting for him in the outer office when he arrived. MacPherson said nobody had called or knocked on the door over the weekend. He said he had gone out for a couple of walks and to get food, but nobody bothered him. He had cleaned himself up and didn't look as hopeless as he had on Friday.

The phone rang, and Freeman answered the call on his assistant's phone. It was from a man with a husky voice and a hint of an accent. He introduced himself as a friend of Chris Thompson and asked if he could make an appointment. *What timing*, thought Freeman. "Of course," he said to the caller. "I'm meeting with someone in my office at the moment. If you give me your name and a phone number, I can call you back." The caller said he couldn't do that, but had some information about Chris that Freeman would want to see. They agreed to meet at 1 P.M.

Freeman unlocked the door to his inner office and he and MacPherson resumed their conversation. Freeman pulled out a pen and a pad of paper. He said he had consulted over the weekend with lawyers he trusted about MacPherson's predicament. MacPherson asked if the phone call he just answered was from one of those lawyers.

"No," Freeman said. "That was somebody else. Now, let's get back to your situation. The first thing is to try to keep you alive. That means finding a place for you to stay while we work this out. Like a safe house. We'll talk about that later. Right now, for starters, you're in a jurisdictional jungle. That's a complicating factor because there's so many law enforcement agencies that might want a piece of you." He said cops with overlapping responsibilities generally don't cooperate well because they don't like to share the glory if everything goes right or the blame if anything goes wrong.

He listed more than a half dozen agencies that could come into play, starting with the military police and the Army's CID. Then there was the FBI, the Massachusetts State Police, and the Boston Police Department. In addition there were other federal agencies dealing with border protection, drugs, and smuggling that might want pieces of the action.

A respected criminal defense attorney he consulted over the weekend suggested the best strategy would be for a lawyer, acting on behalf of MacPherson as an unnamed client, to approach the FBI because the case involved crimes committed on and off a military base. In return for providing information, the client would want to be protected and not identified.

"Obviously," Freeman said, "the FBI is going to demand your cooperation. You'll be questioned about how you know what you know and what part you played in the break-in and theft at the Army base. They'll probably want to use you as bait to lure the soldiers into a trap. There'll be a lot of details to be worked out about how you cooperate with them. And a fair amount of danger." Freeman clicked his pen a few times and looked around like he forgot what he was going to say next. "Oh yes," he said. "Chris Thompson. You said you didn't really know him?"

"Mostly by reputation. I knew from those other guys that he got hurt at the Army base and was in a coma."

"He's dead."

MacPherson looked shocked. "Oh man. No way. Is it another murder?"

"That's what we need to find out. I got a call from his sister. It's been quite a weekend."

"This is some heavy shit."

"There's too much going on all at once related to that Army base," Freeman said. "I need to know why." He had been doodling while he was talking. He leaned back in his chair and tapped his pen on the pad of paper, looking at MacPherson, waiting for an answer. "Well?"

"I don't know what's going on, man, except for the war. If it wasn't for the fucking war, Chris and those other guys would still be alive and those Army dudes might not be smuggling drugs and I would never have gone near that fucking base."

"Yes. The war. It keeps me busy."

"How long before I have to, you know, decide what I'm gonna do?"

"That's up to you. Obviously, you can't stay here indefinitely. I don't want to get too dramatic, but I'm sure you know whatever you do it's one of those big life-changing moments." Freeman said he saw two choices, and both had risks. MacPherson could become an informant or he could try to disappear.

MacPherson looked down at the floor. "I know what it's like to be on the run," he said. "I couldn't live like that for the rest of my life. If the only other choice is cooperating with the FBI, that's what I've got to do."

Freeman said the defense lawyer he mentioned would be willing to work with them to try to negotiate the terms of an arrangement with the FBI. MacPherson said that sounded good, but he wanted to wait a few days before making a final decision.

Freeman said the next decision was where MacPherson would go while the terms of the deal were being worked out. He said Chris's sister Lisa offered her family's Vermont farm, where she lived. Freeman had warned her it could be dangerous, but she said she could handle it. She was eager to talk to MacPherson because the soldiers who were after him could have been involved in Chris's death. MacPherson said he could leave for Vermont right away.

Freeman reached for his phone and called Lisa, who said she'd pick him up outside the office in a few hours.

*   *   *   *

Johnny Dollar meandered into a crowd of students down the street from Freeman's office shortly before Lisa drove by in her pickup truck. Johnny looked like he could be a Harvard economics professor. He was wearing a cardigan sweater over a button-down dress shirt, chinos, and penny loafers with a nice shine. He was carrying a briefcase and wearing glasses. The newsboy flat cap looked a bit odd, but not unexpected in a college town.

Johnny used the group of students as cover after seeing a tall, thin man he recognized on the steps outside Freeman's office smoking cigarette after cigarette. When Lisa stopped in front of MacPherson, he tossed his backpack into the rear of her truck and got into the passenger seat. She stepped on the gas as soon as he closed the door.

Johnny watched them drive out of sight and waited. He didn't see anyone following them. Or him. He lingered a while longer and started down the sidewalk, walking away from Freeman's office. He casually circled the block and checked the street both ways before he took off his cap and went in. Without introducing himself, he told Freeman's assistant he was there for a 1 P.M. appointment. When Freeman came to the reception area, Johnny greeted him by putting a finger to his mouth and then pointing to the door. Freeman nodded, grabbed his coat, and followed Johnny to the street. Once outside on the sidewalk, Johnny introduced himself and Freeman responded with a warm handshake and the unwanted news that Chris had died over the weekend.

"I know," Johnny said. "That's why I'm here."

Johnny and Freeman had never met, but Chris was their common bond and had told them enough about each other to make them feel comfortable. Johnny had a slight accent, suggesting some Hispanic heritage. Freeman asked him about it. Johnny said his father was Puerto Rican and had brought him to mainland America when he was young, after his mother died in a car accident. Johnny said he grew up in Connecticut, where his father had worked in tobacco fields and then a fabric mill.

"It's so good to finally meet you," said Freeman.

"I feel the same way," Johnny said. He looked up and down the street and waited for a cluster of people to pass before suggesting, "Let's walk." They took a few steps and he continued, "I'm probably being overly cautious, but I wouldn't be surprised if your office is bugged."

"What?"

Freeman was stunned. He stopped, turned to Johnny, and asked, "Why would you suspect something like that?" Johnny asked if Lisa had just picked up a man with a backpack. Freeman hesitated. He wasn't inclined to tell Johnny about MacPherson because he was now a client. Confidentiality was a concern. Lisa was a client as well. He asked why Johnny wanted to know about them and how that could be connected to the FBI.

Johnny suggested they start walking again. He didn't want to tell Freeman that he knew Lisa. He said he saw a Vermont license plate on the pickup truck and from what Chris told him about Lisa, he suspected she was the driver.

"Yes. That would have been Lisa."

"And the skinny guy with the backpack?"

"He's a client. So is Lisa."

"I've seen him before," Johnny said.

"So you know him?"

"I don't know his name, but I've seen him before. Where are they going?"

"His name is Ian MacPherson, but I don't want to get into where they're going."

"It might be important."

"Why is that?"

They rounded a corner, and Johnny suggested they cross the street to a park where they could sit on a bench. As they stepped off the curb, Johnny said he had seen MacPherson talking with an FBI agent who was investigating the anti-war movement and the SDS.

Freeman froze. "You're shitting me."

Johnny nudged him to continue across the street. He said he saw MacPherson and the agent together. He couldn't hear what they said, but the conversation had lasted at least fifteen minutes.

As they entered the park, Freeman thought about his advice to MacPherson just hours earlier to cut a deal with the FBI. If Johnny was right, MacPherson was hiding a lot more than Freeman imagined. He felt like a fool. He asked Johnny how confident he was that the man with MacPherson was an FBI agent.

"I know who he is," Johnny said, "and I think you'll know in a minute that you can trust me."

Johnny motioned to a park bench, which was empty, and they sat down.

"I came to see you today because I've got some new information," Johnny said. "I figured Lisa would hire you to go after the Army. I have something for both of you."

He opened his briefcase and pulled out a file folder. It was labeled "Christopher Tucker Thompson." He passed it to Freeman, who thumbed through the pages silently before exclaiming, "Shit man. Holy fucking shit." Then he lowered his voice. "This has Chris's last words."

"Yeah."

"I'd ask how you got this, but I think I already know the answer."

"I'm sure you do."

Johnny said he'd had the file for a while and was waiting for the Army's report to be issued to the family so he could compare them. But when he learned Chris had died, he decided it was time to act. He said he knew the Army was stonewalling Lisa, hoping she and her parents would give up trying to get an official written report.

The file contained statements from Army soldiers and officers who were interviewed by military police about what was termed "the accident." A sergeant who escorted Chris out of the induction room said Chris tried to pull away from him and stumbled on a staircase and fell, hitting his head and face on a wall and the stairs before landing at the bottom, unconscious and unresponsive. What was most startling and important was a statement by an ambulance attendant who rode with Chris and said he briefly regained consciousness before reaching the hospital. The attendant said Chris struggled to talk and told him, barely audibly, that he had been beaten and thrown down a stairway. He quoted Chris as saying they wanted to kill him because he had their drugs and money and was SDS.

Freeman asked if the statements in the file were copies. Johnny nodded. "So the Army's file is still intact?" Johnny nodded again. "And nobody knows copies have been made?" Johnny nodded. "Can I keep this file?" Another nod. "Do you have any problem with me using these documents?" Johnny shook his head.

"The only thing I ask," Johnny said, "is that you don't tell anyone how you got that file."

Freeman said that wouldn't be a problem. He wanted to ask Johnny another question, but wasn't sure where it would lead. He decided to ask anyway. "That statement by the attendant, do you have any idea why Chris might have been killed over drugs and money?"

"No," Johnny said. "How about you?"

That was the comeback Freeman didn't want to hear. He didn't want to talk about MacPherson. He told Johnny he heard that some soldiers at the base had been selling heroin, but didn't know if Chris knew that.

"We never talked about anything like that," Johnny said. "I'll look into it." He checked his watch, shut his briefcase, and got up from the bench, saying he had to leave for another appointment.

"I don't know how you do what you do," said Freeman, "but man, I sure am glad you do it. Lisa's not going to believe what's in this file. Can I tell her I got it from you?"

"Not right now," Johnny said. "Maybe down the road."

Freeman reached out to shake Johnny's hand. Up close, he noticed Johnny's nose was slightly misshapen and the crest of one of his ears was swollen, probably from an old injury. He was surprised at how large Johnny's hand was. He was dressed like a young professional, but his muscular upper body said something else. His clothes looked like he earned his living behind a desk, but he moved like an athlete.

"I've got another question you probably don't want to answer," Freeman said.

"Shoot," said Johnny.

"Do you play sports?"

"I used to box, but these days I just try to stay in shape."

Freeman told Johnny he wanted to stay in touch. He asked if there was a way he could contact him by phone if he needed to ask him a question or talk to him. He suspected the answer would be no, and it was. Johnny said he would check back when he could, but not by the office phone. He asked for Freeman's home phone number and wrote it down. Then he asked if Freeman knew anyone who could inspect his office for listening devices. He said he didn't, but could ask other lawyers. He asked Johnny if he knew anyone.

"I might," he said. "Why don't you hold off talking to anyone else about it. I'll be in touch."

"For myself and Lisa," Freeman said, "I want to thank you. This is going to sound corny, but I'm blown away by your sense of justice and your courage. If you ever need anything, absolutely anything, you know where to find me."

Johnny thanked him. He suggested that Lisa not tell anyone other than her mother and father about the accident file until after the Army produced an official report for the family.

Freeman said he was now worried about Lisa driving MacPherson to her farm. "What more can you tell me about MacPherson?" he asked.

"Not enough," said Johnny. "When I find anything, I'll let you know right away."

"Before you go, I should tell you something I now regret based on what you told me today. I let MacPherson spend the weekend in my outer office because he said he had nowhere else to go."

"This past weekend?"

"Yeah. But I made sure the file cabinets were locked before I left."

"How long was he there?"

"From Friday evening until today."

"Did he ask to stay in your office?"

"No. I offered because he looked so desperate. He said he needed legal help and was on the run. But the possibility that there was another reason is beginning to worry me."

"Did you check the locks on the file cabinets today?"

"Not yet."

"I can tell you this," Johnny said, "which is probably no surprise to you. The FBI and the government will break into offices and steal stuff and plant bugs and make stuff up and do all sorts of illegal shit to stop the anti-war movement. Hoover is paranoid and has put us at the top of his enemies list."

"I've got other reasons to be suspicious about MacPherson," Freeman said, "but I don't feel comfortable talking about them right now."

"I understand," said Johnny, touching his cap lightly in a farewell gesture. "I'll get back to you about checking for listening devices. In the meantime, be careful about using the phone or even just talking in your office about anything sensitive."

"Before you go," said Freeman, "I've got one more question. Is Johnny Dollar your real name?"

"It's one of them."

*   *   *   *

Lisa crossed a bridge over the Connecticut River from New Hampshire to Vermont and then stuck to back roads following rivers and streams through sparsely populated wooded valleys and hills. She slowed her truck and pulled into a dirt turnoff next to a rocky brook. The setting looked like it was once a wonderful place for a family roadside picnic until it became a dumping ground for trash and junk, including broken furniture and appliances. Lisa turned off the motor and pulled the key out of the ignition.

"Let's take a break," she said. She got out of the truck and walked toward the brook. MacPherson leaned out his window and asked, "Bathroom break?"

"You need to go?" Lisa asked.

"No. I'm OK."

"Me too," she said. "This is a break to stretch your legs and breathe some clean, fresh air." She stopped at the edge of the brook. MacPherson got out of the truck and followed her. He reached into his pocket for a cigarette and matches, but before he could light up, she stopped him. "Don't. Don't smoke. Just take a few minutes to listen, breathe clean air, and appreciate nature. If you close your eyes and listen, the stream may talk to you." She sat on a rock, and he watched as she closed her eyes.

So this is what hippies do, MacPherson thought. Is this supposed to be meditation? How crazy is she? Nevertheless, he did as he was told. He tried to listen. He even closed his eyes. He didn't know what he was supposed to hear. He wanted a cigarette so badly he couldn't think about anything else. He hadn't even noticed that the stream had a sound. He hadn't had a cigarette for more than two hours because she asked him not to smoke in the truck. He held the unlit cigarette under his nose to inhale the scent, then put it back in his pocket. He sat on a log and closed his eyes and tried to listen. He didn't hear anything. Then he did. A sound he couldn't identify. It was coming closer. He looked around and then up and there they were, honking geese in formation headed south. They were surprisingly loud as they flew overhead. Then a car—no, it had to be a truck—with a broken muffler—came by and jangled down the road. Then, in the absence of interference, he heard the stream. At first, it sounded like a trickle, but it grew more complex. It produced a variety of splashing and riffling sounds. He was surprised how loud it now seemed. As he listened, he tried to imagine it washing away grim thoughts of the complicated mess he left in the city, but his troubles kept resurfacing, blotting out the brook. He couldn't escape his past and he couldn't stop thinking about how hopeless the future looked. He hadn't told Freeman all of it, and he didn't plan to tell Lisa either. He wondered why she stopped here. What was she up to? She was literally and figuratively in the driver's seat. She had a house in Vermont, a good place to hide. She was smart and good looking and comfortable being in control, something a lot of guys would find intimidating. MacPherson hadn't known Chris, but he wanted to get to know more about Lisa. Their conversation on the ride from Boston had been casual. He figured she must have stopped here to talk about things he wouldn't want to talk about.

A splash and the crack of a rock bouncing off other rocks reminded him he was supposed to be listening for something. He opened his eyes. Lisa threw another stone.

"Do you like tuna fish?" she asked.

"Sure," he said. She had a thermos and a paper bag. She pulled out a couple of sandwiches and passed him one. They ate in silence and shared iced tea and slices of an apple cut into wedges.

"Did you know Chris?" she asked.

MacPherson said he knew of him, but had never talked to him.

"Before we get to the farm," Lisa said, "I need to know what you're going to tell people there about who you are. I have friends who stay at the farm and neighbors who help us and we help them. They'll be curious. It's a small town. All I know about you is what Mr. Freeman told me. It wasn't much, and it wasn't very flattering. He said you were in trouble and had to get away from Boston. He said you were involved in a break-in and vandalism at the Army base and stealing drugs and cash and because of that, soldiers killed two people you lived with and now they're trying to kill you. And they might have killed my brother."

MacPherson looked away, embarrassed. He took his time before answering. "That's harsh," he said. He tried to soften Freeman's description by saying he was only a lookout and the others did the vandalizing and stealing. He told her the soldiers were after him because he was the only one who knew where the drugs and cash were after they had killed the others.

She wanted to know why he had gotten involved. He called it a stupid mistake, the biggest one he'd ever made. It was probably going to wreck his life. She asked what he planned to do about it. He said that was why he met with Freeman, to get his advice. Why Freeman? He said he heard about him through Boston Draft Resistance. He said with Freeman's help, he was probably going to try to stay out of jail by making a deal with the FBI.

She said she was concerned her life could be in danger because he was with her. He said nobody knew he was going to Vermont except Freeman. What if the soldiers found out where he was? What would they do? He didn't know, but he was the only one they were after. Did he know the names of the soldiers or what they looked like? No. He had never seen them, but he said the drugs were found in an office of a soldier named Sanders.

Lisa wanted to scream, but held it in. She stood up, turning away from him. "Does Mr. Freeman know that?" she asked.

"I don't know. I might have told him. Do you know who he is?"

"I've heard the name," she said. "What kind of drugs were found in his office?"

"Heroin."

Lisa picked up the lunch wrappers and the thermos and carried them back to the truck. She wasn't going to tell MacPherson anything. She was more than grateful he just gave her a crucial bit of information. But she didn't trust him. There was no way she would let him get anywhere near the farm and put her and her friends in danger. But she needed to probe for more information.

She pulled some empty plastic bags out of the truck and walked back to MacPherson, who had lit a cigarette. She kept her distance from the smoke. She asked if Chris knew about the raid on the Army base. MacPherson said he knew Chris wasn't involved but that he could have heard about it afterward. What about the heroin and cash? He said nobody knew about that except him and the guys who were killed. And now, he pointed out, she knew about the drugs and cash, as well as Freeman. She asked whether he had any of the heroin with him. He said no. Did anyone else know he was coming to Vermont? "Only you and Freeman," he said.

"What will you tell people at the house about who you are and why you're there?"

"I don't know," he said. "I'm a grad student. We could stick with that. We could say I heard about Chris and you and the family farm from Draft Resistance and I wanted to get out of the city for a while. That's mostly true."

"How long would you stay?"

"I don't know. I need to think about my next move."

"If those soldiers come after you, you won't know they're coming, will you? You don't have anyone to warn you, do you?"

"No."

"Is there anything important that you haven't told me?"

MacPherson exhaled a long stream of smoke. "Not that I can think of," he said.

"Could the soldiers who killed your friends have killed my brother?"

"They weren't my friends."

"Then why were you with them?"

"They offered to let me stay with them while my apartment was being fixed."

"Once again, could the soldiers who killed them have killed my brother?"

"I don't know. I suppose so. Anything's possible. But I don't know of any connection."

The stream babbled in the background. She held out the empty bags and handed him one. "Before we leave," she said, "we're going to pick up some of this trash, the beer cans and bottles and food wrappers and stuff like that around the parking area. Get the cigarette butts and the condoms too. We'll worry about the big stuff another time."

They filled three bags. Lisa dropped the truck's tailgate and sat on it, looking back at the stream. MacPherson lit another cigarette and stood downwind, exhaling smoke into the breeze. "This place looks a lot better," he said, "but it would take years to clean up a whole stream or a river."

"Someone has to start somewhere," she said.

After MacPherson finished his cigarette, Lisa slid off the tailgate and closed it so she was standing facing him. She was close enough to smell his stinky cigarette breath. "I've made a decision," she said. "It affects you. I can't let you come to the farm. It's too dangerous."

He looked dazed and stepped back. "Whoa," he said. "What do you mean? That changes everything."

"What's everything?"

He spread his arms and looked around. "Everything," he said. "Every. Thing."

His eyes flared with anger. "I thought we had a deal. You said I could crash at your farm. I'm just looking for a safe place to chill and take the heat off for a few days."

"You can find some other place."

"I don't know any other place. There's nobody I can call. Do you want money? How much? Because I don't have much."

"There's lots of people you can call and places you can go."

"Oh yeah. Who are those people and where are those places?"

"You know them, but you don't want to call or go there because you'd put people in danger, people you obviously care about a lot more than me."

"I can't go to obvious places where the soldiers will look."

"So you want to bring danger to my place."

"The lawyer said you offered."

"I did. And now I'm withdrawing the offer."

"Right here. In the middle of nowhere. On a back road in Vermont after bringing me here from Boston? You can't just leave me here. You're sentencing me to death. I've got nowhere to go."

"You're so dramatic. You're also dangerous. You're a walking stick of dynamite that could explode at any time."

"That's not fair. I'm an innocent guy, a grad student, who got caught up in something he doesn't understand."

"Through no fault of your own? Give me a break."

"What am I supposed to do?"

"That's for you to figure out. You got yourself into whatever it is that you got into and now it's up to you to figure a way out. I'm not here to save you. I've got more important things to do."

"Like finding out what happened to your brother?"

"That's right."

"And then what do you want? Do you want to put people in jail? Do you want a big payday from a lawsuit? The Army isn't going to give you shit. If you don't get money are you going to kill somebody?"

"We're not far from Hanover," she said. "That's a college town where you could fit in or catch a ride back to Boston. I'll drive you to Hanover if you want. It's back across the river."

MacPherson turned away. He walked into the trees along the stream and lit another cigarette. He took his time to wind down. When he came back, he was subdued. "I'll take the ride," he said.

Neither of them spoke on the way to Hanover. She dropped him at a corner of the Dartmouth College Green. Then she drove a couple of blocks and found a parking space. She walked back on foot, slowing down to blend in behind a group of people, to where she left MacPherson. She didn't want him to see her. She spotted him in a phone booth. He was talking to someone and gesturing wildly with his arms. At one point, he hit the side of the booth with an open hand.

"What a surprise," Lisa said to herself. "You found somebody to call. I'd sure like to know who it is."

*   *   *   *

She returned to her truck and drove to the farm a little over a half hour away. The sun had dropped below the ridge when she pulled into the yard. She didn't need her headlights because the house and barn were illuminated by a bonfire with sparks soaring into the air and drifting on the breeze. Fortunately, they were blowing away from the buildings. The Beatles *Magical Mystery Tour* album was blasting from speakers on the porch. A cluster of people circled the fire. She didn't recognize the ones she could see. The scene made her nervous. But she had something else on her mind.

She got down from the truck and strode into the house. She grabbed the phone and dialed Lincoln Freeman's office. While the call was ringing, she looked around the living room. The couch and chairs had been moved and a drum set dominated a corner where her grandparents' antique spinning wheel had been displayed for years. A couple of large music posters were hanging behind the drums. She didn't see the spinning wheel.

When the phone rang, Freeman was alone, reflecting on the unsettling events of the day, looking out his office window at the street. He went to his desk to answer it. He smiled when he heard Lisa's voice, but her tone sounded off. He asked if anything was wrong. She told him she just got back to the farm and a lot had changed. "I'll be all right," she said. "I called you about MacPherson."

She told Freeman she didn't take MacPherson to the farm because of the danger. She described how she dropped him off in Hanover and watched him make a phone call after he told her there was nobody he could call.

"Did he call you?" she asked.

"No," said Freeman. He started to say more and stopped. "Wait. Give me a minute," he said, "Somebody may have just come into the office. I'll put you on hold." He did and laid the handset on his desk. He picked up the base of the phone and turned it over so he could see the sides and the bottom. He unscrewed the cap on the mouthpiece and looked inside. He didn't see anything unusual. He moved to the outer office, where he picked up his assistant's phone and studied it in the same way. Then he scanned the ceiling and walls. He didn't see anything out of the ordinary, but he didn't know what he was looking for. He returned to his desk and picked up the phone.

"I'm back," he said to Lisa, "but I've got to break away. When are you coming back to town?"

She said she'd probably return to her parents' house in a few days, once she dealt with what was going on at the farm. He asked her to call him as soon as she got back to Lexington.

*   *   *   *

"Hi," a woman called softly through the front porch screen door. She and Lisa knew each other from college and she had been staying at the house for several weeks. "Welcome back," she said timidly when Lisa didn't respond. "This may be kind of a shock seeing all these people here. We didn't expect you. It turns out someone got some Owsley. We're ahhh, tripping. Do you want to join us?"

Lisa shook her head and asked that nobody put any more wood on the bonfire, leading to an awkward silence. The woman agreed and retreated from the door to rejoin the group. Lisa stayed inside. She looked around the house to see what had happened since she left. Quite a few people seemed to have moved in, rearranged furniture, and made themselves at home. She found her grandparents' spinning wheel upstairs in a bedroom. Nothing appeared to be missing.

Lisa pulled a backpack out of a closet and stuffed it with her sleeping bag, some clothes, snacks, and camping supplies. She filled a couple of water bottles and grabbed her tent and went out the back kitchen door into the darkness. After feeling the cold air, she turned back inside for a warm jacket and a flashlight. She looked through the living room window and counted more than a dozen people gathered around the bonfire. She left the house again through the kitchen and started up the trail with her backpack and tent. She didn't need the flashlight. The night was clear and moonlit, unusual for November in Vermont. She reached the clearing at Turtle Rock, gathered wood, and started a fire. She decided not to put up her tent. It was a beautiful night to sleep under the stars and clear her head. Years ago she and Chris had dug a fire pit close to the boulder and ringed it with stones. She wished Chris could be with her now.

She stared into the flames. She loved how different kinds of wood produced such a variety of colors and sparks and sounds. But in the end, no matter where the wood came from or how old or young it was or what distinguished it, it was all reduced to coals that glowed orange, then dimmed and turned to ash and disappeared, blown by the winds, mixing with soil to produce more plants and trees.

She didn't feel hungry, but she dipped into a bag of trail mix as she settled down by the fire. She kept nibbling as she thought back to the scene she'd encountered at the farmhouse. She'd already made up her mind they would have to find somewhere else to live. She'd deal with that tomorrow after they came down from their trip. It would be a bumpy landing.

Lisa knew LSD from personal experience. She had taken a few trips with Chris and friends. She loved the out-of-body transition as the drug came on. For her, it was a step through an imaginary door into a magical kingdom that felt like her celestial home, a home that asked her to leave herself at the door and prepare to experience the unseen. It was a wonderful place to visit. No need for a fuel-guzzling jetliner to get there. Just a tiny pill or a small blot on a piece of paper. As she reflected on the wonders of LSD, her thoughts turned to her most recent trip. It was the best. It was in May with Chris and a mutual friend who was studying Zen Buddhism while working on his PhD in literature. The three of them took mescaline that day.

Their trip began at the farmhouse with music, Bob Dylan's *Bringing It All Back Home* album, before they headed outside to experience the wonders of spring. They stopped at Turtle Rock to take in the view. They were struck by how many thousands or millions of years it must have taken for the forces of nature to shape that rock and place it on the ridge and buff its contours smooth. They studied the lines and cracks in it. They climbed on it and ran their hands over it and were amazed they could feel it breathing. They lay face down on it and matched their own breathing with the stone, in and out, in and out. They pondered how a seemingly inanimate rock could possibly breathe, but after a while they moved on, deciding they should appreciate it, rather than try to explain the inexplicable. They wandered into unfamiliar woods, drawn deeper and deeper by the seductive rebirth of tiny wildflowers, yellow, white, pink, and violet, scattered like a trail of bread crumbs, leading them on. Somebody wanted them to see something. They followed the colors through the forest to a collection of boulders near a hollow in the ridge.

On closer inspection they surmised it could have been a giant's fire ring. They worked their way through the boulders and discovered a glistening pool of water seething with wildlife, a primal swamp, the beginning of life. There was no doubt they had found the source of all creation. They were thrilled with their good fortune and took ringside seats on the rocks. They drank in ecstasy from the fountain of awareness until they realized they were under attack, twitching and frantically waving their arms to defend themselves from swarming clouds of black flies. "Who the hell let these goddamn bugs into paradise?" the Buddhist shouted to the heavens as they rose unsteadily to their feet, as if waking from a dream. They got their bearings and fled.

That evening, they came down gently in the comfort of stuffed chairs and the cozy couch in the farmhouse living room. They reflected on their trip while their bug-bitten bodies recovered. A breathing boulder was far out, but the primal swamp was the highlight. The aspiring Buddhist suggested they had discovered spiritual truth, something mystics had sought since the beginning of time, the answer to one of the great mysteries of the cosmos. "You don't have to go all over the universe seeking awareness," he said. "It's wherever you are. When you stop looking, you'll find it. Paradise is bug city."

Lisa remembered how she and Chris marveled at the simplicity of that observation as they turned it over in their minds. The more they thought about it, it was so true, in so many ways. A moment of acid truth. Such fun. It's here. And then it's not. She really missed Chris. All she had now were her memories.

She put another log on her fire. She had been sitting on a blanket. She unfolded it, pulled it up around her shoulders and reluctantly turned her attention to the urgent matter at hand, those strangers at the farmhouse. She didn't like the idea of kicking anybody out, but most of them were never invited in. She didn't want the farm to become party central. She had to shut it down. She would have to spend more time in Boston and couldn't think of anybody she could trust to manage the farm while she was away. She had depended on her boyfriend Theo for that, but he left for the West Coast after Chris was hospitalized. The garden had already been put to bed for the winter, and she would have to find new homes for the chickens and the goat. The barn cats could stay or leave if they wanted.

If they weren't wild to begin with, they were now.

It bothered her that she'd have to tell people to leave. It would be stressful and contrary to her reputation among the communes that were sprouting in Vermont's mountain towns. Her farm was known as a welcoming place where new arrivals could get help or eggs or borrow a chainsaw or other tools. Some of the communes were barely livable, with shabby shelters thrown together from whatever materials could be salvaged, including cardboard. Many of the young people attracted to the communes were outcasts from urban and suburban areas and knew nothing about rural life or subsistence farming or providing for themselves in a climate where summers were short, winters were long, and mud and bugs had their own seasons.

She thought of her parents, who regarded the communes as a threat. They saw the communes as the forefront of an invading force of hippies and worried about the hippies taking over an entire state that they loved. An array of intertwined causes were rattling the nation—the back-to-the-land movement, the hippie counterculture movement, the environmental movement, the anti-war movement, the civil rights and women's rights movements, the Indian rights movement, and the Black pride movement. That profusion of causes was accompanied by the relentless drumbeat of music, which made parents cringe and got their kids dancing.

Lisa sensed what her parents feared most was change. The proliferation of communes was inspired by a 1954 book written by a couple of seemingly harmless vegetarians, Helen and Scott Nearing, who turned their backs on city life to homestead in southern Vermont. Lisa and Chris were familiar with the Nearings and their book, *Living the Good Life*. It came to be regarded as a bible of organic gardening. Chris had admired Scott Nearing, an outspoken pacifist who was prosecuted for opposing the draft during World War I.

Lisa put another log on the fire and slid into her sleeping bag with the blanket underneath it. Thoughts of the Nearings and Chris, along with questions about what she was trying to do with the farm, swirled through her mind. It was getting late, but she didn't feel like sleeping. She lay on her back and pulled the sleeping bag tight around her neck. The stars were spectacular. She wished she could lay there forever, plugged into the universe, untouched by illusory, inconvenient earthly matters. But that wasn't possible. A shooting star flashed across the sky. She imagined it was Chris, reunited with the cosmos, out there having fun, waving to her. They both believed their spirits came from the heavens and returned there when they died.

She turned her attention back to her utopian dream of an environmentally responsible lifestyle. What was that anyway? She wasn't sure anymore. For the first time, she questioned whether it was desirable or even possible. Why even engage in the futility of trying to save a planet that doesn't want to be saved? How much can one person do? That question could stop a dream before it even got started.

She dwelt on that and Chris's life and death and surprised herself by coming away upbeat for the first time in weeks. Of course. The Nearings. Two people, one book. Rachel Carson, one person, one book. Look at the movements they created. One or two or three people might even be able to secure lasting justice for Chris.

That was a good thought to sleep on.

16

Wednesday, November 13, 1968
Fort Dix

On a chilly, damp day, Bear and Stillman's platoon was ordered to carry out a training exercise in a remote section of woods, not far from an elaborate replica of a Vietnamese village with booby traps and tunnels designed to give trainees a sample of what they would be up against.

During the march, drill sergeants lobbed tear gas canisters at them, testing how quickly they could get their gas masks on while choking and gasping for air. Their unit was ordered to set up a camp with perimeter guards to prepare for a possible attack since they were supposed to be in hostile territory. Stillman and Bear volunteered for perimeter security. Stillman had worked summers as a counselor at a rustic camp in Vermont and was at ease in the woods. He told Bear he didn't think they should wait for the enemy to find them. They should go out beyond the perimeter and catch the enemy by surprise before they could attack. So they went deeper into the woods to scout how an attacking unit might approach. They found what looked like a faint trail through the trees. Stillman stopped at a point where the trail curled around thick bushes and said it looked like the perfect place for an ambush. Bear agreed anyone approaching their assigned part of the perimeter would probably pass within a few feet of them.

Daylight savings time had ended, the rain showers were cold, and it was getting dark. "This is when being Black is a good thing," said Stillman. "You'll have the advantage. You'll blend into the dark. They'll see me first and probably kill me."

"Then they'll shoot me because I'm Black," said Bear. "Some advantage."

They crawled into the bushes, wiggled themselves flat on the wet ground, and lay still, talking in whispers, wondering if they were going to get into trouble and how that might turn out. They had their M16 rifles, which were lethal at three hundred yards but so lightweight that they felt like toys. The first day the rifles were issued, some of the trainees in their unit played with them like kids, pointing them at each other, going bang-bang, bang-bang. Watching, Stillman felt sorry for them and wondered how they'd ever survive in Vietnam. As he and Bear discovered during their training, the M16 was powerful and accurate, but unreliable, prone to jamming.

On this training exercise, anticipating an attack, their rifles were not supposed to be loaded. But somebody in their unit had got ahold of blank rounds and passed them to friends. So Bear and Stillman each had a blank loaded in their M16s. They planned to fire them if the enemy showed up. A half hour later the enemy did show up, a group of three soldiers led by their basic training company commander, a captain who had won a bunch of combat medals in Vietnam. He was about to step on Bear when Stillman fired his rifle and told them to drop their guns. The captain jumped at the sound of the shot, which echoed through the trees. One of the drill sergeants behind him stumbled into the bushes. "You got us," the captain said. "We're your prisoners." Bear and Stillman led them into the training unit's makeshift camp.

The captain didn't talk about the ambush until the trainees got back to their barracks that night. He gathered them as a group under a floodlight at one end of the barracks in the cold drizzle and singled out Stillman and Bear with praise for their initiative. They couldn't believe it. He motioned to a drill sergeant who had a large piece of cake on a paper plate with two forks. The captain dismissed the rest of the trainees and drill sergeants and told Stillman and Bear to stay behind. While they ate cake, he told Stillman he knew he had talked with the chaplain about how to get out of the Army.

"I know you told him you'd do anything to avoid supporting the war."

"That's right."

"That's flawed thinking, son."

"Why do Army officers call everybody son?"

"We're concerned about your well-being."

"You don't need to be."

"It's my job."

"If you're really concerned, give me a discharge. Bear too. And anyone else who wants out."

"You know I can't do that."

"Sure you can. You'd be famous."

"A hero," said Bear. He reached out and offered the last bite of cake to Stillman, who declined it.

Stillman kept his eyes on the captain. "You don't seem to understand what's going on," he told him. "By keeping us in the Army, you're making yourself an accessory to whatever we do to stop the war because now you know who we are. We're the resistance. We're the enemy. As of this moment, if you don't give us discharges, you're a conspirator with me and Bear and responsible for whatever we do from here on out. If we go to the stockade, you go with us."

The captain didn't blink. "Get real," he said, "and show some respect. Both of you. Listen up. I've got some advice that might keep you out of the stockade or worse. Do what you're told, serve your time quietly, and get out. You do that and you can go back to being civilians with clean records. Don't let the Army mess up the rest of your lives. Just follow orders and you'll be fine. You've both got bright futures. Stillman, you're a college graduate. So am I. You should apply to become an officer."

"There's no way that's ever going to happen."

"You worked hard to get that college degree. Don't do anything that will erase it."

"The dishonorable discharge threat."

"That's right. It would dog you forever."

"I'm going for the 214. I like the name, "unsuitability for military service." That sounds honorable to me."

"It's not. It's a general discharge."

"You're never going to make me a soldier. It's just not going to happen."

"It's already happening. Both of you have excellent basic training records that can lead to good duty assignments. You should build on that."

"We're just buying time until we figure out the best way to get out."

"We're time bombs," said Bear. "Tick. Tick. Tick. The Army doesn't know when we're going to go off."

"Keep that up and you'll find yourself in the stockade."

"That seems to be where a lot of people who look like me end up."

"It's their own fault," the captain said.

Bear turned around in disgust, looked to the heavens, and crumpled the empty paper plate in his huge hands, breaking the plastic forks. Then he looked back at the captain.

"How'd I know you'd say that? You people been saying that ever since you hijacked us and threw us in the stinking cargo holds of ships and brought us here in chains. It's how you justify all the stockades you've built to keep us down for hundreds of years."

"Don't blame us for all your troubles. You had one strike against you before you got here. Don't get another." He told Bear he knew a judge gave him a choice between jail and the Army.

"I figured that would be in my file," said Bear. "What did the file tell you about my brother?"

"Nothing that I remember. What kind of trouble was he in?"

Bear glared at the captain. "My brother's trouble was he got drafted and killed in Nam."

The captain swallowed. He said he was sorry. He asked where and when. Bear waved the question off. "What's important," he said, "is everybody who was sent over there, when they saw what was going on, they turned against the war."

"That's not true. We have a job to do and we're doing it."

"I believe my brother. I don't know you. From what I see, all you and your college friends do is lie to justify a senseless, immoral war. You send my Black brothers over there to fight your war."

"I was over there too."

"Then you know in your heart that I'm right. You just won't say it."

"I think we're done here. You're dismissed."

"I'd rather be discharged," said Stillman.

"Me too," said Bear. "Just so there's no misunderstanding. We're never going to serve our time quietly. That's how wars happen."

He and Stillman turned toward the barracks.

"Wait," said the captain.

"Oh my," said Bear, "we musta forgot to salute." He spun around, raised his hand to his forehead, forming a peace sign *V* with his fingers, and snapped off a mock salute. Stillman followed suit.

"You know that's the kind of defiance that's going to get you into trouble," said the captain. "But that's not why I asked you to wait. I was contacted by a soldier who said he needs to talk to you. He wouldn't say why. Do you know a sergeant named Ransom?"

Stillman and Bear nodded.

"How do you know him?"

Stillman said they met him in town during their first day pass off the base.

"Do you know what he wants?"

They shook their heads.

"Does it have anything to do with the anti-war stuff and you trying to get out of the Army?"

They shook their heads again and said no.

"If it's not important enough for either of you to tell me what it is, I'm not going to approve it."

"It might be," said Stillman.

"That's not good enough."

Stillman looked at Bear and asked what he thought. Bear told the captain, "There's something happening on the base that doesn't look right. We asked Ransom to help check it out. He might have found something."

"If something is wrong, how wrong is it?"

"Real wrong. It could involve children."

"Does it have anything to do with my company?"

"We don't think so," said Bear.

"What does it have to do with?"

"Someone taking advantage of children."

"But not anyone under my command."

"Not that we know."

The captain thought for a minute. "I'll approve a meeting with the two of you and Ransom, but I have to be there."

Stillman said he was concerned that Ransom was supposed to be discharged in less than two weeks. "Can you promise us you won't do anything to stop him from getting out?"

"As long as he hasn't done anything wrong," said the captain. "Yes."

"What we're trying to do is right a wrong," said Stillman. "If he has anything to tell us, I'd like you to treat him like a confidential source, the way newspapers do."

"That's fair. We'll consider the meeting confidential. You'll be notified when it's set up. Now you need to get into the barracks. After you salute."

They did.

17

Friday, November 15, 1968
Thompson Farm, Vermont

Lisa was eager to get back to Boston to find out why Freeman wanted to see her. The squatters hadn't protested when she told them they would have to leave, but she was worried they might come back while she was away. Five of them were trying to form a band, friends of the woman she knew from college. Others were following the band and one was AWOL from the Army after being ordered to Vietnam. He said he was going to Canada. She wished him luck and gave him and everyone else a couple of days to leave. One of them was a teenage girl who was pregnant and unsure about what to do. Lisa had spent time comforting her and encouraged her to get in touch with the local social service agency.

With the house empty and MacPherson's fear of killer soldiers fresh in her mind, Lisa turned her attention to self-defense. She had stored in the attic three guns that she had inherited from her grandfather, a 30-30 Model 94 Winchester rifle, a 12-gauge Model 31 Remington shotgun, and a nine-shot .22 High Standard Sentinel revolver. She grabbed a few targets to sight in the rifle and shotgun and fired a few rounds from the revolver. Afterward she cleaned them. Her grandfather and her father taught her and Chris how to handle guns and had taken them deer hunting when they were younger. Lisa shot her first deer with the 30-30. They had eaten plenty of venison on their visits to the farm, but hunting was not part of their lives. The guns used to be kept on a rack in a room used as an office, but when friends started staying at the house, Lisa moved them to an old trunk in the attic where ammunition was stored.

After making sure the shotgun and the rifle were ready for action, she put them back in the trunk and closed it. She still had the revolver and its brown leather holster. She sat on the trunk, holding the gun in her hand, getting a feel for it. It was heavy and had a long barrel. It wouldn't be easy to conceal. She had her handbag and she opened it to see whether the gun could be carried inside with and without the holster. It was a tight fit with the holster. She slid the revolver into the holster and snapped a leather strap to hold it in place. She snapped and unsnapped the strap several times, practicing how quickly she could remove the gun from the holster and be ready to shoot. The holster wasn't designed for quick draws. She reopened the trunk, grabbed a box of 22 caliber bullets and put it in her handbag along with the gun and holster. She was about to shut the trunk when she saw the knife her grandfather had used to gut deer. She picked it up, and underneath it was a shorter folding Buck knife in a black sheath that she and Chris had used for gutting. The folding knife was better for concealment. She added it to her handbag, closed the trunk, and reached for the attic door. Before shutting it, she looked around to make sure there was a clear path to the trunk in case she needed quick access to the shotgun or the rifle when she came back. She felt ready to return to Boston to hunt down whoever was responsible for her brother's death. She didn't know how it would turn out, but thought it best to be prepared for the worst.

Downstairs, Lisa readied the house for an extended absence. She turned off the water so the pipes wouldn't freeze. She thought back to the last time the house was empty. It must have been before she started living there full time after college. After that, locks weren't needed because one of her friends had always been around when she was gone. She didn't have as many friends now. They drifted away after Chris got hurt in Boston. She guessed it was the kind of tragedy they didn't want to deal with. Or they didn't know how.

She checked the kitchen door to make sure it was locked and left through the front door, which she locked with a padlock on a clasp. She looked around to see if she had missed anything. She had left a light on in the living room so it would look like someone was home. She picked up her handbag and backpack and put them on top of a suitcase on the passenger seat of the truck. She had some dress-up clothes in the suitcase. Her parents had scheduled a memorial service after finally receiving the

Army's "accident" report. It was as expected, concluding that Chris was injured when he fell down a stairway. The autopsy didn't find anything that contradicted the Army's finding. Thanksgiving was two weeks away.

She walked to the barn to double-check all the lights were off. The animals had been taken by neighbors, except for the cats. One rubbed up against her leg. "Guard our farm," she told the cat.

She returned to the truck and looked back at the house and barn. She had an uneasy feeling, but wasn't sure why. Maybe it was the squatters. A friend at the social service agency said he would check the farm every few days to look for unwanted signs of activity. She had given him a key for the padlock on the front door and another key for the back door.

She took a mental picture of the farm. It was snowing lightly. It looked like a Christmas postcard. She hoped it would look just as good when she returned. She had lined up a neighbor to plow the driveway.

She started the truck's engine and turned on the heater and the wipers to sweep snow off the windshield. She glanced at the passenger seat to make sure she had her handbag before putting the truck in first gear and starting out the driveway. She stopped before making the turn onto the dirt road. She checked the house and the barn in the rearview mirror, hoping to see Chris or some sign that his spirit was watching over the farm. She wondered if he knew what was going on and how he would let her know if he needed her to do something and how long it would be before she'd see the place again.

18

Saturday, November 16, 1968
Fort Dix

The captain's office was antiseptic clean and formal, with an orderly desk and the president's photo and flags on the wall behind it. The linoleum floor shined like a mirror, and three chairs were set up in formation in front of the desk. Ransom was in one of them, looking sharp in his dress khaki Army uniform. Bear and Stillman were led in by a clerk who motioned them to the empty chairs. He said the captain would join them shortly.

Bear and Stillman, wearing their basic training fatigues, bumped fists with Ransom and razzed him about his pressed uniform as they took their seats. It was the first time they'd seen him in uniform. He said he only had to play Army for a few more days and he'd be free. Bear asked what he found out about the chaplain and his assistant. Ransom said it was bad, but he'd wait for the captain to go into detail. "Looks like you guys once again got yourselves into some heavy shit," he said, "very heavy."

"Cool," said Bear.

"How short are you?" asked Stillman.

"Three days," said Ransom.

"That sets you up for the greatest Thanksgiving ever," Stillman said.

"Dig it."

"Where will you go?"

"Wherever my bike takes me. If the lady in Boston wants help finding out what happened to her brother, I'll head that way, either before or after I go to West Virginia to see my family."

Stillman said he got a letter from Lisa that the memorial service was set for the Saturday before Thanksgiving. He said he and Bear were going to ask for passes so they could go. Bear said he had another reason to go to Boston. One of his cousins in Roxbury had died of a heroin overdose, and he wanted to see the family and find out more.

A side door opened and the captain came in. Ransom stood to salute, and Bear and Stillman followed his lead. The captain returned the salute and sat down behind his desk. "Gentlemen," he said, "tell me why we're here."

Stillman filled him in about the photos he found in the chaplain's office and their plan to confront him and how Ransom followed him and his assistant. "That's how we got here."

"That's quite a story," said the captain. "It raises some troubling questions, such as how you found those photographs. But first, let's ask Sgt. Ransom what he discovered."

Ransom said the chaplain and his assistant got into a military sedan together after they came out of the chapel and drove off base. He watched them stop at a pharmacy before going to an apartment complex and unlocking the door to an apartment. Over the next few hours he saw several men go in and out of the apartment, one of them with a child. Another of the men had what looked like a camera case and lighting equipment and tripods. The chaplain and his assistant came out after about four hours and locked the door. They had their military uniforms on when they went inside, but were in civilian clothes when they came out. A listing of mailboxes said the apartment was rented to Family Films. Ransom said he followed them back to the base, where the chaplain dropped his assistant off in a parking lot at the officer's club. The assistant got into a Porsche and drove off. Ransom said he wrote down the license plate number.

"Is that all of it?" the captain asked.

Ransom said he made a couple of calls to friends to try to check out the chaplain's assistant, a sergeant named Youngblood, and whether he could be a CID investigator.

"Is he?"

"Not as far as my friends could determine," Ransom said. "He was in Nam around the same time the chaplain was. I don't know if you're aware, but the chaplain started an orphanage when he was there."

"I did not know that."

"He has a photo of the orphanage on a wall in his office," Stillman said, "like it was quite an accomplishment to be proud of."

"I'm aware you've been in his office to ask him to help you get out of the Army," said the captain. "How did you find the photos?"

"I was going to use the copy machine and somebody had left the photos in the machine."

"Was the chaplain with you?"

"No."

"Why were you in his office without him?"

"I needed to make a phone call."

"Did he give you permission to use his phone?"

"No."

"Did you make copies of the photos?"

"Yes."

"Do you have them with you?"

"Yes."

"I'd like to see them."

Stillman unbuttoned his fatigue shirt, pulled out a large mailing envelope and put it on the desk. The captain opened the envelope, extracted the photocopies, glanced at them quickly, and put them back in the envelope. "I'm going to keep this," he said, "and I'm going to turn it over to the CID. That could raise serious issues for you if I tell them how I got this."

"Yes."

"We agreed before setting up this meeting that it would be confidential to protect Sgt. Ransom and his scheduled discharge date."

"Yes."

"It looks like you have your own reasons to keep this meeting confidential."

"Yes sir. I'd like to keep it confidential, but I'm sure the chaplain and his assistant know I've seen the photos and made copies."

The captain looked at Bear and asked whether he wanted confidentiality.

"Yes sir."

"Sgt. Ransom, can you identify the location of the apartment?"

"Yes sir," he said. He reached into his shirt pocket and put a folded piece of paper on the desk. "Here's a rundown of what I saw and where, including the date and time and the license plate on the assistant's car."

The captain looked the paper over carefully and put it in the envelope with the photos. He leaned on the desk and stared silently at the envelope for a long time, as though trying to will it to do something.

"Gentlemen," he said, "the confidentiality of this meeting applies to all of us, me included. Understood?"

They nodded.

"To me," the captain said, "that means none of us tells anyone about anything relating to this meeting without the approval of the other three. Do you agree?"

Bear, Stillman, and Ransom looked at each other, nodded, and said, "Yes sir," one after another.

"For me," the captain said, "this is a serious matter that hits very close to home. I'm going to tell you something I've never told anyone. I was a Cub Scout and one of the troop leaders on a campout asked me to sleep in his tent. You can imagine what happened. What he did. Something like that leaves deep scars that last a long time. I think you understand what I'm saying."

They nodded.

"Indications are you've come across a similar situation here, and this time I'm in a position to do something about it. I intend to find out if it's as bad as it appears, and I commend you for bringing it to my attention. I'm going to take the information in this envelope that somehow appeared anonymously in my office and turn it over to the CID and let them take it from there. Is that agreeable?"

"Yes sir," they said in unison.

"I should also warn you that I will not be around to find out what ultimately happens. We're going to have to trust the CID to do the right thing because I'm short. I'll be leaving the Army after your class graduates."

Bear said he hoped the captain would join the Vietnam Veterans Against the War. "That's what my brother was going to do before he was killed. It's the only way to stop this insanity. We can do it."

"I'll take that under consideration," said the captain. "Is there anything else?"

Bear said he had something. He referred to their earlier meeting when the captain advised them to serve their time quietly. "In other words you told us to give up. Well, we didn't and we won't because we've done good and we've already made a difference. Look at what you're doing now about that chaplain. That's because of what we did. If we all try, we can do something great, like end a senseless war and stop the killing. We've got to try. We can't end a war by doing nothing. That's all."

The captain said, "I'll keep that in mind."

Stillman said he had one more question. "There's a memorial service in Boston that Bear, ahhh Simpson, and I would like to attend and we need a pass to do that."

"You're eligible for passes, so that should not be a problem," said the captain. "Who died?"

"A draftee we saw at our induction. He refused induction and he was taken away in an ambulance. The Army told his family he fell down stairs. He was in a coma and died."

"Did you know him?"

"No sir. I've been in touch with his sister, who doesn't believe he fell."

"If he didn't fall, what could have happened?"

"That's what we want to find out. She thinks he was killed."

"Who do you think you are? Private detectives?"

"We're guys just like you, guys trying to do the right thing."

"The right thing will be for both of you to stay out of trouble while you're in Boston and get back here on time."

"Yes sir," said Stillman.

The captain asked whether Stillman and Bear knew each other before they were inducted. They shook their heads no.

"So what brought you together?"

"The government. The draft. The Army," said Bear. "We have a common enemy."

"We were being herded from the induction to the bus to bring us here," Stillman said, "and Bear called me out, ahhh Simpson, for doing something stupid."

"You can call him Bear," said the captain. "What did you do?"

"I lit into an old guy handing out Bibles on the loading dock after we were rounded up to be sent halfway around the world to murder people. I was pissed. Bear told me to back off."

"Good advice," said the captain. "I was curious because you two seem to be friends, yet you come from such different places."

"We are friends," said Stillman. "Good friends."

"Don't get carried away," Bear said.

"We've got the draft to thank for making us friends," Stillman said. "And now we're going to make the Army regret that."

"Once again, I warn you to be careful."

"I played a lot of poker in college when I should have been studying," Stillman said. "Poker's like studying. You learn a lot about yourself and other people. We're playing poker right now, and I like the people I see around the table."

The captain looked from Bear to Stillman to Ransom. "Agreed," he said. "Anything else?"

"One more thing," said Bear. "It's about those guys who went AWOL to New York. We don't know why those drill sergeants aren't with us anymore or where they went, but thanks for that."

"That's a personnel matter we won't discuss," the captain said. "If there's nothing else gentlemen, you're dismissed."

They stood in unison, saluted, and left.

19

Monday, November 18, 1968
Lexington

Lisa called Lincoln Freeman's office using the kitchen phone at her parents' house. His assistant answered and said he would return her call as soon as he could.

"That was quick," said Mary Lou, who was washing dishes.

"He's with a client."

"I hope he's not with a client when your father and I get arrested at one of our anti-war demonstrations. I don't want to spend a night in jail because our lawyer was with a client."

"I'm sure we're a high priority," said Lisa. "He and Chris were close. It's personal for him, as well as for Dad." Lisa grabbed a dish towel. "Dad has really surprised me."

"You mean anti-war Dad."

"He's the one. I really admire how he's handling all this."

"He's a good dad. He always has been. He's still the same dad, doing the best he can. The death of a son or daughter is about the most awful thing that could ever happen to anyone."

"It is. It really is. How are you doing, Mom?"

"I'm OK."

"Really."

"Really. You know I was devastated. But now I have purpose. Chris gave me a reason to live, gave all of us a reason to live. Your father and I are as close as I can remember. It's good. We're good."

"It's brought us all together."

"It really has. Now we've just got to end this fucking war."

"Mom!"

"I know."

They carried on silently with washing and drying.

Lisa's father was at work at the other end of the house in Chris's former bedroom, which he had converted to his new office. His dramatic turnaround to anti-war lawyer and crime fighter was underway. On this morning he was working with incriminating documents he copied and took from his former employer to expose corruption in military contracting.

Art's new home office left no doubt about his changing perspective. His desk faced two posters on a wall above the bed where Chris used to sleep. Chris had created the top poster. It was an old saying, first attributed to Aeschylus, the renowned writer of Greek tragedies. Since his death in 456 BC, many others had also claimed credit for the adage. The poster said:

In war, TRUTH is the FIRST CASUALTY

Below it was a poster with an untitled poem printed on it. Art had written the poem as a young soldier in the Army, serving as a radio operator in Europe during World War II. He had been drafted. The poem read:

> *The radio said yesterday,*
> *   "We're six miles from the town."*
> *Today, excitedly they say,*
> *   that we have gained more ground.*
> *"We crashed and smashed the enemy*
> *   with devastating blows.*
> *And all along the line we blast*
> *   our swiftly crumbling foes."*
> *Announcer pauses for effect,*
> *   then tears the whole thing down.*
> *"In this advance, our forces now*
> *   are eight miles from the town."*

Decades had passed since Art wrote those words. After the war, he chose law school over returning to the family farm. He met Mary Lou and raised a family and lived in comfortable houses in nice towns and worked for corporations and made lots of money. Most people would consider that a good life and a successful career. But the posters reminded Art that he had once been an idealistic young man who wrote about the corruption of war. Now, almost thirty years later, he was preparing to become a whistleblower.

Overcharging the government for the tools of war was nothing new. A federal law was adopted during the Civil War to prevent the Union Army from being ripped off by its suppliers. Since then, the Lincoln Law, as it came to be known, had been used to expose hundreds of millions of dollars of waste, fraud, and abuse in government contracting.

After the end of World War II, the United States competed with Russia to arm the world. The nation's economic health had become so dependent on making weapons that Art believed ending the Vietnam War could plunge the economy into a deep recession. But beyond the dollars, because of Chris's influence, he was far more upset about the price paid in human lives to keep the economy humming.

In his office, Art was arranging the documents he had copied into separate folders relating to payoffs for particular contracts and weapons systems. He built a chronology of everything and was surprised how some of the dates intersected, tying key congressional votes to campaign donations and junkets and other favors for politicians and pentagon officials.

One destination that popped up more than others was a luxurious oceanside mansion in the Bahamas his company used for entertaining. One congressman who chaired a critical subcommittee had been there far more than anyone else. The bills for hosting guests at the mansion and providing for their recreational and cultural and sexual needs were substantial. Art had never been there, but he was aware of what went on. Now, in Chris's bedroom, he could feel his son looking over his shoulder, and he was ashamed for not blowing the whistle a long time ago.

Art planned to present his material to the FBI within a few weeks. This morning he was focused on whether to send the package anonymously or to make contact directly. He had written two cover letters, one for each option. As he considered which one to use, his chest tightened and the pace of his heart quickened. He felt it throbbing in his chest. That had happened a few times in the past couple of weeks. He was concerned enough that he planned to make an appointment with his doctor to talk about it and other health issues that had emerged since Chris was hospitalized. But he hadn't made the appointment yet.

He was inclined to send his corruption package anonymously, but he knew he stood the best chance of it being taken seriously if he worked directly with the FBI to explain the significance and timing of the documents. The problem with that was it would expose him as the source of the documents and could get him arrested for stealing them.

He wasn't naïve enough to believe the FBI would launch a major investigation of the defense industry based on his information. Mostly he wanted to test the government, to find out what, if anything, the FBI would do. He expected very little, possibly nothing. So he made duplicate copies of the documents. If the FBI did nothing, he would turn copies over to the press. He figured there were at most a dozen newspapers in the US that had the resources and the initiative needed to undertake a comprehensive investigation of the military-industrial complex. Art intended to approach the newspapers one at a time. He wasn't going to contact congressional committees. Trying to get Congress to investigate itself would be a waste of time.

Mary Lou was the only one who knew about Art's whistleblowing plan. He was waiting to tell Lisa and Freeman until after he had everything in order. He didn't expect them to object. He wanted to make sure both of them were on board before he contacted the FBI.

*   *   *   *

Freeman returned Lisa's call in less than an hour and suggested they meet for lunch at a restaurant in Arlington, midway between her parents' house and his law office in Cambridge. Lisa knew her father wanted to start working with Freeman on draft-related issues and asked whether he should join them. Freeman thought that was a good idea. As he hung up, she heard cars in the background and wondered why he would call from an outdoor phone booth.

He was waiting outside the restaurant when Lisa and Art drove into the parking lot off busy Massachusetts Avenue. He intercepted them as they got out of their car and suggested they take a walk before going inside to eat. He guided them toward the sidewalk.

"You look nervous," said Lisa. "What's up?"

"Too much." He looked up and down the street. "I wouldn't be surprised if we're being followed."

"Don't tell me it's the Army," she said.

"I don't know, but I don't think so," he said. "It could be the FBI. Let's walk around the block and see how that goes."

"The FBI?" asked Lisa. "Why?"

"Just a minute," he said. He led them silently along Mass Ave to a quiet residential side street, where he slowed down. "We can talk as we walk," he said.

Art asked what made him think they would be followed. Freeman said bugs, "as in listening devices," were found in his office. Art asked how they were discovered. Freeman said he had a friend with access to tools to detect them.

"So that's why you called me from a phone booth," said Lisa.

"Yes," Freeman said.

Art asked, "What makes you think it's the FBI?"

Freeman said he was warned by someone he did not want to identify. He asked Art if he knew who Ian MacPherson was. Art said he knew Lisa was going to take him to their Vermont farm, but decided it was too dangerous.

Freeman said MacPherson had been seen talking with an FBI agent sometime before Lisa drove him to Vermont.

"Whoa," said Lisa. "Why would MacPherson have been talking to the FBI back then?"

"Excellent question," Freeman said, "because . . ." He stopped midsentence, remembering MacPherson was still a client. He stopped walking. "This is tricky," he said. "I don't know how much to tell you."

Lisa said MacPherson told her on the way to Vermont he was going to make a deal with the FBI to save himself from the soldiers who wanted to kill him.

Art was wearing an overcoat, but seemed to be shivering from the cool November wind, shifting his weight back and forth from one foot to the other. Lisa wrapped her arms around him and rubbed his back. "Are you cold Dad?" she asked. He said he was. She suggested they go back to the restaurant to get warm. "No," he said. "I'm OK." His voice was trembling. "If we think this is tricky," he said, "I'm working on something that will complicate everything even more." She asked what that was. He said he'd tell her later.

Freeman said he'd also like to know what Art was up to. But first, he said, he had important news about the Army's report on Chris. "That's why I called. I've got something for you."

Before getting into that, Lisa suggested they turn back toward the restaurant. Freeman didn't object. As they reversed direction, she said she had her own complicating question. She asked Freeman if he knew who Lt. Sanders was. He remembered it was Sanders who ordered Chris removed from the induction ceremony. Sanders also called the family to claim Chris accidentally fell.

She said MacPherson told her during their ride to Vermont that the drugs stolen during the Army base raid came from Sanders's office.

Freeman stopped so quickly she bumped into him. "Oh man," he said. "I've got to give this to you now." He pulled the Army file folder from his leather jacket and handed it to Lisa.

"It has Chris's name on it," she said half to herself as she opened it. She flipped through the pages. "It's the Army file. Sanders wrote the report they sent to us. That's in here. It's got to—holy shit—we haven't seen this statement before . . . Oh God . . . this proves the coverup. They wanted to kill Chris. For something he didn't do. Goddamn. Fucking Army. They hid this from us. They killed Chris. Sanders killed Chris."

She passed the folder to her father, open to the page with the ambulance attendant's statement. Her father's hands were shaking. He read it in silence. Lisa reached out to Freeman and hugged him, long and forcefully. "Thank you," she whispered in his ear. "Thank you so much. How did you get this?"

"I can't tell you, but you've been right all along," he said. "They killed Chris for something he didn't do." They turned to Art for his reaction.

He closed the file and stared at it without moving. Now he looked hot instead of cold. Beads of sweat dotted his face. The sun was bright. A chill wind was rustling dead leaves in the trees and on the street. Art asked, "Where did you get this?"

"I can't tell you just yet," Freeman said. "But it's the real deal. I'm sure."

"How do you know that?"

"I trust the person who gave it to me."

"I'm a little confused," said Art. He spoke haltingly, as though he had to think about each word before he said it. "I might be mixing things up. How do you know Chris wasn't part of the raid?"

"MacPherson. He was the lookout during the raid. He said Chris wasn't there. He came to my office to ask me to represent him."

"This doesn't make sense. This file says the killers thought Chris stole their drugs."

"That's how it appears."

"Why would they think that?" Art was having a hard time talking.

"Because Chris mentioned the SDS raid at the induction ceremony," said Freeman. "Did Lisa tell you she got a call from one of the draftees who was there?"

"I think so."

"The one at Fort Dix," she said.

Freeman interrupted. "Just a minute. Someone's coming."

A woman with a dog on a leash was herding two young children down the sidewalk. Freeman reached out to Art to help him move out of the way onto the grass to let them pass. Art stumbled, but stayed on his feet and exchanged greetings with the woman. He asked about the dog as it raised its nose to sniff the Army file. "He's a good mutt," the woman said. Her daughter said, "His name is Buddy."

Art offered his hand to the dog and said, "Good to meet you Buddy." He watched them move on. Buddy kept trying to turn back toward Art, who took several small unsteady steps in the opposite direction. He seemed to be looking past Lisa and Freeman. His next words came out slowly and slurred and he struggled to keep his balance. "Chris. Oh Chris. There you are. How did . . ."

"Dad," said Lisa, reaching out to help. "What's wrong?"

"Dizzy," he said. "Sit down." The Army file dropped from his hand to the sidewalk. Papers scattered as his knees buckled. Freeman caught him as he fell. Lisa helped lower him to the grass next to the sidewalk. He didn't have the strength to sit upright. They laid him on his back. His eyelids drooped. He looked like he was going to sleep. "I love you, sweetheart," he whispered. "Mary Lou. I love. You. You know. Why. Tell. Chris is here."

Freeman was up and moving to find a phone to call an ambulance. He ran back down Mass Ave toward the restaurant. Lisa sat in the grass and lifted her father's head to cradle it in her lap. She massaged his scalp. His head was heavy. He was half breathing, half gasping, and his head felt heavier with each weary breath. "I love you Dad," she said over and over. The papers from the file trembled in the wind.

20

Friday, November 22, 1968
Boston

The Army gave Stillman and Bear three-day passes for Chris Thompson's memorial service in Lexington. They planned to stay with Bear's sister at her apartment in Roxbury. Peter Ransom, savoring freedom as a civilian, was invited to join them. He said he'd be fine sleeping on the floor.

Nobody wanted to impose on Lisa and her mother. The memorial service for Chris had been transformed into a double shot of pain. Art's life would also be honored. The service would be held five days before Thanksgiving.

Stillman and Bear flew to Boston Friday afternoon. Taking a bus would have saved money, but the plane was quicker. Lisa said she would reimburse them for their travel costs. Lincoln Freeman offered to pick them up at Logan Airport. When Bear heard the lawyer's name, he realized he knew him. After Bear was arrested for rioting, Freeman represented him pro bono, so Bear hadn't had to pay. Freeman was waiting when they landed at Logan. He and Bear greeted each other warmly. Stillman and Bear were in civilian clothes. Their shaved heads had grown out enough to look like crew cuts. Bear was wearing his black beret and leather jacket. Stillman wore a secondhand overcoat. Freeman got right to business, giving them a copy of the complete Army file on Chris's injury.

They went to a passenger waiting area to review the file for accuracy. Stillman and Bear sat side by side and Freeman was behind them, looking over their shoulders. When they got to the ambulance attendant's statement, Freeman told them the attendant was so upset by what Chris told him that he reported it to the Boston Police Department, as well as giving a statement to the military police.

Freeman said he personally interviewed the attendant, who was still shaken by Chris's words and the likelihood that he was beaten by Army soldiers. Freeman had asked him what he remembered. He said Chris had trouble talking because his face was so damaged. He said Chris's injuries were far more serious than the accidental fall reported to city ambulance authorities. It had not been transmitted as an urgent call. He said Chris had been moved before the ambulance reached the base. He was lying unconscious on the pavement outside a building when the ambulance arrived. There was no staircase in sight. A bloody towel was wrapped around his head and there was blood on the pavement. The attendant asked one of the soldiers when and where the fall happened and didn't get an answer. After loading Chris onto a stretcher, as he was about to close the ambulance doors, he said an Army sergeant blocked him and asked whether Chris would survive. He declined to speculate and the sergeant handed him a bag with Chris's wallet and other personal items found in his pockets, saying he went through them to confirm his identity. Then an Army lieutenant came up and asked if he was hurt as bad as he looked. The attendant didn't answer, saying he had to get Chris to the hospital as quickly as possible.

What was odd, the attendant said, was that nobody expressed sympathy for Chris. In his experience, he said, bystanders or people involved in accidents almost always express hope that anyone injured will be all right.

Freeman asked Stillman and Bear how that account squared with what they saw and heard.

"We need to look at the times," said Bear. He estimated an hour passed between the time they heard someone call for medical assistance and when the ambulance left the base with its lights and siren on.

Stillman and Bear huddled over the report shifting back and forth between the ambulance attendant's statement and the soldiers' statements. The times didn't match.

The Army said Chris fell at 10:05 A.M. and the call for an ambulance was made at 10:15. But the attendant's statement said the ambulance call wasn't made until 10:45—forty minutes after Chris was hurt. The ambulance, according to the attendant, reached the Army base at 10:59

and left for the hospital at 11:08 and reached the hospital at 11:13.

Bear and Stillman's estimate of an hour between the time Chris was hurt and the time the ambulance took him to the hospital was on the mark.

"The Army's lying about when the ambulance call was made," said Bear.

Freeman stood up and stretched his back after huddling over their shoulders for so long. "We don't know why the Army's lying," he said. "But we know it wasn't good for Chris."

*   *   *   *

On their way out of the terminal they decided to drive by the South Boston Army Base so Freeman could get a feel for it and Bear and Stillman could see if they remembered anything new.

Freeman led them to his car, a large Chevy sedan showing its age. He called it "the boat." Stillman offered to get in the back. Freeman told them so much had happened since the SDS raid and its aftermath that he was confused about how much they did and didn't know. They only knew what they saw at the induction, that Chris's mention of the SDS had infuriated the officer in charge, a guy named Sanders.

"So you don't know about the drugs?"

"What drugs?"

"OK," Freeman said as he backed the Chevy out of its parking space. "We need to get you guys caught up. Here's the big picture. It turns out the Army base is the scene of multiple crimes related to Chris's death and at least two other deaths. This has turned into a really bad movie and we don't know how it ends."

"Holy shit," said Stillman. "Who died besides Chris?"

"Two student radicals who did the SDS raid," Freeman said. "And then there's a fourth, Chris's father, Arthur. You know he died of a heart attack a few days ago, right?"

They did.

"The Army would consider Art's death collateral damage," Freeman said. "If Chris hadn't been killed, I think Art would still be alive. He was a good guy and a good lawyer who was so devastated by what happened to Chris that he changed his life. He worked for a weapons manufacturer. He quit that job so he could work with anti-war folks. He was planning to help Boston Draft Resistance and me in my practice when he died."

As he drove, Freeman gave them details of the SDS raid—trashing the induction center, stealing the heroin and cash from Sanders's office, and the overdose deaths of two raiders, leaving a third raider on the run. Stillman reminded Bear that Sanders was the lieutenant who ran the induction ceremony.

"So it looks like Sanders is a drug dealer and a killer?" said Bear.

"That's right," Freeman said.

"I don't like Sanders, you know, because of how he did the induction," said Bear. "But there's other ways it could go down. The guys who work for Sanders could be running drugs out of his office and he doesn't even know about it."

"You're right," said Freeman. "We have to consider that."

"The only thing we know for sure is that the Army lies and covers up all the time," said Bear. "So we don't know what we know."

"Right," said Freeman. "And we don't know what we don't know. But we have the evidence to prove what we think we know."

Bear asked whether Chris's death had been reported to the FBI.

Freeman pulled his Chevy to the curb and stopped. "Guys," he said, "I almost made that mistake. That was before I found out my office is being bugged, probably by the FBI."

"You can't be serious," said Stillman.

"I am. It's real," said Freeman. "I had a guy sweep my office, and he detected two listening devices. We don't know for sure who planted them, but I suspect it's the FBI."

"Why would they bug you?" asked Stillman.

Bear interrupted. "Just a minute. Let me think about this," he said. "Hmmm. Why would the FBI be interested in a Black civil rights anti-war lawyer about to tell the world that the US Army is lying to cover up for soldiers who are selling drugs and murdering civilians?"

"Good point," acknowledged Stillman. Then he asked Freeman, "Who makes the next move?"

"There's more that I'm not ready to tell you because it gets into complications with client confidentiality. For our next move at this moment, let's go take a look at that Army base."

The sky had darkened, and Freeman switched on his headlights before pulling back into traffic. On their way Bear told Freeman they might see a friend, a Vietnam vet, at the base. He explained who Ransom was and how he had already helped them with the chaplain.

The Army induction center was in a large building in a row of identical buildings lined up like soldiers in formation. The building appeared desolate under floodlights on a Friday evening, with just a few cars parked near the entrance. One of them stood out, a sleek red sports car. Freeman drove close enough to see that it was an Alfa Romeo with Massachusetts plates, and he continued around the building. "Not much to see here," he said. Stillman pointed out the loading dock where he met Bear and they boarded the bus to Dix.

Freeman spotted a bar down the street and offered to buy them dinner. They hadn't eaten since leaving Dix. The bar had a bright neon sign hanging over the sidewalk above the entrance, The Silver Dollar. As they got close, Bear noticed a motorcycle parked nearby. "Looks like our friend Peter Ransom had the same idea," he said. "If that's not his bike, I'll buy the beers."

Stillman reminded Bear he was old enough to be sent to war, but too young to buy liquor.

The bar was bustling on a Friday night. Music was blasting from a jukebox, but it was hard to hear over the clamor of conversation. They saw an open table and were working their way through the crowd when they spotted Ransom standing at the far end of the bar, engaged in a lively conversation with several soldiers in uniform. Bear gave Ransom a wave and pointed to the open table and then to Stillman and Freeman. Ransom didn't respond. Bear was sure Ransom saw him and was about to wave again when Stillman grabbed his arm. "He may not want anyone to know that he knows us," he said. "Let's sit down and see what happens. Black guys are kind of obvious in this place." They continued to the open table. On the way Freeman stopped a waiter who was carrying beers to another table. He asked for a pitcher and three glasses and menus.

They took their seats and surveyed the scene, a working-class smoke-filled bar, mostly men, almost all white, a lot of them burly, probably dock workers, and some uniformed soldiers. Freeman was the only one wearing a tie. Waiters and waitresses hustled between the tables and the bar and the kitchen to keep up with orders. Many customers called the waiters by their first names. Everyone seemed to know everybody else. The room felt like it belonged to a John Wayne, no-nonsense, America-love-it-or-leave-it crowd. Bear, Stillman, and Freeman felt like foreigners. The wait for service was long enough to make them wonder whether the staff was delivering a message that they didn't belong, that they should go somewhere else. But finally a different waiter delivered them a pitcher of beer, glasses, and menus and apologized for the delay.

The menu offerings were limited. They ordered burgers and fries. While they were talking and eating, Bear and Stillman glanced a few times in Ransom's direction, trying not to be obvious. On one of those glances, Stillman recognized that one of the soldiers with Ransom was Sanders. "You're not going to believe this," he told the others, "but the prime suspect is talking to Ransom. He's looking away from us right now, but it's definitely Sanders. Maybe that's why Peter didn't want to be seen with us."

Bear said he couldn't believe Sanders would remember either of them. "He probably processes hundreds of draftees a day."

"I'll tell you one draftee he'll always remember," Freeman said. "He'll never forget Chris. We'll make sure of that."

Stillman said he'd bet that Ransom came to the bar hoping to meet Sanders or soldiers who work with him to find out why they went after Chris. "I wouldn't be surprised if Peter follows Sanders when he leaves," he said, "just like he did with the chaplain." He told Freeman they were lucky to have help from a combat vet.

They stayed at the bar for several hours. Freeman offered to drive them to Roxbury. Bear and Stillman were sure they'd see Ransom at Bear's sister's house before the night was over. On their way out, Stillman asked Freeman if he would mind stopping at the *Boston World* to try to talk to the editor he called about Chris. Freeman said he'd like to meet him. The bar had a phone booth and Stillman used it to call the newspaper. McAlister was there and said he could spare a few minutes.

The *Boston World*'s newsroom was buzzing at 9 P.M. on a Friday night. It was crammed with desks where white men in ties were banging on their typewriters and jumping on and off their phones and talking to each other like they were competing in a marathon. With copy deadlines approaching, the air was thick with the fog of cigarette smoke. Stillman talked to a clerk who then approached McAlister, a clean-shaven heavy-set man standing next to a desk where a reporter was typing furiously as they talked. McAlister waved to them and indicated he'd be right over. He apologized for only being able to give them a few minutes because he was on deadline. He said he'd been wondering what happened to the draftee who was hurt.

"He's dead," said Stillman. "His name was Chris Thompson, and I'm Jud Stillman, the guy who called you that day." He introduced Bear and Freeman and said they hoped the newspaper would want to follow up on the Army's statement that nothing had happened and nobody had been hurt.

McAlister led them to a darkened office, pulling a chair on rollers behind him. He turned on the light and invited them to sit down. "I don't have an office," he said, "but we can use this one." He pushed the chair he'd been dragging over to Stillman and took a seat behind the desk. "I'm really sorry to hear about Chris Thompson. Was his death related to what happened at the induction?"

"Without a doubt," said Stillman. He introduced Freeman as the family's lawyer.

Freeman told McAlister Chris refused induction and was removed from the room and attacked by soldiers who mistakenly thought he was involved in a SDS raid on the induction station. "When the Army told your reporter nobody was hurt," Freeman said, "that was the first lie and the beginning of a coverup. The Army told the family Chris accidentally fell down some stairs. The family asked for a written report and got stonewalled. When they finally got the report, one critical document was withheld, a statement by an ambulance attendant that Chris regained consciousness and said he was attacked and beaten. Chris worked with Boston Draft Resistance, and the Army knew that. It would take more time than we have now to describe the extent of what else has happened related to Chris's death, but it involves serious crimes, including drug dealing and we believe murder, committed by soldiers. If you're interested in pursuing this, I will talk to my clients, who I expect would be willing to share with you whatever is necessary. You might want to make a preliminary decision tonight because the memorial service for Chris is tomorrow in Lexington. It would help if your reporter could be there to get a feel for the situation. It's a double memorial service, for Chris and his father, who died of a heart attack a few days ago."

"You know how to pitch a story," McAlister said. "You can give the clerk the details about the time and place of the service, and I'll send a reporter and a photographer. I can't promise what we'll do after that. I'm going to have to talk with other editors about pursuing the larger story that would likely have us going up against the military and the federal government."

"I don't know anything about the inner workings of newspapers," said Freeman. "But in my line of work, which is civil rights, I see a lot of courageous people fighting for justice when the odds are stacked against them. They're going up against very powerful institutions. They can use all the help they can get to spread the word, to let people know the truth about what's at stake. That's all we're asking from your newspaper."

"That's why we do what we do," said McAlister. "We provide a place for people to tell their stories. We shine a light on complicated situations and do our best to explain them. That's why a free press is so critical. We'll be in touch. But right now, it's deadline, and I've got to get back to work."

* * * *

Freeman drove them to Roxbury and dropped them in front of the apartment complex where Bear's sister, Rose, lived. The apartment building was surrounded by dirt and broken blacktop and patches of blotchy weeds strewn with trash. Freeman told Bear and Stillman he'd catch up with them Saturday at the memorial service. He said he'd keep his distance from Ransom in case Sanders or his soldiers were at the service.

Bear led Stillman up a grungy stairway to Rose's fourth-floor apartment. She lived there alone with her six-month-old daughter, Melanie. Stillman knew Bear loved Rose, who was just twenty and worked in a restaurant kitchen. Her life had been hard, like a lot of others who grew up in Roxbury. Her boyfriend, the father of her daughter, got terrified at the prospect of a baby and took off. He said he couldn't handle the responsibility. She was a single parent with some help from her mother, who worked as a secretary at a medical office and lived a few blocks away in an apartment with Bear's brother, who had just started high school.

Rose was in her bedroom, trying to catch some sleep before Melanie's next feeding. She heard them open the door. She jumped up and gave her brother a huge hug in the kitchen. She was smiling despite the late hour. Her hair was cut short and she was wearing jeans and a red T-shirt with a large white peace sign printed on the front.

Rose and Bear had exchanged letters since Bear was sent to Dix. She had a sense of an aspiring musician's feelings about being forced to become a soldier. It seemed to her like he had been gone for months. Bear told her that in a few weeks he and Stillman would be sent somewhere else for new kinds of training. They wouldn't find out where until their last day of basic training, and they'd probably be sent to different places.

"When that happens," Stillman said, "it'll be hard. I've kind of gotten used to living with your brother."

"I know what you mean," she grinned.

Stillman was struck by how pretty and self-assured Rose was for a young single mother growing up and living in what many would consider a ghetto. He now knew four Black people, two of them strong women. They were all impressive in different ways. He had the draft to thank for the chance to finally get to know Black folks.

They moved from the kitchen to a larger room, a combination living room/dining room, which had a couch and would become a crowded bedroom for the next few days. Bear and Rose talked about their friends and what was going on in the neighborhood. Rose described the protests that were drawing increasing numbers of people to oppose a plan that would cut a huge swath through Roxbury and other Boston neighborhoods to build an eight-lane interstate highway. Houses, apartments, and businesses would be bulldozed. Some already had. Rose had taken Melanie to the protests. She showed them signs she had made for the next demonstration. One declared "Roxbury Counts" and another demanded "Give Roxbury a Voice." Another pleaded, "Hear Us, We Are Here." She was optimistic the highway plan would be defeated because residents from different parts of Boston were banding together to oppose it.

"You and Mel will overcome," Bear said. "Then, after you block the highway, you can end the draft and the war."

Stillman congratulated Rose for her activism, saying he couldn't imagine how she found the energy to protest, work full time, raise a child, and host a bunch of Army guys on weekend passes on short notice. "Not all guys are bad," she said. Being Melanie's mom, she said, made everything worthwhile. She was about to elaborate when she heard sounds in the bedroom. "You'll have to excuse me," she said, "while I tend to a baby protesting about hunger."

Stillman and Bear had bought a case of beer and opened two cans, wondering when Ransom might get there. It was another couple of hours and a few more beers before they heard the throbbing growl of his Harley outside.

They went downstairs and guided him to a place to park his bike by one of the few street lights that was working. Ransom was upbeat. He high-fived them before he got off. "I think I found a job," he said with a devious smirk. He hoisted his backpack over his shoulder and they led him upstairs.

They had only known Ransom for a few weeks, but it felt like years. They figured out their sleeping arrangements, opened more beers, and sat down. Bear and Stillman insisted Ransom tell them about his new job before anything else.

He had planned to buddy up to soldiers so he could learn as much as possible about Sanders. He was in the bar less than an hour when Sanders showed up and they were introduced. From then on, a lot of the talk was about Vietnam because most of them had served there. Ransom said he told them the truth, that he'd just been discharged after a tour in Nam and needed a job. He was looking for advice because he didn't know much about Boston. Sanders said he knew someone who might have a job where military experience would be a plus. He didn't want to say more until he talked with his friend.

Ransom said Sanders was stiff and a little distant, but overall he appeared to be a typical lieutenant who saw a lot of combat, lost too many men, and was proud of those who survived. "It's hard to know what he's like when he's not in uniform," Ransom said. "I do know he likes performance sports cars and drives a red Alfa Romeo."

"Did you follow him?" asked Stillman.

"Of course."

Stillman and Bear laughed. Ransom said Sanders drove his Alfa to another bar, but didn't stay long. Then something mysterious happened.

Ransom had just kick-started his motorcycle to follow Sanders from the second bar when a stranger approached and asked if he was following the Alfa. Ransom asked why. The stranger told Ransom he wanted to talk to him about it. They agreed to meet at Boston Common Saturday morning. Ransom sped off and caught up to Sanders, who drove to an apartment in Boston's North End, where he parked and went inside. Ransom waited a half hour before heading on to Roxbury.

"It was a productive recon," he said, "and there's more to learn tomorrow. Uhhh, I mean today. Like this morning. What time is it?"

Bear pointed to the kitchen clock, which read 2 A.M. Bear was hungry and asked if anyone wanted to eat. He offered bacon and eggs or pancakes. They settled on pancakes, and he started the preparations.

Stillman wanted to know about the stranger. Ransom said he didn't identify himself. He had a husky voice and was probably in his midthirties. He was wearing jeans and a green hooded Celtics sweatshirt and was carrying what looked like a guitar case. Ransom said he had another person to meet who might provide information. "One of the soldiers at the bar slipped me a piece of paper with his name and phone number. He wants to meet today. I just got to town and my tomorrow, which is really today, is already filling up with meetings."

"You're the one who's making it happen," said Stillman.

"Yeah," he said, "but I'm worried I'll miss the best part of the weekend, the memorial service where I get to see Lisa."

"I know she's looking forward to meeting you," Stillman said. "I talked to her this morning after we got off base. She wants to get the whole team together for a strategy session." He cleared the empty beer cans and filled Ransom in on everything they'd learned that evening from Lincoln Freeman. He set out three more cold ones, along with plates and forks. Rose reappeared as they were about to dig into Bear's stack of pancakes. She had just nursed Melanie and smelled the bacon. She joined the conversation.

Bear brought up Roxbury's rash of heroin overdose deaths and whether they could be connected to Sanders. He asked Rose what she knew about their cousin's death. She said he was unemployed and down and out and died shooting up in a smack house along with a girl he knew. The girl survived. People said it was the same heroin that had killed others. She didn't know who was supplying it, except that street people said a white guy driving a red sports car had been seen a couple of times on streets where it was sold, probably a rich guy from the suburbs coming to the city to feed his habit.

The mention of a red sports car caused Bear, Stillman, and Ransom to raise their beers in a toast. "It had to be Sanders," said Stillman.

"I can't believe he's that stupid," said Bear.

"He could be that cocky," said Ransom. "He's an officer. He probably thinks he's untouchable."

Stillman asked Rose if she knew anything else about the red sports car. She said it had an Army bumper sticker on it.

21

Saturday, November 23, 1968
Boston

The Saturday issue of the *Boston World* had a brief police story that was hard to find on an inside page crowded with other news.

College Student
Presumed Dead
In Suicide Leap

A Boston University graduate student is believed to have died after he reportedly jumped from the BU Bridge into the frigid Charles River near midnight Thursday, authorities said.

The student was identified as 23-year-old Ian MacPherson of Brighton. Police said he left a backpack on the Boston side of the bridge that spans the river to Cambridge. His body was not found during a search by police and firefighters Friday. A suicide note was left in the backpack, according to police, who did not disclose what it said.

A Boston University spokesman declined to comment, other than to confirm MacPherson was enrolled as a student.

22

Saturday, November 23, 1968
Lexington

The morning sky was still dark when the Saturday issue of the *Boston World* was delivered to the Thompson house in Lexington, tossed by a newspaper carrier onto the porch, where it would remain untouched throughout the day. Lisa and Mary Lou had no interest in news. They were overwhelmed with grief. Their family of four had been cut down to two.

They heard the newspaper land on the porch and bounce off the wall. With the memorial service looming, they had hardly slept. Lisa spent the night with Mary Lou in her bed, the one she and Art shared for decades. They hardly talked, except to ask each other if they were still awake. They didn't have much to say. They felt helpless in a world they didn't understand, empty, drained of strength and emotion. They would have to pull themselves together.

The service would take place at the congregational church. They weren't churchgoers. They didn't want to go, didn't want to say goodbye, didn't want to admit that their family, shattered by their government's own Army, could never be put back together. It had been three years since they were at the congregational church. They had been invited by friends for a Christmas eve service. The pastor who would preside over the memorial service was a stranger to them. He had never met Chris or Art. He had asked to talk with Lisa and Mary Lou before the service so they could give him something personal to say. Lisa choreographed the service. She determined the tone, the speakers, and the music. It would be part memorial, part protest.

She and Mary Lou wanted to look nice, but they hadn't talked about what they would wear. It was too much effort. They put it off until the morning. Now the sun was about to rise and they dreaded seeing it. They put off getting out of bed a while longer.

* * * *

Fifteen miles away in Roxbury three young men who had also been up most of the night were asleep in Rose's crowded fourth-floor apartment. Stillman and Ransom were on the floor. They insisted Bear should sleep on the couch. Their Army experience had numbed them to night sounds. They didn't hear Melanie crying for her mom or Rose going to the bathroom and changing diapers. They barely stirred at the sounds of sirens.

Stillman was the first to wake up. He made a pot of coffee and called Freeman to tell him about the stranger who wanted to meet Ransom at Boston Common. He used Rose's kitchen phone, her only phone. Freeman agreed to pick up Stillman and Bear in Roxbury and take them to the Common so they could see who the stranger was before they went to the afternoon memorial service together.

The aroma of coffee drew Rose to the kitchen. She and Stillman exchanged whispered morning greetings. She was holding Melanie on her hip with one hand and grabbed a cup with the other. She set it on the counter and was reaching for the coffee pot when Stillman asked if he could hold Melanie while she poured. She started to say she could do both, but didn't. He asked how he should hold her. She said he could use two hands like a cradle. He said he had never held a baby and reached out nervously. "You'll be fine," she said. "She might cry, but she won't break." He took her and smiled and whispered, "Hi Melanie, my name is Jud. I'm a friend of Bear, ahhh Clarence. Good morning." Melanie looked up at him with a questioning expression. Then she smiled, and he rocked her. "See," said Rose. "Nothing to it. How'd you like to take care of her the rest of the weekend?" He said he wasn't ready to deal with diapers.

Bear rolled over on the couch and stretched. He saw Stillman and quipped, "If the Army could see you now, they might make you a medic."

Ransom leaned up on an elbow from the floor and commented on how good the coffee smelled.

Stillman walked and swayed with Melanie until she spit up on his shirt and he passed her back to Rose. Not long afterward, Freeman knocked on the door and entered with a box of coffee and donuts. Bear introduced him to Ransom, who told him about the stranger and asked if he had any advice.

"Expect the unexpected," Freeman said.

*   *   *   *

Boston Common, America's oldest public park, encompassed fifty acres near the State House, the Massachusetts state capitol. The park was coming alive with people as bright sunlight took the chill out of the air.

Ransom parked his bike off Beacon Street on the north side of the Common near the pond, where he was supposed to meet the stranger. Freeman, carrying Stillman and Bear in his car, parked on the opposite side of the park. Freeman had brought a frisbee with him. They worked their way across the park to an area near the pond, tossing the frisbee as they moved. They spotted Ransom and watched as he approached a man standing at the edge of the pond in a green Celtics sweatshirt with the hood over his head. The stranger pulled his hood back to shake hands.

"Well, how about that," Freeman muttered to himself. "Hello Johnny."

Ransom and Johnny Dollar walked to a bench. They talked for a while before Ransom waved to the frisbee players and motioned for them to join him.

"Mr. Dollar," said Freeman, "nice to see you again."

"Back at you," said Johnny.

Freeman introduced Stillman and Bear. He told them Johnny had been extremely helpful proving the Army lied about what happened to Chris. Stillman asked Johnny if he was in the Army. "Only when I have to be," he said.

Freeman cut off further probing into Johnny's background. "I've got a strategic question," he said. "What do we do now?"

Ransom spoke up. "I'm the new guy," he said, "but Johnny and I have been talking about how I might have lucked out last night when that soldier gave me his name and phone number. I don't know what he wants, but I'm gonna give him a call. Johnny thinks it could be worthwhile."

"Maybe more than worthwhile," said Freeman. "If one of Sanders's crew is willing to talk about what happened to Chris, that would be the jackpot." Since they were all together, he said he had something new to tell them. He got a call a couple of hours earlier from a Boston police detective who wanted information about one of his clients, a BU grad student who committed suicide. He told them the student, Ian MacPherson, had been part of the SDS raid on the Army induction center.

"It looks like another death related to the Army base," Freeman said. "The police found my name in a backpack he left behind. MacPherson wanted me to represent him. He said soldiers were trying to kill him. The detective is coming to my office Monday morning."

"Heavy duty," said Bear. "Me and Jud wish we could do more, but I don't know what."

Freeman said he, Bear, and Stillman should be alert for anyone or anything suspicious at the memorial service, maybe soldiers they might recognize from the bar. He cautioned them not to say anything to newspaper reporters other than what they saw at the induction ceremony.

*　*　*　*

Cars were barely moving and horns were blaring in front of the congregational church on Mass Ave, the main road through the center of Lexington. Across from the church was the Lexington Battle Green, where the first shots of the Revolutionary War were fired in 1775. Young people on foot, some carrying anti-war signs, walked casually among the cars creeping along Mass Ave, encouraging their drivers to honk in support of the demonstrators gathering on the church lawn for the memorial service. Lisa and Mary Lou had contacted Boston area anti-war activists to let them know they would welcome a protest as a tribute to Chris and Art.

Because of the traffic jam, Freeman parked before reaching the church and they walked the rest of the way. On the church lawn a trio of singers, two with guitars, were playing Pete Seeger's protest anthem, "If I Had a Hammer." Many in the crowd, including Freeman, Bear, and Stillman, sang along as they walked.

Inside the church, easels near the altar displayed pictures of Chris and Art flanking Chris's bedroom poster:

In war, TRUTH is the FIRST CASUALTY.

Freeman showed Stillman and Bear where Lisa and her mother were sitting by themselves in the front row of pews. Behind them were Art's parents, the retired Vermont dairy farmers, and Mary Lou's mother. Her father had died several years earlier.

Freeman and Stillman took seats a few rows behind them, but Bear went up and introduced himself to Lisa. He sat down briefly next to her, and they talked for a few minutes. Then he moved back to join the others.

"What did you talk about?" asked Stillman.

"You'll see," he said.

When the pastor walked up to the pulpit to open the service, the church was packed. Johnny got there late and blended in at the back where those who couldn't find seats were clustered.

"Good afternoon," the pastor said, "Thank you for coming. What a wonderful turnout. I expect most of you knew Chris Thompson and admired his passion, his activism, and his dedication to nonviolence, civil rights, and justice. Those of you who knew Art know how much he loved Chris and how he shared that admiration of his son's life. Judging by what I've seen so far this afternoon, inside as well as outside the church, you will not be surprised that this is going to be a nontraditional memorial service."

The crowd erupted in applause.

"With that sign of approval," the pastor said, "let's get started with some music. If you feel like singing, please join in. We'll lead off with a hymn written by Bob Dylan."

The church rocked with applause, whoops, and cheers.

"This song speaks to generations of young Americans," he said. "It's one of Chris's favorites. It's called 'Blowin' in the Wind.'"

The trio that had been playing outside the church took the stage, and the crowd boisterously joined in. The singing could be heard outside the church, even over the honking horns of the cars and trucks on Mass Ave.

More protest and folk music followed, punctuated by Bible readings and recollections from two activists who had worked closely with Chris.

Then Lisa took over.

She thanked everyone for coming. "Before I start," she said, "I'd like to introduce someone who only knew Chris for a few minutes just before he was attacked at the Boston Army Base. His name is Clarence Simpson. His friends know him as Bear. He has a special song for us."

Bear got up and walked to a piano at the side of the pulpit. He addressed the crowd. "This song is for Chris. It's called "They Can't Take That Away from Me." It was written by two amazing songwriters, George and Ira Gershwin. My favorite version was performed by two of the greatest jazz musicians ever, Louis Armstrong and Ella Fitzgerald. But today, it's just me. And I took the liberty of adding a final verse for Chris."

He took his seat at the piano and began performing. The crowd was silent throughout until Bear got to the last verse, the one he wrote.

The way you were so brave
When you fought the draft
The innocent souls you saved
So people could be free

The church erupted with a roar. When he hit the final chord, everyone in the church was standing and applauding, including Lisa and her mother, in a prolonged ovation.

Lisa intercepted Bear as he stepped away from the piano and hugged him, a handkerchief in her hand. She wiped away tears before turning to address the crowd.

"Bear, thank you so much. That was beautiful. I miss Chris. I'm so proud of him. I miss him dearly."

She paused to regain her composure and dabbed at her face again. When she resumed talking, her expression toughened.

"I miss my father just as much as my brother. They were two extraordinary men. I could never have imagined that the horror that took Chris away from us would also take my father. But it did. When my dad saw what happened to Chris at the South Boston Army Base, he changed his life. He quit his job and dedicated himself to war resistance. But watching Chris waste away in a hospital bed was too much for him. My father died in my arms of a heart attack on the day we received proof that the Army lied to us about how Chris was hurt. The Army said he accidently fell down the stairs. That was the beginning of a coverup. I won't go into details here, but I promise you the soldiers responsible for Chris's death will be exposed. And while we're doing that, we will end the draft. And then we'll end the goddamned war."

The church exploded with applause and cheers. Lisa's voice came back stronger.

"The government and the Army and those soldiers will never forget my brother, Christopher Thompson, and our father, Arthur Thompson."

More applause.

"We can't stop there. We're going to go after the shameless politicians and businessmen who send disadvantaged kids to die so they can sell their killing machines and profit from endless war. Those hateful people have no souls. Their world is all about greed. They crave money and power for themselves and for others who look like them. It's built into our society, our government, our economy, the draft, the military. Our country is addicted to war. We need change. Massive change. It's got to stop. We need cold turkey. Cold turkey now. That's right. Cold turkey."

The applause built again and was prolonged, accompanied by shouts of "cold turkey."

"My brother went to the Boston Army Base as ordered because he was drafted. He didn't hide or run off to Canada. He confronted the government. He wanted to challenge the legitimacy of the draft. He went to the base and expected to end up in court or possibly a prison cell. But he was carried away on a stretcher in an ambulance to Massachusetts General Hospital, where he died. His body died, but his spirit is alive. I feel it here. I feel it now."

The church shook as people stood and stomped their feet amid sustained applause and cheers.

"Chris was an activist right up to the end. Bear and another draftee who was with him that day at the Boston Army Base told me Chris was removed from the induction room by two soldiers holding his arms because he refused to join the Army. His last words to the draftees in that room were that they could still stop the war. He called on them to resist. He told them to call Boston Draft Resistance. Resist was what he said as he was dragged from that room. Resist."

Chants of "resist, resist, resist" rocked the church.

Lisa raised her arms to quiet the crowd, and she lowered her voice to a more reflective tone.

"Chris loved coffeehouses and folk music. One of his favorite singers was Joan Baez. Boston is lucky, we're all lucky, this is where Joan found her beautiful voice. I'm sure many of you have seen her, although not as many times as my brother. One song stands out that he loved to hear her sing and that is particularly appropriate for this occasion. It's called 'Joe Hill.'"

Applause spread through the crowd.

"For those who are not familiar with Joe Hill, the man, he was a migrant laborer and union activist accused of murdering two men in Utah in 1914. He insisted he was innocent, but he was convicted and executed by a firing squad in 1915. Joe Hill was also a songwriter whose songs inspired workers fighting for rights across the country. 'Joe Hill,' the song, was originally a poem written about ten years after Joe's death by Alfred Hayes. It was set to music in the 1930s by Earl Robinson and has been performed by many prominent artists. Copies of the poem titled '*I Dreamed I Saw Joe Hill Last Night*' are available on a table as you leave the church. It's a powerful poem that became an anthem for the labor movement. Today I am using it as an anthem for another worthy movement, the anti-war movement.

"Thank you all for coming to pay tribute to my brother and my father and to protest an immoral war. We hope you'll carry on with what mattered most to them. It's time now to close with Joe Hill. I hope it will help you, whenever you hear it, wherever you are, whatever you're doing, to remember Chris and the ideals he lived and died for."

Lisa walked solemnly back to the pew where Mary Lou nodded and held up her handkerchief to show she was ready. The trio took the stage and performed a heartfelt interpretation of the song. Afterward, the hushed crowd filed silently out of the church. Almost everyone picked up a copy of the poem.

*   *   *   *

Ransom had hoped to join the others at the memorial service, but the soldier from the bar wanted to meet at the same time. Ransom had to be patient, had to wait a little longer to meet the woman from Vermont he heard on a phone call in New Jersey, vowing to get justice for her brother in Boston. He was curious about her farm. He'd heard it described as a commune. He wasn't sure how a Vietnam vet would be received at a commune. He parked his Harley on a side street in Boston's Back Bay neighborhood near the Charles River. Thanks to directions from Johnny and Freeman and Bear, he was getting to know his way around the city after just twenty-four hours.

He walked to the Esplanade, a long park on the Boston side of the river with a huge semicircular bandstand in the shape of a shell. It was highlighted in the afternoon sun against a deep blue sky. He thought of his new friends who were at the service mourning a man they never got to know. Fresh out of the Army in an unfamiliar city, he was hoping to help identify that man's killers. Yet it felt right. He scanned the area around the bandstand. He was looking for the soldier, but he was also on alert for anyone or anything that could signal danger. The soldier was scared of something, or acted like he was. He said he'd be jogging in shorts and a yellow jacket. He told Ransom to stroll along the path by the river and he would slow down and walk with him.

Ransom didn't see him until he felt him at his side, coming from the rear. "Nice day," the soldier said. "Thanks for meeting me."

"No problem. What's going on?"

The soldier glanced around before answering. He looked younger now than he did in the dark bar, probably too young to legally vote or buy liquor, and his darting eyes appeared wild, partially hidden under the brim of a Chicago Cubs baseball cap. He was skinny and shorter than Ransom. If they were in a street fight, it wouldn't be fair. Unless the soldier had a gun. Or a syringe.

"This is going to sound weird," the soldier said. "You and Lt. Sanders seemed to be getting along pretty well last night, and I came here to warn you he's crazy dangerous. He's into some bad shit. You don't wanna get mixed up with him."

"Sounds serious."

"It is."

"You seem to be mixed up with him."

"I am. That's why I'm here. Let's keep walking."

"Where?"

"I don't know. Nowhere in particular. I just like to keep moving."

"You look nervous. Is somebody after you?"

"No. It's not like that. It's just Sanders. He makes me nervous."

"Why?"

"I'm in so deep I don't know how to get out without getting killed. You've been to Nam. I'd hate to see you get hurt any more than you already are."

"Do I look hurt?"

"No. But if you've been to Nam, chances are you're hurt. I know. I was there."

Ransom left the statement unanswered as they kept walking.

"Look," said the soldier. "I've got to be honest with you. Sanders asked me to check you out. So in addition to warning you, that's what I'm doing. He probably has somebody watching us right now. He wants me to make sure you're not a cop. Are you?"

"If somebody told you a cop can't lie about being a cop, that's bullshit. Cops lie all the time. Just like presidents and generals and politicians and priests and practically everybody else. No, I'm not a cop. Why are you worried about cops?"

"Because Sanders is."

Ransom stopped, opened his hands, and held them up for the soldier to see. "What you see is what you get. I'm a Viet vet looking for a job."

"I believe you."

They resumed walking. Ransom asked again why Sanders was worried about cops. The soldier took his time to answer. "Look, I don't know you. Like I said, Sanders is into some bad shit. I just don't want you to get in trouble. You seem like a good guy."

"I can take care of myself."

"I expect you can."

"Why are you so nervous?"

"I guess it shows. I'm kind of in a jam. I'm trying to figure a way out. Looking for someone who can maybe help me get out of it. Maybe we can help each other."

"I don't need any help."

"Yeah. I get that."

Ransom stopped again. "This walking without really talking isn't getting us anywhere," he said. "If you need some advice, I'll listen. But you gotta tell me what's going on. Otherwise, I'll see you later."

The soldier shifted his weight and kicked at a pebble. "Please don't go," he said. "I need help. I'll tell you everything." Ransom suggested they sit down on a nearby bench.

He said his name was Leo Miller, a sergeant working for Sanders. He said he was from Illinois, a high school dropout who'd been drafted and recently reenlisted to cash in on an eight-thousand-dollar bonus offered to keep him and others like him in the Army so the war could go on and on and on. He said in Vietnam he worked for Sanders in an infantry unit that took heavy losses, but gave more than it took. He described Sanders as a reckless brutal leader, known as "Wild Bill." He said Sanders persuaded him to work privately on a crew that bought and sold drugs and military spare parts on the black market. He said Sanders shared the profits with the men on the crew. When their Vietnam tours ended, Sanders arranged for some of them to be reassigned to the Boston Army Base with him. Over time, he said, it became clear that nobody would leave the crew alive. Two who tried had died and a third had recently disappeared, leaving just two on the crew, in addition to Sanders.

Miller said Sanders was desperate, under a lot of pressure to come up with money he didn't have because a shipment of his drugs had been stolen. He said Sanders had talked about kidnapping the sister of one of the guys who stole his drugs and holding her for ransom. Miller hesitated. "That's weird. I just realized your name is Ransom, and Sanders wants a ransom."

"Quite a coincidence," said Ransom. "What kind of ransom does he want?"

Miller said Sanders thought the sister might know where the drugs were. "If he can't get the drugs back, he'll make her family pay."

"What kind of drugs," asked Ransom.

"Heroin."

"How much is it worth?"

"At least a hundred thousand."

"Why are you telling me about this?"

"Because he wants me to kidnap the sister."

"And you don't want to do it?"

"No. I haven't killed anybody yet for drugs, and she probably won't come out of this alive."

"I'm sure your drugs have killed more than a few people."

"Yeah, but that's their choice."

"When is this kidnapping supposed to happen?"

"Possibly this coming week."

"Thanksgiving week?"

"Yeah."

"Where?"

"Probably in Lexington where her mother lives or someplace in Vermont where she has a farm."

Ransom asked why Sanders thought the sister knew how to find the drugs.

"Because he's desperate. There were four guys in on the heist. Three of them are dead. We haven't been able to find the fourth, who is supposed to have stashed the drugs in a locker at a train station and has the key. The sister may know where he is. Sanders thinks she could even have the key."

Ransom asked where the drugs were stashed when they were stolen.

"They were at the base. In Sanders's office. It was stupid for him to leave them there. It was supposed to have been for one night, but it was the night the SDS trashed the processing station."

"The SDS stole your drugs?"

"They weren't my drugs. But yes. It was the SDS."

"Did the SDS know the drugs were in Sanders's office?"

"I don't know. I don't know how they could have."

"I suppose it doesn't really matter," Ransom said. "So let's wrap this up. Going back to where we started, what do you want from me? If you want me to kill Sanders, that ain't happening."

Miller looked defeated. "No," he said, "I don't think that's the best way out of this. Suppose you really are a cop. What would you do after everything I've told you?"

"I'd try to save that sister from being kidnapped."

"And what about Sanders?"

"I'd start gathering evidence to arrest him."

"And what about me?"

"You'd be a witness. You'd have to help the cops. You'd probably be asked to continue working with Sanders to get more evidence and be their eyes and ears inside the organization."

"I'd be an informant."

"That's what you'd be."

"Would I be arrested?"

"I don't know. It would probably depend on how many crimes you've committed and how helpful you've been."

"Yeah."

"I have a couple of friends who might have some ideas. I'm going to see them in the next few days. Why don't we meet again, say around here on Tuesday or Wednesday?"

"Wednesday would be better for me. How about noon? How do I get in touch with you if I need to?"

"You can't," said Ransom. "I'll give you a call if I can't make it on Wednesday at noon."

23

Sunday, November 24, 1968
Boston

On Sunday morning, Rose's Roxbury apartment was a replay of Saturday. Freeman showed up with the paper, which carried a story about the memorial service accompanied by a photo of demonstrators waving signs in front of the Lexington Congregational Church. He also brought donuts and coffee, which were both welcomed. Bear, Stillman, and Ransom were packing up their bedding to make space. They had just taken turns in the bathroom shower. Again they had stayed up late, drinking and talking, mostly about Lisa and how to keep her safe.

Ransom had called Freeman Saturday night to fill him in on what he learned at the esplanade. Freeman knew Lisa wanted to get together with Bear and Stillman before they returned to Fort Dix. She also wanted to meet Ransom. Freeman had called her before he drove to Rose's apartment and Lisa invited all of them, including Rose and Melanie, to join her and her mother for lunch at their house. She also asked Freeman to invite Johnny Dollar, but he said nobody knew how to reach him. Freeman had told her it was Johnny who gave him the Army file that revealed Chris' last words, but asked her to keep that to herself. She had not had any contact with Johnny since he surprised her at the farm, and she decided to keep it that way. She didn't want to bother him unless it was absolutely necessary.

Rose had never been to Lexington. Bear had only been there once, for Saturday's memorial service. His second trip, that Sunday morning, was punctuated by a police stop. As if on cue, shortly after crossing the Lexington town line, Freeman noticed a police cruiser in his rearview mirror. The cruiser's lights flashed, and he pulled over. He had his license and registration ready when the officer peered into the crowded car. Bear was in the passenger seat and Rose, Melanie, Stillman, and Ransom were in back. The officer walked around the car, looking at it from all directions. He told Freeman to flash his lights and turn signals before he went back to his cruiser to call headquarters. They sat in the car for over half an hour, long enough for Rose to nurse Melanie, who fell asleep before the officer returned. He asked where they were going and then sent them on their way. "Driving while Black," grumbled Bear. "It'll never end."

The introductions at the house were awkward. Stillman had only talked with Lisa on a phone call, but felt like he knew her. Bear had introduced himself to Lisa at the memorial service. Ransom had heard her on Stillman's bookstore phone call, but had never seen or talked to her. Lisa hugged each of them, and they expressed their heartfelt sorrow about what happened to her brother and her father. They praised her for turning the memorial service into an anti-war protest and for her inspiring speech.

During the meal, Mary Lou offered to take Melanie so Rose could eat with two hands. Mary Lou seemed to delight in snuggling a baby. It had been a long time. The conversation revolved around Stillman and Bear. Lisa told them she would forever be grateful that they called the newspaper and later called her. Without them, Lisa said, nobody would have known what happened between Chris and Lt. Sanders in the induction room. "Everybody in that room saw and heard what happened with Chris, but nobody else did anything about it," she said. "You did. You didn't have to, but you did. Because Jud called the *Boston World* and the newspaper called the Army base, we know the lies and the coverup started that day. I'll never be able to thank you enough. If we had more people like you two, we might have already ended that goddamned war."

Mary Lou stood up from the table, cradling Melanie, and said, "With apologies to Melanie, I have to correct you. It's that goddamned fucking war."

"Mom!" scolded Lisa.

Mary Lou reached for her glass and raised it. "We only served water with lunch," she said. "But it will have to do. I want to toast Jud and Bear."

The others stood and raised their glasses. Mary Lou declared. "To Jud and Bear. To standing tall and making a difference." Glasses were clinked. Stillman and Bear joined the toast, exchanging embarrassed glances.

"What we saw was wrong," said Bear. "Jud was the one who did something."

"You and me," Stillman said. "We're a team. Chris was the one who brought us together that day. Yesterday he brought a lot of other people together at the memorial service." He raised his glass. "To Chris. He'll be making a difference for a long time to come."

The others joined in.

Mary Lou said she had to make one more toast. "I don't think most of you know this," she said. "Arthur made copies of a lot of documents before he left his job so he could expose the corruption of the military-industrial complex, profiting from endless wars. He put a package together and I'm going to give it to Attorney Freeman to decide what to do." Freeman nodded his approval from across the table. Mary Lou then raised her glass and said, "To Art," her voice breaking, tears running down her face. "To my true love Art, making a difference from the grave."

All raised their glasses again.

Mary Lou slumped into her seat, overcome with emotion. Lisa wrapped her arms around her mother, and they sobbed together. Melanie started crying. Rose took Melanie back and comforted her, walking around the table, telling her everything was going to be OK, but not really believing it. On her third lap, she changed her tune. "This is what's true," she whispered to her daughter. "It's going to be up to you, baby. It's going to be up to you." Melanie quieted down, and Rose returned to her seat. Everybody resumed eating. The meal ended in silence.

Rose helped Mary Lou clean up while Lisa and the others moved to the spacious living room, which had two facing couches in front of a fireplace surrounded by other cozy chairs.

They settled into the seats and looked nervously at each other, wondering who would talk first. Four men seeking justice, trying to protect a woman in danger because her brother had been drafted and killed for something he didn't do.

"Before we get started," Lisa said, "as I look around this room, I'm thinking how lucky I am to have such a brave team supporting our family.

Thank you all for being here. Your faces say you have some bad news. Don't worry about me. I felt a lot of love yesterday. I can handle whatever comes today. So throw it at me."

Freeman picked up the ball. He started with the Boston police detective who told him MacPherson was missing after jumping into the Charles River and leaving a backpack with a suicide note. Lisa said she didn't believe it, didn't think MacPherson was capable of killing himself. "If he's dead," she said, "somebody else killed him." She said he struck her as a survivor, someone who would find a way to slither out of whatever messy situation he was in. "He's not a quitter," she said. "He's a snake."

She described her conversation with MacPherson by the stream, when she decided he was too dangerous to take to the farm. He'd accused her of sentencing him to death because he had nobody else to help him. But then, a few minutes after she dropped him in Hanover, he was on the phone to someone. She figured it had to be Freeman, but based on what Johnny discovered, it was likely the FBI.

"I learned firsthand about depression in college," Lisa said, "seeing what it could do to lonely young students. MacPherson wasn't suffering from depression. If he's dead, he didn't kill himself. Somebody else did it."

Freeman said he'd find out more about MacPherson in the morning when the detective was supposed to come to his office. He hoped to see a copy of the suicide note. If MacPherson was dead, he pointed out, the location of Sanders's drugs died with him. When MacPherson wanted to hire him, Freeman recalled, "He was about to tell me where the drugs were hidden, but I told him no, I didn't want to know. I was thinking that could make me a party to the crime. Now that looks like a bad decision."

Lisa suggested MacPherson might have left something in his backpack that could lead them to the drugs. She didn't believe he would kill himself if he could trade the drugs for his life.

She asked how much Freeman planned to tell the detective about MacPherson, whether he would mention the Army raid and Sanders. Freeman said he would get as much information as he could without giving too much away. If the detective pressed him, he said he'd claim attorney-client privilege.

"Why?" asked Lisa. "Why not tell him the truth? Why shouldn't we get the police involved?"

Nobody answered. They looked at each other around the circle.

Ransom shifted in his seat, focused on Lisa and started to say something, but realized Freeman was about to speak. "You first," said Freeman.

"I like Lisa's instincts." Ransom said. "This MacPherson thing is an opportunity to bring the police in. They're coming to us. We don't need to go to them. We just need the right cop. This is a big, complicated, dangerous case. It's going to take more than one cop."

Everyone looked to Freeman.

"I agree," he said. "Look, I've made some mistakes, and we need help. As a rule, lawyers don't team up with the police. But we can't do this ourselves. We know we can't trust the FBI. The Boston police may be our answer. I think you all know my office is bugged. It looks like MacPherson was working with the FBI when the bugs were planted. That was one dumb thing I did. I let him spend the weekend in my office. MacPherson played me."

"I think he's still playing us," Lisa said. "So you'll let us know tomorrow what you think of this detective?"

"Yes."

"Is there anything else?" asked Lisa.

The others looked to Ransom, who shifted forward in his seat on one of the couches and cleared his throat.

"There's more," he said, looking apologetically at Lisa.

He told her about how he got close to Lt. Sanders and his crew at the bar Friday night and one of them warned him Saturday that Sanders was desperate and planning to kidnap the sister of one of the raiders to try to get the drugs back.

"That would be me," said Lisa.

"No doubt," said Ransom.

"When?"

"He said probably this week."

"Do they know where I am?" She stood up, looked at the others, and answered her own question. "Of course they do. I struggled with whether I should bring my revolver for self-defense. I've got it and now I'm glad I do."

"I think we all can agree we don't want a gunfight," said Ransom. "But the way I see it, we've got another reason to get the police on our side. The police would probably side with the Army if it's our word against theirs. But this kidnap plot could work in our favor. Leo Miller, the guy who told me about it, says he wants to get away from Sanders. If he's telling the truth, he should be willing to cooperate with the cops. But there's a lot about him I don't trust. His claim about wanting to expose Sanders is just too convenient. We're supposed to talk again on Wednesday."

Everyone looked to Lisa, who was still on her feet. "So we have a couple of days to find out more about him and Sanders before then," she said. "Maybe Johnny Dollar could help, but it seems nobody knows how to get in touch with him." She looked around the circle. Nobody said anything. "We've got a deadline," she said. "We've got to do something." She set her eyes on Freeman. "I've been wondering if we might be able to use the bugs in your office to our advantage. You haven't removed them, have you?"

Freeman shook his head. "No. They should still be working. Whoever's listening is probably falling asleep because they're basically hearing nothing. Any sensitive business I've been doing outside the office."

"In that case," said Lisa, "let's figure out the best way to wake up whoever's on the other end of those bugs."

*   *   *   *

Freeman drove Stillman and Bear to the airport to catch a late afternoon flight. They had agonized over their decision to return to Dix. If they didn't go back, they'd likely end up in the stockade. They didn't want that, and they didn't want to leave the team in Boston, but they didn't think they'd be needed if Freeman and Ransom got the police involved to protect Lisa. Freeman assured them he'd let them know about any new developments. "I'll find a way to reach you," he said, "even if I have to call a general."

Stillman and Bear said they had one strong reason to return to Dix. The memorial service had reinforced their determination to put out a GI newspaper with Angela Williams.

On the way to the airport, they told Freeman they were also motivated by their brief exposure to the *Boston World*'s newsroom and their meeting with Roger McAlister. "There was so much energy in that place," said Stillman. "I hadn't thought about it before, but when you work for a newspaper, every day is different. The world changes and you have to reflect that. It's a new product, a new challenge every day. It makes me want to be there."

"It's kinda like writing a song," said Bear. "You're looking for truth. You know what I mean? You want to express it with imagination, put catchy lyrics together with the right melody. But having to write a new song every day, that's pressure man, that's excitement."

Freeman said the meeting with McAlister was the first time he'd been inside a newsroom on deadline. "With so many people hustling all over the place, I'd say making a good newspaper every day is nothing short of a miracle. They're so serious about their work. We're lucky to have McAlister on our side."

Stillman reminded Bear they didn't have much time left to finish writing stories for Angela to put out a newspaper before the end of basic training.

"We can write on the plane," said Bear. "It's our first deadline. We'll make it."

In addition to planning their stories, they'd been thinking about what to call their paper. Bear liked "Resist." Stillman favored "Up Yours," with a logo of a mooning bare ass. He suggested they could use the first issue to solicit stories about soldiers who had lost their lives or their limbs in Vietnam. He wanted to put names and faces on the casualties, turn them from Army statistics back into real people.

Stillman told Freeman about Fort Dix calling itself the "Home of the Ultimate Weapon," a name that revealed a lot about the psyche of military commanders. He described basic training as a brutal hazing process designed to strip kids of their identities and their humanity and turn them into tools of war.

"You're all the same. That's what we hear from the drill sergeants all the time," he said. "Over and over, from morning to night, you're all the same."

"Trainees aren't people," said Bear. "They don't want soldiers who think. They want ultimate weapons, mindless grunts they can toss onto the battlefield like grenades and watch them explode. It's kind of messy, you know, with blood and guts splattered everywhere, but that gets white-washed away by the casualty reports, body pieces reduced to numbers so they can draft more kids."

"Wow," said Freeman. "I'm beginning to feel what you're going through."

It turned out Freeman knew Angela. He had met her at a conference for civil rights lawyers and anti-war activists. She had told him about the national anti-war initiative to nurture an underground GI press and the coffeehouse plan. He said he was impressed by her vision, intelligence, and seemingly boundless energy.

Stillman had been surprised how much Johnny Dollar knew about the GI underground press. They had talked about it at Boston Common. Johnny knew the power of information. He said a lot of bigotry was generated by misunderstandings, and he contended newspapers could reduce it by publishing in-depth stories about history and war and racism. Johnny had a vision for an international GI underground paper that would be sent to bases around the world. He said he was working on a plan to trick the Army into paying for it. "Imagine the Army putting out its own anti-war newspaper," Stillman said. "If anyone could manage that, it would be Johnny."

Freeman had only known Johnny a short time but was sure he'd be successful at whatever he did.

They reached the airport and found a parking spot. They still had time before their flight. Freeman asked if they had any thoughts about Lisa's question: How could they turn the tables on whoever planted the listening devices in his office? If the FBI was tapping the phones of lawyers, he said, it would be illegal unless the FBI had gotten a judge to sign off on it first and that was highly unlikely.

"The only thing we know," he said, "is that Johnny detected listening devices. We don't even know if they're still there."

"You could find out," said Bear, "and lay a trap."

"Good idea," said Stillman. "What kind of a trap?"

"I don't know. In the office somebody could say something the bugs would hear that lures whoever planted them out in the open."

"And then what?"

"You're there, waiting for them to show up."

"And then?"

"They're trapped. You got 'em."

"That's when you step out and say, 'Smile. You're on Candid Camera.'"

"Exactly. Gotcha, you bastards."

"What if it's not the FBI, and they've got guns?"

"Then you make sure you've got pictures before they shoot you."

Freeman liked Bear's idea. "What if we say on the phone and loud enough for any bugs to hear that we're going to debug the office on a certain day. They'd want to retrieve the bugs before someone finds them. They'd have to break into the office to do that. We could be ready for them."

"With a couple of cameras," said Stillman, "and a reporter and a photographer."

"And cake," said Bear. "We'd deserve cake for exposing them."

He and Stillman raised their arms, fist bumped, and laughed. They told Freeman about how they were rewarded for ambushing their company commander at Dix during a training exercise.

"I wish you could be around to celebrate if we do catch someone," said Freeman. "But you'll be doing more to end the war by putting out that GI paper back at Dix. We've got you covered here. Say hi to Angela for me."

24

Monday, November 25, 1968
Cambridge

Freeman went back and forth thinking about whether to ask Ransom to join him for the meeting with the Boston police detective. He wanted the detective to feel free to share whatever information he had. He was worried that Ransom might make the detective uncomfortable. But he decided an extra set of eyes and ears outweighed any negatives. Ransom had great instincts. And it couldn't hurt having a Vietnam vet teaming with an anti-war lawyer while dealing with a cop who probably supported the war and had pals who would like nothing better than to put hippie draft dodgers behind bars.

Ransom was waiting on the sidewalk outside Freeman's building Monday morning when Freeman approached with a tray of coffees and donuts. He opened the door, but Freeman reminded him they didn't want to be in the office. "It's such a nice morning," he said, "Let's go to the park where we can have some privacy."

"Smart thinking for a Monday morning," said Ransom. "Afterward we can put Bear's plan into action."

The Boston detective arrived a few minutes later. He was middle-aged, wore a coat and tie under a topcoat, and appeared physically fit. He showed them his credentials. His name was Salvatore Arruda. Freeman introduced Ransom as someone who assisted him in investigating cases. Arruda asked Ransom if he knew MacPherson. He didn't, but was aware of some of his activities. "He does seem to get around," Arruda said.

Freeman led them to the park. One of the benches was empty. He passed out coffees and donuts and asked Arruda how long he'd been with the Boston police. "It seems like all my life," he said. "My dad was a cop and I'm carrying the torch now. How about you?" Freeman said he grew up in South Carolina and was the first in his family to go to college and law school. Arruda turned to Ransom with the same question. Ransom said he grew up in West Virginia and came to Boston after getting out of the Army. "Vietnam?" asked Arruda. Ransom said yes. "Combat?" Ransom nodded. Arruda said he had a son in college and hoped the war would be over before he graduated. "Right on," said Ransom.

Freeman steered the conversation to how much Arruda knew about MacPherson. Arruda described him as a small-time drug dealer who got mixed up in enough stuff that he stayed out of jail by becoming a snitch. Arruda said MacPherson would work with anyone if it helped his cause. "Boston police. State police. The feds. Various gangs. He plays a dangerous game. He seems to like the action. He's also supposed to be quite the gambler when he has a bankroll. It doesn't usually last very long. He lives on the edge. The picture I have in my mind is a Ping-Pong ball, getting batted back and forth and all over the place by anyone and everyone." He said he based that on what he heard from other detectives, as well as from MacPherson. "He seems to know a little about a lot," Arruda said, "and a lot about little." He had only met him once in connection with a recent murder in Roxbury. "It's really a disappearance because we don't have a body," he said.

"Now there's a coincidence," said Freeman. "With MacPherson you're working two disappearances at the same time."

Arruda said an Irish criminal gang was believed responsible for the murder-disappearance case in Roxbury. It was one of two dominant gangs—the other was Italian—that had divided the city into territories where they controlled various types of crime.

Freeman said he wanted to hear about that case, but asked to talk about MacPherson first.

Arruda passed him an envelope. It had the lawyer's name on it. Inside were ten crumpled one hundred dollar bills and a handwritten piece of lined paper that had been torn from a notebook. It said:

Dear Attorney Freeman,

I'm sorry things didn't work out for us. Thank you for listening to my story and for your advice and for giving me a safe place to stay that weekend. I hope this is enough to cover it.

Ian

Freeman turned the paper over and the back was blank. He checked inside the envelope to see if it might contain a key. No key. He wasn't sure if he was disappointed or relieved.

Arruda asked him to explain the note.

"He came to my office on a Friday a few weeks ago," he said. "He wanted to talk about possible legal representation. He said he'd been living on the streets and didn't have any place to stay. He looked awful. I let him spend the weekend in my office."

"Did you know him?"

"No."

"You let someone you didn't know spend the weekend in your law office?"

"Yes."

"Isn't that unusual?"

"Yeah. I guess so. I've slept in the office, but I've never let someone else sleep there."

"Why did you do that for MacPherson?"

"He said his life was in danger, that somebody was trying to kill him. He was desperate."

"Did he say who wanted to kill him and why?"

"That's where this gets tricky because he was a client. At least at that point. He was concerned about confidentiality."

"I can understand answering questions about a client is tricky, as you say, but this client is no longer around and likely is dead."

"Has his body been found?"

"No."

"That would make this easier, if there was a body."

"Yes."

"The newspaper indicated there was a suicide note."

"I saw that story, but it was wrong. Somebody might have mistaken the letter to you for a suicide note."

"Was it in the backpack?"

"Yes."

"Was anything else in the backpack?"

"Now we're getting into a sensitive area for me. The backpack is evidence. I gave you the letter to see, but I'm going to have to take it back and keep it, along with the money, until we close this case."

"I'd like to make a copy before you go."

"Certainly."

Freeman handed the letter back to Arruda. He said he'd like to be more open about MacPherson, "but I don't know you and you don't know me. You're scratching the surface of a complicated, dangerous situation. If we get any deeper into it, we'd have to work together. In my experience police don't usually cooperate with lawyers, unless they're prosecutors. And most defense lawyers don't cooperate with police. If we work together, we need to trust each other."

Arruda said he had already checked out Freeman with a couple of lawyers he knew and respected. "They said your word is solid, and you're good at what you do."

"Thank you for that," Freeman said. "I'd like to make a call or two and get back to you, probably tomorrow. In the meantime, I'd like to ask another question about MacPherson. Were any keys found in his backpack?"

"Not that I know of," said Arruda, "but that's not to say one couldn't be hidden in it. Should I take a closer look?"

"It couldn't hurt."

"What might that key open?"

"I'll tell you if we find it."

Arruda asked why Freeman wanted to talk about Roxbury. Freeman said he was looking into the rash of heroin overdose deaths and was interested in two in particular, a couple of graduate students with ties to the SDS, Roy Hodges and Bruce Franklin. "Their bodies were found in Brighton," he said, "but the heroin was believed to be the same kind involved in the Roxbury overdoses." Arruda took notes, including the students' names, and said he'd get some information.

"Why are you interested in them?" he asked.

"MacPherson said they were murdered."

"By who?"

"By the same people he said were trying to murder him. Soldiers from the South Boston Army Base."

"Do you know why?"

"MacPherson said Hodges and Franklin broke into the base to trash the induction station and stole drugs and cash that soldiers had stashed there. MacPherson said he was with them as a lookout."

"What kind of drugs?"

"Heroin."

"Do you know the names of the soldiers who killed the students?"

"We're working on that," said Freeman. "By the way do you know anything about Chris Thompson, who died after being attacked at the base?"

Arruda said he had read the story in the *World* about the memorial service, and other people he asked about Freeman had brought up Thompson's death.

"Then you know I represent his family," Freeman said. "We believe Chris was killed by at least one of those soldiers who killed the students."

"Well," said Arruda, "this case is taking off. The other guy who disappeared, the one we believe was murdered by the Irish gang a couple of weeks ago, he's a soldier from the Army base."

*   *   *   *

Arruda and Freeman were already acting like partners when they got back to the office and made a copy of MacPherson's note. Arruda promised to be in touch. Ransom and Freeman followed him down the stairs to the street and made small talk on the sidewalk while Arruda went to his car. They waved to him as he drove by in an unmarked dark sedan. Ransom said they should stay on the sidewalk because he expected Johnny to show up. He'd seen him walk by when they were in the park. He was wearing a sweater and sport coat and carrying a briefcase.

They spotted Johnny down the block, motioning for them to join him, which was in the opposite direction from the park. When they got close, he walked nonchalantly away. They followed. He slowed. They caught up. "Nice day," he said. "Just the right amount of chill in the air," said Freeman.

They walked while they talked, initially about Arruda. Johnny had heard of him as a no-nonsense straight shooter, one of the department's best detectives.

Freeman told Johnny that Arruda had another case involving a missing soldier who was presumed dead. They agreed he had to be part of the military drug crew. Then Freeman brought up the listening devices and Bear's suggestion that they set a trap to catch whoever planted them. But first he said they needed to be sure the bugs were still there.

"They are," said Johnny.

"How do you know?"

"I checked."

"How'd you do that?"

"With the same equipment I used before."

"I should put you on the payroll."

"No need for that. I enjoy my work. It's for a good cause."

"If our plan works, we'll soon know who planted the bugs."

"It's the FBI."

"For sure?"

"Yes."

"What do you think about Bear's plan?"

"I like it."

"When should we put it into action?"

"How about today?"

They agreed Freeman and Ransom would be stationed in the inner office that evening with cameras. Johnny said he had one in his briefcase if they needed it.

"You just happen to have a camera with you?" said Freeman. Then he caught himself. "By now I know I shouldn't be surprised by anything about you."

"Tools of the trade," said Johnny. "It's a Leica."

"Whoa," said Ransom. "That's not just a camera. That's a precision instrument. It's the best." Ransom said he had a Nikon, but would like to try the Leica.

Freeman said he would set the trap as soon as he got back to his office. He'd ask his assistant to phone a friend to make a fake appointment to have the office swept for listening devices the next day. He wanted her to use the phone because he didn't know whether the FBI had tapped the phone line or had installed devices to pick up conversations in the office, or both.

Their plan called for Ransom to use the building's back door to slip in undetected late in the afternoon. Freeman would leave a few minutes later from the front door. He'd get in his car and drive away like he was going home. He'd park a few blocks away and return through the back door.

Johnny suggested they get some food and water and a good book in case they had to wait for hours or overnight for somebody to show up. They figured it wouldn't be a break-in because the FBI already had a key to the office, courtesy of MacPherson.

Johnny didn't expect trouble, but said he'd be in the vicinity if they needed help in an emergency. Otherwise, he planned to be invisible.

They returned to Freeman's office building. Johnny followed them in the door, but stopped at the base of the stairs out of sight of the street. He opened his briefcase, handed his Leica to Ransom, and explained how it worked. "Happy hunting," he said as he left.

For Johnny the anticipation of catching FBI agents illegally bugging a law office was akin to winning an Olympic medal. It put a spring in his step as walked down the street. He was confident the FBI didn't obtain a warrant. He had been aware for some time of suspicions that Hoover used his agents for surveillance on political and civil rights leaders as a form of extortion. But as far as Johnny knew, the FBI had never been caught in the act of planting or removing illegal bugs, at least not by anyone who went public with the information. Exposing Hoover's use of agents for corrupt purposes should force him to resign or at the least retire. It would probably still take years to clean up the bureau, but Hoover would be gone.

Johnny was already carrying out another plan that he had not shared with anyone. It required secrecy and skills he learned in the military. It should work perfectly in conjunction with Freeman catching the FBI bugging his office. Before the US became mired in Vietnam, Johnny had enlisted in the Army for military intelligence, focusing on counterintelligence, in part because he wanted to learn about security systems and how to penetrate them or get around them without being detected.

On the way to his car, Johnny thought of his father. They had lived in

Willimantic, Connecticut, known as Thread City, where his dad worked in a fabric mill. His father came to the mainland from Puerto Rico, initially to work on a shade tobacco farm, knowing he would encounter prejudice, but figuring the job opportunities and the money were worth it. Johnny also worked in the fabric mills for a couple of summers when he was in high school. His fondest memories were of him and his father sitting together in front of their old cabinet radio listening to their favorite show, "Yours Truly Johnny Dollar," about a tough wise-cracking freelance insurance fraud investigator in Hartford, the Insurance Capital of the World, about thirty miles from Willimantic. Each episode featured unusual insurance company claims that required Johnny's special talents to investigate. The show inspired real-life teenage Johnny, whose given name was Juan Ernesto Aviles, to pursue the kind of life that the fictional radio Johnny lived.

Following his military service, when Juan Ernesto felt the need to assume identities other than his own, he used Johnny Dollar. It worked, and he stuck with it. He rarely used his real name, although he did use it when he applied for the Boston FBI office-cleaning crew, anticipating a background check. He was relieved when no questions were asked. He needed that job to check out the FBI's power, security, and lock systems and to determine the likely locations of files he wanted to see and copy. His mission was to get in and out alone and undetected, leaving no trace.

*   *   *   *

Freeman's office was dark late Monday afternoon when he let himself in the back door. He climbed the stairs and opened the door to his outer office. He locked the door behind him.

"Welcome back," whispered Ransom, who had arrived through the back door shortly before Freeman left through the front. They nodded, a silent agreement to keep their voices low to avoid detection.

They went into Freeman's private office. The lights from the street brightened the office enough for them to see in the semidarkness.

Freeman had picked up a couple of sandwiches, which they ate, washing them down with coffee. They set out their cameras. Each was equipped with a flash attachment. "There's a switch just outside that door for the overhead light in the outer office," Freeman said. "I'll throw it when we open the door and surprise whoever shows up."

Ransom had a handgun—a 9mm semiautomatic Smith & Wesson Model 39—with him in a small backpack. He didn't want to provoke anyone by wearing it, but wanted it close by. Freeman suggested a bookcase next to the door.

Ransom told him he had talked with Leo Miller again a few hours earlier. Miller claimed he was getting increasingly fearful of what Sanders might do, but was not quite ready to talk with the cops. Ransom said he didn't know what to think about Miller or Sanders. When he talked with Sanders at the bar, he seemed to be a decent guy, considerate of the people who worked for him. Miller, on the other hand, seemed on edge, trying too hard to play the role of a potential informer. Freeman said Ransom's description of Miller reminded him of MacPherson. "He was an enigma," he said. "You could never be sure of anything."

Freeman finished his sandwich and coffee and said he was ready to work with Arruda. He had contacted a couple of lawyers who had high praise for the detective, as well as Lisa, who gave him a go-ahead. One hurdle he anticipated was jurisdiction, with a Boston cop investigating crimes committed on the Army base. But the heroin was stashed somewhere in Boston and the SDS grad students were murdered in Boston and the soldiers were selling heroin in Boston. He said Arruda should be able to figure it all out. He planned to call him in the morning.

It was too dark in the office to read or do any work. A flashlight would probably be visible from the street since they were only on the second floor. Ransom said music would be nice, but a radio could be heard outside the thin office walls. Freeman said he had a good way to pass the time. He reached into one of his desk drawers and pulled out a deck of cards and a cribbage board. "Do you play?" he asked. Ransom lit up. "Deal."

It seemed like they had been playing for hours when they heard the downstairs outside door creak. "Showtime?" whispered Ransom.

Then they heard a bottle break. It sounded like it came from the front steps. They didn't want to look out the window in case the FBI was testing to see if anyone was still in the office. They sat tight. The door rattled again and then silence. "Could've been a drunk," said Freeman. Ransom was thinking back to Vietnam and the military lessons about night vision. It was amazing how much you could see in the dark once your eyes had time to adjust, building what the Army called "visual purple." But it was troubling how quickly that visual purple could be lost after a blast of light. Inside the office, as long as they didn't look out the window, they had no problem seeing their cards or the holes in the cribbage board when they were pegging. They stood up and stretched and went back to their game.

More time passed and they heard a vehicle stop outside, maybe a truck or a van. They heard doors open and close and a clanking noise. Then they heard, as well as felt something hit the side of the building. "A ladder," whispered Ransom. Then the front door rattled and opened and shut. The stairs creaked as someone climbed them slowly. "One outside, one inside," whispered Ransom. "I'll take outside." They got up to take their positions behind the door to the outer office, taking care to move catlike around the furniture. Freeman took hold of the door handle so he could open it quickly while he operated his camera with his other hand.

They heard a key being inserted into the lock on the hallway door. A few seconds passed. The key was turned and the door opened. Someone stepped inside and the door closed. They heard footsteps cross the office and something was moved. It sounded like the chair behind Freeman's assistant's desk. Freeman and Ransom looked at each other as they prepared to make their move. They had agreed to nod as a signal to burst through the door. They heard a sound on the outside wall, like someone was prying something. Ransom pointed to himself and then toward the street, indicating he would take care of whoever was outside. Then he gave Freeman a thumbs-up sign. Freeman returned the thumbs-up and nodded a second before he twisted the handle, threw the door open and hit the light switch. Both cameras flashed and Ransom dashed for the window to get photos of what was going on outside.

Freeman stepped into the outer office. "Hello, Ian," he said. "Welcome back from the dead."

He shot photos of MacPherson stumbling backward with the desk lamp in his hand. Ransom opened the window, forcing it up to get a better angle on whoever was on the ladder outside. He knocked out the screen, which rang wind chimes hanging from a hook above the window. His camera flashed as he moved it outside, getting photos of a man in coveralls jumping off the ladder, sprinting to an unmarked van, and squealing off into the night. The ladder was left behind. Ransom put his camera on Freeman's desk and moved to the outer office to cut off the only escape route for the man holding the lamp. He locked the door.

"Sit down, Ian," ordered Freeman. He nodded to his assistant's desk chair. MacPherson did as he was told after seeing Ransom blocking the door to the hallway like a warrior.

"This is Mr. MacPherson," Freeman said. "Turning our attention to Exhibit A, empty your pockets. Put whatever's in 'em on the desk, your wallet, keys, everything."

While MacPherson complied, Ransom took Freeman's camera to the inner office. He returned with a legal notepad and a pen and put them on a small table between two chairs used by clients waiting for appointments.

"Do you have any weapons?" Freeman asked.

MacPherson shook his head.

"Answer me."

"Just a small knife."

"Put it on the desk and strip."

"Really?"

"Really."

MacPherson lifted a pants leg and pulled a six-inch knife from a sheath strapped to his lower leg. Then he took off his shoes and clothes.

"Underpants, shirt, and socks. Everything. Off."

"Oh man. Really?"

"Do it. Now."

He did.

Ransom picked up MacPherson's clothes, checked the pockets, and threw the clothes in the corner by the coat closet. He collected everything MacPherson had put on the desk, including a pack of cigarettes and a lighter, and set them on the table with the pad and pen.

"Sit," ordered Freeman.

MacPherson sat.

Freeman asked Ransom to get a tape recorder from his desk and bring it out. He did and returned to his post by the door.

Freeman sat in one of the client chairs. He turned on the tape recorder. He grabbed MacPherson's wallet and flipped it open. "Hmmm," he said. "Fake IDs, a couple of credit cards, phone numbers, a rubber. Only one? A picture of a girl, a fair amount of money, a concert ticket stub. Janis

Joplin."

He set the wallet aside and picked up a key ring with three keys. "How many of these are mine?"

MacPherson leaned across the desk to get a close look. "They're all yours," he said.

Freeman put the keys in his pocket. He picked up another ring with three keys on it.

"Whose are these?"

"Mine."

"What do they open?"

"Apartments."

"Whose apartments?"

"Mine and my girlfriend's and a friend's."

"Who's the friend?"

"Somebody I know."

"If you want to spend the night here, we can do that, but in the end we're going to get answers. Who's the friend?"

"A law enforcement contact."

"I want a name and position and employer."

"Frank Martino. Special agent. FBI."

"Where's the apartment?"

"Beacon Street."

"What's the address?"

"I don't remember. I just know where it is. It may be in Brookline."

"What's it used for?"

"Meetings. Instructions. Messages."

"Don't move."

Freeman got out of his chair and went into his inner office. He came back with a street map, opened it and positioned it on the desk in front of MacPherson.

"Show me where the Beacon Street apartment is."

MacPherson studied the map and pointed to an intersection, west of Kenmore Square and Fenway Park. "It's in an apartment building on that corner," he said. "Second floor, facing Beacon Street."

"Does Martino go there?"

"Sometimes."

"Was Martino in the van tonight?"

"No."

"Who was in the van?"

"I don't know."

"Were you in the van?"

"Yes."

"Why were you in the van with someone you don't know?"

"We were supposed to do a job."

"What was the job?"

"We were told to get the bugs out of your office."

"Who told you to do that?"

"Frank Martino."

"What was the other guy doing?"

"Getting the tap off the phone line."

"What were you doing?"

"Getting the bug in here."

"Where is it?"

"In the light on the desk."

"Get it and hand it to me."

He did.

"Did you put it there?"

"No."

"Who did?"

"Somebody I don't know. Just like tonight. The FBI has special people who do that kind of shit."

"When was it put there?"

"The weekend I stayed here."

"Who wanted to bug me?"

"Martino."

"Why?"

"'Cause Washington has this thing about Vietnam. Hoover ordered FBI surveillance on anti-war people all over the country. If they're Black, all the better. He wants to shut 'em down."

"Who gave Martino my name?"

"Me."

"Why?"

"He said he'd make trouble for me if I didn't give him some names."

"What kind of trouble?"

"I have some drug charges hanging over me. He said he'd put me in prison."

"Why did you pick me?"

"He told me I had to get close to activists and agitators and students, like the SDS. I heard about you through Boston Draft Resistance."

"There's no more keys on the table. Where's the locker key?"

"What locker?"

Freeman got up from his chair and circled behind the desk slowly, stopping behind the naked man sitting there. MacPherson didn't move. Freeman was struck by his bony shoulders and how skinny he looked without his clothes.

"Don't fuck with me, Ian," Freeman said, bending close to MacPherson's ear. "You're in a load of shit so deep you may drown. Do you want me to turn you over to the Army guys?"

"No."

Freeman continued walking to the front of the desk and sat back down, looking fiercely at MacPherson, whose head was bowed.

"Look at me," he commanded. "I need answers."

"What about confidentiality?" MacPherson's voice was weak. "You said what I told you was confidential, just between us."

"Your confidentiality ended when you bugged my office. I want that locker key. Lives depend on it and not just yours."

MacPherson didn't respond. He looked around, like he might find another way out that wasn't blocked by Ransom, who was as rigid as a Greek statue.

The phone rang, breaking the silence. Freeman let it ring until the answering machine kicked in. The person who called hung up without leaving a message.

"Who knows you're here?"

"Just Martino and that other guy."

"Where's the key?"

"Will you represent me?"

"I can't."

"I need a lawyer."

"I'm not a cop. I don't need to warn you of any rights."

"I'm not going to answer any more questions without a lawyer."

"You sent me a note with money when you faked your suicide. Why?"

"Because you were nice to me."

"But you didn't return the favor, did you?"

"No."

"Why did you want the cops to find that note and then me?"

"I don't know. I thought you might help me."

"The only way I'm going to help you is by getting that key. Where's it at?"

MacPherson shut down again. Freeman let the silence linger before asking Ransom to go through MacPherson's clothes another time to see if any keys might have been hidden or sewn into them. Then he turned his attention back to MacPherson, who looked pathetic, emaciated.

"Does the FBI know about the SDS raid and the drugs you're hiding?"
No response.

"Do you think you can trade the drugs for your life?"
No reply.

"Did the money you left for me come from the drug vest?"
Still nothing.

Ransom stood up from the pile of clothes. "Got something," he said. He held out MacPherson's jacket for Freeman to see. He was grinning. He took out a pocketknife and cut into the jacket's lining near the zipper. "Bingo," he said, pulling out a key.

Freeman looked back to MacPherson.

"Is that the key to the locker with the vest and drugs and cash?"

MacPherson held up his hands, like a signal of surrender. "I need a minute to think," he said.

"OK, we'll take a break," said Freeman. "You know, Ian, this is a dangerous game you're playing. You're not very good at it. You might want to try something else."

He picked up MacPherson's wallet, cigarettes, lighter, knife, and keys and asked Ransom to join him in his inner office.

"Can you leave the cigarettes and lighter?" said MacPherson. "I need a smoke."

"Get real," said Freeman.

Ransom asked Freeman to stay in the outer office for a minute while he went to the inner office. He looked out the window, glancing up and down the street. He saw one man in a doorway wearing a newsboy flat cap. Ransom reached out the window and gave Johnny a thumbs-up sign. Then he unhooked the chimes from the window. He took them back to the outer office and hung them around MacPherson's neck. MacPherson cringed and twitched as the cold metal chimes hit his bare chest. Ransom gathered MacPherson's clothes and shoes into a bundle. "I don't think you'll be going anywhere without these," he said. "It would be a mistake to try to leave."

He returned to Freeman's inner office with MacPherson's clothes. As he passed through the door, he reached for his handgun and took it off the shelf in a way that MacPherson could see he was armed. He left the door open a crack.

*   *   *   *

Freeman plucked Arruda's card from his Rolodex and showed it to Ransom, who pulled a chair close enough to talk without being heard in the next room.

They agreed to give MacPherson one more chance to answer questions before turning him over to Arruda. Catching him breaking into the office would almost certainly mean having to tell Arruda everything about everything. He'd need a team to take on that many investigations.

Ransom heard a jingle of chimes from the next room and moved to the door in a flash. MacPherson was shifting his position in the chair. "I need to go to the bathroom," he said.

Ransom opened the door and followed MacPherson down the hallway to the bathroom. He checked to make sure nobody else was in it and there was no other way out. He shut the door and waited outside. When MacPherson was done, they returned to the office, where Freeman was waiting for them.

Freeman had his tape recorder on the table. He turned it on after MacPherson sat down. He asked whether the key Ransom found in the jacket would open the drug locker.

"Yes."

"Are the drugs still there?"

"As far as I know."

"How about the money?"

"Some of it."

"Where's the locker?"

"South Station."

"What's the locker number?"

"103."

"When was the last time you opened it?"

"A couple of weeks ago."

"Why?"

"I needed money."

"I'm going to stop there," said Freeman. "You realize we're going to have to turn you over to the police."

"Really? I just gave you what you want. If you let me go, we'll call it even and I'll never bother you again."

"You shouldn't be surprised that's not going to happen. We're not going to take your word that the key opens the locker and the drugs are there."

"Then let's go to South Station and I'll show you."

"We can't do that. The police need to do that and only after they get a search warrant."

"Oh man."

"If you're being straight with us, if you don't try to bullshit your way out of this with the police or the court, as long as you tell the truth, I'll be on your side. I'll testify, I'll write letters asking for leniency. Your only way out of this shithole you've dug for yourself is to cooperate and tell the truth. Do you understand?"

"Oh man."

"Do you understand?"

"Yeah."

"I'm going to call the detective now. He was here yesterday asking about you and that note in your backpack."

"Who is it?"

"A guy named Arruda. You know him?"

"I've met him. Why him?"

"You can ask him." He turned off the recorder and went to his office. MacPherson and Ransom could hear Freeman on the phone, asking for

Arruda, asking that someone give Arruda a call as soon as possible, that it was important because MacPherson was alive and detained in his office.

Freeman returned to the outer office, sat down next to the recorder, and turned it on again. He asked MacPherson why he tried to fake his suicide. He said he wanted to get the Army guys off his back.

"Did you tell the FBI what you were doing?"

He shook his head no.

Freeman suggested the FBI might have helped him get a new identity. MacPherson said the FBI doesn't help anybody except the FBI. He said he had no future, that the FBI had him in a stranglehold, that they'd use him to do their bidding until there was nothing left that he could do for them and then they'd turn their backs and feed him to the wolves. "That's my life sentence for selling dime bags," he said. "I just wanted to have a good time and help my friends get high. I never imagined it would end like this. First it was the Boston police, then the FBI. The cops wanted me to rat out my friends. Then the FBI ordered me to get close to the SDS and the protesters. That fucking war fucks up everything."

Freeman asked him how he thought he could get away with faking a suicide. MacPherson said he didn't think. He just had to do something. He said the newspaper carried a story about his suicide, but the FBI didn't see it. "They didn't even know I was supposed to be dead," he said.

Freeman asked again whether the FBI knew about the SDS raid and the drugs.

"Not from me," MacPherson said. "I didn't know I was going to be part of a raid until that night. By then it was too late. The FBI would have wanted to catch the SDS in the act. I never told Martino about the raid because he'd send me to prison for fucking that up. I fuck everything up. I could fuck up a wet dream."

"Stop," Freeman said sharply. "Stop whining. Stop running. You need to make a decision. Tonight's a golden opportunity to put all that stuff behind you. Cooperate with the cops. Get the FBI off your back. Put those twisted killer soldiers away in a prison so dark they'll never get out. What are you going to do?"

"I know what I should do, but I don't know if I can."

"You can. Believe in yourself."

"I can't."

"You can."

Ransom cut into the conversation by stomping his foot.

"Fuck this," he said. "No more bullshit, MacPherson. You are really pissing me off. You're so weak. Take control of your life. It's decision time. Life or death?"

Faintly, MacPherson said, "Life."

Ransom picked up MacPherson's clothes and put them on the desk.

"Get dressed," said Freeman.

He turned off the tape recorder. The phone rang. It was the Boston police. Arruda was on his way. It was getting close to midnight.

*   *   *   *

Arruda put MacPherson in handcuffs as soon as he reached the office. He took brief statements from Freeman and Ransom about what happened and hauled MacPherson off to the police station to spend the night in a cell.

Arruda caught some sleep at home before returning to the station around noon. He wanted to get enough information from MacPherson to prepare a search warrant application and get it signed by a judge before Thanksgiving, which was two days away. He also planned to talk with Ransom, who had fresh information and a plan to catch the leader of the Army drug crew.

MacPherson was delivered in handcuffs to a Police Department interview room, where Arruda questioned him for four hours. The pieces of the puzzle started to fit into place, and a new piece was added when Arruda asked MacPherson about the territorial dispute involving the Irish gang. The Irish and the Italians had emerged as the strongest of Boston's criminal gangs after murderous wars that started in 1961 and finally settled down over the past year. More than fifty people had been killed.

Arruda was familiar with the history of the gang wars. MacPherson was aware Army soldiers had been selling heroin in Roxbury and had been threatened by the Irish gang if they did not pay to play. The Irish controlled drugs, gambling, and loansharking in Dorchester and Roxbury. The soldiers ignored the Irish gang's demands for payments, and one of them was beaten so badly with a baseball bat that he died while another

Army crew member was forced to watch. That was a few days before the SDS raid on the Army base. So in less than a week, the soldiers lost one of their crew as well as their drugs and their money. The soldier who witnessed the beating was so terrified, according to MacPherson, that he contacted the FBI to go after the Irish gang for the killing. That soldier was now missing and presumed dead.

What jolted Arruda was that MacPherson suspected the murdering leaders of the Irish gang were federal informants, protected by the FBI as long as they provided the kind of tips the FBI wanted. Who would know more about informing than an informant? If what MacPherson said was true, there didn't seem to be any limits to what the FBI would let the Irish gang do. During the drug wars, a lot of the gang's criminal competitors had been killed and the police had assumed the Irish were responsible. Arruda knew a number of cases against the Irish had been dropped because witnesses were murdered or disappeared. As long as the cases appeared to involve criminals killing criminals, police and prosecutors seemed to shrug them off. To imagine the FBI could have fingered witnesses for execution to protect the Irish gang from the Boston police or the Massachusetts state police was astonishing to Arruda. And yet now he was investigating the Irish gang for the murder-disappearance of an Army soldier after that soldier told the FBI he saw another soldier beaten to death by the Irish. That raised the stakes considerably. Arruda knew he should also be investigating the FBI, but that was not possible, not without far more resources than he could ever put together. He wondered who would be killed next, and worried that innocent bystanders could be caught in the crossfire.

25

Wednesday, November 27, 1968
Boston

Lisa parked her pickup truck a few doors down from the bar and noted the time, 7 P.M. The Silver Dollar's neon sign was flashing. She looked at herself in the rearview mirror. She had tied her hair up, leaving some wisps dangling to frame her face. She had thought about lipstick, but that was too much. Underneath, she was still an unvarnished nature girl. She took a deep breath, exhaled through her mouth, and opened the driver's door. She swung out of her seat to the pavement. She was wearing a miniskirt with a low-cut blouse and had borrowed one of her mother's jackets without asking. She was also wearing a bohemian cross-body bag with Native American beading. She could feel the weight of the revolver inside resting against her hip. She was nervous. She hadn't told anyone what she was about to do.

Freeman had called her Tuesday afternoon to tell her about MacPherson being caught. She was thrilled the police were going for a warrant to search the locker where the drugs were supposed to be hidden. "Now all we have to do is connect the drugs and the murders to the right soldier," she told Freeman. He said Ransom and Johnny were working on that. She cut the conversation short, saying she had to tell her mother about MacPherson. She was worried that if she stayed on the phone with Freeman any longer she might slip up and give her plan away. She didn't want him or anyone else to talk her out of it.

She would have felt safer if Ransom or Johnny were backing her up. Johnny inspired confidence with his ability to show up when needed and accomplish just about anything. But she didn't really know Johnny.

Nobody did, and it seemed nobody ever would. Still, she was comforted that he was out there somewhere in the shadows likely aware of what she was doing. She had his phone number if the situation demanded it, but she wasn't ready to call him just yet. She had only met Peter Ransom once, just like Johnny, and was impressed by both of them for different reasons. Ransom had survived unspeakable horrors of war with his integrity and compassion intact. Lisa felt lucky to have him on her side, like he was a gift, like maybe they were destined to meet. He lifted her spirits, gave her hope that she could endure the deaths of her brother and father and somehow come out stronger. She trusted him. She wanted to know more about him, but she couldn't ask for his help with her latest task because the soldiers knew him. She had to go into their hangout alone.

She walked through the door into the smoke-filled darkness of the Silver Dollar. They were at the far end of the bar in their uniforms, talking in a cluster. A few empty bar stools were close by. She took one, hung her bag on the backrest and ordered a beer. It didn't take long for a soldier to approach and ask if she was alone.

"I am," she said. "How about you?" He said he came in to have a beer with soldiers who worked for him. He asked if he could take the stool next to her. They exchanged names. Lisa used her real name. She didn't want to confuse herself with a fake name and screw up whatever was about to happen. His name was Bill, and the name tag on his shirt pocket read Sanders. He asked if she was too warm with her jacket on and offered to hang it up for her. She declined his offer, but took it off and watched him check out her breasts. She hung the jacket on the back of her stool over her bag. She didn't want him to get too close to the gun.

They talked and drank beers for a couple of hours, long enough for the other soldiers to leave. They ordered burgers and fries. Sanders paid. While they were eating, he asked Lisa where she was from. She told him Vermont, that she had come to Boston to visit relatives.

"For Thanksgiving?"

Lisa twisted in surprise and slipped off her stool, reaching out quickly to make sure her bag didn't also slide off and drop to the floor with a thud. She had forgotten about Thanksgiving.

"Are you OK?"

"Yes. I just lost my balance. I was getting ready to go to the bathroom.

Thanksgiving. Yes. Where's the bathroom?"

When she returned, Sanders was smoking a cigarette. She asked him to put it out because the smell bothered her. "No problem," he said, snuffing it. "It's a bad habit. I should quit. I just need to find the right time."

Lisa said she understood. Sanders asked her about Vermont, saying he had never been north of Massachusetts. They talked about Vermont's picture postcard mountains and lakes and streams and small towns and family farms. She told him she lived on a farm that had been in her family for generations.

She asked where he was from—North Carolina—why he was in the Army—he enlisted to be an officer rather than being drafted when he graduated from college—whether he had been to Vietnam—he had—how it was—horrifying—where he worked now—at the nearby induction center where new soldiers are sworn in to the Army—whether he swore them in—he did—how he felt about that—awful, but somebody has to do it—and how long he would stay in the Army. He said he would get out in a few months when his enlistment was due to end. She asked how he felt about the war. He said it was already lost and pointless. She asked whether he had thought about joining Vietnam Veterans Against the War. He had and would go to demonstrations after he was discharged. Why wait, she asked. "Good question," he said, pausing to weigh how to answer. "I've kept my opinions to myself while I've been in the Army because I'm an officer and I have a job to do. Now I'm beginning to rethink that. It seems the only way the war will end is if the soldiers end it. We've got to speak up, but it takes a lot of guts to refuse to fight. Some do. Some won't go out on patrol. Some won't do anything after they've been there a while and quite a few go AWOL. That's when . . ."

Lisa cut in. "I know what AWOL is."

"Yes. Sorry. Anyway, just about anybody who's been to Nam knows we've already lost. The Vietnamese won't stop fighting. They'll never give up their country. So yes, I'll start protesting, maybe even before I'm discharged. I'm sorry now that I wasn't more active before, but it's hard when you're an officer."

She was struck by the apparent honesty of his words. She didn't know how to respond. She stared into her glass. This can't be the same guy who deals drugs and kills people, she thought. She asked him how he felt about the war before he went to Vietnam. He said he hadn't really thought about it because of the draft. "You go because you have to go. You're advised to serve your time quietly and get out and get on with your life."

"If you're still alive," she said.

"Yeah," he said.

He looked like he was about to order another beer and changed his mind. He asked what she planned to do while she was in Boston. She told him she wanted to go to the beach before she left, even though it was almost December. She loved the ocean, the sand, the salt water, the smells, the sounds, the creatures. He asked if she had ever been on the beach at night. She had.

"Would you like to go tonight?" he asked. "It's clear outside. There'll be stars and shadows from the moon. I'm sure there'll be other people there, walking the beach. We can take my car."

If he wants to kidnap me, she thought, he's got me. She said yes.

He lifted her jacket off the stool and held it for her to put on. She made sure to grab her bag before he tried to lift that as well. They walked to his gleaming red two-seat Alfa Romeo. On the way she pointed out her pickup truck. His car was a convertible and he had the top on because it was cold. He asked if she wanted him to take it down. She said to leave it up for warmth, and they headed off into the night south of Boston. She had rarely been down that way, so she paid attention to where he was going in case she had to get away. She was impressed by the comfort of the leather seat and complimented him on his choice of the Alfa. "It's my one expensive pleasure," he said.

She had noticed the Army sticker on the rear bumper. She wondered why his car would be on a Roxbury street where heroin was sold if he wasn't part of the drug ring. It would be stupid for a drug dealer to take this car there. It would stand out like a flag. From what she had seen so far, Sanders was not stupid. It was beginning to look like somebody was setting him up to take the fall in a drug bust. Other soldiers could have been using his office at the base to cover their asses. They would have needed access to his car. She reached for the shift lever, feeling its leather cover with her fingers.

"Do you ever let other people drive it?" she asked.

"Would you like to try it out?"

That was not the answer she expected. "Really?"

"Yeah, really."

"I'd love to."

He pulled to the curb and they switched seats. He explained the shifting and the controls and gauges. Maybe I should kidnap him, she thought as she adjusted her seat. She checked the mirrors and turned the key. The engine sounded strong. She let out the clutch and the car quivered and stalled. "Sensitive," she said.

"Yeah. Not like a pickup truck."

She got used to the clutch quickly and felt secure behind the wheel. "Bet your soldiers would like to drive it," she said.

"I have a sergeant who wishes he had one. I've let him take it out a few times. Kind of like test drives while his car was being worked on."

"Is he going to get one?"

"He says he will when he has enough money."

Sanders said he couldn't remember ever riding in the passenger seat. He ran his hands over everything like he was sizing up a new car. He gave her directions as she drove. He described the beach, named Nantasket, as a beautiful finger of sand extending a few miles into Massachusetts Bay. Along the way one road had a series of curves where she was able to feel how well the car cornered. "Such a pleasure to drive," she said as she parked where he suggested. "Thanks for letting me take the wheel. That was such a treat."

"You're welcome," he said. "It's a fun car. But I'm sure a pickup truck makes more sense on a Vermont farm."

"Not much room for manure in yours," she said, "even with the top down."

They took off their shoes and carried them into the cool sand. Lisa wore her cross-body bag. The lights of Boston's tallest buildings were visible far across the bay. The tide was low, and they could see people through the darkness out by the water. Billowing white clouds drifted across the moon. When they got to the water, small waves drifted peacefully across the sand, depositing a patchy line of seaweed snaking into the distance. They followed the seaweed, walking silently, passing a few other couples, picking up stones and sea glass and shells, examining them in the moonlight and tossing most back onto the firm sand where the tides would determine what went where and when.

Lisa was thinking about Chris, how they had spent so many good times at different beaches, most north of Boston, playing in the sand with tiny buckets and shovels when they were young and later with Frisbees and volleyballs. They loved the salt water and spent a lot of time in it, bodysurfing and swimming and playing games. There were meals on the beach with their parents and later campfires with their friends. At times, the beach felt so comfortably removed from the world that it became a sanctuary where they could rest their weary minds to the rhythm of waves and try to figure things out without distractions.

Lisa was lost in her thoughts when she looked down and remembered she was walking next to a barefoot uniformed soldier who was supposed to be a murdering drug kingpin who killed Chris and might kidnap her. She didn't believe it. She wanted to tell him who she was. She wanted to question him about the Army report on Chris. She wanted to find out how bad he was or whether he might even be good. She knew that Freeman and Ransom and Stillman and Bear, along with her mother, wouldn't want her to do what she was doing. But she was worried about Peter Ransom. If Sanders wasn't bad, she needed to warn Ransom about his next meeting with that other soldier.

"Check this out," said Sanders.

He held up a piece of driftwood. It was worn smooth and shaped like a rifle.

"This is what I've become. Everything I see looks like a weapon," he said and tossed the driftwood into the loose sand above the waterline. "Maybe it'll get burned in a campfire before some kid uses it to play war."

"It must be awful being haunted by war," said Lisa. "What you said about kids is so true. Kids start fighting when they're toddlers, even when they're brothers and sisters or especially when they're brothers and sisters, instead of working things out. It's who gets the candy or the ball, and when they grow up, it's who gets the most money and power. If I had a magic wand, I'd wipe away greed."

"That," he said, "would have to be a mighty powerful wand."

They walked on in silence.

"Do you get high?" Lisa asked

"Sometimes."

"Do you have any with you?"

"No, I hardly ever do. Mostly I smoke when other people have some."

"Me too," she said. "We should probably turn around soon and head back to the car."

They stopped and looked out across the bay to the dome of stars and the lights of the Boston skyline.

"It's a beautiful night," he said.

"It sure is," she said. "And on this beautiful night, I've got to ask you something."

"You've been asking a lot," he said.

She laughed. "Yes, " she said. "I guess I've asked a lot of questions. Now I've got to tell you something. I'm not here by accident. I wanted to get to know you."

"I sensed this might be something like that. Why?"

She turned to face him. "Because from what I'd seen before tonight you're supposed to be a ruthless drug dealer who killed my brother."

He stepped back in shock.

"A drug dealer?"

"Who killed my brother."

"When am I supposed to have done that?"

"Almost two months ago during an initiation ceremony."

"Initiation into what?"

"I don't mean initiation. I mean induction. Into the Army."

"What's your brother's name?"

"Chris Thompson. You signed a report about him."

Sanders looked puzzled.

"What kind of report?"

"The Army called it an accident report. The report said my brother fell down some stairs."

"I remember that. You said he was killed."

"Yes. He was in a coma and died at Mass General. A couple of soldiers who were with him the day he was hurt said you were upset at my brother because he brought up an SDS raid."

"Oh that."

"My brother worked with Boston Draft Resistance and he was going to refuse induction."

"Yes."

"Instead he was brutally attacked and killed."

"How do you know that?"

"We have a statement from an ambulance attendant who heard his last words on the way to the hospital."

"I don't remember any statement like that."

"The Army took his statement, but it wasn't in the report you sent me."

"Oh no. Oh shit."

"What does that mean?"

"If what you're telling me is true, it means I've got, we've got a very serious problem."

"Yes you do, and it's more than my brother's death."

"What else is it?"

"I've talked to someone who was involved with the SDS raid, and the people who did the damage found a large quantity of drugs and cash in your office."

"What?"

"They were in a vest in a filing cabinet, and they took it."

"Do you have this vest?"

"No, but I know someone who knows where it is."

"Have you talked to the police?"

"No, but the police unintentionally found out about it."

"When?"

"Yesterday. It's a complicated situation. At some point the police are going to want to talk to you."

"Yes. From what you say, I'm sure they will. I can tell you this. If there were drugs in my office, it was nothing I knew anything about. What kind of drugs?"

"Heroin."

"Holy shit. I'm sorry."

"No problem. Two of the SDS raiders were found dead of heroin overdoses a week or two after the raid."

"Jesus Christ."

"Can you think of anyone who works for you who could have stashed drugs in your office and killed people because his drugs were stolen?"

"Fuckin' A."

"Is that a yes?"

"Yes."

"Would that be someone who has borrowed your car?"

"Yes."

"His name wouldn't be Miller would it?"

"Goddamn. How do you know so much?"

"It cost my brother his life and others could still be in danger, including me."

26

Thursday, Thanksgiving,
November 28, 1968
Lexington

Mary Lou longed for the peace of snow-covered mountains. She really wanted to go to Vermont for a few days. She was feeling an overwhelming need to escape the Lexington house. It had become the house of gloom, moving from room to room, wanting to see Art, to talk to him, expecting to hear him in the shower or see him in the bedroom or sitting in a chair reading the newspaper or at work on his capitalist corruption project in his new office, the bedroom where Chris grew up. She would go to the door and look inside and see Art's desk and Chris's "First Casualty" poster on the wall. She wanted to go in, but didn't feel the timing was right. It might never be right. She felt like she'd be intruding. She didn't want to disturb anything. She wondered if Art's spirit might have visited the room. She wondered if Chris's spirit had visited and seen that Art had used it as his office. She imagined the two of them, their spirits, in the room together, in a comfortable space where they could relax. But how could they relax when Chris's killers hadn't been caught? And how could Art relax when the corruption package he meticulously put together for the FBI and the newspapers was still sitting on his desktop? Two boxes with two cover letters. She knew now that the package had to go to the newspapers. To send it to the FBI would be an obscenity. But first she had to get the package to Freeman for his review before giving it to anyone.

She wondered if Chris's spirit knew that she and Art had been tear-gassed by police at their last demonstration before Art died. It made them feel that they had been initiated. It was during a march that began at Boston Common. They weren't hit directly by the gas, but they got the taste and the sting of it as the cloud wafted past them. Some demonstrators carried gas masks in anticipation of trouble. Art had told her tear gas was created as a weapon during World War I. Now it was being used on protesters trying to end wars. Anyone who knew anything about the history of the world should have seen that coming. She and Art had talked about buying their own gas masks for future protests, but then he had his heart attack. She wondered if his death could be a consequence of the gas they inhaled.

At the demonstrations, she and Art were surprised at the number of disabled Vietnam vets they saw. Some were in need of medical care, living on the streets, panhandling after being discharged, enraged and depressed that they had been abandoned by their government. Some had combat injuries caused by American weapons, chief among them Agent Orange, the defoliant used to deprive the Viet Cong of jungle cover. Agent Orange didn't distinguish between Americans and Vietnamese or soldiers and civilians or old and young.

After Art's sudden death, Mary Lou started looking at help-wanted ads in the *Boston World*, seeing what was available for jobs. She had taught elementary school after college, then did some substitute teaching while Chris and Lisa were growing up, but had not taught in years. She worried that the world had passed her by and she wouldn't be able to pay the bills. But then Freeman told her that Art had taken out a large life insurance policy after he quit his defense job. Freeman offered to help her sort out the financial consequences of Art's death and take care of the necessary paperwork, and she was grateful.

Mary Lou was sitting at the kitchen table with a cup of coffee, thinking about all that when she remembered it was Thanksgiving. It had always been her favorite holiday, but this year she dreaded its arrival.

Lisa slept late. When she came to the kitchen, Mary Lou put on a pleasant face and asked whether she had a nice evening out. Lisa told her she went for a walk on the beach under the stars and that it felt liberating to get out of the house.

"You looked like you were dressed to meet someone at a restaurant," said Mary Lou.

"I was," said Lisa. "And I did."

"Anyone I know?" Mary Lou asked.

"Only by name," said Lisa. She hadn't planned to tell her mother about Sanders, but she didn't want to hide anything, especially now, after she made it back home alive. She told her about the Silver Dollar and the Alfa and Nantasket Beach and her impression that he could not possibly be the drug-running killer they imagined. She also shared her suspicion that Miller, the soldier who approached Peter Ransom, was the real monster.

Mary Lou wanted to scold her daughter, but said she was proud of what Lisa had discovered and was concerned for Ransom.

Lisa was already reaching for the phone. She called Rose. No answer. She called Freeman. No answer.

"Oh shit," she said. "It's Thanksgiving. I keep forgetting. I'm sorry mom. I'm swearing too much these days. I have to work on that. But first I've got to find Peter. One day somebody is going to make one of those wristwatch phones like Dick Tracy has so you can call somebody no matter where they are or you are."

"Maybe in a hundred years," said Mary Lou.

"I heard he has a TV on his watch in the latest comics."

"That's pure fantasy," her mother said. "I can't believe we both forgot today is Thanksgiving. I don't feel like cooking."

"I know what you mean. We can go to a restaurant."

Mary Lou said what she really wanted was to go to Vermont. She suggested they could both go and check on the farm and spread Chris's and Art's ashes. Lisa said that was a great idea, but she needed to reach Ransom first.

Mary Lou left the kitchen to get dressed. Lisa made herself a large cup of tea and had some leftover oatmeal and a piece of toast while replaying in her mind the conversation on the beach with Sanders. Her new target was Miller. She couldn't remember whether the Army accident file said anything about him. She retrieved the file from her bedroom, spread it out on the kitchen table, and made a second cup of tea. Miller was listed as a participant in the induction ceremony and as one of two sergeants who escorted Chris from the induction room. The file had a statement from Miller, saying he led Chris to a stairway where Chris jerked his arm loose from Miller's grasp and fell. Nobody else saw what happened.

"You're the one," Lisa said to herself. "You bastard."

Mary Lou returned to the kitchen and asked about the Army file on the table. Lisa told her it confirmed what she suspected, that Miller was the only soldier who was with Chris when he was hurt.

Lisa dialed Rose's number again. Rose answered. She didn't know where Ransom was. He hadn't come back to her apartment the night before. One of his packs was still in her living room. Rose assumed he might have spent the night at Lisa's house. Lisa didn't want to alarm Rose. She said Peter was probably with Freeman and she'd let her know when she located him.

Lisa tried Freeman's home phone and he answered. He hadn't heard from Peter since the previous day when he was supposed to have had a follow-up meeting with Miller. She told him about her excursion with Sanders and her suspicion that Miller was the real killer.

"I wish you would've let us know," Freeman said. "We could have backed you up."

"Next time," she said. "Right now, I'm worried about Peter."

"He can take care of himself," Freeman said. "I know he doesn't trust Miller. I'm going to get a message to Sal Arruda, the detective. He needs to know what's up. Even if it is Thanksgiving."

After he hung up, Freeman's first thought was how frustrating it was that he didn't have a phone number for Johnny. He wondered whether Johnny had planted any listening devices in his office so he would know when he was needed. If Johnny had bugged his office, maybe he'd also bugged his apartment. So he said out loud, his neck craned to the ceiling, "Johnny, if you can hear me, give me a call as soon as possible. We don't know where Peter Ransom is. Lisa thinks Miller, the guy Peter's trying to flip, is the real killer. Last we knew, Peter was gonna meet him again. Hope to hear from you soon man."

Freeman felt more than foolish. Here he was talking to the ceiling, hoping the mysterious Johnny Dollar was listening and would materialize out of nowhere to save the day. In the meantime, he picked up the phone and called the Boston police to ask that someone let Arruda know Peter Ransom was missing.

He wondered if Arruda would get back to him. Or ever talk to him again. Two days ago, he woke the detective out of bed at midnight, and now he was interrupting his family's Thanksgiving Day celebration.

Freeman wouldn't be seeing any members of his own family for Thanksgiving. They were spread across the country. His first ancestors to reach North America had been hijacked from their homeland and shipped to South Carolina and sold as slaves. After emancipation, they endured the racial repression and segregation brought on by the Jim Crow laws. That and the civil rights movement of the 1950s inspired Freeman to become his family's first college graduate and then a lawyer. The movement's persistence and strength and the charismatic leadership of Martin Luther King led to the passage of the federal Civil Rights Act of 1964 and the Voting Rights Act of 1965, laws that were supposed to end the Jim Crow era. But some states, among them South Carolina, continued to resist racial reforms. Many members of Freeman's extended family had left South Carolina, but his parents still lived there. He hadn't considered joining them for Thanksgiving because he was so busy in Boston. He'd have to call them later.

Arruda phoned around noontime. Arruda said he had new information and would meet Freeman at his office Friday morning. He said Ransom would join them.

*   *   *   *

South Station was a magnificent building facing Dewey Square with a three-story curved classical front featuring ionic columns. It was built in 1899 as a single combined terminal for the railroads serving Boston. In the early 1900s it achieved prestige as the busiest transportation hub in the world.

On Thanksgiving Day, Ransom and Johnny were surprised at how many people were passing through the cavernous station. They were looking for anyone who would stop at one particular luggage locker. They were positioned on a second-tier balcony where they could be out of sight from the open floor below while keeping their eyes on the locker. They had been conducting surveillance in one form or another for almost twenty-four hours straight.

On Wednesday they adopted a tag-team strategy to protect Lisa and keep track of Miller. Johnny suspected Lisa might want to find out for herself what Sanders was like. So he wasn't surprised when her aging pickup appeared in front of the Silver Dollar in the evening while he was tracking Sanders and his red Alfa. He was concerned hours later when he saw her get into the Alfa with Sanders, but felt better after they switched seats and she took the wheel. His unease returned when they walked off together into the darkness of Nantasket Beach. He shadowed them from a distance, too far to hear what they talked about but close enough that he could be by her side quickly if needed. When they returned to the car after midnight, their body language told him there was no reason to be alarmed. He followed them back to the Silver Dollar, where Lisa shook hands with Sanders before she drove home. Johnny wanted to know what she learned, but he didn't have time to find out. He had arranged to reconnect with Ransom at South Station, which is where they hoped to find some action.

Ransom and Johnny had known each other less than a week, but with their shared military experience, they rapidly developed a trusting friendship. Neither of them believed Miller's story about wanting to expose Sanders. They decided to flush him out. They coordinated their moves with Arruda.

Ransom had called Miller Wednesday afternoon from a pay phone, and they agreed to meet a couple of hours later at Boston Common. When they connected, Ransom told Miller the Police Department had applied for a warrant to search a locker at South Station for the drug vest. The police had the key to locker 103. The key had come from an informant. Miller acted nervous. It seemed genuine. He asked why the police would need him if they already had an informant. Ransom said Miller's cooperation would be critical to link the drugs to Sanders. Miller pressed Ransom to tell him where he was getting his information, but he refused. He said he would provide the same kind of anonymity for Miller if he decided to cooperate with the cops. He wouldn't name him without his permission. Miller asked how he would know when the police got the warrant and what they found in the locker. Ransom said he'd call him as soon as he heard anything. Their conversation was brief, and they went their separate ways.

Ransom didn't need to follow Miller. He already knew he lived in a second-floor apartment of a rented carriage house in Dorchester. Johnny had tracked him there. Ransom waited until Miller was out of sight before he got on his Harley and headed to South Station. He thought about going back to Rose's apartment first, but he didn't have enough time now that he'd given Miller the locker number. Rose was probably at her mother's place anyway, celebrating Thanksgiving with Melanie, but without Bear. Fort Dix trainees didn't get Thanksgiving passes.

Ransom was having trouble keeping his eyes open when Johnny arrived at South Station around 2 A.M. with a couple of cups of coffee. Johnny told him about Lisa and Sanders at the Silver Dollar and on the beach. That woke him up.

"I'm starting to like her a lot," Ransom said. "She doesn't sit still for very long, and she isn't afraid to take chances. This is probably going to come out wrong, but you know what she'd be good at? She'd make a great soldier. She's brave, confident, smart, dependable, someone you could trust on the battlefield."

"She's a lot like her brother," Johnny said. "No fear, even when a little fear, you know, might be good to have."

"She's so different from the girls I've known," Ransom said. "In college most of them just wanted to find a guy to marry to take care of them for the rest of their lives. I don't get the sense that Lisa wants a man for a protector or a meal ticket. Hell, I don't even know if she wants a man. But I'd like to find out."

Johnny was wearing his flat cap and had his shoeshine box with him. Ransom asked what the box was for. Johnny opened it and inside were two cameras, the Leica and a Canon with a motor drive and a zoom lens, along with shoe polish and brushes and rags. "Convenient place to keep the cameras," said Ransom. "Do you plan to shine shoes?"

Johnny nodded, "Yep." He reached for the Canon and raised it to his eye. He shifted his position so he could see through a gap in the metal railing to the lockers below. He adjusted the lens to focus on locker 103 and handed the camera to Ransom. He tried it out. "This should work," he said. "Are you really gonna shine shoes?"

"It gives me cover and gets me down on the floor near the lockers," he said. "I might even make some money. Everyone should want a nice shine on Thanksgiving."

They finished their coffees and agreed to sleep in two-hour shifts. Ransom said he was tired enough to sleep even after the coffee. The only option for laying down was a bench. He stretched out, rolled up his jacket, tucked it under his head, and closed his eyes. Johnny let him sleep until sunrise before waking him. "Nothing yet," he said, and then took his turn on the bench. Ransom let him sleep until noon. They took turns for the bathroom and to get something to eat.

Refreshed by midafternoon, Johnny went down on the floor with his shoeshine box. He couldn't see Ransom from below. That was good. But there were uncertainties ahead. They didn't know how many people Miller had working with him. He would probably send one or more of them to retrieve the vest. They didn't expect Miller would show up unless it was to check for trouble. Other uncertainties were what the soldiers would do with the vest: where they would take it and how difficult it would be to follow them. Another question was whether any other shoe shiners would show up and create trouble because Johnny was intruding on their turf. He hadn't seen any so far. He managed six shines in two hours before he returned to the balcony, and he hadn't seen anyone stop near the locker. Soon darkness descended on the city and foot traffic through the terminal picked up. He and Ransom considered it a prime time for Miller to strike.

They had noted when they saw cleaning crews and police officers on the terminal's main floor. The cleaners made their rounds about every three hours and a police officer walked the floor every two hours or so. At 8 P.M., when nothing should have been happening, Ransom saw a man in blue coveralls pushing a green trash barrel on wheels toward the luggage lockers. He checked the Canon to make sure it was ready for action. Johnny picked up his shoeshine box and headed for the stairs. Before he made it to the floor, indoor emergency lights started flashing and alarms sounded. Fire alarms.

Ransom aimed his camera on the area around locker 103. The man in blue coveralls was in his range of vision. He pulled a crowbar from the trash barrel, inserted it behind the locking mechanism on the door of 103 and pried. Ransom could see the veins standing out on his neck, but not his face. The locker door buckled, and he forced it open. He reached inside and pulled out an olive drab vest. He stepped back to look at it, giving Ransom a good view of his head in profile as the lights flashed. He fired off a few photos. The man turned away from the locker, exposing his face to Ransom. He got a few more shots. It wasn't Miller, but Ransom thought he remembered the face from the Silver Dollar.

The man left the trash barrel and moved quickly toward the doors that faced Dewey Square. People below were scampering like ants all over the main floor where the lights were flashing. Alarms were still sounding. Ransom stood up to get a better view. He kept his lens focused on the man in blue and got photos of him handing the vest off to another man in a black jacket wearing a dark baseball cap going in the opposite direction. Ransom switched his focus to the man in black. He had his jacket collar raised high around his neck to obscure his face. Someone bumped into him, and he turned far enough for Ransom to see his face. It was Miller. He fired off a couple of photos and his film ran out. Miller elbowed his way through the crowd to get to the door. Ransom looked for Johnny. He must have seen the handoff because he was following Miller.

Ransom dashed down the stairs and worked his way to the locker. It was empty, except for the crowbar. He laid his jacket over his hand and picked up the crowbar, thinking it would preserve fingerprints. He put it in his backpack, which was on the floor. He checked the trash barrel. It was empty except for a few cigarette butts and a matchbook at the bottom. He tucked the Canon in a pocket on his backpack and reached into the barrel for the matchbook. "Silver Dollar." He heard two gunshots and headed for the exit.

When he reached the doors to the street, his heart was pounding and a police officer was down on the sidewalk, groaning and clutching his midsection. Johnny was bent over him with his head close to the officer's face, talking to him. Other people surrounded them. Johnny looked up and urged them to call for an ambulance, as well as the police. He reached into his shoeshine box for a rag and saw Ransom. He shouted that the officer got one shot off and thought he hit Miller. He motioned for Ransom to keep going.

Ransom sprinted down the sidewalk, but didn't see Miller. He had parked the Harley nearby. He and Johnny had agreed that if they got separated, they'd meet at a parking lot in Dorchester close to Miller's rented carriage house. His heart was still racing when he got to his bike, and he was shivering. He put his jacket on and zipped it up. He strapped his backpack to the bike, stomped on the kick-starter, and the Sportster roared to life. He pulled into traffic and wondered what, if anything, they had accomplished beyond proving what they already knew and getting a cop shot.

*   *   *   *

Ransom rode slowly by Miller's carriage house. Miller's muscle car—a Shelby GT 350 Mustang that Johnny had seen him drive—was parked off to one side. Another car, a big sedan, was parked in front. He noted the number on the license plate. He wouldn't be surprised if it was stolen. Lights were on in the second-floor apartment, and through the windows he saw two people inside hurriedly moving around. One seemed to be struggling to walk, using his arms for support. Ransom continued to the parking lot meeting place, where he left his bike. He grabbed his backpack after checking to make sure the gun was still in it. He circled back near Miller's place on foot and settled into a position behind a bush between two houses across the street from the carriage house. It gave him some cover with a good view of the front of the building. He could no longer see what was going on inside because window shades had been pulled. He wished he had some coffee and a two-way radio with enough range to stay in touch with Johnny. He expected Miller had to be wild with rage over the way things went down at South Station, especially if the officer's shot hit him. Miller must have discovered by now that the vest was empty, no drugs, no cash. He had exposed himself as a heroin dealer, and he was probably wounded. What would he do? He didn't have much time to think because the cops might already be on their way. Miller needed to get out of town fast and find a place to hide.

Ransom heard a car approaching, slowly. It was a police cruiser, and it stopped between him and the carriage house. A searchlight flashed on and swung around to shine directly at him. He was blinded. He covered his eyes with his hands. "I can't see," he said. "Could you aim that down, please, below my eyes?" The searchlight beam eased toward the ground. The officer told him to approach the cruiser with his arms outstretched and his palms open. He walked toward the cruiser and was told to stop a few feet away and to slowly turn around in a complete circle. "Why are you here in the bushes at this location on Thanksgiving?" Ransom said a police officer had been shot at South Station, and he thought he knew who did it. He said the suspect was probably across the street in the carriage house. The officer asked him for his driver's license and told him to move slowly. He reached into his back pocket and pulled out his wallet while watching the windows across the street. He handed his license to the officer, who glanced at it and muttered "West Virginia" as if he was annoyed. He turned off his searchlight and asked Ransom what he was doing in Boston. He said he was a Vietnam vet recently discharged from the Army and working with a lawyer as an investigator on a case that was linked to what happened at South Station. He said he was also cooperating with Detective Arruda. The officer asked whether he was armed, and Ransom said he was.

"I'm going to drive around the block," the officer said, "while I request backup. For now, go back where you were until I tell you to come out."

"Just so you know," Ransom said, "I think those guys across the street are watching us. I've seen the curtains shift. One of them appeared to be limping and may be wounded from the shooting."

"Thanks. That's good to know."

The cruiser pulled away slowly. Ransom didn't want to take his eyes off the carriage house in case whoever was in there decided to take a shot at him. He walked sideways back to his vantage point.

Another car came up the street past the cruiser, going the opposite way. It was a gray VW Bug. It was Johnny. His tires were oversized, and his car was souped up. It was obvious from the sound of the engine. Johnny signaled to Ransom that he saw him and drove on without stopping.

Ransom was surprised Miller and whoever was with him had not tried to get away yet. The inside lights were still on, although he hadn't noticed the curtains move for quite a while. The only outside light came from a streetlight down the block. The guys inside had to know the cops would be closing in. He wondered what their escape plan was or whether they had one. They could be tending to Miller's wound or setting booby traps. They certainly knew how. Military service in Vietnam was like going to booby trap trade school.

"Hey Peter. It's me."

The voice came from behind him. It was Johnny. He crept forward, staying low. "Are they in there?" he whispered.

"Somebody is. I've seen two of them through the windows. One seems to be limping. Maybe wounded."

"The cop at South Station said he got off a shot and was sure he hit the guy who shot him."

"How's he doing?"

"Looks like he'll live. I left when the ambulance got there."

"Did you see Arruda?"

"I didn't, but the cop talked about him. He said Arruda warned him something might go down and gave him the locker number."

The police cruiser approached again. The officer drove by without stopping.

Johnny said he'd move to the back of the carriage house so they'd have that escape route covered. Ransom asked if he was armed. He was. He crept out of sight.

The lights remained on in the carriage house. Ransom couldn't believe they were still in there. If they'd tried to leave, he was sure he would have seen them. He told himself to stop thinking and start listening. He didn't hear anything coming from the carriage house. After a while he thought he saw movement in the darkness behind the house. He figured it was Johnny. Then he saw a door open on the side of the house near the Mustang. Someone stuck his head out and then started out the door, cautiously at first, carrying what looked like a duffle bag. He put it inside the Mustang. He went back to the house and came out with another bag. He put in the Mustang and opened the front passenger-side door and left it open. He went around to the driver-side door, opened it, got into the seat, took hold of the steering wheel, and turned the key. The beautiful, limited edition Shelby GT exploded in a thunderous blast of flames and broken glass.

Ransom felt the concussion across the street, grabbed his pack, and ran toward the carriage house. At the same time, a second man came out of the house, hobbled past the burning Mustang to the sedan in front, and threw himself in. The engine caught just before Ransom got to the driveway. The tires squealed and the car jumped back in reverse, almost hitting Ransom. He pulled the crowbar from his pack and swung it at the driver's window, shattering it. The startled driver looked out through the broken glass as he slammed the car into gear and sped off. It was Miller. In less than a minute two police cruisers, their lights flashing and sirens sounding, screeched to a halt in front of the burning Mustang. Ransom was in the backyard with Johnny, who was laying on the ground, holding his head.

One officer leaped from his cruiser and ran toward the flaming car. On the way he shouted to Ransom and Johnny. "Don't move. Keep your hands where I can see 'em." He slowly circled the jagged mass of twisted metal and stopped where the driver's door and seat used to be.

What remained of the body of the man who turned the ignition key was grotesque, and he was on fire.

27

Friday, November 29, 1968
Boston

T he *Boston World* published a story inside the front section of its Friday morning edition.

Police Officer Shot;
Man Dies in Blast

A police officer was wounded in a shooting at South Station on Thanksgiving, and in a related incident a short time later a man died in a car explosion in Dorchester, according to law enforcement authorities.

Police said a suspect is being sought in connection with both incidents.

The police officer, who was not identified, was shot near an exit door at the transportation hub after a fire alarm was activated, police said. A half hour later, police said, a Shelby GT 350 Mustang parked next to a Dorchester house exploded, killing a man as he started the car.

Immediately after the blast, authorities said, another man sped away from the house in a stolen dark late-model sedan. Both men may have been together at South Station earlier in the evening, police said. They were not identified.

The wounded officer was reported in serious condition at Massachusetts General Hospital late Thursday night.

28

Friday, November 29, 1968
Cambridge

A cardboard box—the kind that moving companies use to pack books and dishes—was delivered to Lincoln Freeman's law office at midmorning on Friday. His assistant put it on her desk and knocked on the door of his private office to ask if he was expecting anything. He wasn't. He was meeting with Arruda and Ransom to go over the events of the previous day and decide what to do next. Freemen went to the outer office to check the box. There was no return address. He was reluctant to open it, considering the Thanksgiving explosion in Dorchester. He picked up the box. It wasn't heavy. He gently shook it. Nothing rattled. He asked Arruda to take a look.

The address label had been typed on a piece of paper that was attached to the box with packing tape. The box had a fitted top that extended an inch down the ends and sides. Packing tape had been used to seal the top to the box. The box had hand-size cutouts on opposite ends for lifting it. The cutouts had been covered with cardboard and then with tape. Arruda lifted the box and held it to his ear. No sound. He turned it over and examined all sides before putting it back on the assistant's desk.

"I understand why you're nervous," he said. "I'm a little nervous myself. I could call our bomb squad, but they'd probably just want to blow it up. It doesn't feel like it has timers or explosive materials. It would be a shame to destroy it if it contains important information. I'd say you should open it, but only after I get a few blocks away from here."

The others laughed nervously. Ransom joined them.

"I'm going to open it," Freeman said. "Does anyone want to leave the room?"

"I could go for coffee," his assistant joked.

"All right," said Freeman. "Here we go."

He pulled out a pocketknife and carefully cut the tape that attached the top to the box. He eased the top off. It had crumpled clusters of newspaper across the top. He picked out the clusters, exposing three narrower boxes, each with its own top. He picked out one of those boxes, put it on the desk and carefully lifted one corner of the top to peek inside. He saw what looked like a government document. It had his name on it. It also had an insignia: FBI. He eased the lid back on and set the smaller box back inside the big box and replaced the top.

"It's related to one of my cases," he said. "Looks like I've got some reading material to catch up on."

He carried the box into his office and set it on the floor behind his desk. He and Arruda and Ransom resumed their strategy session.

Before the packing box was delivered, Arruda told them the police had identified the dead man in the Mustang as a soldier assigned to the South Boston Army Base who was now presumed to be a member of the drug crew. They wondered whether any other crew members could still be alive, besides Miller.

Arruda suspected the Irish gang was behind the bombing of the Mustang. It looked like another case of criminals killing criminals that would likely never be solved or prosecuted. Since Miller owned the car, he was probably the intended target.

The locker at South Station was just as MacPherson described it. Arruda had obtained a search warrant for it the day before Thanksgiving and removed the drugs and what was left of the money before replacing the empty vest for Miller to find.

Arruda said he would apply for search warrants for the Mustang and for Miller's carriage house. Ransom cautioned him to be wary of booby traps.

Arruda asked about a "mystery man" who had tended to the wounded officer and then showed up in Dorchester just before the explosion.

Freeman told him that was Johnny Dollar. He didn't know much about him, but he had been helpful as an investigator on some cases, including the death of Chris Thompson. Arruda wondered if he had a medical background because it was likely he'd saved the wounded officer's life. Freeman didn't know about medical training, but said Johnny did have an impressive range of skills.

"Do you think his real name is Johnny Dollar?" asked Arruda.

Freeman said he didn't care. "Besides being smart, he's a guy who's true to his word and devoted to justice. His heart's in the right place. That's all I need to know."

"Was he hurt last night?" Arruda asked.

"His bell got rung pretty good," said Ransom. "He had trouble hearing and he had a couple of cuts and bruises from the blast, but he didn't want medical treatment."

Arruda asked if Johnny had been in the military. Ransom and Freeman said they didn't know or care. What they were worried about was Miller, where he was and what he would do now that his gang was gone and his military career was obviously over. Arruda said the car Miller drove away from Dorchester had been stolen. He had asked the department to alert hospitals to report anyone seeking treatment for a bullet wound, but had not heard anything back. Ransom was most concerned that Miller might go after Lisa for revenge or money or both. He said he went to her Lexington house Thursday night after Miller got away from Dorchester, but nobody was home and he didn't see any signs of trouble.

Freeman shuffled through his Rolodex and reached for his phone. He dialed the number for the Vermont farm and Lisa answered. She was there with her mother. He filled her in on the Thanksgiving events and the likelihood that Miller was wounded and could be looking for her. Ransom asked to talk to her. Freeman handed him the phone. He asked how long she expected to be in Vermont. She told him through the weekend. He wondered if she would mind if he rode to the farm. She was eager to have him do that. She said she and her mother would feel a lot safer with him there. What she didn't say was that she was interested in more than safety. She told him he should come up soon because snow was expected over the weekend. He said he'd try to be there by nightfall. He asked if there was anything he could bring. "Just you," she said.

* * * *

Ransom was thrilled to be out of the city with the wind in his face, even if it was frigid. He'd longed for the freedom of the road. It was good to feel the Sportster's power at his fingertips, having it surge through his body when called upon to pass cars and trucks or to accelerate through curves on Vermont's hilly winding roads. The afternoon sunlight sparkled off his bike like a kaleidoscope. He'd washed the grime off the Harley before leaving Boston. He was heading into danger, but he was overjoyed. He felt like he was preparing for a date to make a good impression.

He was wearing clean clothes for the first time in days, thanks to Rose. She'd gone to the laundromat that morning to wash her and Melanie's things, along with lots of diapers. She included his clothes without asking. He had stayed at Rose's apartment for a week. She treated him like family. His laundry was folded and stacked on the couch next to his pack when he stopped by to tell her he was leaving for Vermont. It turned out Rose was at work, and Melanie was with her grandmother. He left Rose a note, telling her where he was going and writing the phone number for the farm. He thanked her for her hospitality and pledged to return if she ever needed his help for any reason. He wrote that Melanie had to be the luckiest girl in Boston to have Rose for a mom. He said she inspired him with her civil rights and anti-war activism. He wrote he hoped they would see each other and Bear again under better circumstances. He left the note on the kitchen table next to a vase of flowers he bought for her.

When he reached Vermont, he was surprised by how similar the landscape was to West Virginia. It was strange that traveling to a farm he had never seen to protect a woman he had only known for a few days was like going home to the state where he grew up. He liked her and wanted to make sure she was safe. He felt an obligation to protect her for her brother, a man he had never met who had been killed for something he didn't do. Ransom had been discharged after a ghastly war halfway around the world only to be drawn into a criminal drug war in one of America's oldest cities. He hoped that pattern wouldn't continue to repeat itself. He wanted desperately to be free of war, to leave memories of the Army in the rearview mirror. He questioned whether that was possible in a world that seemed dedicated to endless war. He wondered about love, which he hadn't felt in a long time. He wondered if love was even possible in a society so deeply split between war and humanity that it was at war with itself.

He felt cheated that he'd been unable to go to the memorial service that Lisa had choreographed. Miller had spoiled that for him. He read about the service in the *Boston World*, but from talking to Freeman and Stillman and Bear, the newspaper story didn't begin to capture how well she handled herself while performing a balancing act exposing deep emotions. They said she had the crowd on their feet with the whole church rocking.

He hoped Bear and Stillman were doing OK back at Dix. He'd been so busy he hadn't been able to say goodbye to them. He expected they were working with Angela to put out their underground GI paper before basic training ended in less than a week. He was sure their newspaper would promote the 212 discharge that Stillman and Bear wanted. The last time he talked to them about what they were going to write, they had been excited to learn that Jerry Garcia, the leader of the Grateful Dead, a popular West Coast band, was kicked out of the Army on a 212 discharge in 1960. Garcia was judged to be irresponsible, unreliable, immature, and unwilling to accept authority. Desirable qualities indeed for anyone trying to get out of the Army.

They had talked about that at Rose's apartment, and about their own revised approach to the Army. Bear and Stillman now imagined themselves as ultimate weapons, forged at Fort Dix, disguised as Trojan horses, patiently lying in wait for the right times and places to launch sneak attacks to turn the Army against itself.

Ransom noticed he was getting close to the town where Lisa's farm was. He was anticipating an attack from Miller and was thinking about what he needed to be ready, including a full tank of gas for his bike. He pulled in to a general store, where he gassed up, bought a steak, some ammunition, and a bottle of red wine. The store had postcards with quaint pictures of the Vermont countryside. He bought three—one for his sister, one for his parents, and another for his brother, who was still in college with a student deferment. He had encouraged his brother to do whatever he could to avoid the draft and Vietnam.

The store was less than fifteen minutes from the farm. As he turned into the driveway, Ransom saw a state police cruiser parked in front of the house. Oh shit, he thought. He hoped Miller hadn't beaten him there.

Lisa's pickup was between the house and the barn. He parked his bike next to the cruiser and leaped off. He saw a state trooper inside the house behind the porch door. He was relieved when he saw Lisa step around the trooper and come out to meet him. She hugged him, catching him off guard. He returned the hug.

"I trust I'm not too late," he said.

"No, no, no," she said. "The trooper came to check on us because the state police got a call from the Boston police this afternoon. They said Miller might be coming after us. We've just been telling him what we know." She eased back slightly, her hands still on his arms. "Peter, it's so good to see you."

She hugged him again, like she didn't want to let go.

As they embraced, he felt her relax in his arms and said, "It's really nice to be here. I'm so glad you're safe."

*   *   *   *

The dining room table in Freeman's apartment was covered with documents, all from the anonymous packing box delivered to his office earlier in the day. He had taken it home so he could go through it uninterrupted. He figured it had to have come from Johnny, and after digging into it, he was sure it had. He was also certain he would never reveal that to anyone. How could he? He didn't even know who Johnny was.

How did Johnny do it? Did he have help? Where did the documents come from? Did the FBI know?

The box contained a treasure trove of what appeared to be internal FBI paperwork documenting abuses of power and a national surveillance program using listening devices and lies and dirty tricks to discredit and neutralize nonviolent protest groups and civil rights and anti-war activists and organizations, particularly Black student organizations.

Freeman wasn't surprised, since he'd been a target, but he was energized to have proof. Some of the paperwork showed FBI agents were also spying on families of politicians and other prominent leaders.

Taken together, the documents were evidence of a war—a dirty war waged by Hoover throughout the country. He wasn't using surveillance for criminal prosecutions. He was using it for power and job security. He seemed to be engaged in a high-stakes game of blackmail, letting some of the country's most powerful leaders inside and outside of government know that he had embarrassing information on them, but withholding it so they would be terrified to challenge him about anything.

Freeman was exhausted after going through the documents. He grabbed a beer from his refrigerator and sat back down at his table.

He had opened Johnny's box, but it felt like Pandora's, with Hoover's disgusting secrets spilling out, contaminating his apartment.

Much of the material concerned Massachusetts citizens, including surveillance reports on some members of the Massachusetts congressional delegation, led by Sen. Edward Brooke, the first Black man ever elected to the US Senate, and Sen. Edward Kennedy, who lost his brothers to assassinations.

The box contained FBI memos related to the bugging of Freeman's office. The paperwork said a confidential informant supervised by Special Agent Frank Martino had identified Freeman as a key anti-war activist. The informant was obviously MacPherson.

Another set of documents identified an unnamed leader of the Irish gang as a federal informant and Martino as his handler. Freeman planned to send copies anonymously to detective Arruda as confirmation of his suspicion that Martino was letting the Irish run wild.

But what about all the other explosive information Freeman now possessed? Who do you call when the FBI is suspected of widespread corruption? What would happen if he called senators or congressmen heading powerful committees only to discover Hoover had photos and wiretap transcripts of them and their girlfriends and their criminal friends?

It was getting close to midnight. He picked up the phone. He dialed the *World* and was somewhat surprised when someone answered. He asked for the newspaper's mailing address.

29

Saturday, November 30, 1968
Thompson Farm, Vermont

Darkness would give Miller the chance to get close to the farmhouse without being seen. Peter would have to fight off sleep until the sun rose. He wished Lisa and Mary Lou had a dog, but all they had were barn cats. He kept his handgun within reach, as well as a classic anti-war novel, *Johnny Got His Gun*, written in the 1930s by Dalton Trumbo, one of Hollywood's highest paid screenwriters who was blacklisted from the movie industry under political pressure in the 1940s for suspected communist influence. The Vietnam War rejuvenated sales of Trumbo's book, which Peter was trying to read to stay awake. He'd grabbed it for one dollar off the outdoor rack of used books at the store in Wrightstown where he first heard Lisa on her phone call with Stillman. The determination he heard in her voice that day made him want to get to know her. Now he was spending the night in the second-floor bedroom where her brother used to sleep. All because of a chance meeting with a couple of Army basic trainees in a dingy New Jersey bar. If the coffeehouse hadn't been bombed, he wouldn't have been in the bar that day.

Lisa and her mother were in separate bedrooms down the hall. Earlier, outside his bedroom door, as Lisa was about to go to her room, he had assured her everything was going to be all right. They looked longingly into each other's eyes. She reached for him, leaned in, and they exchanged a kiss, their first. They whispered goodnight, and he watched her walk down the hall. She looked sexy in the most unlikely outfit, brown bib overalls and a yellow T-shirt. She reached her door, turned, and smiled. She kissed her finger and sent the kiss his way. He caught it in both hands, like a softball, and kissed it in return. He mouthed a silent thank you and then goodnight. He stepped into his room, closed the door, and didn't move, savoring everything about her. He was smitten. He missed her already.

He hadn't been with a woman since Vietnam, and those encounters— "short time GI"—lasted a matter of minutes. Sex was a booming business in Vietnam and had no doubt flourished in wartime everywhere in the world going back to the beginning of time. Being propositioned in Vietnam, where sex was an emotionless financial transaction, had made him yearn for a return to civilian life where he could build a relationship with a woman and sex would be an expression of love. In his dreams, he could not have imagined a finer woman than Lisa for building a relationship.

It had already been a long night. The room had a straight-backed chair, which he put in front of the window so he could scan the area between the house and the barn and see the dirt road through the trees. He had opened the window a crack so the air would keep him awake, but then it was too cold, so he kept opening it and closing it. He put his book and his gun on the bed next to him. Earlier a set of headlights had crept by in the darkness on the road. Somebody was out late. He hoped it wasn't Miller, and the lights didn't return. The road was dirt with hardly any traffic. He had only seen three cars and trucks pass by since he arrived. He had tried to read Trumbo's book, but it was difficult to concentrate. All he could think about was Lisa's beautiful smile in the hallway and her touch on his arms to draw him into the kiss. The chair was so uncomfortable and chilly in front of the window that he moved to the bed for a while, but didn't lie down, worried he'd fall asleep. He knew he'd been reading the same pages over and over, but had to do something to stay awake. He'd put on his jacket and propped a pillow behind his back against the headboard to stay upright, but had nodded off so many times his neck was aching. He moved back and forth between the chair and the bed until dawn brightened the sky outside his window. He was relieved when he heard Lisa and her mother moving around. He set his alarm clock for three hours, turned off the light, stretched out on the bed, and was asleep within seconds.

His alarm was loud enough for Lisa and Mary Lou to hear in the kitchen. They had left a washcloth and towels for him by the bed. He washed up and shaved in the bathroom. When he returned to the bedroom, a breakfast tray with a plate of bacon and eggs and toast and a cup of coffee was on the bedside table. He felt as welcomed as he would have been back at home in West Virginia. He dug in to the breakfast offering. He was more than comfortable with Lisa. He was attracted to her in a way he had never felt before. After the brutality of war, he'd wondered if he'd ever be capable of love. He believed he had his answer and hoped Lisa felt the same way. He was lucky. He'd been wounded, but not seriously enough to be sent home. That could be considered unlucky because he got patched up and sent back to his unit, which was frequently at half strength because so many others had been killed and maimed.

Those ghastly memories reminded him he had a job to do. He finished his coffee and looked around the room. On a bureau were framed photographs of Chris and Lisa and their parents. He picked up a picture of Lisa, probably when she was a teenager. She was in the woods with one knee on the ground, holding a rifle in one hand and lifting the head of a young deer by its antlers. Her expression looked like a forced smile, proud of the shot she had made and sorry for the life she had taken. He assumed it was her first kill. He knew the feeling.

*   *   *   *

Bear and Stillman walked briskly through the Fort Dix–Wrightstown gate on a day pass, feeling exhilarated. They saw Angela's van parked down the block. She opened the door, waved, and held up two large sheets of paper. Their first underground GI newspaper.

They hustled down the street, anxious to see what they never could have done without a lot of help from her. They had decided to name their paper *Resist.* They had written their material longhand with pencils, and mailed it to Angela to type and lay out for printing on the mimeograph machine. They were overjoyed with the result. It was two legal-size sheets of paper, printed front and back, and it looked professional. Its most prominent feature was an essay across the top titled "You're Not All the Same," which Stillman and Bear had cowritten. The essay encouraged soldiers to join the GI movement, a growing anti-war crusade within the military that coincided with the expanding coffeehouse program. The essay played off the boast that Fort Dix was the Home of the Ultimate Weapon. It noted that weapons are likely to jam or backfire, especially when they are capable of independent thought. The essay contended the Army's tactic to isolate and silence anyone who defied orders was no longer effective because so many soldiers had turned against the war. Individual acts of resistance were turning into group protests. The essay said 1968, the deadliest year yet in Vietnam for American soldiers, had reached a tipping point, where the Army was about to be at war with itself. More soldiers were refusing orders to go to Vietnam, and more soldiers already there were refusing to fight. The essay applauded their courage because the consequences of resistance were so severe. Military stockades had become so overcrowded that conditions were inhumane. The government couldn't build them or expand them fast enough to confine all the soldiers refusing to fight or follow orders. It was clear the US would have to withdraw from Vietnam or its Army would collapse. The only question was how many more American lives and body parts would be lost before the government stopped lying and admitted the obvious.

The essay proposed creation of a new anti-war medal—the "Up Yours" commendation for bravery—to recognize soldiers for acts of defiance. "The Army calls it insubordination or worse," the essay said. "We call it bravery."

Angela told Bear and Stillman their essay was her favorite part of the paper. She said it was good enough that it should have had their names on it as the authors. But that would have earned them one-way tickets to the stockade.

The paper had a number of other stories. One was about the bomb at the Wrightstown coffeehouse and the Army's efforts to keep it shut down if anyone tried to reopen it.

Another story highlighted recent rebellions at two military stockades. One was at Fort Dix, where the stockade was known as The Pound because it was only fit for dogs. The other was halfway around the world—the Army's notorious Long Binh Jail in South Vietnam—known as LBJ, by chance the initials of President Lyndon Baines Johnson, whose term was about to end. Both installations had twice as many prisoners as they were designed to hold and were considered obvious examples of racism because the percentages of Black soldiers were so high. They also demonstrated the growing strength of the GI movement because so many soldiers were confined for refusing to fight or for going AWOL. The uprising at the Long Binh Jail effectively destroyed the facility.

The paper also had a brief item called "Unsuitable Jerry." It elaborated on Grateful Dead founder and lead guitarist Jerry Garcia's discharge for unsuitability because the Army couldn't turn him into a soldier. Others who wanted to follow Garcia's example were advised to check out Army Regulation 635-212.

Resist also had a few letters to the editor sent by fans of the first Fort Dix underground newspaper that was called *About Face.*

"I hope the letters encourage others to write," said Angela. "I rented a post office box for our address. Wouldn't it be nice if it fills up."

"I wish we could be around to find out," said Bear.

"You'll find out," said Angela. "I'll make sure of that. We need to keep this going. You have great ideas. Your paper's a big improvement over *About Face.* I think it can really take off if you're willing to stay with it. No matter where you go, we can do it by mail or over the phone."

She said she had just signed a lease for a new location for the coffeehouse and expected to open it before Christmas. *Resist* would be prominently displayed at the coffeehouse and soldiers would be encouraged to take as many copies as they wanted back to the base to give to their friends.

"My plan is to print an initial run of five hundred copies, but only after you proofread the copies I just gave you," she said. "After that I'll keep printing as long as people take them. At some point, we'll want to produce a second issue. That will probably depend on how fast our mailbox fills up. In the meantime, you should be thinking about possible stories for the next issue. You guys are the ghost editors."

"I like the sound of that," said Bear.

"I looked for a newspaper job after college," said Stillman. "I never expected to find one in the Army."

"Gentlemen," said Angela. "I'd like to buy you a beer. Congratulations."

They crossed the street to the same bar where Stillman and Bear met Ransom on their first foray into Wrightstown. Nobody was there except the bartender. He didn't remember them. He served them three beers without questioning Bear's age. They took stools at the bar.

They mentioned Ransom, and Angela said he had been a coffeehouse regular. She asked if they knew how he was doing. They told her how he had helped solve a couple of cases for a Boston lawyer who knew her, Lincoln Freeman. Angela remembered meeting Freeman at a conference and said she hoped she would see him again. Stillman said Freeman knew someone who had a vision for a national or possibly international GI newspaper.

"That wouldn't be Johnny Dollar would it?" she asked.

"You know him?"

"Not exactly. I got a call from somebody using that name. He said Lincoln Freeman gave him my name. He said he figured out a way to have the Army unknowingly pay for a national anti-war underground paper. He asked if I'd be willing to work with him on that. Is he for real?"

"He was when we met him in Boston," Bear said. "Unless there's more than one of him, which could explain a lot."

"What does he do?"

"Just about anything that's necessary for truth, justice, and the American way," said Stillman.

"Superman, huh?"

"And just as elusive," said Bear. "He doesn't talk about himself, at least not to anyone we know."

Angela said, "I'm going to take a wild guess that Johnny Dollar is not his real name."

"You wouldn't be the only one," said Bear.

*   *   *   *

The *World's* newsroom was bright and appeared spacious on a Saturday afternoon, a dramatic contrast to the last time Freeman was there. That was the night before the memorial service, when the smoke-filled newsroom had editors and reporters on deadline buzzing like bees around a hive.

It had only been a little over a week, but so much had happened. Freeman saw Roger McAlister come out of an office and eagerly approach him with his hand extended. "Welcome," the editor said. "It's good to see you again."

"Same here," Freeman said. "It looks so much different in daylight without all the reporters and editors."

"It's easier to think and talk on a weekend without so much going on," he said. "They actually gave me an office a few days ago. It's the one we were in the last time you were here."

"Does that mean a promotion?"

"We'll see. It's an outgrowth of our first meeting. The managing editor figured I should have more space and privacy, considering the importance of the issues. Hell, look at what's happened in just the last week."

"You don't know the half of it."

"Then let's get to it." McAlister got two cups of coffee and led Freeman to his office. They went over the Thanksgiving incidents at South Station and Dorchester and the likelihood that Boston's Irish gang was responsible for the bomb in the Shelby GT and possibly the deaths of two other soldiers for intruding on the gang's turf. Freeman brought up the suspicion that one of the Irish gang's leaders was a federal informant protected by the FBI. McAlister said he had not heard that, but noted that the Irish gang had emerged strong and relatively intact from the criminal gang wars. "Maybe they had some help," he said. "That would be a hell of a story if the FBI's protecting a criminal gang and letting it kill off its competitors. But that story would be almost impossible to get."

Freeman said one reason he asked for another meeting was to encourage McAlister to investigate corruption in the FBI. "The FBI bugged my office," he said. "We caught them in the act." He gave him a brief rundown. They agreed a story about FBI bugging would have to wait until after the paper wrapped up the Army story that began with Chris Thompson's murder and exposed the other killings.

"I've got something else for you," Freeman said. He opened his briefcase and pulled out a thick folder of documents. He explained Art's effort to expose military contracting corruption, implicating weapons manufacturers, top Pentagon officials, and members of Congress. He told McAlister he'd give him the documents as long as neither he nor Art were identified as the source to anyone, even inside the newspaper. He said he wanted to establish a trusting and confidential source relationship with McAlister, and nobody else. The editor agreed.

*   *   *   *

Johnny set up his shoeshine kit on the sidewalk near the FBI office where

Martino would pass by.

It had been nearly a week since MacPherson was caught retrieving the bug from Freeman's office. Johnny figured MacPherson had probably been released from jail, which had been a safe spot for him while Miller was on the loose. Would Martino still be MacPherson's handler? Would Martino still be supervising the Irish gang informants? Would Martino be booted from Boston or from the bureau? What use was he now that he'd been exposed? Well, maybe he hadn't been exposed yet, but those documents ought to get to the newspaper soon enough.

Maybe the Irish gang would give him a job. He'd taken good care of them, and they of him. Johnny had seen Irish mobsters deliver cases of wine and Cuban cigars to Martino's house on several occasions. Or maybe the mob would put him into permanent retirement.

On the sidewalk as dusk settled in, Johnny had just finished with a customer when Martino walked up behind him and said, "Hey Johnny."

"Be right with you," said Johnny without looking up.

"You're under arrest," said Martino.

Johnny wheeled around. "What'd you get me on copper?"

"Failure to be around when I needed a shine the other day."

"You'll never take me alive."

"I don't do this for everybody, but you could make that shoeshine charge go away by giving me one now."

"Sounds fair. Step right up."

Martino put his foot on Johnny's shoeshine box. "Haven't seen you in a while," he said. "Where you been?"

"Busy in other parts of the city. How about you?"

"Getting ready for a change of scenery. Alaska."

"Holy shit. Why Alaska?"

"That's where the bureau wants me."

"So it's not a vacation?"

"No. I'll be there for a while."

"Is it like a special assignment?"

"Johnny, you know I can't talk about things like that."

"Right. You ever been there?"

"Alaska?"

"Yeah."

"No."

Johnny had been there when he was in military intelligence, but he wasn't about to tell Martino that. "Do you fish?"

"What?"

"Do you fish, like with a fishing rod?"

"Done it a few times. Caught more beers than fish. Why?"

"I hear there's good fishing in Alaska."

"I'll keep that in mind."

Johnny finished the shine. "Those shoes look so good that you should go dancing," he said. "You better be careful though. The women might mistake you for Fred Astaire."

"Not where I'm going." Martino pulled three dollar bills out of his pocket and handed them to Johnny. "Thanks for the shines and the conversations. It's been good to get to know you."

"Thanks. Same here. When do you leave?"

"If I told you, you know what I'd have to do."

"Then I withdraw the question."

"Goodbye Johnny."

"A friendly word of advice," said Johnny. "Get bug protection." He touched the tip of his cap and gave Martino a farewell wave.

*　*　*　*

Late afternoon winds swept dark clouds down from Canada into Vermont, the leading edge of a cold front that was predicted to produce the first significant snow of the season. Peter and Lisa were preparing to use it to their advantage. The temperature was falling, but they were sweating as they cut pine branches and carefully placed them across a long narrow ditch they dug with shovels and a pick axe in the woods about twenty-five yards from the farmhouse to create a booby trap for Miller or anyone else from his gang who might be helping him. Earlier Peter and Lisa had walked the road, trying to anticipate where Miller might park and how he would likely approach the house through the woods. The place where they dug was an educated guess. The ditch was about a dozen feet long, three feet across and two feet deep. They hoped the storm would dump enough snow so that it would build up and blanket the covering branches, concealing their trap. The ditch didn't have any sharpened punji stakes at the bottom, and it wasn't deep enough to stop anyone for more than a few seconds. It was designed as an early warning signal. They weaved baling twine from a stake in the ground at one end through the pine branches the length of the ditch and attached the twine to three large cowbells hanging by leather collars from a nearby tree. Anyone falling in the ditch, or quite possibly a deer, would hit the twine, ringing the bells and alerting anyone within hearing range that an intruder could be closing in. It wasn't perfect, but as Lisa told Peter, it was what Vermont farmers were known for doing—improvising with whatever materials were at hand.

The cowbells were Lisa's idea after Peter said he wanted to build defenses to alert them to Miller's approach. She and Chris had discovered the bells in a corner of the barn when they were young. The bells were rusty, but still produced strong tones that could be heard from a distance.

Lisa and Peter made other cowbell alarms for the front and back doors of the farmhouse, as well as a couple of doors on the barn. They finished their work as darkness blanketed the valley. They closed up the barn and headed back to the house. As they walked, Peter put his hand around Lisa's back, saying they made a great team. She reached behind his back, only her hand was lower than his. She squeezed his butt with approval. As they neared the house, they could see Mary Lou through the kitchen windows. They stopped before going in and turned to each other.

"I think we're ready," he said.

"Yes," she said.

They kissed, their bodies pressed firmly into each other. He eased away and raised his hands to embrace her face. He kissed her forehead.

"It's a pleasure working with you," he said.

She tugged him back into her midsection, kissed him again, and said, "You too."

They didn't want to let go, but it was cold and getting colder. Lisa opened the back door to the warmth of the kitchen woodstove, the aroma of fresh baked bread, and Mary Lou spreading apple slices in a pie crust. They left their muddy shoes by the door, stripped off their jackets and gloves, and put them on a coat rack around the corner. "It smells so good in here," Peter said. He asked Mary Lou what he could do to help. She pulled a canvas log carrier out of a large wooden box near the woodstove and sent him to the cellar to retrieve firewood stored there. "Three or four loads should fill it," she said. "That'll give us enough for tonight and tomorrow."

Lisa headed upstairs to take a shower while Peter went to the cellar, which had a dirt floor and a massive wood furnace that wasn't being used this weekend. Cords of split wood were stacked along the fieldstone foundation wall. Three loads in the canvas carrier filled the wood box.

Lisa returned to the kitchen looking refreshed and warm in a loose ankle-length granny dress. Peter took a turn in the shower and shaved before he came back down wearing clean jeans and a new plaid flannel shirt he had bought in Boston.

For dinner, they had the steak and wine that Peter had picked up at the store and potatoes and green beans that Lisa had grown in her garden. Mary Lou's bread was served with dinner, and later her pie for dessert. Peter volunteered to clean up. Lisa helped him and showed him how to operate the woodstove and where the ashes were stored outside away from the house in an old oil drum. She told him that wood ashes were good for gardens. He said he was surprised that burning wood was not as messy or smelly as the coal his family burned in West Virginia.

After dinner, they shifted to the living room, where they told Mary Lou about the early-warning cowbell defenses. Mary Lou knew they were necessary, but she was unnerved. "Can you believe what we've come to," she said. "Think about it. What does that say about our country? Here we are in beautiful Vermont defending ourselves against American soldiers who killed my son and my husband, and now one of them wants to kill us. Who could ever even imagine that. It makes you wonder how this world can possibly survive."

"Mom," said Lisa. "You're right of course. We're in a world of perpetual war. But let's look ahead and try to think positive. If we're going to spread Chris and Dad's ashes tomorrow, let's focus on their lives. Let's remember how good they were, how both of them tried to make the world a better place."

"Honey," said Mary Lou, "I love you—"

The phone rang. Peter and Lisa looked at each other and sprang to their feet.

Lisa said she'd answer. She picked up the phone after the fourth ring. It was a neighboring farmer she'd lined up to plow snow. She relaxed. He had plowed their driveway during storms when nobody was at the farm. He'd seen lights in the house and was checking to see if they wanted him to plow tomorrow. Lisa thanked him for calling and said they'd take care of it themselves. After she hung up, she admitted she hadn't even thought about putting the snow plow on the family tractor. "I guess I've been a little distracted," she said.

"Don't worry about it," said Peter. "It's probably better if we don't plow. Tracks in the snow will make it easier to find anyone who shows up."

Mary Lou looked worn out. She said she would go along with whatever Lisa and Peter wanted to do. She struggled to push herself up out of her chair and went to the kitchen to get a glass of water. She checked the locks on the back and front doors and said she was going up to her bedroom to read before going to sleep. "I feel safe with you two in charge," she said. "I'm not very good company tonight. I don't think you'll mind me leaving you alone." She said goodnight and climbed the stairs slowly, using the railing for support.

"I love you, Mom," said Lisa. "We're ready. We'll see you in the morning."

They heard her bedroom door close. Lisa told Peter she was worried. Her mother seemed to have aged ten years in less than a week. Peter assured her that Mary Lou was strong, but both of them could see she was exhausted and depressed.

"Think about what she's been through," he said. "Look at what you've both been through. You're a very strong woman. I think you know that. I bet you got a lot of that strength from your mother. This waiting for Miller to do whatever he's going to do wears everybody down, but it should be over soon. Then you and your mom should take a vacation, go somewhere you've never been before to recuperate. A change of scenery would really help."

"What soldiers call R and R?"

"That's right. Rest and relaxation. We could add a third R for rejuvenation."

"Would you come?"

"Where?"

"On R and R and R with us?"

"If you asked me."

"I'm asking."

"Yes. Absolutely, I'll be there. I know some of what you've been through, and you know some of what I've been through. I think we could help each other with all those Rs."

Lisa reached out and took his hand in hers. "Thank you." Her expression was one of deep appreciation. "You've been a lifesaver."

"Thank you," he said. "I feel the same way about you."

"It feels like we're becoming a team."

"You've been an inspiration to me," he said, squeezing her hand, "the way you took charge and held everything together when you lost your brother and then your dad. I lost a lot of fellow soldiers in Vietnam. I lost my innocence in Vietnam. I saw the most horrible things people can do to each other, absolute cruelty, over and over. I was nervous about whether I could come back from that. Then I heard you on the phone that day with Jud, vowing to get justice for Chris. I knew I had to meet you. Then you did that beautiful memorial service like a maestro. I heard all about it. I'm so sorry I missed it. You managed to turn your personal tragedy into a beautiful loving tribute. I can't think of anywhere I'd rather be right now than here with you."

They were standing by the couch in the living room, looking tenderly into each other's eyes. They embraced. He whispered, "We can take on whatever's coming. You're right. We make a terrific team."

"I think my mom senses something happening between us."

"I hope she approves."

"I'm sure she does. She told me yesterday how relieved she was when you said you were coming up here. She likes you a lot."

They kissed.

A door opened. They froze. They heard footsteps upstairs and another door opened and closed.

"The bathroom," Lisa whispered.

Peter stepped back. "There's a little wine left," he said softly. "Would you like to finish it off?"

"That would be a perfect ending to a wonderful day," she said. "Wait. Think about that. About what I just said." She brushed her hair back from her face. "What a crazy thing for me to say. Here we are, on alert, preparing to be attacked, and I called it wonderful. It's because of you."

"I know what you mean. It's hard to describe the emotions and how they fit together and strengthen each other."

"If it wasn't for the deaths of my brother and my father," she said, "you and I would never have met."

"I'm so sorry I didn't have a chance to know them. But I'm getting to know them through you. They were both destined to make the world a better place. And they did. It reminds me of something my parents taught us about camping. They always told us to leave a campsite in better shape than when we found it. They said we should leave no trace, no evidence that we'd been there. Just like all kids, we wanted to carve our initials wherever we went. We weren't allowed to do that."

"It's such a temptation," she said, "to let someone, anyone, know you've been somewhere, as though it validates your existence. I can't wait to meet your parents."

"I'm really looking forward to introducing you to them."

"Leave no trace. That's the way we should all live our lives. It would force us to lose our sense of self-importance. Wouldn't it be a better world if everyone could do that?"

"And a kinder world."

"And a cleaner world."

A toilet flushed. A door opened and closed upstairs. Then another.

"I think it's time for the wine." Lisa smiled.

Peter went to the kitchen and came back with two glasses, a little more than half full. Lisa was on the couch. He handed her a glass. He loved her smile and her eyes. He thought of them as windows to her soul. He sat on the couch facing her.

"What shall we toast?" she asked.

"To the end of armies and war and cruelty and hatred forever."

"And to the beginning of kindness," she said.

They raised their glasses, clinked, and sipped.

"To the beginning of us," she said.

"Our next chapter," he said.

They clinked and sipped.

They put their glasses on the coffee table, turned to each other, and hugged.

"I can't believe how happy I am, how right it feels being here with you," he whispered.

"Me too," she said. "It seems crazy, but I feel like I know everything's going to be all right."

Peter pulled back and looked deep into her eyes. "Speaking of crazy," he said, "I was thinking before that we might play cribbage tonight. But that's not what I'm thinking now."

"We do have cards and a cribbage board." She smiled again. "But I don't think I could concentrate on the game."

Lisa grabbed both glasses and handed one to Peter. "I keep thinking about the mix of events and emotions that brought us together to this place at this moment," she said. "It feels like magic."

"It does and it is. We're two very lucky people." He raised his glass. "To luck and magic."

They clinked and finished the wine. They stretched out side by side on the couch, their arms around each other, their noses touching.

"Thank you," he said, "for letting me get to know you, for letting me into your life."

"You should be careful what you thank me for," she said. "My life can get pretty complicated, and who knows what will happen tomorrow."

"I think we're ready," he said.

"Me too," she said. "So before tomorrow, let's celebrate tonight."

"Tonight," he said, "feels just right."

She put her hand on his thigh. "That it does."

They kissed and stroked each other tenderly.

Peter lifted his head and asked if she had noticed what was happening outside.

"I bet it's snowing."

"It's so beautiful," he said, "watching it come down with the porch light on. It makes me want to run outside and throw snowballs."

She sat up and looked. "Sorry. There isn't enough snow yet. We'll have to wait for tomorrow."

"But it's calling me now," he said. "We could go outside and walk and feel it on our faces. What do you think?"

She said she had an idea. "Wait here," she said as she got up. She opened the front door, walked to the edge of the porch, scooped up a handful of snow, came back to the couch, and sprinkled the snow on his face. "There you go." She giggled.

"Oooooo," he said, "that feels so good."

"Now for my next trick," she said.

"What's that?"

"It's what Vermonters always do."

He sat up, looking serious, and asked, "What exactly is it that Vermonters always do?"

"They improvise, silly." They shared a hearty laugh and another hug.

"Whoops," she said, raising a finger to her mouth. "That was a little loud. I think we should fill the woodstove and take our celebration upstairs. To your room. I'd suggest my room, but we'd have to be awfully quiet because it's next to my mother's room. What do you think?"

"I can't imagine anything I'd rather do."

They untangled themselves, and he offered his hand to help her off the couch. "Thank you," she said. "You're so kind." She leaned in close and whispered, "I really mean that."

They hugged, and he looked outside again, mesmerized by the glittering falling snow. "This is the first snow I've seen since I was shipped to Vietnam. It's . . ." he hesitated, considering the right word. "It's purifying."

"Yes," she whispered, "and it's magic. If I've learned one lesson since Chris and Dad died, it's that you never know how much time you have. We should make the most of ours. Let's stoke the stove."

30

Sunday, December 1, 1968
Boston

Sunday's edition of the *World* had a brief follow-up story on an inside page.

**Soldier Sought
In Connection
With Shooting**

A soldier from the South Boston Army Base is being sought by authorities investigating the shooting of a police officer on Thanksgiving, authorities said.

Sgt. Leo Miller, a Vietnam veteran, was last seen driving a stolen car away from a Dorchester house where another car exploded less than an hour after Boston Police Officer Glen Baker was shot at South Station. Baker was reported in stable condition with an abdominal wound at Massachusetts General Hospital Saturday.

Another soldier from the Army base, Sgt. Alan Reed, was identified by police as the man who died when the car exploded in Dorchester as he tried to start it.

An Army spokesman declined to comment.

31

Sunday, December 1, 1968
Fort Dix

It had been three weeks since Bear and Stillman went to the chapel early on a Sunday morning. That was when the chaplain's assistant threatened them, claiming to be working undercover on a child abuse investigation.

They moved toward the chapel doors in a line with other trainees. The plaque on the wall where the chaplain's name had been engraved was blank. They sat in a pew. A man poked his head out from a curtain behind the pulpit. He said the chaplain had been delayed for a few minutes, but would be out soon. He wasn't the assistant who threatened them. That was encouraging.

The chaplain finally appeared, and his face was a new, older one. He introduced himself and apologized for the delay. He said he was sorry the previous Sunday's service had to be cancelled at the last minute. He said it was due to a death in the former chaplain's family. He had been assigned to take over the position because the previous chaplain would not return.

Neither Bear nor Stillman paid attention to what was said after that. Their job was done. The pedophile chaplain was gone. They expected the Army would lie about what happened. No surprise there. Whether the chaplain would be prosecuted or reassigned somewhere else was beyond their control. Stillman leaned over to Bear and whispered, "I don't pray, but if I did, I'd say a prayer of thanks to the captain. He was true to his word."

Bear nodded his agreement and whispered back, "Yeah, but he'll never let us out of the Army."

32

Sunday, December 1, 1968
Thompson Farm, Vermont

Peter jerked awake, his head cocked. He listened intently and then propped himself up far enough to look out the window. The weather had celebrated the first day of December by turning Vermont into a winter wonderland, concealing their early warning system. He'd put his faith in the cowbell alarms to warn them overnight of any trouble. He thought of Lisa and relaxed when he realized her warm body was still next to his. She stirred, and they turned toward each other.

"Good morning," she said.

They kissed.

"I'm so glad you're still here," he said.

"Where else would I be?"

"It's so nice to wake up with you."

"I wish we could stay here all day."

"That makes two of us," he said. "We got what we wanted outside, enough snow to cover our ditch. It's beautiful, almost as beautiful as in here."

She raised herself up to look briefly out the window and then pulled the blanket back over them. "This is what I love about Vermont," she said. "All the seasons are so wonderful in their own ways."

"The people too," he said and kissed her forehead.

"Last night was wonderful," she said.

"Beyond words," he said.

"How did you sleep?"

"The best I've slept in a very, very long time. How about you?"

She kissed him. "Wonderful. It seems like that's the only word I know this morning."

It was chilly in the bedroom, but not so cold that they could see their breath. It was warm under the covers. Neither wanted to move. Finally Lisa got up and wiggled into a nightgown she had grabbed last night on their way to his room. "I hear Mom in the kitchen," she said. "Feels like she's ready to start the day. I'll be back in a few minutes. I'm going to go to the bathroom and get dressed. I'd like for us to go downstairs together if that's OK with you."

"We can hold hands."

"I'd like that," she said. She kissed him before she left and closed the door behind her.

He got dressed and put on an extra shirt before they went downstairs together, holding hands, where the woodstove radiated welcoming heat.

Mary Lou was wearing an apron and stirring a pot of oatmeal. She appeared to have regained some of her energy and spirit. "Good morning," she said cheerfully. "You two look happy. It must have been a good night."

"It was," they said at the same time and laughed.

Peter poured himself a cup of coffee and topped off Mary Lou's cup. He offered to start some water for Lisa's tea, but Mary Lou had already made the tea.

"Breakfast smells delicious," he said, "and the stove sure makes the kitchen cozy."

"It's a special kind of heat," Lisa said. "It sets a mood."

"What a way to start the day," said Peter. "My introduction to Vermont is nothing short of amazing."

The table was set with bowls and plates and silverware for the oatmeal and a platter of French toast and bacon. A jar of homemade maple syrup was next to the platter, along with a dish of blueberries Lisa had picked and frozen last summer.

Mary Lou announced breakfast was ready. Peter watched Lisa mix maple syrup and blueberries into her oatmeal, and he did the same.

Mostly they ate in silence, thinking about someone without a seat at the table. Leo Miller was an ominous presence. They were hoping the phone would ring with good news. They wanted to hear from the police calling to tell them Miller had been caught. A call from the general store could be a warning that he was on his way. Lisa had asked the owner to let her know if anyone inquired about where she lived.

Peter was hoping for a call from Johnny. Before leaving Boston, he had asked him to try to find someone to check Miller's military records to look for anything that would help them understand why he did what he did and what he might do now. He told Johnny he'd like to locate Miller's parents to see if they would be willing to talk to their son. Peter wanted to take Miller alive, maybe even convince him to surrender. He and Johnny had worked closely together for a week without any disagreements. Each seemed to know how the other would react in fast-moving situations. Johnny had given Peter a phone number to get a message to him if it was ever necessary. Peter hadn't felt the need to use it yet.

On Friday afternoon, after the state trooper left, Peter had scouted an area of several acres surrounding the farmhouse, the barn, an old sugar house, and other smaller outbuildings. He'd put his Harley in the barn and moved Mary Lou's car behind the barn so anyone approaching the house shouldn't see either one. Lisa had found enough scrap material to make the cowbell alarms and came up with an oversized funnel that would work as a megaphone to talk to Miller from a safe distance. Peter had consulted with Lisa and Mary Lou and strategically positioned the shotgun and the rifle in the house so they would be loaded and available if needed. Lisa would keep the revolver with her.

Peter cleared the breakfast table and did the dishes and checked the woodstove to see if the firebox needed wood. He didn't add any. He was worried about the possibility of a struggle in the kitchen, where someone could get seriously burned.

He was thinking about going outside to experience the snow when the phone rang. Lisa looked at Peter, each knowing what the other was thinking, and she answered. It was Johnny. She welcomed his call and passed the phone to Peter.

Johnny said one of his associates had come up with some information. Miller's personnel file contained minor disciplinary actions, but nothing serious. No indication of drug running or weapons sales. But there was an unresolved incident in Vietnam involving his company that was under review and seemed like it could become a big deal. It was a reported massacre of Vietnamese men, women, and children. It appeared an entire village was torched and its inhabitants killed. The early death toll was estimated at more than one hundred, and possibly hundreds more. The name of the village was My Lai. It had happened in March, six weeks after the Viet Cong launched their Tet Offensive. Johnny said the My Lai body count was praised as an outstanding job by Gen. William Westmoreland, the commander of US forces in Vietnam for the last four years. Westmoreland considered body counts a vital measure of his strategy to fight a war of attrition using search-and-destroy tactics.

At My Lai, several American soldiers tried to stop the slaughter and protect some of the villagers. They failed. So did the Army. It had been nine months since the massacre, and Johnny said it was still under review by high-ranking Army officials. It looked like a coverup. There was no doubt Miller's company was responsible for My Lai. Whether he participated in the killings or whether he was even at My Lai was unclear from his personnel file. Peter and Johnny agreed that if Miller was there that would really fuck him up.

Johnny gave Peter a phone number for Miller's parents. He didn't know if it was a good number or if they even lived there anymore.

Peter told him he wished he'd also asked if someone could check Lt. Sanders's personnel file. Johnny said he did have it checked. Sanders had a clean record of service and no involvement at My Lai. In fact, he said, Miller and Sanders were never in the same unit in Vietnam. It appeared they didn't know each other until they got to Boston.

Johnny said he'd probably be leaving Boston soon, although he'd be back if Freeman needed him for anything. As for where he'd be going, Johnny said he wasn't sure, but the phone number he gave Peter would still work for getting a message to him.

After the call, Peter thought back to his first conversation with Miller when Miller tried to convince him Sanders was a drug-dealing murderer. He had described Sanders as "Wild Bill," a reckless brutal platoon leader who gave worse than he got. He had likely been describing My Lai.

Peter told Lisa and Mary Lou what Johnny had discovered. He asked them what they thought. Their view was that Miller had killed before and would most likely try to kill again.

"The Army taught him to kill and sent him to war," said Lisa. "Is it the Army or the war that turns people into murderers? I suppose it's both. But how do you get over that? Living with murder on your conscience? I can't even comprehend a massacre. I mean that's genocide."

"As I understand it," said Mary Lou, "we don't really know what he did or didn't do over there. But we know what he did in Boston. He killed Chris and probably others and he shot a police officer. It's hard to forgive all that under any circumstances."

Lisa asked Peter what he thought about Miller's situation.

He ducked the question. He was dialing the phone number Johnny gave him to reach Miller's parents. He said he hoped it wasn't too late. A woman answered. Peter identified himself as a Vietnam veteran. "Oh, do you know Leo?`" the woman asked. He said he did.

"How's he doing?" she asked.

"Not well," said Peter. He asked who she was.

"I'm Leo's mother."

He asked whether her husband was home.

"Why," she asked, "what's going on?"

"Leo's got himself into trouble with the police."

"Is it drugs again?"

"Drugs do have something to do with it. Can you tell me if Leo's dad is home?"

"His stepfather is here."

"Is it possible for him to get on this line so I can talk with both of you at the same time?"

Peter could hear her shouting for someone. A man clicked in on an extension phone. He identified himself as Sam, Leo's stepfather. Peter asked Leo's mother for her name. She said Roberta.

"Are you aware that Leo is on the run from the police?"

They said no.

"Can you tell me when you last heard from him?"

"It's been months," said Roberta.

"Do you know where he is?"

"The last we knew he was in Boston," she said. "Why is he on the run?"

"He's wanted for shooting a police officer."

"Oh no."

"Oh shit."

"Goddamn."

"Is the officer OK?"

"He was hurt pretty bad, but it looks like he'll live. Look, I'm sorry to catch you off guard with this call, but a minute ago you mentioned drugs. Does Leo have a drug problem?"

They said that from his letters they assumed he took drugs in Vietnam because it seemed everybody was taking drugs, even opium and heroin. "Leo told us people took whatever they could find to cope with what he described more than once as hell on earth. He also mentioned that Vietnam offered business opportunities. We weren't sure what he meant, but we took it to mean buying and selling drugs and just about anything else on the black market."

Sam and Roberta said they were relieved when Leo got out of Vietnam alive. They said he had a tough childhood, mainly because his father was an abusive alcoholic. When he was in high school, Leo intervened in a fight between his parents to protect his mother and he knocked his father unconscious. His father tried to have him arrested. That's when Roberta and Leo moved out of the house. Leo, who was an only child, dropped out of high school and enlisted in the Army, rather than being drafted, because the Army told him he could get the job he wanted. The problem was the Army put him in the infantry, even though the recruiter promised he'd be a mechanic because he liked to work on cars.

"He was really bitter about that," said Roberta. "But what happened was the Army lied to Leo. He said the Army always lies. He said the soldiers had a saying that, if you'll excuse my language, the Army fucks its own. We've only got one letter since he got to Boston. It was short. He'd said it was nice to be back in the world—he called the United States the world—and he bought a special kind of Ford Mustang built for racing."

Peter asked if Leo ever wrote or talked about a massacre in Vietnam. They said he wrote about soldiers having to do awful things he didn't want to talk about. But he didn't get any more specific than that. He just said it was hell on earth. They asked Peter if he knew whether Leo was involved in a massacre. Peter said he didn't. They asked how well he knew Leo. He told them he'd only met Leo a few times. They asked why he was calling now.

"Leo is probably trying to find me and a family I'm with. I'm calling you from their house in Vermont. I think Leo was wounded by the police officer he shot a couple of days ago and is desperate. He probably needs medical treatment and money. He may think he can get it here. He may also want revenge against me because I was cooperating with the police. It's a complicated situation. I'm here in Vermont with the sister and mother of one of the people he killed. It looks like your son killed him because he thought he did something that he didn't do."

"Oh no."

"Oh shit."

"It's complicated," said Peter, "and I thought I'd reach out to see if you might want to talk to Leo if he shows up here."

"Are you afraid he might try to kill you?"

"That's a possibility I can't ignore."

"And the family you're with?"

"I don't know. He talked about kidnapping the sister to get money."

"How do we know we can believe you?"

"I can give you the name and phone number of a Boston police detective who knows about all of this. It's Sunday, but the department can get a message to him."

"Please do."

He gave them Arruda's contact information, as well as the phone number at the farmhouse.

"Before I hang up," Peter said, "I'd like to know whether you might want to talk to Leo if he does come here. I don't want anyone to get hurt, but I've got to defend myself and the family who lives here. I wonder if you'd want to try to maybe calm him down by talking to him."

"I don't know," Leo's mother said. "I'm not thinking very good right now. You caught me off guard with all this. But of course I'll talk to Leo if he'll talk to us. I've got to support my son."

"He's potentially facing several murder charges, as well as drug charges and shooting the cop," said Peter. "He could help himself by surrendering without a gunfight. Then maybe he could get help to deal with whatever damage the Army and the war did to him."

The other end of the line was silent. Then Roberta said, "Thank you for calling. I'm glad you did even though it's very hard for us to hear what you said about the trouble Leo's in. Please, I'm begging you, please don't shoot my son. He's had a hard life."

*   *   *   *

Early in the afternoon, Lisa and Mary Lou set out from the house through the fresh snow to make their last climb to Turtle Rock with Chris and Art. Lisa wore a backpack and cradled in her arms a hardwood box that held Chris's ashes. Mary Lou had Art's box, identical to Chris's. Peter followed a respectful distance behind. Lisa was leading the solemn procession, walking at a slow pace, making sure it wasn't too fast for her mother. It reminded Peter of a scene at airports in Vietnam where soldiers respectfully carried the bodies of dead soldiers to transport planes for return trips to American graveyards.

They walked past the barn and crossed the meadow. The sunlight reflecting off the snow was so bright they wore sunglasses. They'd thought about wearing snowshoes but put on winter boots instead because the snow wasn't that deep. Peter was also concerned that snowshoes would be cumbersome if Miller showed up and he and Lisa and Mary Lou had to react quickly. Peter wore a barn coat and boots that were kept at the farmhouse for visitors. He stopped and turned to look at the footprints they were leaving. Miller would know how many of them were walking the trail. Peter felt for his handgun. It was in his coat pocket.

They reached the woods and started climbing the old logging road that weaved up the ridge. They were passing through a cluster of birch trees when a gunshot shattered the stillness. They jumped, crouched, and scanned the area. Another shot. And another. They looked and listened intently, trying to assess where the shots were coming from. As the booms faded, Lisa relaxed. "We're far enough away that we're OK," she said. "It's deer season. They're either lousy shots or they're at *beer* camp or both."

It wasn't surprising that hunters were out. They would welcome the snow that made it easy to track their quarry.

The funeral procession proceeded up the ridge. The old road narrowed to a footpath as it wound through a section of tall white pine and maples. The snow was beautiful. Lisa had described the clearing around Turtle Rock to Peter. He'd thought he'd seen it in the distance a couple of times. This time, he was right. The boulder, about fifty yards ahead, was much more imposing than he expected. Lisa stopped. She turned around and asked her mother, "Are you ready?" Mary Lou didn't respond immediately. Then she nodded silently. It looked like the way some people bow before entering a church. Peter also nodded, and Lisa led the way to the clearing.

Peter hadn't noticed any wind down by the farmhouse. But when they reached the clearing, a cold breeze was blowing into their faces from the west. They were all wearing knit winter caps, covering their ears. He was thankful for that. He was struck by the view across the valley past the far ridgeline to mountain tops in the distance. He wanted to say something, but he didn't. He wanted to get close to the boulder to check it out, but he didn't.

Lisa turned to Mary Lou and asked, "What do we do now?"

"I don't know," she said.

"Peter?"

"Ahhh, give me a second." He looked around the clearing before answering. "We know Lisa already crafted a magnificent memorial service that will be remembered for a long time. This place is like a church, but it's different. It's peaceful and powerful with a stunning view and that massive rock. It blows my mind. There must be a reason it's here, all alone. I assume that's Turtle Rock."

"That is our Turtle Rock," said Lisa. "As you pointed out, it's a special place. It has a mystical dimension. I'm going to start a fire."

She took off her backpack, laid it down, and pulled out a plaid blanket, newspaper, and kindling. She put Chris's box on top of the pack. She knelt and cleared snow from the fire pit she and Chris had made many years ago and lit a small fire. She spread the blanket on the snow near the fire and put her pack on it with Chris's box. Mary Lou walked onto the blanket and sat down with Art's box in her lap. Lisa moved to the edge of the clearing to retrieve snow-covered wood she had stored there. Soon the fire was blazing. Mary Lou and Art and Lisa and Chris were together on the blanket.

Peter moved back toward the edge of the clearing. He wanted to give them space and time alone. He told them he was going to backtrack down the trail to make sure nobody was following them.

Lisa and Mary Lou sat quietly, caught up in their personal memories. After a while, Lisa reached out for a stick and used it to shift the burning logs while adding a couple of new ones.

"Remember when we used to come up here for overnight camping?" she asked her mother. "We did it for a lot of years."

"I loved the breakfasts," said Mary Lou.

"I thought we should have a picnic table up here."

"That would have been too civilized."

"I agree. I've changed my mind. But it would have been more comfortable, and it would have been easier on Dad doing the cooking."

"Your father loved making those breakfasts, even when he spilled something."

"He was always spilling something."

"If he was here now, he might spill his ashes."

Neither of them said anything for a while. Then Lisa asked, "Do you think we should spread their ashes or bury them?"

"Do you have a shovel?"

"Yes."

"I don't know."

"Me neither."

"It's windy up here."

"Is that good or bad?"

"I don't know. It probably only matters if we're on the wrong side of the wind."

"Then we'd wear their ashes."

"We could bury them now and come back in the spring to spread them on a calm day."

"That would give us an excuse to be with them again."

"In the spring we should be able to tell them how everything turned out. It's all so unsettled now."

"You're right. Let's spread their ashes next spring."

"OK. Here's another question. Should we bury them here or do you think they'd rather be in the house for the rest of the winter?"

"I think they'd want to be here. It's quiet and safe, and they can keep an eye on what's happening in the valley."

Lisa reached for her pack and pulled out a folding shovel. She started digging next to Turtle Rock. The soil wasn't frozen yet, but the digging was easier the deeper she dug. She put the boxes in the grave side by side and covered them with dirt and then snow so nobody would know they were there.

"Do you know who named Turtle Rock?" she asked her mother.

"You know, I don't," said Mary Lou. "I never even thought about it. It's been Turtle Rock ever since I met your father. What else would anyone call it?"

Lisa thought back to the mescaline trip last spring when she and Chris felt Turtle Rock breathing. "It named itself," she said, "by becoming what it was."

"Isn't that what we all want to do?"

"You mean become our true selves?"

"Try to find ourselves, who we are, why we're here, what we're supposed to do about it. All that jazz."

"This is starting to sound like a college philosophy course."

"The course at Turtle Rock."

"That's better than the curse at Turtle Rock."

"Sounds like a horror film."

"One that we've been living."

"We've got to change that."

"We will," said Lisa, "with Peter's help."

"I'm glad he's here," said Mary Lou. "I don't think we should always depend on men to help us, but I feel so much safer with him here."

"So do I, Mom. And he's good-looking."

"You make a nice couple."

"It's happened so fast that it almost feels unreal."

"It looked real when you came downstairs this morning. You two lit up the kitchen."

"I like being with him."

"It's good to see happiness again," said Mary Lou. "You don't need my approval, but I approve."

"Thank you, Mom. That means a lot."

"Peter's been gone a long time."

"He has, but I don't worry about him. He inspires confidence that he can deal with whatever happens."

"I like that he called Miller's parents," said Mary Lou. "That was very thoughtful."

"Yes. After all he's been through, he's very sensitive."

The campfire burned quickly. The wood was mostly pine. Only glowing coals were left.

"Are you ready to go back to the house?" Lisa asked.

"Let's go back the long way," said Mary Lou.

"We might miss Peter."

"He shouldn't have any trouble following our tracks."

Mary Lou picked up the blanket and folded it into the backpack while Lisa used the shovel to smother the fire with snow. Lisa was glad nobody climbed on Turtle Rock. It was still pure, white and untouched. As it should be. Who would ever suspect it was a secret sentry, watching over the remains of her brother and her father? She wanted to touch Turtle Rock, but she dared not disturb it. God help anybody who would ever consider violating this sacred ground, she thought. There was no telling how a big rock that can breathe would react.

Mary Lou retreated to the top edge of the clearing. She looked past Turtle Rock to the distant mountains, wondering what would happen next, what the rest of her life would bring. She wanted 1968 to be over. It had been so violent, so filled with hate and tragedy, from the assassinations of Martin Luther King and Bobby Kennedy to the protesters ruthlessly beaten in Chicago to the deaths of Chris and Art. Underlying it all was the war and the draft. The war had generated a worldwide convulsion of protests, but the government just kept sending more kids to die. More than a half-million American servicemen and women were now in Vietnam. She'd heard on the radio that more than sixteen thousand had been killed in 1968 so far. And thousands more had been wounded and disabled. And what for? So the rich and powerful could get richer and more powerful. She had given Art's military-industrial corruption documents to Lincoln Freeman to review and pass on to the editor at the *World*. Maybe those would lead to meaningful change. Probably not. But at least she and Art had tried. That was what was important.

As she looked out from the stillness of the clearing she thought it was such a shame that humans seem determined to make such a mess of such a beautiful world.

Lisa snuggled up against her. They wrapped their arms around each other. Lisa heard the squawks first. "Here come our friends," she said. The squawks grew louder, and then they heard the drumbeat of their wings. Two ravens swooped low over Turtle Rock and then swept up, riding the wind currents effortlessly in circles above them around and around and around, higher and higher until they could hardly be seen. Lisa and Mary Lou were looking straight up, their necks strained, until the ravens disappeared into the clouds.

"That was amazing, Mom. They've never done that before. Never. I think they just told us Chris and Dad are up there somewhere, and it's time for us to let go. Maybe the ravens gave them a lift, showed them the way."

"It doesn't make sense," said Mary Lou. "But when I'm here, I can feel the presence of Art and Chris like no other place in the world. You're probably right, but I don't want to leave just yet."

"OK," said Lisa. "A few more minutes."

Distant clanging cowbells shattered the stillness. Somebody or something had crossed the ditch.

"We've got to go, Mom." Lisa grabbed her backpack, took Mary Lou's hand, and led her down the path as quickly as she could. Soon they heard another single cowbell. "Somebody's in the house," Lisa said.

*   *   *   *

Peter knew Miller had found them before he heard the cowbells. He had veered off the path about halfway between the house and Turtle Rock and circled through the woods to check the road. That way he wouldn't leave any additional tracks coming down off the ridgeline for Miller to see near the house. If Miller thought they were all up on the ridge, Peter figured he might be able to surprise him on the trail.

He found Miller's car parked on the side of the road where he and Lisa had expected it would be. The car was a station wagon with New Hampshire license plates. The hood was warm and the tailpipe hot. Footprints showed Miller was headed for the house. Before Peter could look inside, he heard another car approaching and ducked behind a tree. It was a gray VW Bug, but it didn't sound like one. Peter waved Johnny to a stop.

"Hey man," he said. "I didn't expect to see you here, but I'm sure glad you came." He started to brief Johnny on the situation when they heard the cowbells at the ditch. Peter said he had to get back up the ridge to warn Lisa and Mary Lou before they ran into Miller. Johnny said he'd park farther down the road and circle back to help. Peter looked inside the station wagon and told Johnny what he saw—trash, food wrappers, drink containers, a pile of stained bandages or towels, stains on the driver's seat, probably blood. Behind the driver's seat was a military metal ammunition box with the top open. It was empty.

Johnny drove down the road and Peter jogged back up into the woods toward the Turtle Rock trail. When he reached it, he was breathing hard. He didn't see any new boot prints. He kept jogging and intercepted Lisa and Mary Lou on their way down. It took him a while to explain what had happened while catching his breath. Lisa and Mary Lou were thankful Johnny was down below.

Peter asked how long it would take either of them to get to the nearest neighbor's house where they could call the state police. They estimated fifteen minutes. They knew where a spare house key was kept if nobody was home. Lisa wanted to stay with Peter. Mary Lou offered to hike to the neighboring farm. Peter suggested she ask the police not to use their sirens and that she keep going if she heard shots. He asked Lisa if she was armed, as they had planned. She was. They were near a split in the trail. Mary Lou took the left fork, and Peter and Lisa proceeded cautiously down toward the farmhouse with Peter in the lead, maintaining distance between themselves in case of gunfire and scanning the woods for any sign of Miller.

Peter saw him first. He edged behind a tree and signaled Lisa to do the same. She was wearing her backpack and had her revolver in her hand. Miller was dragging one leg as he struggled up the trail. He was carrying an M16 in one hand and using the other to grab and lean on trees to steady himself. His bad leg was wrapped with something dark around his thigh. He was wearing a long-sleeved shirt. He wasn't dressed for the snow. No coat. No hat or gloves. Peter couldn't see what he had on his feet. He signaled to Lisa that he would say something when Miller got closer. The distance between them closed slowly. Fifty yards. Twenty-five yards. Fifteen yards. Ten yards.

"Leo," Peter shouted. "Stop. It's Peter."

Miller raised his rifle and fired a burst of rounds. The recoil jerked the barrel up, and Miller lost his footing. The bullets zinged skyward through tree branches, and Miller fell sideways into a young tree that bent slightly but kept him upright.

"Leo. Don't do that again."

Miller fired off two more rounds, individually this time. One round hit Peter's tree.

"Leo. Did you see the note I left for you in the house? I talked to your parents this morning."

Another shot rang out.

"Leo. I don't want to shoot you. Your mother wants to talk to you."

No answer. Peter peeked around his tree. Miller was still leaning against the sapling.

"Leo. Drop your rifle so we can talk."

No answer.

Miller was still holding the M16, but it was pointed to the ground.

Peter was silent for a while, letting Miller take stock of the situation.

"This doesn't have to end here, Leo. Please lay down your gun. We can go back to the house, tend to your injuries, and talk."

"Why?" said Leo. "There's no future for me."

"That's not true. We want to help you. Your mother loves you and wants to help you."

"I'm a killer. The Army made me a killer. Nobody wants to help a killer."

Miller was gasping as he talked. He seemed to be in a lot of pain.

"You deserve help, Leo. Everybody who was in Nam deserves help."

"You don't know what I did there."

"I know about My Lai."

Silence.

Peter heard a tree rustle. He peeked and saw Miller use the sapling and his rifle for support to lower himself to the ground. He sat with his back against the sapling, his injured leg outstretched, the M16 across his lap. Behind Miller, Peter saw a shadow moving carefully among the trees. Johnny.

"The Army wants to cover it up," said Miller. "Blame it on a few grunts."

"That's the Army way," said Peter. "Fuck the Army. All you can do is tell the truth."

"It was so awful there's no word for it. You can't make it go away."

"Maybe if you get some help, you can ease the pain."

"It's like burned into you, man."

"I know what you mean."

"It'll never go away."

"For a lot of us."

"Fuck the Army."

"Right on."

"What now?"

"Why don't we go to the house and get you fixed up."

"I'm having trouble walking. That ditch was a killer. Nice job."

"It was an alarm, just to let us know you were coming."

"Glad it didn't have spikes."

"Just wanted to slow you down."

"Cowbells were a nice touch."

"Thanks."

"I don't think I can get back up."

Lisa peeked out from behind her tree. "I can get a sled," she said.

Miller twitched and grabbed for his rifle. "Who's that?"

"My name is Lisa," she said. "I'm Chris Thompson's sister."

"The guy who raided our offices?"

"He didn't raid your offices."

"Then how'd he know about it? The Army kept it quiet."

"He was just saying what he heard."

"He was trying to make trouble."

"Yes," said Lisa. "That's right. He was. He was trying to stop the war. He was trying to help people like you."

"I don't know what to think."

"Chris is gone, and now I'm trying to help you so nobody else gets hurt. If you put your rifle on the ground and push it away, I'll get a sled and we can take you to the house."

Miller shifted his position and nudged his rifle aside, first with his hand, then with his foot, groaning as he pushed.

Peter leaned out from behind his tree and asked if he had any other weapons. He said he didn't.

Peter and Lisa looked at each other. Peter nodded and pointed in the direction of the house. Lisa mouthed, "Ready."

She put her revolver in her coat pocket and stepped out from behind her tree so she and Miller could see each other.

"Leo," she said, "would you be more comfortable lying down?"

He coughed, painfully clutching his chest. He said he'd stay where he was because lying in the snow would be too cold. Lisa slipped her backpack off her shoulder, reached inside, and pulled out the blanket. "This should help," she said. "It's a blanket." She started walking guardedly toward him.

She unfolded the blanket when she got close. "I'm going to drape it around you, over your shoulders," she said, moving cautiously as she did.

"Thanks."

"I have a water bottle. Would you like some?"

"Yes. Please."

She gave him the water.

"Thanks."

"Now I'm going to pick up your rifle and take it with me," she said.

"OK."

"I'll be back in a few minutes with the sled," she said, turning her back to him and starting down the trail with his M16. She waved to Johnny as she went by. He held his position and gave her a thumbs up. She thought back to the day when he showed up down by the barn. What she saw first was his shadow. She had come to think of him as the family's unseen guardian angel, always nearby in the shadows.

After seeing Johnny backing up Peter, Lisa felt she could relax, at least a little. She tried to erase the tension of the confrontation with Miller from her body, and her thoughts turned to her brother. She imagined him walking down the trail with her through the snow, as they'd done countless times before. "We did it, Chris," she said softly. "We got justice for you." She continued the conversation as they walked. "We couldn't have done it without Johnny. He's here now, backing us up. Then there were two guys who were with you at the base that day when you were attacked, they helped us. They're in the Army now, and because of you, they're part of a new military resistance movement. They just put out a GI underground newspaper. You ain't dead yet, you know. Just like Joe Hill, your spirit lives on. Attorney Freeman helped us. It'd take too long to tell you all that he's done. He's a good man. Dad is another good man. He quit his job, and he and Mom started protesting the war before he lost his life. There's another good man who's come into our lives and helped us and is still helping us. His name is Peter Ransom. He's an anti-war Vietnam veteran. He's very brave, sensitive and kind. He's been protecting me and Mom, and he's up there on the ridge keeping an eye on that soldier who killed you."

She neared the barn and stopped before going inside for the toboggan. She turned to her imaginary brother.

"Can you believe I'm here at the farm holding an M16?" She raised the weapon for him to see. "Of course you can. It's a symbol of everything you were fighting against. We took it away from that soldier. He gave up his gun." She looked around the barnyard and turned back to her brother.

"You and I love this place. It's a family place. It's where our history is. It's where we grew up. You know you'll always be with me, Chris, especially when I'm here. Now that you know we got the guy who killed you, it's probably time for you to go. I hope you'll stop by from time to time. I hope Peter and I can make a life together, and I hope it can be here. If that happens, you'll be with both of us.

"Mom and I were just up at Turtle Rock. We built a fire and put your ashes and Dad's ashes in the ground. The ravens came by, and they said it's time for you to take off. While you're gone, we'll do our best to handle things down here. I love you, Chris. Rest in peace. You deserve it. I hope you can find a place without war."

THE END

Epilogue

Wednesday, December 4, 1968
Fort Dix

Army graduation ceremonies were held at the conclusion of two months of basic training. At Fort Dix, the Army gave each trainee a yearbook filled with pictures of their training, as well as individual head shots. It might be the first and only yearbook some would ever receive. The cover was embossed with an image of a helmeted foot soldier sprinting with his rifle, poised to shoot. The yearbook was titled:

**The United States
Army Training Center
Infantry
Fort Dix, New Jersey
The Home of the Ultimate Weapon**

Bear and Stillman were stunned. They hadn't seen the yearbook coming. The Army had outdone itself with absurdity. What a thoughtful reminder of eight weeks of forced fear and loathing and racism and brutality and deprivation of constitutional rights before sending the country's young sons off to kill or be killed. Why not also give them lollipops, since most were too young for beer?

What Bear and Stillman wanted most after enduring the graduation ceremony was to find out where the Army would order them to go next. They didn't expect good news.

Bear—as well as many other Black and Hispanic trainees—got what he expected after experiencing the prejudice on display during basic training: orders to go to Fort Polk in Louisiana for advanced infantry training, a stepping stone to Vietnam.

For Stillman, it was Fort Bliss in El Paso, Texas, for advanced missile and air defense training. That would surely qualify as absurd. The Army was sending an unpredictable Ultimate Weapon to Bliss. How could that go wrong? Imagine the ways.

Afterword

More than two million young Americans were drafted into the military during the Vietnam War. The draft was terminated in 1973 when the US withdrew most of its combat forces. By that time an estimated four hundred underground anti-war GI newspapers had been produced by American servicemen and women at US bases around the world, contributing to a rolling widespread mutiny. All the military services were stunned by breakdowns in discipline and morale created by opposition to the war within their ranks. In the Army, the resistance was generated mostly by draftees who at great personal risk defied orders or refused to fight or went AWOL or deserted at unprecedented levels. In the most extreme instances, overzealous combat officers were attacked and killed by their own troops. America had no choice but to leave Vietnam before its armed forces, the most formidable in the world, collapsed.

Nearly sixty thousand Americans died in the war. Overall military and civilian casualties were counted in the millions.

Acknowledgments

My education as a writer has been through on-the-job training. For that, I am indebted to so many people, places, and events that I can't begin to name them all.

I could never have completed this debut novel without my wife Debbie, a nurse practitioner and an insatiable reader who never goes anywhere without a book. I don't outline; I write by feel, and her patience gave me the time and space over many years to figure out what I was trying to do. I lost track of the number of times she read all or parts of this book and let me know how it was going.

A number of colleagues from my newspaper career were early readers of this novel and offered indispensable advice. Chief among them was Larry Roberts, a sensitive, insightful award-winning news editor and writer who said he didn't know anything about novels, but faked it really well. He informed me that Grateful Dead cofounder Jerry Garcia, a brilliant guitarist, got the same Army discharge as I did. The discharge was for unsuitability for military service, effectively an admission that the Army couldn't turn us into soldiers. I'm in good company in that regard.

Larry Williams, another former newspaper colleague, offered valuable guidance and constructive criticism. He served in the Air Force during the Vietnam era. Strat Douthat, a reporter and friend, was one of my early readers who offered suggestions and set a fine example by writing a novel after he retired from working decades for the Associated Press.

While writing this book, I reminded myself of lessons learned from another journalist, executive and friend, Mike Waller, a gifted plain-talking former editor, publisher and CEO of *The Hartford Courant* who is a genius in long-form journalism. He read an early draft, as well as the final manuscript, using a magnifying glass because his eyes were failing.

There were times when I felt lost and didn't think I could complete the book. On one of those occasions by chance I met the accomplished adventure novelist Peter Heller. We were in the same place for a week and talked nearly every day about writing. He gave me much-needed confidence and encouragement to keep going.

I was also influenced by two brilliant people I met in the early 1970s. One was Jerry Griswold, a rascal, a college professor, an authority on children's literature and the author of many books, as well as one of my closest friends for fifty years, although we were usually separated by thousands of miles. The other is Basil Paquet, a conscientious objector, Army medic, Vietnam veteran and poet who created a publishing company for veterans to tell their stories. He understood what I was trying to write more deeply than anyone.

Last and most important is a brave, articulate young man who was the inspiration for this book, Robert "Mike" Ransom. He was a college classmate who was opposed to the war before he dropped out of school and was drafted and then died in Vietnam. I was shocked by his death and began participating in anti-war protests. What later impressed me profoundly were the letters he wrote during a sixty-five-day period between March 7, 1968, the day he landed in Vietnam as an untested Army lieutenant, and May 11, 1968, the day he lost his life in a surgical hospital as a combat-hardened and respected battlefield leader. He died of wounds he had received eight days earlier when an enemy land mine detonated. He refused medical attention until other injured soldiers in his squad had been treated.

Mike's letters chart how the Vietnamese were both hated and admired by American soldiers as they began to understand that the Vietnamese could not be defeated because they would never give up their country. Mike's letters were made public by his parents, who became active in the anti-war movement after his death. An additional letter was written to his parents by a nurse who cared for Mike as he lay dying. She wrote:

"I have never written a letter like this before. But then, in my six years of nursing I have never met as courageous an individual as your son... Mike fought hard, terribly hard, to overcome his wounded condition. But, strong as he was, his body could only endure so much. Mike was never afraid and although I'm sure he realized what was happening, he never, never lost his smile or his courage."

Anyone who wants to understand a soldier's transformation in combat during the Vietnam war might start with Mike Ransom's letters. They were published as "Letters from a Dead GI" by the *Washingtonian Magazine* and are available on this website:

https://www.washingtonian.com/2015/05/26/letters-from-a-dead-gi/

Mike's gravestone is inscribed with two lines from a 1943 poem that his parents admired, "The Young Dead Soldiers Do Not Speak," written by Archibald MacLeish:

"We leave you our deaths.
Give them their meaning."

About the Author

Lyn Bixby was drafted within weeks of graduating in 1969 from Colby College in Waterville, Maine. After being discharged from the army, he found a job at a suburban Connecticut daily newspaper as a copy boy, was promoted to reporter, and spent most of his career at the state's largest newspaper, *The Hartford Courant*, primarily working on its special projects desk as an investigative reporter focused on corruption. Some projects gave him opportunities to dig into issues later raised in this debut novel.

During his newspaper career he received a range of writing awards, including a shared Pulitzer Prize.

Born in New York City, Lyn lives in Northern Vermont, with his wife Debbie. They have two sons and three grandchildren.

We Grow Our Books in Montpelier, Vermont

Learn more about our titles in Fiction, Nonfiction, Poetry and Children's Literature at the QR code below or visit www.rootstockpublishing.com.

9 781578 692118